REBIRTH

OF

DEAD ROSES

T·B· Ellis

Printed in the United States of America
Published by Elite Press Publications: St. Louis, MO
Edited by Erica Anderson
Book Cover Design by Kreationsk
Formatting by Sophie Hanks
Contact author at info@tbellis.com or visit www.tbellis.com

This is a work of fiction. Names, characters, places, and incidents either are the product of the author's imagination or, are used fictiously, and any resemblance to actual persons, living or dead, events, or locales is entirely coincidental.

ISBN 978-1-7362084-0-3

DEDICATION

This book is dedicated to my mother and son, who were my source of motivation during the writing process. This book was inspired by my grandmother in Heaven who is my guardian angel.

Contents

TO FALL OR NOT TO FALL

1. Men are like buses. When you miss one, another one comes in fifteen minutes.
2. People come into your life for a reason, a season, or a lifetime.

That's what my Grandma Rose told us to mend our broken hearts and to keep our egos intact regarding the male species.

Those words always stuck to me like honey, until recently. I don't believe in prayer.
Even if I did, no amount of prayer could help me, so I'll have to accept my fate.

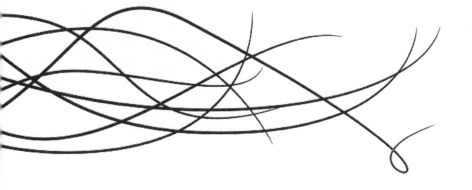

A
Lonely
Winter

Chapter 1

If I were a Christian, I would have surrendered on my hands and knees. I would have prayed for mercy right in the back seat of the soccer mom SUV where I was, knees cramped from the position of the passenger seat. Instead, my hand was glued to my cell phone, finger positioned to answer his call with timely precision. I blocked out the music that was blaring through the speakers, as well as the chit chat amongst the driver and front seat passenger. My mind was focused on one thing and one person only.

"How many times did you try to call him?" asked Kandi.

Songs from the *"I Love My 90's R&B"* Spotify playlist blasted from the speakers as Kandi lowered the volume.

"Steph, I said how many times did you try to call him?"

I paused before answering. It didn't matter whether I had called him once or ten times. He had not responded to my text messages or calls. I hadn't heard his raspy voice since my lunch break 13 hours prior. He told me he was hanging out at Benji's house after work. I never had a problem with him hanging out with Benji because I knew he was a good guy. I knew I would be hanging with my friends too, celebrating Kandi's 35th birthday. I had texted him to let him know we had safely arrived at the Karaoke Bar six hours prior. I sent him videos of Jamie and Kandi channeling Brandy and Monica's "The Boy is Mine" on the microphone and myself belting out Aaliyah's "Four Page Letter". I sent him a cute short video of myself with my duck lips poked out while I played with the bouncy curls from the blonde wig that I got from him the month prior. He didn't laugh at our silly videos nor tell me that I looked cute. He didn't even tell me to be careful at the bar and on our way home like he usually did. I knew something was up when Kandi pulled up to my condo close to 2:00 AM and Ronaldo's car was nowhere in sight.

"I don't know. I probably called over twenty times," I answered.

I could see her look back at me through her rearview mirror with pity.

"Hey what's his number? I'll try to call him and see if he answers," said Jamie.

"The phone is going to voicemail now so the battery must be dead. I'm waiting on him to call me when he charges it up," I said defensively.

"But he ain't called you all night and his phone wasn't dead at first."

"Don't you think I know that Jamie? Look, you're not making this situation any better. Can you just be quiet, please?" I asserted. "And Kandi, you will make a right at the next stop light."

Jamie added, "Okay I'll be quiet, but I'm just saying the only thing open at this time of night is--"

"Girl stop being negative and hush up like she said!" Kandi interrupted.

"I know that's just the liquor in her talking, so I'll give her a pass," I said.

Kandi and I had met in the first grade. We instantly became like sisters. Jamie joined our sisterhood a year later when she used her grandparent's address to attend school in our district. We became inseparable and began to reference ourselves as the "Three Amigas" during our first year of Spanish in High School.

I had a secret that I didn't plan to reveal to them until the right time. I didn't plan for that moment to be the right time, but Jamie forced me to let the cat out the bag.

"For your information, Ronaldo is about to propose to me sometime during the holidays so there was no way he is out cheating on me right now as you are trying to imply!"

"Propose?" Kandi yelled out. "Say what? How did you know? Did you find the ring?"

I reconfigured my body and leaned in closer to the middle console. My heart smiled again for a moment as I tried to forget the situation at hand. I recalled my reaction two days prior when I figured out his secret plan. I overheard him on the phone with his cousin Mark who lived in his hometown of Michigan.

I heard Mark yell out, "So you're gonna do it right before the holidays?"

Ronaldo quickly took him off speakerphone when I walked into the room. I put two and two together, which equaled an engagement ring and holiday proposal. At least, in my mind it did. He had been secretive in the weeks before that, but I was glad there was a legitimate reason. I immediately went to the bathroom and released silent screams in the mirror. I performed the Cabbage Patch and the Running Man in the mirror, then jumped for joy.

"Well, I didn't actually find a ring. I overheard his cousin mention something that gave the secret away," I offered.

I saw Kandi smile from the rearview mirror.

"Aw sis, I'm so happy for you!" she exclaimed.

Jamie replied, "Yeah that's dope Steph. I'm happy for you too, but that's even more reason why he might be out creeping tonight. He may have to tell his mistress they can get it in one last time before he is officially off the market." She barely got the last words out before she laughed at her own attempt of a joke. I playfully smacked her in the back in the head which made her laugh even more. Kandi shook her head in Jamie's direction.

"Didn't we just tell you hush? Anyway, there has got to be an explanation for tonight. Like I said earlier, he probably passed out at his friend's house," said Kandi.

"Thanks sis. And yes, I am hoping that is the case. As a matter of fact, the house is coming up so slow down."

Kandi followed my instructions and we cruised down the dusky street until I saw Benji's old school Monte Carlo parked in the driveway. Rather than praying, I hoped for the appearance of Ronaldo's vehicle to be safely parked outside. To my disappointment, there were no other vehicles in the driveway or in front of the house. My heart sank deep down into my chest again. I immediately called his phone, which was once again routed straight to voicemail.

"Dang, I can't believe this! Where is he?" I asked, exasperated. "I hope nothing happened to him."

"Go knock on old boy's door and see when the last time he heard from him," said Jamie.

"She can't go knock on this man's door at 2:00 A.M.," Kandi shouted.

It was rather early in the morning to knock on someone's door, but this was an emergency. The house was pitch black, so it was apparent that nobody was still awake. I did not want to wake his wife and kids up at that hour. It wasn't like he had been missing for 24 hours.

"Okay I'm done, I'm not saying anything else about it. Heck I hope he is okay too, but I did see the police out tonight. You know they are real quick to stop a black man who is driving alone at night."

"I thought you wasn't saying nothing else about it?" I asked Jamie sarcastically. "If he got locked up, he would have used his one phone call to reach me by now."

All kinds of thoughts swirled through my mind, but I had to remain positive. I was not going to believe the worst had happened to him. I would not accept that fate for him, especially not when our relationship was headed to a new level of commitment. He had to be okay for my sake.

"Hey, you're right. It's too late to knock on Benji's door. Just take me back home and hopefully he will be back when I get there."

On the ride home, I checked the internet on my phone for any accidents, police shootings or any crimes that could have taken place that night. Luckily, I found nothing, which was a relief. I did my best to dismiss Jamie's accusations, but they continually slipped in and out of my mind. Neither one of them commented when we pulled up and he still was not there. I hated that Kandi's birthday celebration ended on such a gloomy note, but it wasn't my fault.

When I entered my home, the heat warmed my body from the frigid cold that had enveloped me as I had walked to the door. I slipped off my Ugg boots and placed them neatly by the door. I walked past our living room table which displayed pictures of Ronaldo and me. Once I found out he was about to propose; I imagined adding our wedding photos to the table. I moved upstairs and changed into a warm Christmas-themed Snuggie that Mama got me for Christmas the year before. I removed my wig and skillfully placed it on the mannequin in the bathroom. I was disappointed that my phone had not rang in the time since I walked in the door. I kept the light on and laid across my side of the bed on top of the sheets. I checked my phone once more and got excited when I heard a text come through, but was disappointed to see it was only Kandi letting me know that she and Jamie had made it home safely.

I was tired beyond words but did everything I could to keep my eyes open. Part of me wanted to sleep it off with the hope that this was just a bad dream, and when I woke up, he would be in the bed next to me. I was never the clingy type, however, I didn't want to sleep knowing that my future fiancé was nowhere to be found. Once again my mind drifted to the worst case scenarios and I was tempted to call around to hospitals and even jails although I had already checked the media outlets for current events.

To keep my mind focused on the positive, I considered how and where he had planned to propose. I was surprised I hadn't already walked down the aisle with someone's son. I deserved to be a wife more than the high school tramps who slept with the entire basketball team or the neighborhood hood rats with six kids and six baby daddies. It irked my existence when I saw those types of women post their engagements on social media. Their wide grins and raised hands to show off their new engagement rings ruffled my feathers and I longed for the day that I could flaunt my engagement pictures to the world too. I always wondered why men decided to turn those garden tools into housewives. My thoughts continued to consume my uncertainty.

. . .

I entered an unfamiliar territory that neither frightened nor enlightened me. The sun's beams scorched down on my bare caramel brown shoulders. My eyes were somewhat shielded by the sheer white covering that hung over my face as the long goddess braids draped down and met the top of an all-white off the shoulder gown. The soft fabric clung perfectly to my curvaceous shape and I transformed into a Nubian Princess. The dress was short in the front but felt longer in the back. My unusually long and narrow feet appeared two sizes smaller in the Cinderella inspired glass slippers. I wasn't sure how, but a white bouquet of roses, blinged out with sparkling silver studs magically appeared. I was compelled to grasp it and I never wanted to release it. I heard familiar voices calling and speaking to me in the distance. I moved forward and followed the direction of the voices. Soft elevator music serenaded me on my journey and I found a stream of multicolored rose petals scattered neatly on the fresh grass. As my feet glided across the petals, I saw a man dressed in a white tuxedo in the distance. It had to be my Ronaldo, but I wasn't sure why his face was blurry and his features were distorted. Even his long dreadlocks were no longer visible, but it had to be him, and it had to be the wedding day that I always dreamed about. I held my head up high and twisted my hips as I eased down the aisle toward him. I still heard voices yelling out to me, but nobody was there. The white chairs that were intended for my wedding guests were all empty. There were no bridesmaids, groomsmen, or officiant at the altar and no sign of Mama either. As if things were already strange enough, all of a sudden there was intense thunder and lightning. The sun faded to pure darkness in a split second and the invisible voices grew louder. The trail of roses and empty chairs disappeared along with my mysterious groom. I was now all alone in the dark in unknown territory.

"If you don't know God, you better get to know him!" screamed an eerie high-pitched voice from somewhere in the darkness. "Did you hear that Stephanie? If you don't know God; you better get to know him before it's too late!"

I didn't know God by any means so I flung the bouquet down to the ground and ran as fast I could in the opposite direction. I didn't know exactly where to run but I had to get away and not look back.

I jumped up to a sitting position as sweat drizzled down my neck and back. The back of my onesie was soaked, although my slumber was brief. I had intended to wait up for Ronaldo. I didn't realize that I had dozed off. I checked my phone which had no missed calls or texts. The time was 6:06 A.M. I resided as a single tenant in the bed, as he had not arrived home to occupy his space next to me. I called his phone again assuming that it should have been charged up by that time, wherever he was. There was no answer.

I jumped up and jogged down the stairs, expecting him to be laid out on the couch.

The couch was empty and there was no sign that he had come home. Sheer panic came over me as I recalled the dream of darkness and a disappearing groom. I reluctantly turned on the television for the early local news to ensure no foul play had gone on the prior night. I specifically watched for the latest accidents and shootings. Although some incidents were reported, none were in areas where Ronaldo would be. As a matter of fact, he didn't travel around town much anyway. He had only been living in town for four years, and didn't have many friends. He had no family at all in the area. The absence of his name and picture floating across the screen was a relief. I logged onto Facebook for any possible information. Sometimes Facebook got news before the media outlets and I was disappointed that I hadn't thought to check there first.

To my surprise, Ronaldo had posted a picture of himself within a fifteen-minute period. He was seated inside of his car - the same car my friends and I had been looking for all night. His fingers displayed the peace sign and his caption read:

Good morning World, today marks the 1st day of my new life! Wish me luck; I'm about to be a happy man again!

My panic subsided as I realized he was alive and unharmed. Did he plan to surprise me with the engagement ring later that day? It wasn't his birthday so that had to be the only reason why that particular day would mark the first day of his new life. But wait, what did he mean when he said that he would be a happy man again? Wasn't he already happy? Why was he able to make a Facebook post but not pick up the phone to call me or text me back? I was ecstatic that he was safe but I had a problem with him staying out all night so I didn't hesitate to reach out to him again.

That time the phone rang three times before it went to voicemail. Something was going on and I needed answers. I called back three more times and he still didn't answer. My body started to tingle as I felt in my gut that he had sent my call to voicemail intentionally.

I threw the phone down and watched as it bounced across the comforter. I sat on the edge of the bed, remembering two years prior sitting in the same spot as he professed his love to me while kneeling before me. He told me that he loved me and that one day soon he would be kneeling with an engagement ring. I wished he was there again in the same spot so I could kick him in the face. How dare he disrespect me and not come home and not even tell me beforehand? I laid back down in the bed and sent him several texts then waited for his reply.

Two hours went by and my phone finally rang. I sprang for the phone immediately, assuming it was him.

"Hello."

"Good morning baby. You know, you didn't let me know you made it home last night," said Mama.

"Good morning. Sorry, it was a long night, so I forgot," I said unenthusiastically.

"Was everything okay?" she asked.

"Yeah all is good. I'm still just a little sleepy," I offered rather than the truth.

"Okay, well you can lay back down and call me when you're ready to go."

I replied, "No that's okay. I'm about to start getting ready now so we can still meet for breakfast and then go to the mall after that."

"Sounds like a plan, see you soon."

"Okay cool," I said as I hung up the phone.

I sluggishly moved to the bathroom to brush my teeth and shower. I was no longer confident about an engagement. There was no way a man should be gone all night and all morning with no explanation. The only things open during those hours were legs, just like Jamie had insinuated. My woman's intuition had failed me and there seemed to be something else going on that I had no idea about. I knew that his recent behavior was slightly off, but I assumed he was just nervous about proposing to me.

I stared at my complexion in the foggy mirror as I dried off. I grew up as a skinny little girl but I had definitely filled out since my younger days, dubbed as 'thick' in the eyes of most men. I had nothing to blame except my love for food and cooking, which was taught to me by Grandma Rose. I jiggled my belly fat, a vast difference from my flat-belly days. Kandi and Jamie complained about their belly flab too, but it was different for them. They had given birth to children. Kandi had one daughter, Kayla, who was twelve years old. Jamie had two daughters, Jamiya and Jade, who were twelve and sixteen years old. I, on the other hand, couldn't use childbirth as an excuse.

I noticed my boobs had started to sag a little too. Ronaldo never complained about my body. Perhaps he grew dissatisfied with my fat belly, sagging boobs and the double chin that was developing. He probably wanted a woman shaped like a coke bottle, perky breasts and washboard abs. I decided I would search for a girdle to flatten my tummy.

I also put on black Adidas stretch pants and a matching black sweatshirt. I knew the color black would make me look slimmer.I positioned my face closer to the mirror to examine my face. It was amazing to me how much I resembled my Grandma Rose. We both had black curly medium length hair, cute little button noses, big almond shaped eyes and high cheekbones. I gathered myself and decided on black Adidas stretch pants and a matching black sweatshirt for my attire. I knew the color black would make me look slim. I went through my wig collection to see which personality I wanted to be that day. Atomic Red was what I wore when I wanted to feel hot and sexy, but I didn't feel hot and sexy. Curly Sue came in handy when I felt bubbly and energetic, but that was definitely not my vibe either. I wore Slick and Chic with the deep middle part and strands that cascaded down my back whenever I felt girly and flirty. Another choice was a burgundy short bob. I called it Cherry Blossom, but I wasn't feeling that either. I stopped short of going down the wig lineup and just decided to go natural. I brushed my hair up into a ponytail and tied it in a bun. I grabbed my makeup kit, but it only took me a split second to decide against that too. I settled on just wearing lip gloss. I wasn't big on jewelry other than earrings. I could never live with chapped lips and bare ears. I couldn't help but think about Ronaldo again and what he meant by his Facebook post or why he failed to come home. To think of it, Ronaldo was the main reason I lived for fake hair and makeup. Before I met him, I seldomly wore eye shadow and lipstick, and I kept my hair in a natural style or braids. He slowly introduced me to fake hair for his own personal pleasure.

I was still so anxious to see what was going with him. Another forty-five minutes had passed, and he still hadn't arrived home nor had he called or texted me back. I decided to wait another fifteen minutes before calling him back. Those fifteen minutes couldn't pass fast enough though.

I began to get nervous. I didn't care about being sent to voicemail because I was going to keep calling until he answered. I had worked myself up with all these possible scenarios but there had to be some kind of explanation for all of this. He had to come back home at some point and explain his actions and whereabouts.

I knew I had my work cut out for me with him in the beginning. I recall how he was late to our first few dates. I told him the next time he was late that he had to bring me a dozen roses. On date number four, I sat on the bench outside The Cheesecake Factory, twiddling my thumb waiting for him to pull up. It was a beautiful spring day. Fifteen minutes from the time I sat on the warm bench, a tall dark figure emerged from the opposite direction. He wore a red long-sleeved shirt, jeans and white Air Force Ones as he hid behind a bouquet of flowers. He stood in front of me, lowered the flowers and said, "So sorry to keep you waiting again. That is why I have the flowers you asked for. I will make sure this is the last time I will be late."

I smirked at his sweet gesture although I wasn't really impressed with his choice of clothes nor the flowers. I specifically asked for roses but he got daffodils. I nodded politely and said, "Well, thank you for the flowers. I really hope this will be your last time being late."

"It will be. I don't want to keep messing it up with you. I really like you. I'm just not used to all this dating and stuff you know, but I am truly sorry."

His eyes were bloodshot red; like he was on the verge of crying. The serious look in his eyes was so sincere that it made me forget about the clothes and flowers. I saw potential in him to be molded into what I needed him to be.

With five minutes left, I entered my little bumblebee colored Camaro. As I drove off, I briefly looked in the mirror, appreciating my own natural beauty. I got mad at Ronaldo all over again. How dare he not come home all night and not tell me what was going on? How dare he disrespect me like that?! He had me worrying and going crazy for nothing. I wanted to rip out each dreadlock from his little peanut head. I counted down the final minute although I didn't even know exactly what I was going to say.

The wait was finally over. My Bluetooth had become faulty, so I dialed him from my phone. It rang continuously.

"Ugghhh!" I exclaimed and hung up the phone.

I came to a stop at the traffic light and decided to check Facebook again. There was a green circle by his name, indicating that he was active online. I surmised that it was true that he saw my calls and blatantly ignored me.

"Really!" I can't believe him!" I screamed to myself.

The rage I felt was replaced by hurt. Before pulling into the parking lot of the restaurant I called again just to see what would happen. The phone rang again three times before someone picked up. All I heard was music and background noise.

"Hello!" I yelled into the phone. "Hello?" I exclaimed.

No one answered. The phone went dead.

Chapter 2

The family portrait that hung on the living room wall of my childhood home told an indirect story of three generations. I was at the bottom of the portrait in a black and white puffy dress, a black bow on the right side as I gave a crooked smile. My cheek bones sat high on my face, underscoring a pair of cute and chocolate colored eyes. My first hair relaxer was captured in time and sleekly pulled up into a ponytail that was off centered, dangling with Shirley Temple curls. A lovely pair of pale hands with fuchsia nail polish were resting upon my shoulders. It was Mama, Shirleen. Her matching fuchsia colored lips seemed fake as if they were airbrushed onto the portrait. Her usually distinct freckles were covered with blush. Her almond shaped eyes were of a hazelnut hue and her strands of sandy brown hair were styled in an updo, with the back cascading down her shoulders. She wore a black and white dress shirt with an attached black vest. To the side of Mama, Grandma Rose stood tall and strong. She looked nothing like Grandma Rose, and I looked nothing like Mama.

If you looked at us but didn't know us, you would think that my grandma gave birth to me because I looked more like her than Mama. Grandma Rose's jet black hair was styled in classic finger waves. It was as if each wave had its own story to tell. She wore no makeup or lipstick, only lip balm. She wore a fitted cashmere sweater with her favorite brooch: a golden rose. Her cheek bones were just as high as mine when she laughed or smiled, but she opted not to show them in the photo. Grandma Rose anchored herself as the foundation and protector of our little unordinary family since the fathers and grandfathers were gone.

I recall the day when Mama came home carrying the package of pictures from Olan Mills. Grandma Rose was whipping up her famous macaroni and cheese and fried chicken that day.

"Sho Nuff?! Miss Janie did what?" she shouted in response to whatever gossip her younger sister, Auntie Mae, had relayed to her about the folks back home in Tennessee.

I listened as she carried on, shouting and laughing as I distractedly struggled with math homework at the kitchen table. I probably should have gone to my room to concentrate but I loved the aroma of greasy chicken and melted cheese smothered over noodles. I memorized her recipes and techniques more than the formulas in my math book. It was unfortunate that my deceased father's mathematical abilities bypassed me. At least I was great at spelling, English, History, and I couldn't forget Art.

Mama walked in with her work purse in one hand and the pictures in the other. She did not want to bother Grandma Rose while she was on the phone so she laid the pictures on the table.

"Hey Mama," I said. She walked toward me and kissed me on the forehead.

"Hey baby. Are you almost done with your homework?"

"Not yet," I sighed.

"Okay, let me know when you're finished so I can check your answers and then we can all look at the pictures together."

Once I had completed my homework, we looked over the pictures. There was a huge 11x14 that we hung up in our living room. The other photos were wallet size. I preferred the poses we did on the wallets better than the pose on the larger picture, but that was between Mama and the photographer. Mama had me to do the honors of writing our names and the year on the back of each individual picture. My wrist ached the following morning from the monotony of all that writing:

Rose Vernice Carter, Shirleen Carter, and Stephanie La'Rose Carter1994

I had to write it thirty-two times in my newly learned cursive handwriting. I would rather have racked my brain at that amount of math problems instead.

"Are we sending these pictures out?" I asked.

"Yeah I'll have mama send them out to her folks in Tennessee. The rest I will hand out to my co-workers and I can give June Bug his picture at the wedding this weekend," said Mama.

. . .

The day of cousin June Bug's wedding was a beautiful and sunny October day with a temperature in the low seventies. It was my first time attending a wedding and I was excited. I dreamt of wedding cake all night although I had never eaten it before. My pink and white floral Easter dress from that year was what Mama laid out for me to wear, along with some stockings. What I really wanted was a spanking new dress, fresh out of the plastic, that my body had never touched before. I mean, that was my first wedding for God's sake! In my dream, I wore an all-white dress with an abundance of ruffles, accented with lace tights and patent leather white dress shoes. My hair was long and straightened. It flowed down my back and was adorned with a pink headband.

I heard Grandma Rose yell out, "Hurry up! We have to leave in twenty minutes to catch the bus on time."

"Okay, I'm almost done. Steph you almost done?" Mama yelled out to me from the bathroom.

"Yes!" I shouted.

Why do we have to catch the bus today to a wedding? I thought. I wondered why June Bug didn't pick us up instead of allowing three women dressed to the nines to ride public transportation. I resented the fact that neither Mama nor Grandma Rose had a car and not even a driver's license at that time. Luckily, Mama finally got both some years later.

I drifted into the remembrance of my dream, where I had arrived at the wedding in a pretty pink limousine that matched my headband. The photographer snapped pictures of me as I exited from the limo and I prepared to showcase my grand entrance into the church doors.

I came to as I realized the three of us had arrived to the bus stop, which didn't have any benches like the bus stops on television. The fabric of Mama's purple flared dress fluttered up and around from the breeze, no matter how much she pulled it down. She clutched a professionally wrapped gift from Famous and Barr in her other hand. It felt that we were a bit overdressed for the setting, as others who waited at the same stop were dressed down. The other people that waited at the bus stop fit in with the atmosphere as they wore down to earth clothes and shoes. We looked out of place like a group of Caucasians standing in line for a Public Enemy concert.

Grandma Rose wore her comfortable flats, but with a long colorful skirt with a floral design and a silk blouse with a big bow in the middle. She kept checking her watch for the time. I looked down the street every 15 seconds or so, hoping to see the giant machine coming down the road. I was jealous as I watched the people in their cars pass by. I tried to ignore the stares from those who saw us standing there in our Easter Sunday clothes in mid-October.

"The bus is late!" Grandma Rose exclaimed.

"Well you know a black wedding don't start on time no way so we won't miss nothing," said Mama as she pulled her dress down once more.

"I hope not but this bus is never late. It should have been here five minutes ago according to the bus schedule."

"Maybe there was an accident," I chimed in. Before they could reply, a young woman who carried a sleeping baby in her arms leaned in and asked, "Excuse me miss, what time do you have?"

Grandma Rose looked down at her watch again before looking back up to say, "Eight minutes past four."

"Okay thanks," said the young woman as she rubbed her baby's back and stepped back into her original spot.

"What time is the wedding supposed to start?" I asked.

"At 4:30 baby," said Grandma Rose.

Mama chimed in and said, "No it starts at four o'clock but like I said it won't start on time anyway."

"You told me it started at 4:30!" yelled Grandma Rose.

"No I didn't. I said four o'clock like the invitation stated. Maybe I said it would probably start at 4:30 and you got confused."

"Oh my God! I know I'm old but I'm not crazy. I asked you what time it started and I know what you told me chile! You better hope it don't start on time because I gots to see my June Bug say *I do!*"

I hoped she was right too because that would be my first ever live wedding and not just the same fake wedding on the soap operas I watched with Mama. I wanted to see the train of Rhonda's beautiful gown glide down the aisle and I wanted to see if June Bug would cry when his bride came floating down toward him. I looked again for the bus but it was nothing but cars of people staring again. Mama rolled her eyes, let out a sigh and turned her head slightly.

"Your precious June Bug should have come to pick us up then," Mama muttered

Grandma Rose and I were still able to make out her words even though she tried to be discreet. She was never good at whispering. I rolled my eyes and sighed too because I could sense what was about to come next.

"Excuse you! He did offer to pick us up, but he had to be at the church early and I didn't want to come that early. You know I don't wanna be around dem ugly folks no longer than I have to be. So, he offered to have Stanley pick us up but I didn't want nobody coming out of they way to get us." She retorted as she rolled her neck toward Mama. She stared in her face awaiting her response.

"Why did you do that? Who cares if Stanley was coming out of his way or if we had to be there early? You are complaining about being late but if we had got a ride with him you would already be there. Besides, you are like June Bug's mother, he should have made you take that ride with either him or Stanley."

"Chile, can't nobody make me do nothing."

I quickly interrupted the match that was about to ensue among them, "It doesn't matter now, the bus is coming now," I said.

When we finally got on the bus, we were treated somewhat like royalty. The others at our bus stop let us board first. I guess we looked like we were going somewhere of importance. I didn't mind the special treatment at all. I guess Grandma Rose's face almost cut the bus driver sharp as he apologized profusely for the delay. He claimed there was a fatal accident that caused the streets to be blocked off which created a slight traffic jam. I had told them there was probably an accident of some sort, but I never thought it would be a fatal one. How ironic it was that I had just learned the definition of the word fatal. Grandma Rose and I were watching the five o'clock news and the black lady with the puffy hair and coke bottle glasses reported that there was a fatal car accident on the highway and I asked her what that word meant. It was sad to hear that someone had lost their life on that beautiful October day, but I hoped they would go to Heaven and not Hell.

I sat next to Grandma Rose on the bus and Mama sat behind us. I prayed that the wedding hadn't started yet. For one, I had counted down the days to attend my first wedding and my counting would have been a waste of time if we missed the ceremony. Secondly, Grandma Rose would never let Mama forget it if she missed her nephew's wedding.

She never confessed it, but I think Mama was slightly jealous of June Bug. Grandma Rose loved him in a different kind of way that I really couldn't explain, but I could feel it. We were all so shocked when he came home with Rhonda and announced her as his fiancé two years prior. Grandma Rose immediately questioned the authenticity of their relationship. I didn't know why because those years with Rhonda had been the happiest I had ever seen him in my ten years of life at that time. Rhonda proved that she really loved him and vice versa. She was a nurse who was also a part-time interior decorator. Rhonda also had one son who was close to my age. June Bug always wanted us to meet up and play together. June Bug was so attached to the boy that he referred to him as his stepson even before they got engaged. I was sure I would finally meet him at the wedding or at least the reception.

Mama pulled the strings at the top of the bus to alert the driver that we would be getting off at the next stop. There was no limo to hop out of like in my dream, but I pranced down the mini staircase of the bus. I was all ready to make my wedding debut and to witness a wedding live and in the flesh. When we got off the bus, we saw a group of people outside the church. I knew Mama wanted to do her "I told you so" victory dance but of course she didn't.

"See, I told you black weddings never start on time." Mama's eyes shifted in Grandma's direction. Grandma Rose couldn't help but to smirk.

"Well thank goodness then," she said.

There seemed to be some commotion going on amongst the bystanders outside the church. Two ladies in matching bridesmaid dresses wore frantic looks on their faces. They paced back and forth as one looked down at her watch. If Rhonda stood with them, I would have thought they were triplets. I assumed one was an older sister and the other a young sister as the resemblance was undeniable. It looked like the others were guests who were waiting for the ceremony to begin. As we got closer, Rhonda's apparent older sister noticed us. She ran over to Grandma Rose and almost tripped herself over the hem of her long dress.

"Ma'am have you talked to June Bug?" she exclaimed, without greeting us.

"Not since this morning," answered Grandma Rose. "He should be here already."

"No ma'am, he's not here. Nobody has talked to him since earlier. His best man said he was on his way an hour ago, but he hasn't made it yet.

Mama interjected, "Did someone beep him?"

"Yes, and he has not called back yet."

It's weird that June Bug would be late to his own wedding I thought. For a moment, I wondered if he got scared and decided to leave Rhonda at the altar. I felt sorry for Rhonda at that point. What if she had to look her family and friends in the face to tell them she got stood up on her wedding day? All the money spent on the wedding would have gone down the drain. But I knew June Bug would never do that to her so there had to be some explanation to his tardiness.

"Sho nuff? Well he told me he had to be at the church early so I don't know why he's not here yet unless he got stuck in traffic," replied Grandma Rose.

Mama interjected, "Oh yeah, remember the bus driver said there was an accident that caused a lot of traffic? Yeah, he probably got caught in that traffic too."

"Whew! Okay thanks. That makes sense, maybe he did get stuck in traffic. I guess he will be here soon I hope."

"Yeah, June Bug'll be here soon, he wouldn't miss his own wedding," stated Grandma Rose in a matter of fact way.

"You're right ma'am. And I'm so sorry I didn't introduce myself. I am Rhonda's sister, Rolanda.

She motioned for the other sister to come closer and she introduced her too.

"This is our little sister, Shonda. I knew your face from a picture June Bug showed us. He spoke very highly of you." Rolanda went on.

"Oh, did he? That's my June Bug. And it's nice to meet you Rolanda and Shonda. This is my daughter Shirleen and my granddaughter Stephanie."

"Hey nice to meet you all. Welcome to the family I should say," said Rolanda as a smile replaced the frantic look on her face.

Mama and I both smiled and returned the greetings.

She turned to Shonda and said, "They said it was a bad accident on the way here so we think he still may be caught in the traffic."

The worry disappeared from Shonda's face.

"Oh okay. I knew there had to be something crazy going on. Let me go back in and check on Rhonda. You guys can come inside with me and be seated," said Shonda.

When I walked in the church it was nothing like I expected. The weddings on the tv shows I watched were elaborately decorated with flowers, ribbons on the church pews, and candles. It wasn't totally absent of decorations, but it was not as fancy as I expected. My old Easter dress was fine to wear that day after all. We all took seats at the front with me placed between Grandma Rose and Mama. The church was filled with an adequate amount of people but most of them were Rhonda's family and friends. Grandma Rose had relocated to the Midwest away from her home town in Tennessee when she was only eighteen years old. We had no family members in town. Auntie Mae was scheduled to drive up to the wedding but her husband caught a bad case of the gout, so she wasn't able to make the wedding.

Time never seemed slower as we waited for the groom to arrive. I started to get impatient and looked around to see if I could spot Rhonda's son. June Bug only referred to him as his stepson when he spoke of him so I didn't know his government name. I never really cared to ask but the few times we were supposed to get together something always came up.

Thirty minutes had passed by and I grew hungry for the wedding buffet and the three-tier wedding cake that I had dreamed about. I could taste the crispy but greasy fried chicken and the soft buttery rolls that would melt in my little mouth. My favorite type of cake was usually yellow but the wedding cake in my dream was a lemon cake with pink icing. It was so moist and fluffy and I couldn't wait to taste the delightfulness in real life. I kept looking back to see if June Bug had arrived but he didn't make it. I realized that I left his wallet size picture of us that I put in a cute little frame on the kitchen table. I had forgotten it since we were rushing to catch the bus. I had planned to give him the framed picture as a wedding gift from me since I had no money to buy him anything.

As we waited, I imagined myself as a bride on my own wedding day. I knew I would wear a fitted white long-sleeved lace wedding gown with a long train attached. I wanted to wear my hair in a corn roll in the back with Shirley Temple curls cascading down the front over my left eye with a princess tiara and a white long veil. I envisioned holding a bouquet of white roses in my hands. My colors would be pink and blue. I longed to see my future husband start crying once he saw the doors of the church open up for me to walk down the aisle toward him. I wanted June Bug to walk me down the aisle as he was the only male figure in my life.

My thoughts were interrupted by a loud wail that came from an area to my left. I assumed it was the part of the church where the members of the wedding party were.

"NO, NO, NO, NO, NO!"

Everyone looked around in confusion. Some guests even stood up. Nothing more could be heard except loud and intense cries. The next few moments happened in a blur. All of a sudden, a short, slender black man walked up to the three of us and requested that we follow him to where the cries originated. It appeared that he was the preacher who was going to perform the ceremony based on his attire: a black suit with a white collared shirt, bible in hand. Grandma Rose asked him, "What is going on sir?" He didn't answer. He only motioned for us to continue following him. We ended up in a small room. Rhonda was on her knees in a beautiful beaded wedding gown. She wore the same type of veil I wanted to wear, and her long and bone-straight hair was draped down her back. Something felt uneasy about that moment as Rhonda was keeled over. Her screams went in and out of sync with Boyz II Men's popular hit "End of The Road" which played on a small stereo in the corner. I felt my heart pause and skip a few beats as I took in the dreadful words that that came out of Rolanda's mouth.

Tears filled my eyes as I heard Grandma Rose let out a cry that was even louder and deeper than Rhonda's. Mama grabbed Grandma Rose immediately and the two embraced as they cried in unison. I stood there shocked and numb; so numb I didn't feel the urine that cascaded down my legs. The sweet melody of a dream wedding faded to black and the chorus became a nightmare that I couldn't awake from.

. . .

The church we stood in expecting a wedding was the same church in which we laid June Bug to rest a week and a half later. When I saw his limp and unrecognizable body laid in the casket, I knew it was real and not just a nightmare. He didn't own any suits but luckily Grandma Rose still had one of her brother's suits. My great-uncle Buddy was June Bug's daddy and had died long before I was even thought of. His old suit fit June Bug perfectly, as if it were destined to be his wardrobe for eternity. Mama argued that they should have buried him in the tuxedo that he should have gotten married in, but Rhonda objected. She said it would have been too hard on her to see him with the same tuxedo that he never got a chance to wear. Mama understood that and left the situation alone.

His skin appeared darker than it was in life form and his already stocky body looked somewhat swollen. I began thinking of times he would come over to our house and fall asleep on the couch. I would get bored and stick Q-tips up his nose. It was hilarious to me because he would stir a little then just turn his face away. He never fully woke up. Grandma Rose caught me once since my uncontrollable laughter got the best of me. She spanked my hand and told me to stop meddling. I only bothered him like that as payback for when he would try to tickle me. I hated to be tickled. It had a way of making me laugh but also uncomfortable because I felt like I had no control. Even as a little girl I liked to be in control of most things. June Bug and I would laugh hysterically as I would try to tickle him back but it seemed my hands could never do the trick.

The memories I shared with him came to surface and the tears I couldn't cry at first could no longer be stopped. My tears erupted in an uncontrollable manner. I was at the mercy of my own tears and not only was I sad, I was angry. My Grandma Rose lost her nephew by blood and her son by heart. I was confused that Mama hated the extra attention he received but she was just as, if not more, distraught than Grandma Rose. I was angry that my cousin who was like a father figure to me had been taken away suddenly before I could properly say goodbye to him.

How could God take a man's life on his wedding day? How could God take away a woman's future husband on her wedding day? How was June Bug the only person that died from the accident and not any of the others involved? Why had God taken away my own father before I could talk? Why had he also taken the only other man who was the next best thing to a father? Would he take away all the men that I would ever love? I questioned if there really was a God. I felt like no one could really answer my questions.

My faith died right along with June Bug in that accident. He always joked and said he would be on TV one day. The night of the wedding, June Bug made the ten o'clock news, reported by the black lady with the puffy hair and coke bottle glasses. The headline read:

Fatal Car accident on the intersection of Gates Street and Pearland Blvd leaves 6 injured and 1 man dead.

Chapter 3

"That omelette just hit the spot." said Mama as she gulped down her cup of water.

"I knew you would love it."

I took a bite of my turkey sausage.

"I'm glad you suggested this place. But you barely ate your food which never happens. Are you still thinking about what happened with Ronaldo?" she asked.

"Yep. He actually introduced me to this restaurant, but I can't let it stress me. There has to be a good explanation. I hope it's not because he was with another woman."

"No, we are not going to speak that into existence. He does have a lot of explaining to do though. All you can do is pray for the situation. Speaking of prayer, you know the church's annual Christmas service is coming up so make sure you invite Kandi and Jamie and especially Jamie. That child really needs a blessing."

She started to discuss the new speakers coming to service that year, but I barely listened to her. I gazed out the window wondering what was really going on between Ronaldo and me. It was weird that he answered the phone and didn't say anything. We hadn't had any major arguments, so I didn't understand the logic. How could I be preparing for an engagement when I didn't even know what was going on with my relationship? My thoughts got interrupted by an elderly man at the window.

"I'm going to use the bathroom real quick before we go, be right back." said Mama as she motioned to leave the table.

An old man standing outside put my thoughts on pause as our eyes met for a moment through the window. He was putting on his winter gloves, which were the same shade of blue as his coat and hat. He was a handsome older gentleman with a light complexion. I smiled at him but for some reason wished I hadn't. He continued to gaze at me even after he finished putting his gloves on. He stared at me like I was a celebrity, and he was star-struck. I looked down and grabbed my phone to avoid looking at him any longer. I still had no missed calls or texts from Ronaldo. Our waitress finally came back to the table and said curtly, "Here is your bill but somebody already took care of it for you." She resembled a video vixen with lengthy false lashes, long Brazilian hair, full collagen injected lips and an even fuller chest and behind.

"What do you mean?" I inquired.

"I mean somebody paid it for you!" she snapped.

"Who paid for it?" I asked.

"I don't know; it was some old man," she said as she walked off.

The waitress had given us poor service the entire visit. She took her precious time coming to take our order, barely checked to see if we needed extra syrup or napkins and she gave us drinks without straws. I wanted to complain to the manager about the service, but I knew Mama would tell me not to. She would say that we didn't know what struggles that young lady had going on at home and that we should just pray for her. She wouldn't want to risk her losing her job for something small. I really didn't care at that point; I wasn't in the mood to be disrespected by anybody else. I decided I would call in later to report the waitress to the manager without Mama knowing. I checked the name on the receipt since she had not introduced herself when she came to serve our table. Gabrielle Abby was printed at the bottom. I felt something stapled to the back of the receipt and flipped the paper to find a church business card. At that point, Mama was returning from the restroom. She had a slight grin on her face as she sat down. As she slid into her seat she said, "On my way back from the restroom I ran into an old guy I used to know."

"You must like him; you came back smiling. Is he married?"

"I heard he got married some years back, but I also heard he got divorced so I don't know for sure. And I was not smiling either."

"Oh yes you were. You should have got his number to see what's up with him." "Chile, I'm not thinking about that man. But he gave me his business card. He has a plumbing business," she said.

"Well alright now, he got his own business. I like him already. Speaking of people we used to know; I went to high school with our waitress. I didn't even recognize her at first but when I saw her name on the receipt it clicked. She used to be so skinny with short nappy hair and a gap in her teeth. She looks like a whole new person now with all that work she got done. She is probably still bitter because Karl embarrassed her in front of everybody after she tried to bully me on the bus." I chuckled at the memory of the childlike foolishness.

"What? You never told me you got bullied on the bus!"

"Yeah, I know, it didn't last that long though.

I explained to Mama how the bus was always full when I got on because I was at the last stop. It was my first day as "Fresh

Meat" and there were no more seats left except the seat next to her but she wouldn't move over to let me sit down. As the bus driver pulled off, I was still in the aisle. The driver yelled at me to sit down. Gabrielle finally moved over but I barely had enough room to sit down so I was hanging off the seat. The following day, the only empty seat was directly behind her. As I approached her to go sit down, she stuck her foot out to trip me. Some kids started laughing and that's when Karl told her to leave me alone. He told her she was jealous of me because I was pretty, and she was ugly. He made fun of her gapped tooth and came up with every nappy hair joke you could think of. Someone in the back yelled out, "Let's call her Nappy Gappy!" Everybody on the bus started laughing and making fun of her and the incident got around the school. From that day forth she became Nappy Gappy to the entire school, but she never tried to bully me again.

"What? I wish you would have told me you had a problem on the bus back then but I'm glad that Karl looked out for you. The Collins family did a good job raising him and Kandi. I guess she remembered you and that's why she gave us bad service. I hope she didn't spit in our food."

"And that's why you pray over our food at all times right?" I said sarcastically. "Oh, I forgot to tell you that we got a free meal too. She said some old man paid for our food."

Somehow that triggered me to move my head in the direction of the window again . The old man was still standing there, watching me in awe. It was like he was trying to study my soul.

"Oh my goodness, this man has been staring at me all this time. Do you know him?"

I looked straight ahead to avoid looking at him again. Mama tilted her head toward the window. "I don't see anybody." she said.

I was afraid to look, but I quickly whirled my eyes in his direction but he was gone.

"He was just standing there. I know I'm not tripping."

"Well I didn't see anybody, so I guess you were tripping. But anyway, give glory to God for the gentleman who provided us a free breakfast. We are now full and appreciative! I'm going to leave the young lady a $5 tip. She would have gotten more if she hadn't bullied my daughter in high school."

"She doesn't deserve a tip because she was horrible!"

"I know but she is probably going through something in her life right now and you know two wrongs don't make a right." She pulled a five-dollar bill from her wallet and dropped it on the table. I shook my head at her but said nothing else, as I had learned to pick and choose my battles with her. We both got up to put on our coats so we could leave. Mama proceeded to the exit and I swiftly grabbed the five dollar bill from the table and placed in my coat pocket as I headed out the door.

Mama decided to hop in the car with me, leaving hers at the restaurant so we wouldn't have to take two vehicles to the mall. I saw Nappy Gappy through the window of the restaurant. She walked over to our table and inspected it for a tip. She must have been delusional to think she was going to get a tip from me with that stank attitude. I saw as she scanned the table for a few seconds. She rolled her eyes and stomped away like a little kid when she realized there was no cash waiting for her at the table. I was completely amused and laughed so hard on the inside that a giggle escaped my lips. Mama looked at me like I was crazy.

"What you laughin' at chile?"

I paused. I wanted to tell her that I snagged up the $5 bill but I decided to tell her later. I had no time to hear speeches about doing the right things for Christ.

"I just thought about something Jamie said last night," I lied.

Little did she know; the internal waves of laughter drowned out the sinking uncertainty in my heart about Ronaldo for just a moment.

Chapter 4

It was 8:15 PM when I pulled into the parking lot of The Japan's Steakhouse. The lot was packed as expected on a Saturday night. I drove down multiple aisles with no luck of an empty space. I was blasting tunes from my Jodeci station on Pandora. Just as I turned the volume down, I spotted a minivan backing out in the next aisle so I sped around to reach the spot before someone else got it. Luckily, nobody was coming, and I was able to slide right in. I parked the Camaro and pulled down the visor to make sure my lipstick was still intact. I was glad to get out of the house to take my mind off Ronaldo. I still had not heard from him and it had been over 24 hours since we last spoke.

After Mama and I had left the mall, I took a surprise trip to his job because he was always scheduled to work on Saturdays. I didn't see his car in the parking lot but one of his female co-workers had just come outside for a smoke break. I sat in the car a bit and debated if I should attempt to interrogate her or not. She didn't really seem like the friendly type, but I could ask her first instead of going inside the building. I bundled up before I exited the vehicle to go out into the cold world.

"Hey, excuse me, did Ronaldo come to work today?" I asked. She took a puff from her cigarette before answering. She looked confused as she said, "He got fired two weeks ago." This was news to my ears because he got up every morning at the same time. He put on his work clothes and headed out the house every day as if he were going to work.

"Fired? Do you know why he got fired?"

She took another puff from her cigarette as she shivered from the cold winds that blew into her face. I didn't understand why she was outside without a coat. She stared me in the eyes as she said, "Girl I don't even know but it seemed like he was trying to get fired," she said. She took one more puff and hurried back inside before I could ask anything else.

I knew Kandi's birthday dinner celebration could help take my mind off my current trouble. I had gone from girlfriend to possible fiancé to an "it's complicated" relationship status in the matter of 24 hours. I opted for the same wig from the night before, whom I had graciously named Blonde Bombshell. I applied red lipstick because I needed a confidence booster. I decided to wear a gold sweater over dark denim jeans with black leather boots and a black leather coat. Before I got out of the car, I had to take a moment to push any thought of Ronaldo out of my mind. I wasn't going to let him ruin my night out with Kandi and her family. I grabbed my mace and Coach wristlet and held my head high as I strutted inside the building.

The smell of sautéed onions and garlic tickled my nose as soon as I opened the door. There was a crowd of people in the waiting area, and it was quite noisy. I couldn't spot anybody I knew. As I continued to walk towards the bar area, I heard Jamie's infectious laugh and spotted her holding a shot glass in her hand at the bar. I saw Kandi's family seated at a table near the bar conversing and drinking. Kandi was closer to the bar with her new guy Hakim. He was whispering something in her ear when she spotted me.

"Hey sis!" she shouted out.

"Hey sis! Happy birthday!" I shouted back.

I got close enough so we could exchange a tight hug.

"You look so cute!" I said.

"Thanks! You too!" Kandi exclaimed.

Hakim reached out to me for a hug which surprised me. I had only met him a few times and we had never exchanged hugs before.

"Thanks for coming out," he said.

"No problem, I wouldn't miss my girl's birthday dinner." I looked over at Jamie. Our eyes locked.

"Hey sis!" we both said in unison. As we embraced, I could smell the same scent of Burberry perfume that I wore. I had forgiven her for her cheating accusations from the night prior. I always forgave her for speaking her mind.

"Girl you got to take a shot with us! Let me get you one!" Jamie said excitedly.

"Yes, I need a shot too but hold on. Let me speak to everybody else real quick." I walked over to the table to speak to Kayla, Karl, and Mama and Papa Collins. Kayla was my beautiful goddaughter. She was so focused on the game she was playing on her new iPhone. Karl and Kandi were the only children to Mama and Papa Collins. In my mind they were the epitome of what family should be and I longed for that type of family during my childhood. It couldn't get any better with a son, a daughter, two parents, a big house and a dog. Personally, I could do without the dog, but it was a blessing that her parents had been married for over 30 years. Karl looked just like Papa Collins, who was tall, dark and handsome. Kandi looked like a younger version of her mother. They both stood about 5'4, light brown complexion, hazel eyes, dimples, and jet black hair that reached the middle of their backs. Karl noticed me coming over and stood up to give me a hug.

"Hey Steph, how are you doing?"

"I'm okay, how are you?"

"I can't complain."

"Okay good. It's so funny that your name came up today. You won't believe who I saw at The Breakfast Den this morning."

"Who did you see?" asked Karl.

I laughed before I revealed the person's identity. "Nappy Gappy."

He laughed upon hearing the nickname that he had helped coin for her.

"But she is not Nappy Gappy anymore. She got that gap fixed and that hair was laid, fried and dyed to the side," I joked.

"Oh yeah? That's good for her. But now you got me feeling bad. I never thought my little jokes would have spread around the school like that."

"Don't feel bad, she still got a nasty attitude after all these years. She needs to get over it and get a life."

I noticed Mama Collins motioned for me, so I ended my conversation with him and went over to her.

"Hey! How are you?"

"Nice to see you beautiful," she exclaimed. I leaned down to hug her in her seated position. Papa Collins had just taken a phone call so I gave him a quick hug so as not to interrupt his call. I nudged Kayla and she quickly gave me a hug and got right back to what appeared to be Candy Crush on the phone.

Jamie came over with what appeared to be a porcelain shot glass. Jamie was 5'11 on a normal day but stood over 6' with her brown stiletto boots that night. Her mocha chocolate skin glistened from the bright restaurant lighting. She always wore a short pixie cut that nobody could rock better than her. She wore the same leopard print jumpsuit that I almost wore but I decided against it to avoid showing off my kangaroo pouch. She didn't possess abs of steel by any means, but she was much more confident in her body than I was.

"Here you go," said Jamie.

I took the glass and gulped down the drink without asking what it was. It went down smoothly and wasn't too strong.

"Ooh this is good stuff!" I proclaimed.

"I knew you would like it. The bartender just schooled me on it. It's called Sake. He said it's Japanese liquor made from fertilized rice or fermented rice or some kind of rice girl. I forgot exactly what he called it, but I love it too. I've been drinking the blue raspberry flavor but there are other flavors too."

Kandi came over as she overheard us discussing the Sake.

She chimed in and stated, "I feel so sophisticated drinking Japanese liquor on my 35th birthday weekend!"

"You mean your 21st birthday for the 14th time!" I exclaimed.

"Oh yeah I forgot, that's right. I'm still 21 in my head," laughed Kandi. We all laughed together and mingled some more while we waited to be seated. During the wait, I continued drinking the Sake. One shot turned into three, then three turned into six. My legs started to feel wobbly, but I continued for a total of eight shots.

Hakim and Kandi kissed each other from time to time. They looked very comfortable together already. Her parents didn't know the truth about how they met. She didn't want them to disapprove in the beginning so she told them they met at the grocery store in the produce section.

About fifteen minutes went by and Hakim went to check on the table to see how much longer it would be. It wasn't until he walked away, that I noticed that he and Kandi were color coordinated. Kandi wore a long black velvet dress with a burgundy blazer of the same fabric and a pair of stunning burgundy and black floral boots. Hakim wore black pants and a shirt with a burgundy velvet blazer as well with black loafers. I was shocked to see matching blazers after just six months of dating. He came back and said, "Our table is getting cleaned now so we will be seated next."

"Thanks for checking baby," offered Kandi. He sat down and they kissed again.

I was glad that no one asked about Ronaldo's whereabouts. Kandi and Jamie were already aware of the confusing events and we agreed not to talk about it at dinner. I had told Ronaldo about the dinner earlier that week and I even had an outfit planned for him to wear. I always wanted us to dress like twins or at least color coordinate like Kandi and Hakim but he thought that was corny. So, I had set aside a nice Polo sweater and dark denim jeans to match mine.

Sounds of shouting and screaming ensued suddenly. Two workers and a manager ran through the bar frantically toward the dining area. Some bystanders stood up and followed them toward the chaos.

Kandi yelled, "What the heck is going on?" We all stood up to look through the opening to the dining area. The workers were pulling a woman holding a cell phone as she elbowed them and tried to turn back around.

"Let me go! Get off me!" she screamed to the employees. "I'm showing these pictures to my brother! You don't deserve him anyway!" yelled the angry woman to another woman who was still seated.

"Come on ma'am, you have to leave the premises now," said the manager.

People laughed, oohed and awed at whatever was happening.

"Get that ghetto heffa out of here!" yelled the woman who was still at the table. She hurled a piece of chicken at the other lady's back. That piece of chicken barely went the distance, but she tried it. "Forget you and your brother!" she said as she sat back down in her seat. The guy next to her kept his head down with embarrassment and didn't say a word.

The managers continued to escort the angry lady out. Someone in the crowd asked what happened. She openly volunteered the information as she was almost out the door. "Oh that lil trifling tramp in there cheating on my brother and I videotaped her and snatched that lace front off her bald head!"

"Dang, I feel like I'm watching an episode of Cheaters: Sisters Edition," Kandi said.

"Right!" I exclaimed.

"That dude probably told her this meal was too expensive to leave so they had to stay to at least catch the shrimp," Jamie said jokingly. They all laughed and shook their heads in disgust of the situation.

"That sister was a little out of line though. Her brother and his lady may have an open relationship or something that she doesn't know about," said Kandi.

"Well true but she couldn't just see that and not address it," Jamie said.

"Yeah but she still didn't have to act all ghetto in a public place like that," Hakim chimed in.

"Party for Kandi, your table is ready," interrupted the hostess.

"Whew about time!" exclaimed Mama Collins.

We had to walk past the alleged cheating woman. At that point she was on the phone with someone retelling the details of the incident. The guy was still silent with a look of embarrassment on his face.

"This is your table here. Enjoy," said the hostess.

We all sat down, and Hakim pulled the chair out for Kandi. It made me think about my relationship with Ronaldo again. He didn't automatically pull out chairs and open doors. I had to remind him most of the time. I could tell that he didn't like being told how to treat me, but he had to learn eventually. I wanted to stop thinking about him, it didn't matter whether the thoughts were good or bad. I ordered two Amaretto Sours, hoping the buzz would erase him from my mind.

"Sis, you going hard on the drinks tonight. You trying to bring in the holidays early I see," said Jamie.

"It's your fault for giving me all those shots when I came in."

The short Japanese chef with a gold tooth and ponytail hanging out of his hat, rolled his food cart over to our table.

"Welcome to Japan's Steakhouse, how are we doing tonight? Are we celebrating anything special tonight?' the chef asked.

"Yes, it's my birthday weekend!" yelled Kandi as she waved her arms in the air.

"Awesome! Turning 18 I bet," said the chef jokingly. "But I heard there was something else special going on at this table tonight."

Hakim intervened, "Yes there is."

He got up and pushed his chair back and motioned toward the ground with a small box in his hand. Kandi looked confused until he kneeled and grabbed her hand.

"Oh my God!" she whispered.

Hakim was shaking a bit, but he mustered up the nerve to say, "Baby, I've been so happy since you came into my life. You accept me for who I am, and you don't try to change me. I know it's been a short period of time, but I love you already. I want you and Kayla to be part of my family and I want you to be my wife so will you marry me?"

He opened the box to a beautiful princess cut diamond ring. Kandi's eyes and mouth were opened to the fullest capacity and she screamed "Yes, Yes! I'll be your wife!"

Everybody clapped and screamed in awe for the newly engaged couple.

Jamie jumped up and yelled, "Congratulations sis, I'm super happy for you!"

Kandi's parents clapped and nodded with approval too. Karl didn't look too pleased though. It looked as if he didn't want to mess up the vibe for his sister and everybody else, so he forced a fake smile. I was surprised that Kandi didn't cry happy tears of joy during her proposal. We always talked about how we would cry when our future husbands proposed to us. I was also shocked that the engagement occurred after only six months of dating. I knew Kandi always talked about finding the perfect step-father for Kayla and she deserved happiness. Kandi was such a caring soul and one of the most understanding people I knew.

Ronaldo and I had been together for three whole years and I was just cabbage patching in the mirror with thoughts that I would be the one getting a holiday proposal. As a matter of fact, I always thought I would be the first of the Three Amigas to get married.

"Did everybody know about this?" Kandi asked.

Before anyone could answer, Hakim said, "No it was all my surprise. I wanted your closest family and friends to be here at your favorite spot to give you the best birthday gift ever."

"Aww that's so sweet baby. I love you!" Kandi exclaimed and their lips collided once more.

The rest of the night went better than planned. The chef did an amazing job with the food and entertainment. The newly engaged couple were all smiles and giggles. Most of the entourage was in good spirits too. Once the food was gone, I was just ready to go get in my bed. I waved the server down to ask for the bills, but she had them in her hands already. I was the only one who had my debit card out. I handed it to the waitress right away without even checking my bill.

"Come on y'all, we need to take a group picture really quick!" Jamie yelled out.

Everybody got up and started to crowd around the newly engaged couple, except for Karl. He headed to the front of the table with his cell phone and said, "I'll take the picture."

Kandi held her hand out to display the new diamond and Hakim placed his arm around her. The rest of the party huddled around them as Hakim snapped a few different pictures.

As the server walked past, Kandi yelled out to her, "Excuse me, can you take a picture of us so my brother can get in the picture too?"

The server was about to respond but Hakim interjected, "Oh that's okay, you know I hate taking pictures."

"Boy, come get in the picture. This is a special day for your sister," demanded Papa Collins.

"That's right daddy, tell him," Kandi said.

Hakim sighed but went ahead and handed his phone to the server to take the picture. He rolled his eyes at his dad and came over and stood next to me. I was sure he would have a serious face or fake smile on the picture. After three clicks of the camera everyone dispersed back to their seat and the server headed to me. She whispered, "Sorry but your card declined, do you have another card to use?"

"Are you sure?"

"Yes ma'am. I ran it twice to make sure."

"I just used that card at the mall earlier with no problem, but I do have another card you can use, one moment."

"Okay," said the server.

"Is everything okay Steph?" asked Kandi.

I reached in my bag and grabbed another card to pay with and handed it to the server.

"Yeah everything is fine."

That account had more than enough money in it to pay for that bill so I didn't know why a hold would have been placed on the account. I really needed to leave so I could check to see what was going on with my account. My thoughts were interrupted by Hakim standing up to get everybody's attention.

He said, "I just want to thank you all for making this the best birthday and engagement celebration ever. My future wife and I will always remember this day."

"Aww, that's so sweet baby," Kandi told him with a big grin on her face.

The server came back to give out change and receipts. I got nervous and hoped there was no issue with the second card. She smiled at me with reassurance and politely handed me the receipt to sign. I gladly signed the receipt with a sigh of relief.

"Hey guys, I'm really tired. I'm going to head on out now," I said.

"Wait we all headed out so let's just leave together, I see my uber ride should be here in five minutes," said Jamie.

"I'm glad you're getting an Uber because you are drunk."

"Wait a minute now, you weren't too far behind me yourself. You sure you don't need to hop in the Uber with me?" Jamie chuckled.

I laughed too, "Girl no I can handle my liquor, I will be just fine."

Everybody walked out together, gave hugs and said goodbyes. I think I stumbled a little bit to the car.

"Are you sure you don't need an Uber to come take you home?" asked Karl.

Before I could reply, Jamie jumped in and said, "That's why I didn't drive, I knew I was getting lit tonight. As a matter of fact, my Uber is pulling up now. Bye everybody and congrats again Kandi and Hakim, love y'all!" She staggered toward the little blue vehicle.

"Did you want to ride home with Karl and come back to get your car tomorrow?" asked Kandi.

"No that's okay. I'll be fine, I promise."

"Okay, well text me when you get home," Kandi insisted.

"Okay I will and congratulations again to you. I love you." I waved goodbye to everyone.

I turned the heat up to the max and opted for the club mix on the radio instead of my Pandora app. The volume was up so loud at first; it made my head spin. I probably did need a ride home instead of driving. But the time was 10:15 PM on my dashboard and I estimated I could get home around at around 10:30 PM. After a few minutes of driving, the phone rang. I answered right away, hoping it was Ronaldo.

"Are you sure you are okay?" asked Jamie.

"Yes, I am just fine," I told her sarcastically.

"Okay, well you were drinking a lot more than usual tonight and I know you were wondering what's up with Ronaldo---"

Before she could finish, I interrupted, "Girl I told you I'm fine. I don't want to talk about him right now. I'm just glad he is alive so that's all the matters now. Our girl just got engaged and we didn't even see it coming. Everything is fine, trust me."

"I know right, I was so shocked. We joked with her about online dating and what do you know? She goes off and finds a husband from a free dating site. I may have to go on loveconnect.com and get my girls a step daddy now," Jamie joked.

I chuckled at her. "Girl you are so silly! But yeah, as long as she's happy then that's all that matters."

"Right and I think she really is, but my phone is about to die. Text me when you make it home."

"Okay I will. Goodnight."

I turned up the volume to the max to keep me awake from all the Sake. I couldn't understand how some people got turned up on booze and others like myself were tranquilized.

When I turned on my street I wondered if I would see Ronaldo's car parked outside the condo. A melancholy gloom loomed over me as I pulled into the garage. When I entered, I knew someone had been there because the light in the foyer was turned on. I also noticed a cup on the table that wasn't there before.

"Ronaldo, Ronaldo!" I screamed his name in case he was still inside. I marched up to my bedroom which somehow seemed unfamiliar. I realized I still had my coat on when I saw myself in the dresser mirror. My eyes then gravitated toward the top of the dresser that formerly housed two cologne bottles, a man's watch, and an old wallet. Those items were now absent and the area was left vacant. I looked around the room some more to see if anything else was missing. All my things were still intact in the same spots as they were before I left the house. The only place left to look was the closet, so I slid the closet door back. The closet was filled with dresses, blouses, skirts, jeans, sweatpants, high heels, boots, and tennis shoes. The other half was bare and naked now. Before I left for the evening, there were still tennis shoes, Polo Shirts, jeans, a few slacks and button-down shirts.

I stepped back, and this was the moment when I officially knew that he had left me. He took all his belongings right before Christmas and he left me remnant and alone. I slid down to the floor, curled up and began to bawl. I quickly got overheated as I still had the thick leather coat on. It was the same coat he got me for our first Christmas together. The precious memory forced me to sulk in my tears even more than before.

"What did I do? How could you do me like this?" I asked myself out loud.

I tried to think about what I could have done so bad for him to betray me in that manner. I was patient and understanding with him. He was sort of a diamond in the rough when I met him, but I saw past all of that. I envisioned helping him reach his full potential which would make him love me in that longing way I wished to be loved. Since he had no real family in town; I wanted to be his everything so he would have no reason to ever go back to Michigan. Had I nagged him too many times when he forgot to open the car door for me? Had I gained so much weight that he was no longer attracted to me? Did I not give him enough attention? Maybe I had put too much pressure on him to be who I desired. He did tell me on more than one occasion that I acted more like his mother instead of his girlfriend. I begged to differ though. I only wanted the best for him emotionally, physically, spiritually and financially. Speaking of finances, a light bulb instantly went off in my head and I thought about my card declining. I hopped up quickly from my sympathy ball and grabbed my laptop. I moved so fast that I initially typed my password wrong. When I finally got past the password screen, I clicked the Safari icon to go my bank's website. The usually fast high-speed internet connection crept along like a thief in the night. My heart ached like an infected wisdom tooth.

"C'mon hurry up," I yelled at the screen. Time seemed frozen just like the computer screen.

"What the heck? Did he take my high-speed internet with him too?" I yelled.

Finally, the website came up and I was able to enter my user ID and password. The account appeared on the screen. The total available balance was zero dollars. My mouth dropped in disbelief. I saw the six transactions from my purchases at the mall which only totaled a little over five hundred dollars.

Then I saw the most recent transaction was a withdrawal of six thousand dollars, which I hadn't authorized.

I wanted to throw the computer to the ground just like he did my heart. The blood from my fragile heart spilled and splattered all over the shiny hardwood floor. I could no longer let out a tear or a wail or anything and my face grew numb. The numbness trickled down throughout my whole body and shut down all my defenses. I couldn't cry anymore. I refused to cry again since another man had left me alone in the deep pits of darkness while I struggled to find light. The sudden sound of the ringing telephone bought back a small glimpse of light, but it was still entangled within the webs of reality. It was probably Mama since I didn't call or text to say that I was back home yet. I couldn't bear to speak to her at that moment. How stupid would I sound if I told her that I added his name to my checking account?

I recalled him sitting on the couch with my head in his lap as he massaged my scalp.

"Hey baby, since we go half on the bills; it would be easier to have our money combined so we can do auto bill payments from a joint account," he said.

"Oh yeah?" I asked.

"Yeah, I mean we already live together, and we do everything together. It's just like another step in our relationship."

I leaned up toward him and poked out my lips for a peck.

"Well since you put it like that, I guess we can."

I had no reason not to trust him, so I was ecstatic about taking another step in our relationship. It assured me that he wanted to marry me one day.

The day I made that disgraceful mistake was only two weeks prior on a cloudy Saturday morning. His alarm clock sounded off like a siren at 8:00 AM and he got up out of bed immediately to stretch, then walked over to my side. I did not move a muscle. He placed his large hands on my shoulders and started rocking me to pull me out of my slumber. I slowly opened my eyes up at him like a cute little baby and then closed them back in the same manner.

"Get up baby," he said as he shook me again but more gently.

I mumbled something and turned my warm body in the opposite direction.

He sighed at me and said, "I know you're still sleepy, but we need to go to the bank to have my name added. You know the bank closes at noon, so we need to get there before my shift at work starts."

I still didn't say a word at first. I briefly wondered why we couldn't open a separate joint account. The thought was interrupted when he reached over and planted a sloppy wet kiss, oozing of morning breath, on my right cheek.

I heard the concern in his tone and felt the urgency in his kiss.

"Okay baby I hear you. I'm getting up," I said as I cautiously turned my body around. I directly faced his dark-skinned torso. I could almost see his ribs through his bare skin. His hirsute chest wasn't something I admired much, but I never told him. I preferred a smooth chest.

"Do I need to cook more?" I asked. "I'm supposed to be fattening you up, not making you skinnier," I jokingly said about his appearance.

"Naw, you cook more than enough but you eat most of the food by yourself and barely leave any for me," he said. I laughed and playfully hit him in his empty belly.

"No, I do not," I said, my voice still raspy. I sat straight up in the bed. I considered the possibility of us opening a brand-new joint account together. I wished I would have thought of that sooner but since I didn't I just went with the plan that we originally discussed and settled on being satisfied that we were moving to a new level of trust.

He hadn't made a deposit yet, so all of that money was mine. Then again, I couldn't call the cops on him because I had legally added him as an authorized account holder. This was my own fault. How dare he take all the money out of my account, come get all his belongings and leave me without a trace or an explanation?

I quickly unbuttoned the coat and threw it down in the middle of the floor. I ran into the hall and down the stairwell. I didn't know why, but I was just compelled to run although I had nowhere to go. As soon as I made it to the living room, I noticed the photos of him and I on the coffee table. That was the same coffee table that he put together on his own and surprised me with one day after work. There were two 8x10 photos of us taken the prior year on my birthday which was also Valentine's Day. He stood behind me with his hands wrapped around my waist in the first picture. In the second picture, which was my favorite, we were positioned face to face. I smiled from ear to ear because I had finally convinced him for that one time to color coordinate with me. He displayed a wide grin on his face. Was that the smile of the devil himself who had preyed on his unknowing subject? He only agreed since we were taking professional pictures. We were both captured in time with his red sweater and my red mini dress that represented our so-called love on Valentine's Day. I grabbed each picture off the table and threw them face down on the hardwood floor. I pretended the pictures of him were his real face and I stomped the cracked glass with my boots until I couldn't stomp anymore.

Chapter 5

On Monday morning, the chirping alarm sounded like music to my ears. I wanted to get up and get out of the house so I could be busy. My mind kept wandering to the darkest of places. I turned the alarm off and jumped up to get ready for work. When I looked in the mirror, I had swollen semi-dark circles under my eyes. My eyeballs were still slightly red from all the crying. I got myself dressed up in the best outfit I could find to look better than how I felt.

I got to work about five minutes before my shift started. I tried to be chipper and not think about the ill-fated weekend. I looked sharp, donning a navy-blue blazer and matching bottoms, accompanied by a blue and white striped bodysuit underneath and Simply Vera Wang booties of the same navy blue family. I stopped by the cafe and grabbed a cinnamon roll and orange juice. I greeted my co-workers as I passed them and tried to seem as normal as possible.

I logged into the computer at my start time and impatiently waited for the systems to load up. I sighed as I waited, more so because I wasn't sure how I was going to get through the day. Thoughts of Ronaldo kept racing through my mind, and I needed answers. My thoughts were interrupted by a pounding on my office door, which I figured would be my co-worker Liz.

"Come in," I yelled.

"Good morning!" Liz quipped. "Did you hear about the email yet?"

She closed the door behind her and took a seat in the leather chair across from me. She took a sip from her usual morning cup of tea. She was a heavy set older Italian woman with tight black curls. She took me under her wing when I first came into the department. She had such a genuine presence about herself and the two of us became an unlikely pair of work buddies.

"Good morning! And no, what email?" I asked.

She leaned forward into the chair and said, "It's bad news chicka."

"I can't afford any more bad news." I thought.

"Oh lord! Go ahead and tell me."

"Well this department is downsizing at the end of 4th quarter to only 25 employees. So, the average top 25 sellers will be saved and the rest will be out of work when 2020 rolls around."

"Wow! Are you serious?"

"Dead serious. You can check the email yourself when you get time." She took another sip from her tea.

I felt somewhat hopeless. I was not a naturally competitive person. I did like my job but not in a sense to compete for it. The career was handed to me on a silver platter. I came into the company as an intern with the High School Internship Program my last two years of high school. I got hired on with an entry level telemarketing position after my senior year. They even offered me tuition reimbursement for college, but it had to be a degree in telecommunications. Telecommunications was never my desired degree program, but I didn't want to turn down a free education and massive bank roll. My peers were bringing home paychecks from The Gap, Dollar Tree and Payless Shoe Source with just a little above minimum wage. I, on the other hand, was making twenty dollars an hour by my sophomore year of college.

I tried to get Jamie and Kandi hired on, but they did not pass the aptitude tests with the scores needed to get an interview. The testing had been waived for me and I got an automatic interview after high school graduation. I was nervous, as I had never been on a job interview before, but I had memorized all the tools we learned in the Program. I remembered to smile, make eye contact, no gum, ask questions, sell myself and show interest in the position. I also knew that I had to wear a skirt or dress below the knees and no cleavage could be shown. Over the years, I did my job the best that I could; not too much or too less. In 2013, I eased my way into an executive sales position complete with my own small office. I felt that position came to me by chance or perhaps affirmative action, but Mama told me it did not matter how it happened. She told me to be grateful that I was one of God's favorites. I was certain I was not one of his favorites.

"Well I believe you. I just didn't see this coming. Did you?"

"Nope, I was blindsided by the announcement. It's going to be a war zone in this office now." I wish it was based on seniority because I would have it in the bag then," said Liz.

"I know right. You got thirty years with the company, right?"

"Yes ma'am I do and you're not too far behind me."

The thought of losing the only job I had since college weighed heavy on me.

I bent my head down and wrapped my hand across my forehead. I seriously wanted to sob right at my desk. People say when it rains it pours and it was most certainly pouring down on my parade. The last person who needed to hear about possible unemployment was a woman who was recently robbed blind of six thousand dollars. My head hung low and I took a few deep breaths to calm down.

"Oh, it will be okay sweetheart. Don't stress yourself over this. All you can do is do your best and if it's meant to be then it will be," said Liz.

How sweet of Liz to think I was moping because of the recent email. She was blind to my entire circumstance and it was best for her to see it that way.

"Yeah, you're right. I can't stress off something I can't control," I said as I lifted my head back up.

"That's right; we will just work as hard as we can and pray about it. Now how was your weekend?"

I paused at the question. I wanted to tell her what happened to gain some sympathy but on the other hand I was embarrassed.

"Oh, my weekend was kinda busy. I did Karaoke, went out to breakfast, dinner and did some Christmas shopping at the mall," I offered. It was mostly the truth, but that was none of her business. "What about you, how was your weekend?"

"Oh, I didn't do anything fun like you. I just cleaned out my closet. I had so many old clothes and shoes that I haven't worn in years. I threw most of it in the garbage. My closet was almost empty when I got done," Liz chuckled.

I chuckled too and took a sip of my orange juice. At least I wasn't the only one with an almost empty closet: half empty just like my heart.

Chapter 6

I was so depressed after Ronaldo left but I didn't want to admit that. I especially didn't want to say that I was depressed over a no-good man who took my money and left me right before Christmas. Christmas in 2018 was not so merry at all. I knew I would be alright though. I was raised by Grandma Rose and Mama, who were the strongest women I knew. I kept it all bottled inside because thinking about it did me no good, but it was so hard not to think about it. All that I could really do was move on with my life.

I had endured much emptiness in my lifetime, but I was still functional. I began feeling less functional as before. The reality of being a childless, unmarried woman started to weigh down on me. I didn't want to do anything or go anywhere and especially not for the holidays. I had to turn down some invites because I knew I would see all the women celebrating with their husbands and their kids. I had no children to wake me up on Christmas morning to open gifts; not even a foster kid or a step-kid. I just wanted to hibernate inside like a bear.

Most of our family lived back in Tennessee, which were Grandma Rose's family, and Mama had no idea on the whereabouts of her deceased father's family. As a matter of fact, we didn't know much about her deceased father either except for his first name. History repeated itself with me because I didn't know much about my deceased father's family either since he grew up in foster homes and never knew the names of his birth parents. Mama said he had a void in his life that was filled by filthy needles. She hoped that being a father could help him overcome his abandonment issues, but he overdosed by the time I turned two, so I have no recollection of him. Not even one solid picture to compare our features. But, you never miss what you didn't have so I wasn't affected by his absence especially when June Bug was alive. However, I was careful to ensure that my future children would not be cursed like me and Mama and it was of great importance to me to have a father figure in their life.

After Grandma Rose passed away, it was just me and Mama for the holidays. I had grown accustomed to that but sometimes I longed for something more. Luckily, I was blessed with Jamie and Kandi who became my sisters despite not sharing the same blood. Their families always welcomed me with open arms. Jamie's childhood home was packed with three generations all living under the same roof. Something was always popping off at her house like yard sales, barbeques, birthday parties and water balloon fights. She moved out after she had her first daughter, but her grandparents still lived in the same house. Her grandparents were the sweetest, especially her grandfather who had an affinity for me. He would always tell us stories of his younger days when he was a wild man before he met his wife. He would have me and everybody else on the porch rolling over with laughter. I always wished I had a grandfather like him but I didn't, so I enjoyed Jamie's grandfather instead.

I always wanted to have a big family as well. Maybe not as big as Jamie's family but more like the ones on television like Family Matters and The Cosby Show. I was drawn to the idea of black families who lived in the same house with a mom and dad just like Kandi and her family. Although it was just parents, two kids and a dog, their life was similar to that of the TV families I watched. I never had that for myself, so I wanted to provide that to my children one day.

Since Grandma Rose passed down all of her recipes; I had planned to share some with Ronaldo so that we could cook and invite Mama over. I saw matching Santa Claus and Mrs. Claus aprons that I was going to buy for us. But thanks to him any joy that was given to my world had been taken away by him.

On top of that, the career that had been graciously given to me could also be taken away. The office, the desk, the telephone with the intercom and the voicemail that made me feel somehow important in the corporate world might no longer be mine. If I wanted to keep those office perks, I would have to bust my butt to maintain the job. I was no suck up and did not kiss nobody's behind for nothing, so I really hoped my hard work would pay off. If I didn't, I had nothing else to fall back on. I figured there was no need to dwell on what may or may not happen. Whatever was going to happen was going to happen. Besides, I knew Mama would pray for me; even though that wouldn't help it was nice to know someone was looking out for me.

"Girl you need to get out the house and ease your mind! It's Christmas Eve. We got plenty of drinks and food over here," said Kandi over the phone.

"No, I don't even feel like leaving the house tonight, I'm on my period and I'm just not in the mood."

"Are you sure? I want you to come to take your mind off of things. You can even bring Mama Carter too. You know y'all are just like family."

"Well she is already headed to the Christmas program at her church. She actually tried to get me to go with her, but

I told her the same thing I told you. She kept telling me that the House of the Lord will heal my wounds but I'm not really trying to hear that right now. I just want to eat, drink some wine and go to sleep."

"Well she does have a point, but I also see your side too."

"Thank you. If I do change my mind, I will let you know but I doubt it."

"Okay I understand. Well call me if you need anything. I love you and Merry Christmas."

"Love you too sis."

During the late night to early morning, a light dusting of snow swept over the rooftops of Helen Hills Condominiums. The temperature dropped drastically overnight, and it was a partially cloudy Christmas morning. The cool air seeped through my window sills, causing moments of involuntary shivering. I laid in bed with my knees bent in an awkward position. I had awful cramps all morning. I considered myself lucky compared to most women since I barely got cramps. Generally, they were extremely mild and didn't last long. I tried to lay still and hoped the pain would eventually cease. That was one of those times when I really longed for a partner next to my side. He could massage me where the pain was, go fetch some water or just be there for moral support. Yet I was alone, and the pain was so intense I thought I was dying. I did not want to die young with no offspring but at least I could reunite with my Grandma Rose. After a series of never-ending grunts and groans; the discomfort and pain finally dwindled down enough to briefly fall asleep.

By noon, I was up and out the door headed to Mama's house to help with our mini holiday dinner. My back was killing me, but I tried to be strong and assured myself that the pain would subside. I decided to rock a long red wig with a middle part that I named Red Hot Mama, just for the sake of holiday spirit, I guess. The usual red and green Christmas attire was replaced with all black from head to toe like I was dressed for a funeral. A sweatshirt and joggers were comfortable enough for me since some of my clothes had gotten a little snug.

We opted for just a small turkey, dressing, macaroni cheese, greens, and yams. Mama had the turkey in the oven since that morning and only had the dressing left to prepare. I really wasn't in the mood to tackle the side dishes, but I couldn't renege since I had already promised Mama I would do it. When I pulled up to the house, I jumped out and grabbed a shopping bag with Mama's gifts out of the trunk. In the bag was Mama's new all white church suit, a faux fur coat, and a Michael Kors purse. When she opened the door, she was wearing an ugly red Christmas sweater with matching leggings and slippers. Her short, cropped cut hair was covered up with a red, green and white scarf.

"Merry Christmas!" she exclaimed as she grabbed me for the tightest hug.

"Merry Christmas Mama."

"Here let me take this bag from you. So, do you want to open up gifts first or start cooking first?"

"We can cook first. You know I'm hungry."

"Of course you are little miss greedy!"

Spending time with my Mama on Christmas put me in better spirits. I was glad we changed plans and moved our dinner to her house instead of my condo. It was something about that house that provided a sense of comfort to me. It was the same house I grew up in with Mama, Grandma Rose and June Bug before he moved in with Rhonda. Mostly everything in that house was updated except Grandma Rose's room which was the exact same as if it were frozen in time. Grandma Rose put up a big tree every year with frilly garland that I hated, along with round ornaments, red ribbons and our black angel at the top. Mama felt like we didn't need a big tree anymore, so she had a small one that she got from Dollar General. That tree was free of the garland and ribbons but the beautiful black angel still made her appearance at the top. Although it was a small tree, it was still decorated with love. We headed off to the kitchen to get the meal prepared and Mama made sure her Christmas music was loud enough.

The euphony of Mariah Carey's voice from "All I Want For Christmas" belted from the stereo as Mama cut up some celery and onions. She watched me prepare the macaroni and cheese the exact way Grandma Rose had taught me. I could tell by her smile that she was proud.

"Oh, I didn't get a chance to tell you about the Christmas program. So, it was really nice and those little kids did such a good job in the play. We had guest speakers and a young lady sang a solo that bought the house down."

"Sounds nice. I'm glad you had a good time."

"Yeah I really wish you would have come. I know you would have really enjoyed it."

"Yeah maybe next year and I'm really sorry I---"

The strong cramping sensation stopped me mid-sentence. I hunched over the counter with a disoriented look on my face. Mama rushed to my side asking, "What's wrong baby? Are you okay?"

I wanted to answer but the pain had paralyzed my tongue.

"Come let's sit down."

She grabbed my arms and guided me to a seat at the kitchen table. "I'm cramping. It hurts so bad! Oh my God! Oh my God!" I moaned loudly.

She had never heard me complain of cramps before, but she always kept a bottle of Midol pills in her purse for relief. Poor Mama looked so scared to see her one and only child in so much pain. Within an instant, her motherly instincts kicked in and she went into caretaker mode. What was going on with my body? Something was not right with me. I screamed, grunted, and begged for any type of mercy to stop the pain.

Chapter 7

Silence and shame fueled the vehicle on the way back home from the hospital the night after Christmas. Speeding drivers passed Mama's tiny car multiple times on the curvy roads. I saw as some of the passengers looked over into her car window. It felt as if they were looking past my Mama who was driving but looking over at me with disgust. The consistent loss of blood drained my body not only physically but also mentally. The darkness of the cold night outside the window was a replica of my soul. Despite what I had been through I could not have been more grateful that she was there every step of the way transforming, from mother to nurse in the blink of an eye. There was no speaking nor the radio playing until we almost got back to her house.

"So, are you gonna to try to contact Ronaldo and tell him about this?"

I hadn't even thought of that before as I still tried to process what had transpired.

"Umm I suppose I should try to reach out to him somehow. But at the same time, he won't care anyway so I probably shouldn't."

"That son of a b---". She stopped dead in her tracks before she finished the sentence.

"Mama, were you about to curse?"

"Lord forgive me. I'm sorry. Yes, I was but I had to catch myself because the devil is a lie!"

I had not heard her curse since she turned her life over to the Lord a year after Grandma Rose passed away. She had told me back then, "I am without a mother and a father on Earth, so I adopted the Heavenly Father as my guardian. The church bench will now be my alternate residence." I remembered the day like it was yesterday.

"I'm just upset at him because you have to go through this all alone. But you will be okay. God does not put something on you that you can't handle. Your Grandma Rose always told us that too, remember?"

"Yes I remember." Then I laughed for the first time in days at the memory of some of her catch phrases.

"But my favorite saying was men are like buses, you miss one and it's another one coming in fifteen minutes."

Mama and I both broke out into laughter as we recalled the many moments she said that to us. She was so serious about it too, like she had firsthand experience.

"Yes, yes, yes indeed and also people come into your life for a reason, season or lifetime."

"Yep I remember that too," I said.

Mama glanced over at me, "Baby I hope it's not too soon to say this to you. But everything happens for a reason and God's rejection is often God's protection. Ronaldo wasn't the right one for you and one day you will find the one that is worthy of you."

She was right, it was too soon for me to hear that. Even if she was right, I didn't want it to be right. One day could be ten or fifteen years from now and I didn't want to wait that long. I yearned for my own family now, not one unknown day in my unforeseen future. Suddenly I thought that our baby could have saved our relationship. Had I known I was pregnant just a few weeks sooner I could have stopped everything from happening. Ronaldo would have been ecstatic to find out he would be a father. He always wanted to be a father and to be a better one than his own father. He would have never left me had he known I was carrying his unborn child. I then considered reaching out to him again to tell him of our loss. Maybe he would feel sympathy and come back home with the money he stole from me and realize that he still loved me. Maybe that would prompt him to kneel on one knee and propose to me like he promised. On the other hand I didn't even want to give him the satisfaction of knowing. He didn't deserve to know anyway after what he did to me. The doctor said the miscarriage was more than likely caused by a high level of stress, so technically it was his fault that my unborn baby died on Jesus Christ's birthday.

I remembered that I couldn't contact him anyway because his number was disconnected the last time I tried to call him, which was the day after his disappearing act. That was probably the best bet for him because what I had to say was nothing pretty at all. He even had me and the Three Amigas blocked from his social media so I had no way to thrust my rage upon him with vowels and consonants of vulgarity.

"And there is something else I need to tell you too," said Mama as she made a right turn.

I had no idea what she was going to say, and I really wished we could go back to the silence. Instead, I replied, "Okay, what is it?"

"Well I don't want you to feel alone in this 'cause you are not alone." She took a deep breath and a pause before she continued.

"I had a miscarriage before. I was at home by myself, so I had nobody to help me at all."

"Wow, I'm so sorry to hear that Mama." I reached over and gave her a side hug. "I can't believe you had to go through that alone. I had no idea."

"Yeah to be honest, I just blocked it out of memory. But I survived it and I'm okay and I know you will be okay too."

When we arrived back home, I just wanted to lay down and go to sleep. I didn't care about the Christmas gifts that still sat under the small tree. I already knew that Mama bought me clothes that I could wear to work and probably a new purse or shoes. The best gift that I could have ever received would have been a husband and baby but that was now out of reach.

I recalled my all-time favorite Christmas gift as a seven-year-old girl. It was a baby doll named P.J. Sparkles. The commercial advertised the Caucasian version but of course I got the African-American one. I was the happiest little girl in the world when I unraveled the sparkling wrapping paper that unveiled the box I had prayed for. Too bad prayers like that could no longer be answered.

P.J. had long stands of jet-black hair matched with a Chinese bang and a pink bow around her head. She also had a small heart over her chest and jewelry that sparkled so sweet and tender when I hugged her tight. I was P.J's mother and took her everywhere I went even to the bathroom. I hid her under the bed when I had company over because I did not want anybody else to play with her. I walked past the Christmas tree envisioning that happy little girl who was nowhere to be found now. I was so discombobulated like I didn't know if I was coming or going.

"Let me get you a towel, some clean underwear and pajamas," said Mama.

"Okay, and actually can you bring me a gown instead?"

"Sorry. I don't have any that are clean right now."

"I'll just get one from Grandma Rose's room."

I started to walk away towards her old room before Mama could offer another alternative. The door was closed but when I opened it, the cold air hit me in the face. The room had been preserved in the same manner since her death. The burgundy and white striped sheets and matching comforter set was crisp and pristine. Grandma Rose worked at a hotel up until she retired, so fixing beds was something she mastered. Directly above the bed hung an exquisite painting of a bouquet of sorbet roses in a distinguished glass vase. It was the prettiest painting I had ever laid my eyes on.

I used to tell her that I heard monsters in my room in an effort to sleep in the room with her. She let me come in sometimes under one condition. I had to lay with my feet at the bottom of the bed and in the opposite direction as her.

"Side by side sleep is only for women and men," she would say. I understood the rules and when she dozed off, I would lay on my back at the bottom of the bed and stare at the painting with P.J. by side. The body of roses danced an illusion on the canvas that captivated me.

On top of the chest of drawers was the same rose shaped brooch that she wore in our family portrait. It was light as a feather when I picked it up and examined it. It was tarnished now after all the years that went by, but it was still a great memory to hold on to.

I got lost in time as I reminisced. I snapped back as I realized I came in the room to get a gown. I moved my fingers down to the third drawer from the top and there laid multiple sleeping gowns in different colors, designs and fabrics. Each gown represented a place and a time with Grandma Rose. The one on top right was the one she wore when she dozed off on her pillow and woke up in the clouds of heaven. It was a soft cotton material, white with green and yellow flowers throughout. I shuffled through a few more and opted for the one that was fifth from the bottom. It was a gray thermal gown, which was great for cold wintry weather. After I showered, I found Mama knocked out on the couch. The lights were out, and This Christmas was playing on the big television screen. There was a red and green plush throw folded on the couch, so I unfolded it and draped it over her. She looked so peaceful and I didn't want to wake her up. I still gave her a goodnight kiss. I could not believe that life had been given and taken away from me and Mama right in that same house.

Instead of going to my old room, I snuck back into Grandma Rose's room. I got under the cool covers and hoped my body temperature would warm them up quickly. I laid in Grandma Rose's old spot and not at the foot of the bed. The mattress springs felt tender on my back and it was nowhere near as comfortable as my own bed.

The Mother's Day before Grandma Rose slipped away from us, Mama wanted to surprise her with a brand new mattress because she had complained of an aching back. Mama was so excited because she got approval for a credit line of $5,000 at the newly built furniture store a block away from her job. In addition to the mattress she also bought a new headboard, box spring, nightstand and dresser too. It must have been an old woman's dream to come home to a newly furnished bedroom. Mama set the delivery up for the morning time so that Grandma Rose would be at church. I thought it was a brilliant idea because she would be so surprised when she got back home.

Her reaction was not what I expected though. I waited anxiously in the hallway for her to shout out, jump up and down and thank Mama profusely for upgrading her room. I did hear shouting but it wasn't the kind that was expected.

All I heard was, "I can't even believe you had some strange negros coming up in my room tryin to fix something that didn't need no fixin!"

After that, Mama exploded. I assumed she was offended after all the hard work she went through. Grandma Rose was finicky about people being in her room but I thought she would get over when she saw the new bedroom set and mattress. I wasn't at liberty to take sides between them so I moved outside to get some fresh air and waited on them to finish their match. I think Grandma Rose won the battle like most times since Mama eventually stormed outside with two duffle bags on each of her shoulders. She slammed the screen door so hard I was shocked the glass didn't break into tiny fragments.

"C'mon let's go!" she said to me in a hurry.

"Where we going?" I asked in confusion.

"I don't know but we can't stay here no more! I'm gonna get us our own place to live. It's been long overdue anyway."

My body froze. Mama was already at the bottom of the steps. She looked back and saw me still sitting on the steps and yelled, "I said let's go!"

At that point I didn't ask any questions and my frail sixteen-year-old body leaped down the steps and followed her trail.

The nightstand and dresser from the bedroom set was still there, but the new mattress was returned and the old one was put back at Grandma Rose's request. Luckily, Mama had only put the old mattress in the basement until it could be discarded. I never really understood why she was so attached to that old mattress, but I understood we all have our own quirks.

I stretched my long legs out on the ancient mattress. My body was so exhausted, yet I was unable to doze off right away. My life seemed blurry and I hoped it was all just a bad dream and not my reality. I was distraught to my core in thinking about losing my baby. At the same time, it was hard to mourn a baby that I didn't even know existed yet. Strangely enough, I still loved it because it grew inside of me and I had helped to create it. The images of the hospital and the foreign doctor who tried to explain everything to us were fuzzy in my mind so I tried to forget. It was hard to understand his thick accent using medical terminology. But there were a few things I definitely understood.

"Lost so much blood. I'm sorry...baby no survive," he said.

He looked at me like I was crazy when I said, "Are you sure it was a baby? I never missed my period."

"Yes, very sure. You miscarry. Sorry." I still didn't believe him. Nothing he said to me made sense; especially that one thing that caused my numbness. I blocked it out and I couldn't trust the words of someone who could barely speak the English language. I knew he said it when Mama left to go to the bathroom but I didn't receive it. I decided to bury those words deep down under the sheets and blanket to never resurface and hurt me again.

I tossed and turned, but still couldn't get comfortable. I got up to turn the TV on in hopes the sounds would soothe me to sleep. I pushed in the small knob at the bottom to power it on then turned the tuner to Channel 30 KDNL.

As I walked back toward the bed, I decided to try my old spot at the foot of the bed. It seemed my body's indenture was still carved into the spot even though I was ten years old the last time I slept there. That was the same night I got my first menstrual period. It was on a warm Sunday afternoon in August, a week before I started fifth grade. It was just a regular day and I played hopscotch and kickball outside with some neighborhood kids. After I ran and played, I noticed wetness inside of my underwear, so I dashed inside the house for the bathroom. It was weird since I knew I didn't pee on myself, but I thought maybe I had. As I approached the toilet and pulled down my orange shorts, I saw my underwear lathered with blood.

"Of my God!" I said to myself as I stood there in shock for a moment. Mama was not home at that time, but Grandma Rose was in the kitchen."

"Grandma Rose! I need you right now. I have a problem!" I yelled from the bathroom.

She scurried her way to the bathroom. She asked, "What's wrong wit you chile?"

"I think I'm dying! I'm bleeding!" I exclaimed.

"Let me come in," she said.

I partially pulled up my underwear and shorts. I'm sure there was a look of disgust and confusion on my face.

As she approached me, I pointed downward and said "I'm bleeding down there."

She chuckled a bit and said, "Gal ain't nothin wrong wit you. You just got your period."

I was a bit relieved that I wasn't about to die a bloody death, but I didn't want to have a period either. The health teacher had talked to us about menstrual cycles in school. I had only partially listened. Or maybe I thought I was exempt from the menstrual cycle of things.

"Ain't I too young?" I asked.

"That's not my call to make. That's a call for Mother Nature. But you gon be just fine chile. Why don't you just soak in the tub right now and I'll bring you a pad. When you get out of the tub, call me and I'll show you how to use the pad."

"Okay thanks. Can you call my Mama at work and let her know?"

"Yes, I will let her know that her daughter is becoming a woman."

She headed out of the bathroom so I could get in the tub. Before she made her exit, she turned to me and said, "And baby you must keep yourself very clean down there so you don't walk around smelling like fish, okay?" I didn't understand how I could smell like fish if I hadn't eaten any but I just nodded.

She let me sleep in her bed that night. I didn't have to foster up an elaborate monster in the closet story or any other foolishness. She hugged me so tight that night and told me, "Goodnight, don't let the bedbugs bite."

I giggled at the silly rhyme and replied the same back to her. From that moment on we told each other that rhyme every night before bed whether in person or by phone, up until the day she died. Before we dozed off she asked, "Where's P.J.? I didn't see you bring her in here.

My eyes tightened right before I dozed off.

"I don't need a doll anymore. I'm becoming a woman now."

Chapter 8

The sound of a ringing phone annoyed me so I put it on silent. The ding and dongs of doorbells startled me. The lights and sounds from the TV screen were too bright and loud. The silence of quietness allowed me to think through my emotions.

I didn't want to talk to anyone. Text messages were fine since I didn't have to verbally speak. Mama got the hint after I ignored her phone calls but did reply back to her texts. She sent five prayer messages in just one day which was overkill. I had a series of missed calls from Kandi and Jamie too and I eventually texted them to let them know I wasn't ready to talk yet and of course they understood.

The darkness was so deep, and the solitude was so real. I wanted to cry but the tears would not fall. I just wanted to lay in bed and do nothing. I constantly thought of the family that I almost had. Maybe that was not meant for me.

I didn't even have an appetite or desire to cook, which was very uncommon for me. I couldn't fathom going to the grocery stores, malls, restaurants or even gas stations. I didn't want to see all the happy couples and families shopping and eating out together as a family. Even if I went to the gas station; I would probably see a nice-looking guy parked next to me with his woman in the car as he pumped the gas. That would make me jealous since I no longer had a guy to pump my gas.

I felt so lonely and incomplete in the cold world. I got chills just looking out the window as I saw the white snow draped over the tree limbs and plastered all over the ground. I despised the cold weather and wished I stayed somewhere warmer. The heat was turned up to an extreme 85 degrees which provided warmth around my frigid body. There was so much doom and disaster around my room with the clothes, shoes, paper, and trash that decorated my bedroom floor. The bedroom was as disheveled as my mind and my heart. People used to say that I was a bit OCD. Maybe I was the O and 1/4 of the C but a person with OCD would never be caught amongst such chaos. In the five days since I had left Mama's, I was no longer living, but merely existing. Luckily, the rest of the place was in good condition except the broken picture frames of Ronaldo and I on the living room floor. I still hadn't caught the urge to clean that mess up.

. . .

The other two amigas insisted that we get together for a lady's night. I wasn't prepared to go out in public just yet, so they recommended that we meet up at Kandi's condo to have a Vision Board Party. They really knew how to help cheer me up. I was the one that suggested us doing vision boards a couple of years before that, but we never got around to doing it. The first time I saw someone host a Vision Board Party was on Facebook. I thought it was inspiring, and a great way to speak things into existence. My own existence had gone through so many changes and challenges, so I definitely needed the positivity back in my life.

Kandi took her job as hostess for that night very seriously. She had our poster boards already laid out on the table with our names scribbled at the bottom and a pair of scissors on top. She selected poster boards that were respective to our favorite colors; pink for me, purple for her and red for Jamie. She had three stacks of magazines neatly lined up in the center of the table, *Essence and People* amongst the top. I expected to have snacks, but I only thought of the basics like chips and dip. I stood in shock to see an entire buffet of food: Shrimp cocktail, chicken wings, potato skins, deviled eggs, spinach artichoke dip, chicken salad, and even the lemon and strawberry filled cupcakes that I loved so much were spread across the kitchen island.

She left the door unlocked for Jamie and me to get in just in case she was still in the shower when we arrived.

"Dang, sis wasn't playing with the food I see," Jamie said as she grabbed a piece of chicken off the platter.

"I know. She is trying to get us fat, but I'm all for it tonight," I said as I grabbed a lemon cupcake.

I heard feet shuffling toward us. Kandi appeared from around the corner. She wore a lavender crop top, gray sweatpants with lavender furry slippers. Her hair was pulled up into a messy bun. As she scratched her scalp, my eyes were drawn to her left hand, which displayed her new engagement ring. It looked perfect on her slender finger. I realized I hadn't seen her in person since her engagement. I always thought I would be the first of the Three Amigas to get hitched. Kandi and Jamie had a phase in their twenties where they were known as female playas. Jamie had juggled dating four different men at the same time before. Kandi was a close runner up with three men at one time. It was all in fun for them; they were not having sex with all of them. They were just young, free spirited females not looking for commitments at that time. I on the other hand, was always a one-man type of woman. I knew men got away with cheating the game, but I wasn't a man. I loved the one on one partnership with my mate and I believed in playing fairly. I didn't want to give my heart to a man for him to turn around and renege on me for other women so I would never do that. Kandi got caught up one time and broke the heart of a really sweet guy who spotted her coming out of a restaurant all hugged up with another guy. That incident led her to give up her playa card but she was now about to score and be out of the game completely.

"Hey y'all!" Kandi shouted once she made it into the kitchen.

"Hey sis!" we shouted out in unison as we stuffed our faces.

She came and wrapped her arms around me, squeezing tightly as she whispered, "I'm so glad you came out tonight."

The sincerity of Kandi's hug was full of humility and good grace. I could sense that she just wanted me to get back to my old self. I was disappointed that I felt envy towards her for about the engagement. After all, we all deserve happiness. It shouldn't matter who got it first.

Jamie was the first at doing the rebellious things like drinking, smoking, having sex, and having a baby. Kandi was the first at milestone moments. She got her driver's license first and her first car before Jamie and me. She got her first high school job and moved out on her own before we did. Kandi and I started college at the same time at the University of Missouri but she received her Bachelor's degree in Social Work one semester sooner than I had. I was always the last to do everything in the group so I always hoped that getting married would be the one thing I could accomplish first.

"I'm so excited to do our vision boards tonight!" exclaimed Kandi as she made her way to grab some shrimp.

"Me too. We finally get to do them now after all this time," I said.

"Are you taking shots at us?" Jamie asked jokingly.

I smirked. "We'll all I'm saying is someone suggested doing

this like two years ago and if I recall nobody else wanted to do it."

"Not me, I had never heard of it before, but I was open to it. It was all her fault," Kandi said as she pointed her finger toward Jamie.

"I admit that I really wasn't feeling it at first. Some grown folks cutting out magazine pictures and pasting them on paper did seem like I was going back to third grade or something," laughed Jamie.

Jamie and I started to load our clear plastic plates with more food while Kandi got drinks out of the refrigerator.

Kandi pulled out some Seagram's flavored coolers. The Jamaican Me Happy was our favorite.

"Ooh girl, give me one of the those!" said Jamie.

"It's not like third grade though. You gotta open your mind and look at the bigger picture. It's more than just playing copy and paste. The whole idea is to speak positive things into existence for your life. And not only that, it's just a fun new way to identify New Year's resolutions and goals since seeing things visually on paper can help motivate a person," I explained.

"Well alrighty then lil Iyanla Fix My life. We gonna call you Stephanie Vanzant tonight. And Kandi over there gonna be Oprah. Instead of saying 'You get a car, you get a car!' she can say 'You get a poster board, and you get a poster board too!" Jamie exclaimed as she pointed her fingers at us mimicking the famous scene from *The Oprah Winfrey Show*.

We all burst out into gut wrenching laughter. I realized that I hadn't laughed that hard or even at all in a very long time. Ronaldo and I had many laughs together but never the kind that made you cry a little nor the kind that made you fall out on the bed and kick your feet up. I looked at Kandi who was also filled with giggles and I wondered whether she and Hakim had those kinds of moments during their new romance.

We indulged in the smorgasbord of appetizers before we began our task for the night. The "Mary J. Blige" Pandora station took us down memory lane as the 90's hip hop and R&B serenaded us. We twisted and twirled our bodies to the music while we cut out items from the magazines to represent on our vision boards. I peeked at Kandi's stash of pictures and saw clippings of flower bouquets, wedding dresses and a picture of a sandy beach. I wasn't able to see what Jamie cut out yet, but I could assume it would be pictures of money, credit cards, a rich man or something along those lines.

"This station is jammin tonight!" exclaimed Jamie.

Kandi and I both nodded as we continued our labor of cutting. The next song that came on was "Real Love" by Mary J. Blige and we all rose to our feet with no hesitation and began to boogie to the beat.

"Do y'all still remember the steps?" Kandi asked.

"Girl no, not after all this time," replied Jamie.

"I think I remember the first part of it," said Kandi.

"Well let's find out! We're gonna follow your lead," I said.

When the first verse dropped, my mind and body reverted to my elementary days when Jamie, Kandi and our old friend, Charmaine, would stay after school for an hour to practice our talent show dance. It took us a month to learn the steps. Charmaine was adorable with her baby teeth, caramel brown skin, and curly hair. Her older sister was our choreographer since she had taken professional dance lessons. We all agreed to wear black biking shorts, pink t-shirts and plain white tennis shoes which we called "white girls" for some reason. Charmaine showed up on talent show day with a lime green shirt instead of a pink one. Apparently, her sister told her she was the lead dancer and needed her appearance to stand out a little more than ours. Looking back on it now, that was kind of shady, but we didn't care back then. We just wanted to have fun, dance to one of our favorite songs and win certificates for free ice cream and pizza. But even more than that, I felt Mary's pain on that song. She sang about a search for a real love that she hadn't found yet.

It felt like the harder I danced the easier it would be for Mary to find her "real love." That sounded so ridiculous as I looked back on it, but those were the thoughts in my young mind. I also believed that Grandma Rose would have been just a little softer and happier if she had found real love. If Mama had found real love after my dad, I thought it would have replaced the empty place in her heart for the deceased father that she never knew. I also believed I would be on the same journey to find real love one day.

It was amazing how my legs and arms mimicked rhythms learned from the early nineties. Jamie and I followed behind Kandi and the way we kept up, I believe we could have been back up dancers for Mary J. Blige. The only thing missing was our pink tops and biking shorts. Our movements flowed naturally up until the end of the first verse. None of us could remember the rest of the dance routine so we freestyled for the rest of the song. Going back down memory lane with my girls was a great remedy to help with the recent mishaps in my life. It was a perfect ending to my six weeks of leave from work.

We continued to laugh, sing, dance and fill up our poster boards. Kandi presented hers first which overflowed with wedding related items. The clippings were cut out and pasted so neatly and well organized.

"So, as you all can see, my vision for the year is to plan a successful wedding with no wedding planner. I want to do it all myself since I have been planning my wedding in my head since I was ten." She laughed at herself.

I remembered being about seven years old planning my own wedding in my head. However, I was totally discouraged after June Bug's accident on his wedding day. It left a bad stigma attached to it that I couldn't release. I became more concerned about the long-term idea of marriage versus the wedding itself. I would be satisfied with going to the courthouse or even getting married in my home, alone with close family and friends.

She continued with her presentation. "I want us to go on a nice honeymoon to either Jamaica or some kind of island. Then I want us to find a bigger home to live in and work on giving Kayla a little brother or sister. So that's my vision for 2019."

I almost cringed at the mention of her wanting another baby, but I had to hold it together. Kandi and Jamie only knew one side of my story and not the whole thing so I couldn't fault her for wanting to have another child.

"You need to put some pictures of some money on there to pay for all that sis," Jamie joked.

"Naw, let me borrow some money from you," Kandi playfully shot back.

We all laughed. "Go ahead Jamie, I'm gonna go last," I said. Jamie cleared her throat several times as she got up from her spot. holding her poster board.

"So, this year I have a lot of visions. One, I want to make sure that my daughters are always happy." She pointed to a picture of two little girls laughing and playing together. "Secondly I want a new car. I want it to be red cause I always wanted a red car. Plus, y'all know I'm a hot girl! Muy, muy caliente!"

Kandi and I shook our heads at her for always being extra. There were various types of red cars and even SUVs on her board. Next she pointed to a section of pictures of black men in business suits and ties.

"Thirdly, I see a rich man coming into my life to fund my red car and to help take care of me and my girls. Ching ching! I also see peace and harmony in my life cause I'm tired of having to check somebody every day. I'm trying to turn my life around. So, I need zen and relaxation you know cause it be stressful out here in these streets. And overall, just looking to be happy and have a better year than before. And that is all."

She took a bow like she was some kind of performer and we gave her a brief round of applause before my turn came up.

My board consisted of many images and it was rather sloppy compared to Kandi's board, but had more images than Jamie's. I found random pictures of black women smiling. They all looked so happy and full of life and that was how I wanted to feel again. I spelled out J.O.B. in the left corner, which represented the guarantee of my current position at work by fourth quarter. And lastly the word L.O.V.E was spelled out in center with a picture of a diamond engagement ring. There were no images of baby clothes, strollers, or advertisements for diapers. It should have been there front and center, but that would have been a nasty reminder of recent tragedy.

Before I even spoke anything, Kandi said, "Oh I love your board, it's so unique."

"Thank you. So, my board is pretty self-explanatory. I need to ensure that I don't lose my job for one. And more than anything I just want to be happy again. I want a husband you know. I thought Ronaldo was going to be my husband, but he turned out to be scandalous. I just want to find my forever person and live happily ever after. I don't want to grow old and die alone."

The thought of my Grandma Rose dying alone in her room without love came to my mind. Rhonda who lost the love of her life on her wedding day also came to mind. I was afraid of finding love and then losing it or even worse; never finding real love at all.

The tears began falling from my eyes. I wasn't just crying tears for myself, but for my unborn child. I was so close to having everything I always wanted, and it was snatched away from me so suddenly.

"I feel like I'm part of a generational curse and I want to break it," I said, wiping my face.

Both of my friends came and surrounded me forming a group hug. I felt pitiful and hated it. I had to pull it together as we were having a fun filled night before I got all emotional.

"It's okay. I know you will find love again one day," said Kandi.

"Yeah girl you will. You're muy caliente just like me, you can get any man out here."

I smiled at Jamie's joke as I broke the embrace. I calmly wiped my face.

"Thanks y'all. I love you both."

They both chanted in unison, "We love you too!"

"You know what, I got an idea. I'll be right back," Kandi said as she scurried off.

"Oh lord, what famous idea does Miss Oprah have now?" Jamie asked.

There was no telling what Kandi was up to, but it would be something with good intentions, whatever it was.

She ran back in holding her MacBook Pro and said, "So I think we should set you up an online dating profile."

I laughed at the thought of it just like I laughed when she set her account up the summer before.

"Sis, I can't do online dating. I mean I am desperate but not that desperate," I said.

"Well hold up, are you saying that I was desperate when I did it?" asked Kandi.

"No, no, no it's just not my style."

"I don't know Steph. Maybe you should. I mean, this chick got a whole fiancé in just six months," said Jamie.

"Facts," exclaimed Kandi as she held up her ring finger to justify Jamie's comments.

"I don't know. You just got lucky but that would probably not happen for me. I would probably get some psycho trying to sniff my panties or something."

"Girl you got to be open-minded. All I'm trying to do is help you make your vision board become a reality. As a matter of fact, Jamie may find her rich businessman on here too so let's set up an account for both of yall!" exclaimed Kandi.

"Hey I'm with it!" Jamie said. "If I meet a psycho, it's okay cause I'm a little crazy too! Sign me up baby! My rich husband is still out there waiting for me.

The online dating world was not something I was accustomed to. Online dating was another form of serial dating which normally wasn't my thing. My longest relationship lasted eight years and it was with my high school sweetheart, Dante. We started dating when I was a senior. I always thought he was handsome when I walked by him in the hallways. He was definitely my type back then: Light skinned with a curly box cut, tall and thuggish, but smart. We happened to be in the same advanced placement English class, which was the first time he ever spoke to me. He started to make small talk with me as we sat in the back of the class. It took him a few weeks to finally ask for my number. I screamed for joy inside and wondered why it had taken him so long. I knew I liked his style and his demeanor, so I had no problem talking to him outside of school.   Online dating, on the other hand, would be much different. There was no way to know whether the person behind the keyboard was actually the person in the picture or a catfish. I was also more of a traditional type of girl and the whole process of chatting with multiple guys that I didn't even know didn't sit too well with me.

"I mean what do you have to lose?" asked Kandi.

I thought long and hard and I had nothing to lose but there was also the thought of not gaining anything either.

"Nothing to lose and if we do it together it will be fun," said Jamie.

"Yeah she's right. It will be fun and different for you. Let's get you back out in the dating scene to find your new man and leave Ronaldo in the past where he belongs," said Kandi.

"Right, forget about granddaddy. It's time to move on."

We usually coined a nickname for all the guys we dated based on something unique about them. Jamie believed that nobody under the age of sixty should be walking around with the name Ronaldo, so she nicknamed him Grandaddy. The thought of leaving him behind and moving forward with my happiness was the final push I needed to convince me. A famous quote crossed my mind: *The best way to get over one is to get under another.*

"Okay, I'll play the online dating game. Sign me up!" I said.

Chapter 9

The time off work was much needed and refreshing. I felt somewhat confident that I could come back and lead the month with strong sales. I was determined to be one of the twenty-five still standing when this thing was all over. As I walked to my office, I passed by two co-workers who were shocked to see me. They didn't probe or ask questions, they just welcomed me back. I felt that my absence was possibly missed. When I walked into my office, there was an Edible Arrangement on my desk. It displayed chocolate strawberries, bananas, and pineapples. I did not expect that but I knew who the culprit was. The note card that accompanied the goodies read:

You were missed but glad to have you back!

I sat down in my comfortable leather chair and looked around at the place. I was filled with gratitude at realizing I was one of few black women who held a position for a Fortune 500 company. I needed to put my blood, sweat and tears into this to make up for my absence. I had been out of the office the entire month of January and the first week in February. I quickly logged into my computer so I could get on the ball. I was glad I had saved my passwords on a sticky note in my desk because I had forgotten them all. I ate some fruit from the arrangement while I waited for the system to load. There was a knock on the door.

"Come in," I said.

"Hey there stranger!" exclaimed Liz as she peeked in slowly.

"Hey there Lizzy Wizzy! So glad to see you!"

She pranced over to me and welcomed me back with a tight squeeze. "So glad you are back. How are you?"

"Thank you and I'm doing better. I was getting bored cooped up in the house, so I was ready to come back and get busy so I could take my mind off things. By the way, thank you so much for the Edible Arrangement. That was so sweet of you!"

"Oh, you're so welcome."

I smiled at Liz as I continued working to get my systems pulled up on the computer.

"So, what have I missed around here?"

"Well let me take a seat first."

When she sat down, I noticed she had lost weight since the last time I saw her.

"Okay well, yours truly is number one in sales for January." She said as she did a little raise the roof dance for her accomplishment.

"Well look at you! Congratulations! Just so you know, I'm coming for your spot in February!" I said jokingly.

"I wouldn't be mad, as long it's me and you in the top five every month, I would be good with that."

"I know that's right Liz. It's just so stressful to even think about it so I try not to."

"Yeah I understand but all you can do is try your best."

"Yeah, you are right. But has there been any office drama lately?" I perked up in my seat awaiting the gossip. My life was so jacked up, it was good to hear other people's drama for a change rather than living in my own.

"Oh yes ma'am!" She hit her hand on the desk. "How could I forget? So did you know that Larry and his wife had got a divorce?"

"I didn't but are you talking about White Larry or Black Larry?"

"Oh sorry, I was referring to Larry Rogers."

"Oh no. He used to always talk about her when I would see him in the cafeteria. She even made cookies and brownies for the office sometimes."

"I know she was a sweet lady. But he was having an affair with a woman that he met on an online dating site."

My mouth dropped. "Shut the front door! I can't believe that!"

"I know right, but wait, it gets better." She cleared her throat before she continued, "Well apparently he wasn't the only one cheating."

My mouth was still wide open. "Say what?!"

"Yep he caught his wife with some man in the house when he got off early one day. That idiot has been going around the office telling everybody his business, but I guess he just needed to vent and get things off his chest you know."

"Wow, that is so crazy."

"Yes, but you never really know what's going on in other people's relationships. They can look so happy to the world but be miserable inside."

"That is so true. But why was he on a dating site when he had a wife? It's funny that you mentioned that because my friends convinced me to go on a dating site too. I've been on it since this weekend actually."

"Oh really? So, you and your guy are no longer together?"

I had forgotten that Liz didn't know all the particulars of my current situation. We had the best work relationship but that never really extended outside the office walls. We shared a quick text or phone call related to work or a certain television show that we both watched, but never too much personal information was given. I didn't tell her about the miscarriage or Ronaldo. I simply texted her and told her that I had some personal issues going on and I had to take time off work. She understood and didn't pry for details.

"No, we are not together anymore. My friends thought it would be a good way to meet new guys and to officially move on. Plus, one of my friends is an online dating success story so I decided to give it a try."

"Oh, I understand. Well I'm sorry to hear about your breakup. I know those can be real messy at times. Have you met anyone yet?"

"Well no I haven't officially met anyone, but it was so crazy that I had so many messages from guys that were giving me compliments on my pictures, sending their phone number, asking to meet up. It's overwhelming; I wasn't expecting to get so many responses in less than forty-eight hours."

"Well I'm not surprised; you are a very beautiful young lady."

"Aww, thanks Lizzy Wizzy and I see you shed a few pounds."

Liz smiled, "Yes I did! I started working out a little. I don't want to be an old, fat slob." We laughed. Liz got up and stretched and said, "Well let me let you get to work and see if you can really take my spot."

Finally, my computer had completely loaded everything that I needed. I was ready to get busy but I noticed I had over four hundred emails.

I smiled. "We shall see. Thanks again for the fruit, talk to you later." She smiled and gave me a thumbs up before she made her exit.

It was refreshing to hear about another successful online dating connection even though it came about inappropriately. I did have access to an array of men of all nationalities, backgrounds, occupations, and age groups. I could chat with and meet people from the comfort of my own home and not just hope for chance encounters with a cute guy at the bar. I felt Grandma Rose's stern presence again. If she were still in the physical realm, she would tell me "See there chile, I told you many, many times before that men are just like buses..."

Chapter 10

Mama always made the best tacos, so I was anxious for a Taco Tuesday with her. The aroma of the sautéed onions and taco seasoning hit me as soon as I walked in the door and it made me even hungrier than before.

"Hey Mama. It smells so good in here." I kissed her on the cheek while she was still at the stove stirring the taco meat.

"Hey baby, the food is almost done."

"Okay cool." I took off my coat and hung up in the closet. For some reason I realized it was the same coat that Ronaldo had bought me for our first Christmas together. I had intended to sell it or give it away but never got a chance to. I only picked it up off the coat hanger that morning because the inside fur was so warm to wear on such a cold day.

"So how was your second day back at work?"

"It's been an adjustment. I had forgotten some of the sales prices, so I had to refresh myself on that."

"That's understandable, you were gone for a while, but I know you will get back into the swing of things soon." I pulled up a seat to the table.

"Yeah I will." I agreed. "And how was your day?"

"My heavenly Father woke me up to see another day, so I am truly blessed and highly favored."

I already knew she was going to give a response with some type of religious context. "I know that's right Mama! Say that!" I said sarcastically. I quickly changed the subject. "Hey, did you ever call that man you ran into at the Breakfast Denn?"

She was in the process of filling our taco shells with meat and cheese.

"Nope! And can you get the sour cream out the fridge and grab us something to drink? I got lemonade and tea." I got up as requested.

"Why did you say nope like that?" I asked.

She turned around and looked at me, "How did I say it?"

"I don't know, it was kind of like you were shutting down and you didn't want me to ask about him."

"I don't really see a need to call him. He has his own plumbing business so if I ever need his company's services, I will contact him but other than that there is no reason to contact him."

"Well you said he is not married anymore, and you're not married, so maybe y'all could go out sometimes." I offered.

She moved to the table with our taco plates which resembled a dish from the Food Network. I handed her a can of lemonade and sat the sour cream down in the middle of the table for both of us to enjoy.

"Steph, can you please just leave it alone? I'm not calling him nor going out with him. End of story, okay?" I didn't know why she was so defensive about the subject, but I obliged to close the book on any further questions.

"Okay, end of story then." I bit into my first taco. It was pure delight. I had eaten a small lunch that day, so I was overdue for a good meal. "Mama, I love your tacos so much. I know mine are good too, but you really put your foot in these."

"Yep. Your Grandma Rose always taught me to put my foot in anything that I cooked, and she taught you the same too."

"Facts! One thing I can say about us is that we can throw down on some food."

"True, but you need to start cooking again. I always hear you going out to get fast food or asking me what I'm cooking."

"Well it's just easier to stop and grab something sometimes. It's not like I have a family to cook for, it's just me at home now."

What she didn't know is that I would have my meals planned and pre-prepped for the whole week if I had children and a husband to feed. I must have developed a sad look on my face after her last comment.

"Baby I'm sorry. I wasn't trying to make you feel bad. I understand that it is just you at home so naturally you're not going to cook as much. But I pray for you every night baby. I know you want a family of your own to cook for and I pray about it every night."

I sighed. "Thank you, Mama." However, in my mind, I had concluded that there was no need for her to pray since it hadn't worked in all this time. My cell phone vibrated with a text from Jamie.

Jamie: Hey sis, I got a date lined up already for this weekend. I told you I was muy muy caliente!

I laughed out loud because I could hear her voice as I read her text. Jamie was playing no games; She was on the search for that rich husband by any means. I hadn't even started a solid conversation with any of the men from the site yet. I only replied thanks to the ones who had given me compliments.

There were a few who were fairly attractive and some that looked like grease monkeys. Jamie's text reminded me to check the site because I hadn't logged in all day to see any new messages.

"So, Jamie just texted me and told me that she is going on a date with a guy from the site this weekend."

"That fast? That girl doesn't waste any time I see. She needs to come on to church and get her a nice church man."

I wanted to recommend that Mama find a nice church man too, but I refrained.

"I could probably get a date this weekend too! I have fifty new messages from today alone. I must say I'm kinda flattered."

"They could all be some crazy or fish catting you."

I wanted to laugh so bad and tell her it was called catfishing, but I kept a straight face and let her continue.

"And I know you heard what I said. You and Jamie need to come down to the church and meet a nice church man who loves the Lord."

She wanted a response, so I had to give her one. "Mama just because a man goes to church that doesn't make him a saint. We both know the ones in the church are the worse sinners sometimes."

"But we have a Singles ministry for those who are single and looking for marriage which is what you want right?" I hated when she made good points. However, I had heard stories of married ministers, preachers, and members of the clergy who had cheated on their wives multiple times and sometimes with women from the same church. Those images tainted my mind, and I considered all men of the church to be low down and dirty.

"Yes Mama, that's what I want."

"Well the church would be a better place to meet someone. I don't like the idea of y'all doing that online dating mess.

You tell Jamie to make sure she gets his full name and driver license number and give it to you just in case."

"Okay Mama, will do." I needed to change the subject fast to avoid any more negative talk about the dating site. Although I was apprehensive, Kandi and Hakim's success was a positive reminder of the possibilities. Even Larry Rogers from work had made a love connection online, so I had a tiny glimpse of hope.

Mama and I enjoyed the rest of our evening together as we watched a Lifetime movie on the couch just like the good old days. We always watched closely during the first fifteen minutes as we sized up the characters and took a guess at who the psycho killer in the movie would be. I had curled up and gotten so comfortable that I dozed off toward the end of the movie. Mama covered me with one of my favorite blankets from childhood which kept me so warm and cozy that I slept there through the night.

The morning sunrise shone in through the thin curtains and awakened me. I grabbed my phone off the table to confirm the time. I had about twenty minutes to spare before I had to get home and get ready for work. I continued to lay with my eyes opened. I looked around the living room, which Mama had transformed into a modern living space with throw pillows, unique lamps, throw rugs, and modern paintings. The paintings were nice, but nothing stood out more than our family portrait that still hung over the fireplace. I always wanted to get that photo recreated into a painting and title it as Mi La Familia. It represented two strong mothers who raised daughters without the presence of a father.

Although I received much love from Mama, Grandma Rose and even June Bug before he passed, I always felt the void of not having a dad or grandad around. When I was younger, I loved to escape to Jamie's grandparents' house or to Kandi's house where I could revel in the same atmosphere as men of the household. They took out the trash, they disciplined us, they worried about us talking to boys, and more than anything they were present.

As I laid on the smooth, velvet sofa engrossed in my thoughts, I heard movement in the hallway. I figured Mama was up and headed to check on me. I sat upright just as she walked in with a confused look on her face.

"Good morning, how long have you been up?" she asked.

"Not long and good morning. You still look sleepy; how did you sleep?"

She sighed, "I did not sleep well at all. I'm gonna be so grumpy at work today."

"Get you some coffee to help wake you up," I suggested.

"Yeah I'm going to need it today. How did you sleep on the couch?"

"I slept like a baby honestly. I always get the best sleep here no matter which room I sleep in."

"Well I guess it's like a place of comfort for you. I usually sleep pretty good too, but I had a bad dream that kept me up."

"What happened in your dream?"

"Umm, I don't really want to talk about it. It's getting late anyway. I need to start getting ready for work and you better get your car warmed up so you can get home and get ready for work too."

"Okay. I'm going to get up in just a few minutes, but I think you should talk about the dream because it may make you feel better instead of holding it in."

"Stephanie, I don't have time to talk about no foolish dream. Now hurry up and get going cause I don't want you to be late for work. You know how morning traffic can be."

"Okay, okay, okay." I got up walked to the window, pressing the button to remote start my car. I then folded my blanket. I still had on the plaid black and white slacks and white button-down blouse from the day before. I think Mama told me to put on a gown but I was too sleepy to move. She stretched her legs forward in the recliner as she waited for me to leave. I reached for my black booties to put on my feet, but I was still curious about the dream that was such a big secret.

"So, Mama, you don't have to tell me all the specific details of the dream, but can you at least give me a brief summary?"

"You know, you can be very persistent when you want to be." She shook her head at me, but she was right. I thought I had gotten her to break her silence, so I didn't want to ask anything more or less at that point. I finished putting my booties on as I awaited her story.

"Well since you insist, I'll tell you. I was looking for my father's grave at the cemetery in the middle of the night and your Grandma begged me to stop looking."

"Oh wow, okay.

"Yeah it was pretty interesting." Mama said as she looked away. I had pried enough so I decided against asking anything more about it.

The weather app showed that the temperature would be in the single digits that day. I hated the fact that I still had to wear that leather coat but it was the heaviest and warmest coat that I had in my possession . I dreaded walking out into the cold, but I bundled up accordingly.

"Do you have any gloves or a hat?" asked Mama.

I checked my pockets and felt the softness of a leather glove in my left pocket. I pulled everything out of my right pocket. There was neatly folded five-dollar bill along with a receipt with a church business card stapled to the back. I unfolded the receipt and glanced over it, noting that it was from The Breakfast Denn Restaurant, dated December 7, 2018. Gabrielle Abby was printed for the server's name. I chuckled.

"Are you serious?! Remember the waitress from The Breakfast Denn who had tried to bully me in school?"

"Yeah. I remember and I guess it's a good thing you never told me about that back then. You know I wasn't no joke before I got saved."

I chuckled. I could envision her along with Grandma Rose hopping on the school bus to curse out Nappy Gappy for messing with me, the bus driver for letting it happen and any kid who thought it was funny.

"I know Mama, you have come a long way. But listen, I meant to call and report her that day. I took the tip you left for her on the table. I'm so mad that I forgot to follow up with that, but it's too late now."

"Really, Steph? You took the five dollars? Mama laughed at my pettiness. "Girl give me this, I'll throw it away." She grabbed the receipt from my hand. "Now, bundle up. And hurry up so you're not late for work. Love you chile." She leaned in and gave me a kiss on the cheek.

"Love you too Mama. Hope you sleep better tonight."

Chapter 11

Online dating had taken me on a new journey and the paths were endless. I felt like a celebrity on the site. I had been addicted for the several days since Jamie told me she already had a date. I didn't even leave my office for lunch. I sat in the chair and scrolled through the messages replying to everyone at least once. Jamie told me I didn't have to reply to the ones I didn't like. I felt like the courteous thing to do was to at least say thanks to them for their comments. My screen name was my middle name, LaRose, but without the apostrophe. I had posted only two pictures: one selfie inside my car and the other a full body image. Kandi had taken the photo of me wearing a floral print maxi halter. We were at the Essence Festival Convention Center the previous summer on our girl's trip to New Orleans. I appeared somewhat slimmer in that photo with my faux locks pulled up into a bun, which gave me a sophisticated look. I couldn't even keep up with the number of times the men described me as beautiful, gorgeous, sexy or pretty. I usually had a weakness for such verbal affirmations, but it was bittersweet not to have the same physical attraction toward the individuals. It was unbelievable how many crackhead looking dudes tried to shoot their shot. They couldn't possibly think I would be interested, but I guess all was fair game on a dating site where the people behind the computer screens were mere strangers. I did see a nice profile of a dark chocolate brother who wore a short fade, his chin adorned with a long but skinny beard. He was absolutely gorgeous and looked like he could pose for one of those business magazines for black men. His message read:

MetAlex: Hello my dear LaRose, my name is Alex. Your pictures caught my attention and I just had to reach out to you. I honestly felt that we had a lot in common once I read your profile so I hope we can chat some time soon and see where things could go.

I had just pulled up the phone number on my work computer for my next potential sale, but I wasn't one hundred percent ready to close the deal just yet. There was a notification on the dating app alerting me that I had a new message. I assumed it was Alex, to whom I had just responded. I took a quick peek and it was him. I reviewed the series of messages on my screen, including my original response:

LaRose: Hello Alex, thank you for the kind words and maybe we can chat soon.

MetAlex: Ok that would be my pleasure. My number is 314-555-5551. Can you call me now or no?

LaRose: Sorry not now, I'm busy trying to make my coins at work right now but I'll text or call you later.

After my last reply, I turned my notifications off and put my cell phone in my drawer. I got kind of excited at the thought of talking to him later and even more excited at the thought of going out on a first date with him. Jamie had a date already so it was only natural that I wanted one too.

I was supposed to be focused on closing that sale, but my mind was all over the place. My eagerness to talk to Alex shifted a bit as I had to come back to reality. He was on a dating site with access to many beautiful women and he probably ran that same line down to many with the hopes that someone would eventually fall into the trap. My mind had traveled back down memory lane to the fall of third grade. I learned a small lesson regarding the male species according to Mama, Grandma Rose and June Bug.

My class had returned from recess, reluctant to transition from being outdoor savages back to indoor scholars. My teacher, Mrs. Lee, gave us five minutes to sharpen pencils, get paper, sip water from the fountain or whatever we needed to do to be equipped for the second half of the day. My Number 2 pencil, decorated with pink glitter and a white eraser, was dull so I made my way to the pencil sharpener. I spun that handle with fast stroking pride until I had a sharp and pointy tip. When I walked back toward my desk it seemed my area had been violated somehow and a piece of notebook paper was folded up on my desk.

"One minute left," said Mrs. Lee.

I was excited and nervous at the same time to see what the folded paper was all about. My neighbors on each side of me were not seated yet so I had time to review the secret note without lurking eyes. I grabbed the paper which was folded rather neatly. I moved it down toward my lap to make it less obvious what I was doing. In big, printed letters, the note read:

Will you be my girlfriend? Circle Yes or No from Bryan.

I blushed so hard, it felt like my face had turned the same color pink as my pencil. Bryan was not ugly, but he was not drop dead fine either. He wore a low-cut hairstyle, and had funny "yo mama" jokes, but never about my Mama of course. He always wore sneakers that could never stay tied. I never thought of him as anything other than a little goofball, but he was kind of a nice goofball that had potential when he got a fresh haircut and wore jeans with starched creases.

"Okay, your five minutes is up now. Please open your Social Studies books and start reading the next chapter," announced Mrs. Lee.

I pulled out my book and flipped the pages to start reading, but I could not stop thinking about Bryan's note. I was afraid to look over in his direction. I wondered if he stared at me while I put my head down to read. The words from the black and white pages blended to gray and I could not comprehend. All I could think about was my response to his note. Usually the notes from the boys would include "maybe" as an option. "Maybe" would at least let them down easily in hopes that it would eventually become a yes. I had only received two other notes in my lifetime and circled maybe on both. But Bryan had to be so direct, requiring a yes or no. I was too young to have a boyfriend in the eyes of my Mama, Grandma Rose and June Bug. So, I kept flip flopping in my mind between yes and no, so I decided I would keep the note a secret and sleep on my decision overnight. I still maintained no eye contact with him for the rest of the day.

The next morning, I had my answer. Kandi got to the table as I was almost done with my cereal and apple juice. Her eyes were lit up like a candle and she approached the table like she had something epic to tell me.

"Guess what girl?" she said as she happily plopped down her tray.

I thought she had just seen MC Hammer, as excited as she was. "I don't know, what is it?" I asked.

"I got a boyfriend now."

My eyes got bigger as I could relate to the elation on her face because I was about to have a boyfriend too.

"Really? Who is your boyfriend?"

"Bryan," she said. There were two boys in our grade by the name of Bryan, but I assumed she was speaking of the one who wasn't in my class.

"Bryan in Mr. Gentry's class?" I asked.

"Nope. I'm talking about Bryan from your class. He just gave me a note asking me to be his girlfriend. I told him yes!"

"Oh wow," I said. "I can't believe you have a boyfriend now!"

"I know me either!" she exclaimed.

The bitter sister in me wanted to tell her that he gave me the same note after recess the day before, but I would never crush Kandi like that. She always gave me the gummy bears out of her lunch and invited me over to play at her house. I never knew she and I would still be best friends over twenty-five years later, but even if not I would never steal any joy away from her.

At the dinner table that evening, I told my family about the incident, but I left out the part where I had circled yes on the note. June Bug laughed at first. "Just like a man to try to be a playa. He probably got it from his daddy," he replied. "You too young for a boyfriend anyway. I say you can start dating when you about thirty-five," he joked.

We all laughed at him.

Grandma Rose interrupted, "Well he sho nuff right. Y'all kids nowadays are too young to be talking about boyfriends and girlfriends. You got the rest of your life for that anyhow."

"That's right baby, you are too good for that lil crumb snatcher anyway," Mama assured me as she put away the dishes.

I was disappointed that my best friend ran off with the boyfriend that I had just walked into. It made me angry and I hoped he tripped on his untied laces, fell on his face and cracked his teeth. Kandi found two weeks later that he had actually given that same note to multiple girls and she just happened to be the first to say yes. I still never told her that I was one of those girls.

She broke up with him on the playground at recess right before a kickball game and my wish was granted. His shoes came untied as he ran from second base to third which caused him to trip, fall, and chip one of his front teeth.

. . .

"Girl what are you doing?" asked Jamie when I answered the phone on that Friday night.

"Nothing. Laying across my bed on this dating site. It's become my guilty pleasure even though I don't trust any of these men. It's so fascinating."

"I know, me too! I feel like I'm addicted to it. My date for tonight got cancelled though so I'm trying to see what I can get into because the girls are with their other grandma this weekend. Do you want to go out and have a drink?"

"I have been stressed out at work this week so I think I may take you up on that offer. Where do you want to go?"

"The Daiquiri Factory."

"Okay I'll be ready in an hour."

The Daiquiri Factory was a small, low-key spot where we hung out from time to time. Ant, the owner, was lifelong friends with Jamie's family. He always made sure we were taken care of and the bartenders always hooked our drinks up. The atmosphere was laid back and casual. We found an empty table not too far from the bar.

I was dressed in a black sweater, jeans, and combat boots. Jamie's look was more club inspired. She had set it off in all black with thigh high boots, a leather pencil skirt and a sheer lace top that had her boobs sitting high and mighty. I was surprised that she was so scantily dressed on cold winter's night. Many of the guests stared as we walked in because she was a bit overdressed.

"So why did your date get cancelled?" I asked.

"One of his family members had an accident and he had to take them to the hospital."

"Oh okay, were you planning on wearing that outfit on your date?"

"Yeah, why?" she asked as she took a sip from her daiquiri.

"I mean, your breasts are out, and the skirt is pretty tight. I mean you look good don't get me wrong, but it may have been much for a first date."

"What are you trying to say? Do I look like a---?"

"No, don't even say it! That's not what I'm saying." I cut her off because I was not trying to imply that she looked like another word for a garden tool.

"So, what are you saying then sis?"

"Well men can get the wrong idea sometimes on a first date and I just think you should be a little more covered up."

"Well it doesn't matter if you're covered up or not. If a man wants to try you, he will try you. They better not mess with me though cause I stay strapped." She bucked her eyes and stuck her tongue out as a way of shutting down my previous point.

Jamie typically kept a gun with her for protection, but she left it in the car that night since we were at a familiar spot. She was like the rough neck of the group since Kandi and I both were terrified of guns.

"And besides, I wear a uniform every day at the hotel, so I just felt like putting on some nice clothes tonight. Plus, we were going to meet up here for our date, so you know my people was gone look out for me up here."

"Yeah you right. My bad, I think my Mama got into my head with all the negative stuff she says about dating sites. She told me to have you get the guys license plate number before y'all went out just in case something happened to you."

"Steph why you ain't tell Mama Carter that I'm something like a private detective out here in these streets? I already got background checks done on him, I know his address, government name, and all that. I be on my p's and q's. But what about you? Have you talked to anybody off the site? What's going on with you?"

"Well there is one guy that gave me his phone number today, but I think he just running game on me and a whole bunch of other chicks too."

"Umm duh! He is. Did you forget he is on a dating site looking for something? You are not the only one he is conversing with right now but you can be if y'all meet and y'all have that connection." She sipped some more of her drink.

"Girl I love talking to you. You keep it real with me cause I overthink things too much."

"Yes, yes, yes! You do overthink way too much! You be stressing me out sometimes. Just relax and talk to that man and see what's good with him."

I smiled at her and felt reassured by her brutally honest words. I picked up my phone and sent him a text:

Stephanie: Hey Alex, this is La'Rose, I'm saving your phone number, you can save mine too and I'll be in touch soon.

He responded immediately:

Alex: Hey La'Rose, can I call you now or no?

He continued giving me third grade vibes with the yay or nay questions.

Stephanie: Sorry not now, I'm out having a drink with a friend.

Alex: Where y'all at? I can come meet you. No pressure but I just really want to see you in person if only for five minutes.

"This man is off the chain. Look at what he just sent me!" Jamie grabbed my phone and read the message then started typing.

"What are you doing?" I said as I reached for my phone.

"I'm telling him where you are so we can meet him face to face." She pulled the phone closer to her so I couldn't reach it.

"I don't even know that man yet. I'm not ready to meet him now!" I exclaimed.

"There's no better time than now." she said.

All I could do was shake my head at her. I mean I wanted a date with him but on my own terms, not a spur of the moment meet and greet at a bar. I was not mentally prepared to meet my first online prospect on such short notice. I wished Kandi wasn't at home sick. I'm sure she would have been on my side. My phone went off immediately after she sent our whereabouts. She looked at my phone and handed it to me as she said, "Read this."

Alex: Ok I can't wait to meet you. I'll be headed out shortly.

I rushed to the restroom to freshen up and to ensure I looked my best. As I walked it, there was a female applying lipstick in the mirror at one of the two sinks. Another female was in one of the stalls. They were engrossed in conversation but stopped once I walked in. Generally, I would have spoken but the one at the mirror didn't seem too friendly and seemed to ignore my presence in the tiny space, which only had two bathroom stalls. I approached the second mirror and pulled out a tube of lipstick to put on a fresh coat, as I had smeared the majority of it on my drinking straw. I began to feel like a nervous schoolgirl thinking about Alex. He seemed so well put together based off his profile, but I wondered if he was too good to be true. Apparently, he had two kids already per his online profile which was good. He mentioned being a romantic and he still believed in chivalry which I found amazing to hear since I didn't have that experience with Ronaldo. I didn't even know how far Alex had to drive to reach The Daiquiri Factory, so I hoped I was worth the drive in case he had a long drive.

The female in the stall had finally come out, and her friend moved closer to the door so that she could wash her hands. She, unlike her friend, smiled at me and said, "That color lipstick looks really cute on you."

"Thank you," I responded with a slight smile, pleased with the compliment.

"Your welcome." She finished washing her hands as I proceeded to put on some gray eyeshadow. I had quickly scanned her up and down to find something to compliment her on. She did have on a gray sweater dress that had potential to be really cute but it looked cheaply made. Her earrings were plain silver hoops, and her straight hair framed her face, bumped from being styled in a wrap. I didn't see anything I could compliment her on that really that stood. As they were leaving, they continued their conversation.

"But like I was saying, he's gonna forget all about her after I'm done with him tonight."

"I know that's right Shay." They both laughed and gave each other a high five before they walked out the bathroom.

I continued prepping myself until the door swung open again and Jamie appeared.

"Steph you look fine already, you don't have to put all the makeup on."

"I know but I just want to make a good first impression."

"What did I just tell you earlier? Stop overthinking and just do. Come on girl."

I sighed at her but looked one last time in the mirror. I was satisfied with my look: a high level of cute mixed with classy.

When we got back to our table, we sat there for about thirty minutes waiting on Alex. Jamie was on drink number four at that point and I had just finished my first drink.

"I got a good buzz tonight. You sure you don't want another drink Steph?"

"Not right now. I'll get another later." I said.

My phone rang and I could see it was Alex.

"Hello?" I answered.

"Hello is this La'Rose?"

"Yes, it's me. Are you outside yet?"

I could barely hear him over the noise from the bar. I pressed a finger to my left ear as I asked louder, "Are you outside yet?" I still couldn't hear so I got up to go closer to the front entrance away from the music and noise. Once I got to a quieter place, I asked the question again.

He answered, "No not yet, I'm about twenty minutes away."

"Oh, okay cool. Well I have big curly hair today so you can't miss me. I'll be sitting near the bar with a black sweater on."

"Oh yeah? Well I'll be the darkest guy in the building wearing a black sweater too."

I laughed playfully adding, "Oh, we twinning already I see." I expected him to laugh at my corny joke, but he didn't even muster up a fake laugh.

"Okay we shall meet soon," was all he said. The call ended. I didn't know whether he ended the call or his phone dropped. I had expected him to have a deep voice, but the baritone was barely there. Maybe I was tripping. My thoughts of Alex faded when I saw a tall and sexy muscular man walk toward me. His muscles literally bulged out of his red and black plaid Polo shirt. He also sported a red puffer vest, black creased jeans and black Timberland boots. To top it all off, he wore a red baseball hat with the brim facing backwards allowing a full view of his beautifully chiseled face. I appreciated a man in a suit, but I had a weakness for the rugged look as well. The fresh yet rustic scent from his cologne captivated me as he walked by. His hazelnut eyes were dreamy, consuming me as we locked eyes for a brief moment when we passed each other. I knew a man that fine was already married or in a relationship. As I got closer to our table, I saw Jamie dancing in her seat to the song, "Tipsy"which was the perfect song for her at that moment.

"He said he is about twenty minutes away," I told her.

She nodded okay as she continued to sway her hands in the air to the music.

Twenty minutes had gone by and there was no sign of Alex, but I kept looking back to see if I would see him. I did see the girl from the bathroom with the cheap looking dress and she appeared to have tears in her eyes. Her friend joined her and they walked arm in arm together in the direction of the bathroom. I wasn't sure what happened, but she was clearly upset. I checked my phone again. It was getting late and I was ready to go. Jamie was across the table from me, faded in her own little world.

I felt a tap on my left shoulder. I turned around slowly and before me stood the guy whose picture I had been seeing on my phone. He looked just like the picture except there had to be a miscalculation in the height that was on his profile because he definitely wasn't 5'8. The long beard that was seen in his pictures was even longer in person and had been carefully twisted into a single braid, secured with a rubber band at the end. I couldn't deny it, he was a handsome man.

"Hello there." I said. I wasn't sure whether I should stand up for a hug or not. Nobody gave me any rules or protocol on how to greet a person that I met online. Apparently, he knew the rules. He leaned in and extended his arm giving me a firm handshake. His hand felt supple, nails manicured with black polish. I was flabbergasted but obliged. He gazed into my eyes and said, "It's nice to meet you."

He spoke eloquently, but the baritone was lacking.

"It's nice to meet you as well." I gestured towards my tipsy friend. "This here is my friend, Jamie."

She waved at him from her seat, but he proceeded to shake her hand as well.

"Hi Jamie, nice to meet you."

"What's your name again?" she asked as she gave him a weird look once she noticed his fingernails.

"It's Alex."

"Oh okay. Love the nails." Her statement was dripping with sarcasm. I laughed hysterically on the inside.

"Thank you." Alex removed his leather jacket and hung it on the back of the chair as he took a seat at the table. He was wearing the black sweater he mentioned, but it was a bit snug by my standard. It was clear that he thought it was fashionable. He pulled his chair a little closer to me and smiled, revealing a beautiful set of pearly white teeth.

"You are more beautiful in person than in the pictures." I lowered my jaw as I blushed.

"Thank you. And thanks for coming out to meet me on such short notice."

"Oh no problem. I was at home and had no plans for the night anyway."

"Okay cool, do you live close by?"

"Umm, not too close but not too far either. My mom lives about five minutes away from here so I actually figured I could stop and see her too while I was in the area."

"Oh okay, it's kind of late though. Do you think she will still be up this time of night?"

"Oh yeah, my mom is a night owl so I know she will still be up. Plus, I'm the only child so we are super tight. She would totally wake up to see me."

"I'm the only child too!"

I started singing the 90's tune, "Something in Common" by Bobby Brown and Whitney Houston. He laughed at my corny joke that time. He seemed cool despite the black nail polish, tight sweater and the not-so-deep voice. I understood that at my age nobody was going to perfect so I would accept a few flaws, as I had some myself. He moved closer, looking deep into my eyes before he spoke again.

"You have such a pretty smile." he said.

I blushed again and responded, "Thanks Alex," I enjoyed the flattery but it made me feel a bit uncomfortable. Before I could change the subject, Jamie hit the table with the palm of her hand. I looked up at her and she had her finger pointed in the direction of the bar.

"Girl, why is Hakim over there with some chick all up in his fac?" I knew she was tipsy, so I had to confirm for myself whether the guy she pointed out was indeed Hakim. I turned to look for any sign of him. I spotted a guy who had the same build as Hakim, but I also saw the chick with the cheap dress from the bathroom. She was in his face as Jamie had claimed. It was dimly lit inside the establishment, but from that view, if this guy wasn't Hakim, he could pass for a twin brother if he had one.

"What the heck?" I turned back to Jamie. "That is a little too close for an engaged man."

"Too close for comfort," said Jamie as she started to rise from her chair. I already knew the next moments were not going to be pretty.

"Hey Alex, I'm sorry. We will be right back." I said as I got up to follow her. With a confused look, he asked, "Is everything okay?"

"I hope so, but I'll be right back though, I promise."

The two of us cleared the path toward the bar to Hakim and this woman. As we got closer, I saw as he gulped down a glass of whatever he was drinking. The female was still very much in his personal space and her eyes were red. Up close, he didn't seem that interested in whatever she was trying to say to him which was a relief to me. However, Jamie didn't care.

"Hey Hakim, how you doing?" she asked in a condescending drunken manner. He looked up, shocked to see us. I couldn't tell whether he was guilty or innocent by his response to seeing us. The woman looked at us, disgusted that she had been abruptly interrupted.

"Hey y'all, what's up? How y'all doing?" said Hakim.

"I was doing good until I looked up to see my bestie's fiancé all up in some random chick's face!"

He shook his head and was about to explain but the female intervened.

"A random chick? Girl bye! I've known this man for YEARS!"

Jamie ignored her, speaking only to Hakim with a louder tone. "Like I said! I look up to see my bestie's fiancé all up in some random chick's face!"

"It's not even like that Jamie, calm down. Shay is my ex." Hakim responded.

"Girl you don't even know what you talking about!" exclaimed Shay.

I knew I had to chime in at that point because I was the only rational one. Jamie was drunk enough to cause a scene if she wanted to.

"Hold up, hold up! Jamie, calm down. Let's hear what he has to say," I said, concerned.

I noticed that her friend with the sour attitude was over at a nearby table talking to a waitress.

Jamie wasn't having it. "Naw, forget that! He has no right to be disrespecting my friend like that!"

The anger in Hakim's voice rose. "Nobody is disrespecting your friend! I love that girl. I just told you this woman is my ex. She is mad that I am engaged to your friend. Ain't nothing going on over here on this end, period!"

He seemed pretty convincing to me, but I couldn't tell whether that was an act to cover up his actions or if he sincerely told the truth.

"Whatever Hakim, you know you still want this!" Shay bragged.

"No! I don't want you no more! It's been over for real so just leave me alone."

"I know you don't mean that," she said as she seductively caressed his face.

Jamie reached over and smacked her hand away. "Didn't he just tell you to leave him alone?" Shay looked appalled at the fact that Jamie had smacked her hand. She instantly grabbed a glass from the bar and flung the remaining liquid at Jamie. It all happened in a blur. Jamie didn't even have time to duck or move, as the drink splattered across her face. She was close enough that it splashed Hakim too.

There was no time to be rational or think of a master plan. It was war against Shay, and I knew her friend was going to notice the commotion and come over so I had to have Jamie's back too. Hakim got up and tried to break them apart, but Jamie became an uncontrollable monster and nothing he could do could stop her. The next moments happened so fast, but all I know is I got my licks in on Shay, but mainly I had to fight off her friend. In one moment, I had Shay in a headlock as Jamie punched her. Someone grabbed me and loosened my grip on Shay, which I looked up and realized was her friend, which caused a second scuffle to ensue. I was somewhat relieved as I was pulled from the fight, as I had lost my breath, and although the fight lasted for seconds, it felt like an eternity. My body ached, reminding me that I was no longer a spring chicken. Despite all this, I still had some fight in me and wanted to make sure Jamie was okay.

"Let me go! Let me go!" I yelled as I was being carried away.

"Just calm down lil mama," said a deep, sexy voice. "You're too cute to be in here fighting anybody." I looked up and the voice turned out to be from the sexy muscular guy I had seen earlier. I was so embarrassed. I had only gotten into two fights in my entire life, and hadn't been in a fight since high school. I felt so out of character. In that moment, I was a bit more concerned about the impression my ratchet behavior had made on him, but it was too late to turn back the hands of time. I tried to put it out of my mind because I was still convinced that a man that fine had to be spoken for.

"Let me go, I have to check on my friend!" I said calmly as I tried to loosen his grasp around me. He didn't reply nor did he loosen his hold on me. He was even stronger than I had envisioned.

"Your friend is okay, and the owner is escorting the other girls out now," he said. His voice invoked such strength and masculinity. I wanted him to say more.

The commotion had died down and I saw Shay and her friend get escorted out of the building just as he said. Shay had no idea that Jamie had a personal relationship with the owner, and they would definitely ban her and her friend from ever coming back there.

"Okay, can you let me go now?" I asked.

He finally let me go and I sprinted straight toward Jamie. Her hair was messy and disheveled, which sparked me to consider my own mane. I patted the top of my head and felt a smooth stocking cap instead of the pretty bouncing curls that I had before the fight. The embarrassment I felt heightened as I wondered whether my wig fell off because it wasn't secure enough, or if one of those chicks had pulled it off. It was just my luck that the one time I had run out of wig glue that my wig would come off in the midst of a fight.

As I got closer to Jamie, I didn't see any bruises or blood, which was a great indication that we won the scuffle. I wasn't proud of my actions, but I was glad the night ended with some kicks and punches and not gunshots. It was a blessing that Jamie had left her gun in the car that night. I didn't think she would have used it, as she only carried it for protection. She would never do anything too crazy to risk being away from her girls, but she was really drunk and I was just thankful that it didn't escalate to that.

"You okay?" she asked as I walked toward her.

"Yeah, I'm good. Are you okay?"

"Yeah. I just can't believe that just went down."

"I know, I never thought we would be fighting like we were in high school again. And your behind got a skirt and heels on."

"I know, I was trying to stomp her with these heels too." We both laughed in unison as I looked around peeping out the scene. The owner of the place frantically walked over to us, "Are y'all okay?" he asked. He was a big, tall man who resembled a gorilla and wore a permanent scowl on his face that could scare little kids. In reality, he was such a gentle giant behind that exterior.

We both replied, "Yes, we're okay."

"Man, I don't even know what happened, but my bartender said ole girl threw a drink in your face. I was like aw naw, she gotta get up out of here for messing with you."

Jamie gave him more details about the situation, but the bass from the music and my own thoughts drowned them out. I realized that Hakim was gone. I wondered if he had gone outside to check on Shay and her friend. My thoughts shifted to my innocent friend who was at home, sick in the bed. I wondered how she would feel when she found out that her two best friends played detective and started a fight with her fiancé's ex-girlfriend.

Once they were done talking, Jamie tapped me on the shoulder and asked, "Hey, where's your new boo, Alex?"

I had completely forgotten about Alex during all the commotion. I looked over at our empty table which I saw was an indication that I had run him off. He was probably headed to his mom's house to tell her how he wasted his time coming out to hook up with a ghetto hood girl who started fights at the bar. That was the opposite of who I was, but it was probably too late.

"His coat is gone so he left already. Oh well. Let's get our coats and get out of here too," I said.

"Okay good. I don't like him for you anyway. He seems too metro sexual. But yeah, let's go. Ant gone walk us to the car. Which one of us is gonna tell Kandi about tonight, Me or you?

"Umm you!" I laughed. "You started this Jamie!" We both cackled at the aftermath of it all.

After we grabbed our things, people stared as we headed toward the exit with Ant. I was sure they labeled us as the troublemakers of the night, but that didn't stop Jamie from strutting in her sexy outfit, drunken spirit, disheveled hair and all. Myself on the other hand, walked out shamefully with my toffee brown stocking cap on display. I just wanted to hide in a corner on the other side of the world. I could definitely say that night made me forget about Ronaldo, the miscarriage, and my job uncertainty.

We spotted Hakim near the exit. He stared at us in disbelief as he just stood there with his arms folded, shaking his head at us. Someone tapped me on the shoulder right as I was about to cross the threshold of the entrance. Maybe Alex hadn't left after all... I thought. I turned around, expecting to see him. It turned out to be the brawny mystery man who had pulled me away from the fight. He held my wig, which had been named Chanel, up in the air and twirled it around with his finger. "Ain't you forgetting something lil mama?" He said with a wink.

Chapter 12

I had officially been back to work for a month and things were pretty much back to normal. I was putting in twenty hours of overtime each week to increase my sales productivity. I even worked on my birthday although I usually took the day off in prior years. I decided to bust my butt at work instead. Besides, turning a year older and being unwed on Valentine's Day without a child was nothing to be celebrated as far as I was concerned.

I got up a little earlier than normal that day to view the sales matrix for the previous month to see where I stood on the list. The sales matrix was posted on a bulletin board right in front of the area manager's office. I felt like a teenage girl who was waiting to see if she made the cut for the cheerleading team. There were two people already searching for their name and ranking on the list. I stood back and patiently waited for them to finish. Before they walked away, they exclaimed, "Yes. we made it!"

My heart was in turmoil as I approached the board. I quickly scanned the list for my name.

"Number 35?? Are you serious?" I sighed, rolled my eyes and stormed away. There had to be a mistake somewhere. I had worked plenty of overtime so it made no sense. I should have looked at Liz's number to see where she stood, but I was so discouraged with myself I forgot. My stomach was in knots, so I skipped breakfast and decided to log onto social media until it was time to log in for work.

After two minutes of scrolling down my timeline, I got mad at myself. Every time I went down my timeline I would see old friends, co-workers, school mates, and family posting pictures of more exciting things than what I had going. They did the things I wanted to do like being in relationships, getting engaged, getting married and having babies. This time it was our old friend Charmaine from elementary school. I had accepted her friend request a few years prior although I was still a little salty about how she pretended to be the star at the talent show. She tried it, but she was definitely no Beyonce. I guess I only accepted to see how her life had turned out compared to the Three Amigas. Apparently, her life was going better than mine.

I came across a picture of her with her husband. They were standing in front of a fireplace inside a well-established looking home. He stood directly behind her, his arms wrapped around her waist with his hands holding her round, pregnant belly. He wasn't much to look at, so I assumed she was either with him for money or he was a real gentleman. I hoped her baby grew to look like her instead of him. She was cheesing like a Cheshire cat with those same baby teeth and gums as she did in the fourth grade. She was always pretty even in school. She was tall, thin, had caramel brown skin, and naturally curly hair. Most people would have liked the post and left a comment to congratulate her, but I closed the app, pretending I never scrolled past the picture.

I felt like I needed to vomit. *Am I being too dramatic?* I wondered. Maybe I was, but throwing up is always good when you want to get something out of your system. When I was done, I could take a bathroom selfie and post it as it would be the most interesting part of my day. Before I dug myself deeper into a ditch of self-pity, I pulled it together as I heard shuffling outside of my office.

"Hey, good morning chicka! How are you?" Liz said as she crept into my office.

"Good morning Lizzy Wizzy, I'm good and yourself?" I said, although I wasn't really okay.

"Oh, I'm fine. Just dropping some breakfast off to you this morning. I know you love The Breakfast Denn."

"Oh my goodness! Thank you so much! I haven't been there in a while either. This is right on time! How much do I owe you?"

"Don't worry about it, I'm just returning the favor. I got you the biscuits and gravy meal."

The aroma from the bag drifted through my nostril, stimulating my appetite.

"You literally just made my morning, cause it did not start off good."

"Aww, is everything okay?"

"Well, I'm not in the top 25 yet."

"You've only been back a month. You still got a few more months to improve. I haven't even checked my ranking yet."

"Yeah, I know, I just expected to be in a better position since I worked overtime."

"I have faith in you. I know you will make the cut when it's all said and done." She looked so sure, but I wasn't.

"Thanks for the kind words girl. And thanks even more for this breakfast," I said as I took a bite. It was so delightful.

Liz smiled at me as she took a sip from her morning tea.

"You are so welcome, and I have been meaning to ask you what's going on with loveconnect.com?"

"Well I met one person but that didn't work out."

"Why what happened?"

"Well he ghosted me after I got into an altercation at the bar."

"An altercation at the bar?"

"Yeah, umm it's a long story. Basically, he met me at the bar, and we talked for a short time and then I kinda got into a little scuffle and when it was over, he was gone."

"Oh wow! I can't believe my precious Stephanie was in a scuffle," said Liz.

I laughed at the memory. "Right. I'm too old for that but anyway he didn't even try to stop it. He didn't check on me after the fact to make sure I was okay or anything. I tried to call him later that night and he didn't answer and then I texted him and do you know what he told me?"

"No, what did he say?"

"He sent me this long paragraph and basically called me a ghetto ratchet chick that he didn't want to be involved with."

"Oh no! He hadn't got the chance to get to know the sweetheart that you are." replied Liz.

"I know right? I wanted to assure him that he was wrong about me, but I understand that first impressions are important. Maybe it was meant for him to leave anyway. His fingernails were polished and looked better than mine anyway. Plus, I think my voice was deeper than his." I chuckled at the comparisons.

"Oh my, a man with fingernail polish. Times are changing, I see."

"Well I guess I missed out on going to get mani/pedis with him. What a loss huh?" I asked sarcastically. "I have seen some other cute guys but I'm hesitant now. Plus, there is this one guy that has been messaging every day for two weeks straight. He is like a bug-a-boo and he just is not my type.

"What is your type?"

"Not him. He kinda looks like a nerd, a cute nerd though but not my normal cup of tea. Plus, his screen name is Nathan4Christ and I don't do men in the church. They are the worst sinners and hypocrites to me. I also think they would be so boring. They just aren't for me."

Liz interrupted, "Well I don't think you're right about that. Not all men who go to church are hypocrites. I understand you have a type, but sometimes the type you like is not the right type for you. Just keep an open mind and keep looking. As a matter of fact, remember I told you Larry Rogers was having an affair with a woman he met online?"

"Yes, I remember."

"Okay well apparently he and the woman are getting married now."

"Umm is his divorce finalized yet?"

"I don't know but he has been going around the office bragging about it now."

"Wow! Him and his wife were married for over twenty years and he is marrying someone else already! I cannot with these men!" I said as I shook my head.

"Yep, so people really can find love through the internet. You had one bad experience but there is nothing wrong with trying again and again until you get it right."

. . .

PaperBoy35 was handsome but his lips were gigantic. SantanaStan was decent looking but he was too short. Brandon04 had the biggest watermelon shaped head I had ever seen. I didn't even bother reading their profiles as I wasn't interested. Besides, they did not check the box to indicate that they were looking for marriage or whether they had children already. I had never really considered being a stepmom before then, but most guys my age probably had at least one kid anyway.

The task of sorting through possible prospects was a daunting one. I had to delete the ones who were only looking for friendship, or casual dating. I even deleted the ones who were looking for a relationship because I wanted more than just a relationship. There was no need to waste my time since those two things were my ultimate goals. Nathan4Christ continued to message me every day even though I never replied to him. I began to use Jamie's method of only replying to the ones I was interested in. He wasn't eye candy per se, but he also wasn't bad on the eyes either. He wore Malcom X framed glasses that made him look rather intelligent, but his smile was goofy. I speculated that he could be a tech savvy computer nerd. I only saw his thread of messages but had never actually read his profile so I decided to check it out.

My name is Nathan and I am looking for my future wife. I strive to be the perfect man of God for my future wife. I am saving my seeds for you and you only. I will protect you at all costs and I will cherish every waking moment with you. I will help you fulfill your dreams and desires in life. I can't wait to meet and spend quality time with you. I am deeply passionate about life, love and artistry. I attend Sunday service every week and bible study most weeks. I also enjoy bowling, going to the movies, going out to eat, and traveling. I have been a commercial real estate broker for ten years now. I am looking for someone to pray with, have fun with and to grow old with. I do have one son who is also my world and I would love to start a family with my future wife as well.

I absolutely loved his profile minus the bible school, Sunday service, and praying references. Nathan4Christ sounded too good to be true and a major snooze fest. I couldn't see having any fun or excitement with him. Not sure why he continued to send me messages when my profile mentioned nothing about Christ or bible study. For what it was worth, I nicknamed him "Church Nerd."

I was still determined again to stick to my vision board plans of finding a mate and being settled down by the end of the year. I had given up, but I was willing to put some more fuel to my fire. I had allowed one bad incident with Alex, AKA Mani/Pedi, to deter me. I had to remind myself that I knew of two success stories that came from the online dating world: Kandi and Hakim and Larry Rogers and his new cyber fiancé.

I was a little broken at some points, somewhat torn and nearly cracked in the middle. However, I was a dope chick, especially compared to others. I was smart, pretty, funny, kind, and thoughtful so I just had to put my best foot forward and someone had to like me on a deeper level.

Chapter 13

Laterite was one of the top bridal shops in town. Our appointment for our dress fitting was at 10:00 AM sharp. I had set my alarm for 8:30 AM and I only hit snooze once. I wanted to arrive on time so I didn't have to hear Kandi's mouth. She seemed somewhat distant with me and Jamie after the confrontation with Hakim at the bar.

I called Jamie to wake her up so she would arrive on time as well. She didn't answer my call, but she texted me instead.

Jamie: I'm already up!

Stephanie: Ok see you soon!

There was usually no traffic on a Saturday morning, so I timed myself based on the ETA from Google Maps. On the way, I ran into traffic that was caused my construction work that wasn't accounted for by the navigation. This forced me to take a different route, causing me to arrive six minutes late. When I pulled into the lot, I saw both Kandi and Jamie's cars. I hurried to the entrance, and when I opened the door, it was pure bridal bliss. The dark cherry hardwood floors shone beautifully to my half awakened eyes. There were racks and racks of brightly colored gowns that hung neatly. A petite White woman walked toward me and smiled.

"Hello there, good morning."

"Good morning, I'm here for an appointment with Kandice Collins."

"Okay great, I'll take you on back now."

"Thank you," I said as I smiled back at her and proceeded to follow.

We walked past aisles of colorful bridesmaid and prom dresses before reaching the wedding gowns. I felt like I was on an episode of Say Yes to the Dress. The sea of white dresses hung abreast on the sales racks with plastic coverings over them. It was such a magical place that I was ecstatic to explore. When I was a little girl, I would dream of being locked inside a store overnight, left to discover and play with whatever I wanted to while nobody was there. What a great dream it would be, to be all alone in the bridal boutique. I wanted to try on as many gowns as possible just for the heck of it before I woke up. I loved them all; mermaid styles, ball gowns, strapless, spaghetti straps, one shoulder, lace, tulle, and bling. It was a sweet reminder of my childhood days playing dress up with Mama's dresses and heels. My thoughts were interrupted when the lady stopped and pointed to my party in a private seating area.

"Here they are, ma'am."

"Thank you," I said as I saw Kandi, Jamie, Mama Collins and Kayla seated on a brown plush leather couch.

"Good morning y'all."

Before anyone else could respond, Kandi declared, "You're late, but good morning to you too!" I would have been offended but she was just giving me a hard time.

"Girl I'm not even ten minutes late." I went down the line and gave each of them a hug.

"How are you late and you called me this morning trying to make sure I was up?" asked Jamie. They all laughed.

"Forget you Jamie, I had to take a different route due to construction."

"I was just messing with you, I figured that. But come on! Squeeze in and have a seat," Kandi said as she tried to move over to make space for me between her and Jamie. The leather of the couch was rather plush beneath me. As soon as I sat down, Kandi cleared her throat for an announcement.

"Okay, so now that we're all here, I just want to thank you guys for giving up your Saturday morning for me. I'm so super excited to find my dress today and helping y'all find a dress too. We will all be wearing white, not just me."

"White? Why are we wearing white too? Are you sure you want to do that?" questioned Jamie.

"Umm, yes I am sure. I saw some pics on Pinterest with brides and bridesmaids who were all white and it looked so dope. Plus, it's different and I want to do something out of the norm."

"Well I'm just double-checking cause I don't want to outdo you on your wedding day with my white dress," said Jamie. All of us burst into laughter.

"Chile please, you will not look better than me. Trust and believe!" Kandi shot back.

Anne, the woman who had greeted me on arrival, reappeared with a tall and slender black woman. The black woman had a roll of measuring tape in her hands.

"Excuse me, is everyone here now?" asked Anne.

"Yes, all are here," answered Kandi.

"Okay, well I want you to meet Bianca, she is going to be

your consultant for the day. Anything you need she will take care of. With that, I'll leave you ladies to have some fun! Thanks again for shopping with us."

We all waved and greeted Bianca and thanked Anne before she walked off.

"Hi ladies! Like she said, my name is Bianca and I'll be here to help you find exactly what you are looking for. Now, who is the bride to be?"

Bianca's voice was chipper and animated. Either she really loved her job or she was excited to be working with women who actually looked like her.

Kandi raised her hand proudly and yelled, "The bride to be, that would be me!" she rhymed.

"Okay great, nice to meet you! And what is your name?'

"Kandice but you can call me Kandi. This here to my right is my mother and that's my daughter next to her, Kayla, who is my maid of honor. And these two are my bridesmaids Jamie and Stephanie."   Bianca was so excited, I thought her eyes were about to pop out of her head. She smiled when she spoke, exposing all her teeth and gums.

"Okay great! Nice to meet you all, now do you already have some ideas in mind, or do you need to look around?"

"Well, I know I want all of them in white dresses. As for me, I want a dress with the most bling possible, a sweetheart neckline and lots of tulle."

She nodded her head with amazement. "Okay got it. I can definitely help you all with that. Let's get some measurements first."

It took three hours of trying on countless dresses before Jamie, Kayla and I finally decided on a white dress with a sash. The process was tiresome and overwhelming. I wanted to trade places with Kandi. I wanted to be the one searching for the perfect wedding gown. I had thought about the dress

I wanted since I was a little girl. Kandi on the other hand was more impressed with the bling and embellishments, but became so indecisive once she actually tried them on. She got frustrated and decided to take a fifteen-minute break to regroup. Mama Collins had received a business call, so she stepped away for a moment and Kayla left for the restroom. The Three Amigas were finally alone for a moment.

Jamie cleared her throat before she spoke. "Hey while we got a second alone, I just wanted to talk to you about something sis." Kandi turned around with a curious look on her face.

"Okay I'm listening."

"Well I just noticed that you have been a little distant with us since the bar incident. I mentioned it to you before and you chalked it up as being so busy. But you haven't hung out with us since then. I saw on Facebook that you went out several times with Hakim and some other couples, so I felt some kind of way about that, and Steph did too."

Why did she have to bring my name up too? I did agree with her though. Kandi claimed that she wasn't mad at us about the fight. She claimed she knew about the ex-girlfriend already and that she wished we would have come to her first instead of taking matters into our own hands. In my opinion, Jamie was the one who took matters into her own hands, literally.

I did feel abandoned when Kandi didn't ask what I wanted to do for my birthday, nor did she try to help me plan anything like in the years prior. At first, I thought maybe she was busy with wedding planning but she made time to go hang out with other couples. Kandi looked shocked about being put on the spot. She paused for a moment as she thought of how to respond.

"Well um, I'm sorry that y'all feel that way. I mean I did hate that things got physical and I wished y'all would have come to me first. But I know you thought he was doing wrong, and you had my back. I can't get mad at that. So, to clear the air for the last time, I am not tripping off that and I'm not trying to act distant toward either of you."

"Okay glad to hear that," I chimed in. "But what about you making time to hang out with other people and not us. I mean you didn't even try to plan nothing for my birthday. I didn't make a fuss about it since I was working so much anyway, but I did feel a bit slighted."

"Well Steph, I asked you about your birthday and you told me you were working. Besides, I have a whole wedding that I'm planning without a planner. It was Hakim's idea to hang with the other couples. He saw how stressed I was from all the wedding planning and he wanted me to get out and have some fun with his co-workers and their wives, especially since I am about to be a wife soon."

"Oh, so does Hakim want you to diss us and start hanging with his friend's wives?" Jamie asked. She rolled her neck slightly and shifted as she put her hand on her hip.

Kandi burst out in laughter. "Oh my God! Y'all are funny. No, they are not replacing y'all, okay? And I'm sorry that I made y'all feel like that so can we just drop it?"

"Aww! Apology accepted," I said.

"Hmmm. I guess I accept your apology," Jamie said jokingly. We all moved in closer and did a group hug in our white bridal gowns. Once we released from our embrace, Jamie inquired, "Does he have any cute single friends? Forget his married friends."

Kandi smiled, "He actually does have a single friend whom I really like but he just went through a bad breakup and is not ready to date right now. As a matter of fact, he was there the same night y'all had the fight at The Daiquiri Factory."

"Oh really? What does he look like?" Jamie asked.

"He is nice looking. Tall, muscular, brown skinned, hazel eyes...but he is really low key. I don't know Jamie. You would probably be too much for him."

"Girl I need a man that keeps to himself and not out here for everybody."

"What about your online dates? I thought you had met a few that you liked," said Kandi.

"Yeah I did but they ain't rich enough for me. Remember my vision board called for a rich man? I'm still looking. So is Hakim's friend rich?"

"Girl stop acting like a gold digger. If a man is working and trying his best, that's all that matters. A man can be rich as the heavens but treat you like trash. Money ain't everything." I added.

Jamie sighed at me. "So, you're back on your Iyanla Vanzant lectures today I see."

"Yes, I am beloved!" I replied to her.

"Y'all so silly! But anyway, Jamie I don't know his finances like that. But he is a marketing executive that travels a lot, so I assume he makes good money. Oh, and his grandfather pastors at that big church by The Breakfast Denn spot that you love, Steph."

"Oh yeah, he sounds like he may be rich or close to it. You know those First Families be balling out of control," said Jamie.

"Girl I can't with you!" Kandi said as she turned back to admire her dress in the mirror.

"Hey Steph, you saw him. He was the one that pulled you out of the fight and found your wig."

My heart skipped several beats. "Are you serious?" I asked.

"Yeah, Hakim told me he found your wig."

"Man, that is so embarrassing. I actually saw him earlier in the night and I thought he was fine, fine! I didn't know he was Hakim's friend. Sorry Jamie, I saw him first so I'm calling dibs on him!" I joked.

"Fine, you can have him. I would probably be too ghetto for his church family anyway," said Jamie. We all laughed.

"I just thought about it. He is going to see me at your wedding and be like 'That's the girl whose wig fell off.'" I said.

"Girl, ain't nobody gonna be trippin off that and you're actually gonna get to see him at the engagement party," said Kandi.

"Oh, I forgot about the engagement party. Is he part of the wedding party too?" I inquired, hoping she would say yes.

"Yep."

"What about Karl? Is he going to be a part of the wedding too?" Jamie asked.

Kandi lowered her head a bit before answering. "No, he's not."

"Why not?" she asked.

"Well for one, he's been acting strange since the night of my engagement. We were both at my parent's house for Christmas Eve, but I haven't seen or talked to him since. I found out he told my parents that he doesn't support my relationship. He says I barely know the man that I'm marrying. Since he doesn't support us, there is no need for him to be in the wedding party."

"Wait, what? I know he is very protective of you, but you are so happy now and everyone sees it. I can't believe he is tripping," I added.

"Girl yes, he is tripping, and I got too much going on to worry about that right now."

Jamie chimed in, "Now that I think about it, he was acting strange that night at the engagement. Man, that's so crazy."

"It could be more to the story. Maybe he is jealous that his younger sister is getting married before him." I added.

"Hmm, I never thought of that. It could be possible, but I don't really want to invite him to my engagement party or wedding since he's not supportive."

"I hope you're not talking about your brother!" snarled Mama Collins as she quietly snuck back into our private area. Kandi gazed at her reflection in the mirror. She turned around, stunned that her mom had caught the end of our conversation.

"Sorry Ma, but yeah I was talking about him."

"I understand you want him to be more supportive but the way to do that is to give him time. Not inviting him will only make things worse between the two of you."

Kandi knew better than to argue with Mama Collins, especially in front of us, so she responded, "Okay Ma."

Within a few seconds, Kayla returned from the restroom with Bianca trailing behind her, flashing those teeth and gums.

"So, Kandi, are we going to say yes to this dress?" exclaimed Bianca.

Kandi twirled around twice then stared at herself in the full-length mirror. She scrunched up her nose with a look of disapproval.

"Naw, I'm not ready yet. I need to see more dresses."

No
Spring
Fling

Chapter 14

Rows of blooming red and yellow roses highlighted the arrival of spring along the business districts and neighboring gardens. I swallowed the fresh and crisp air like it was a bottle of refreshing water as soon as I stepped outside. The transition from winter's bitter wrath to the calming luxuries of spring always made me feel special. The scent was sweet yet pure and inviting. It was as if my mind, body and soul were entering a rejuvenating experience and the newness of life reminded me of the days during my elementary years when I no longer had to walk to and from school swaddled in bulky coats and thermals. Instead, I was less restricted, wearing only a windbreaker or perhaps no jacket at all.

The warm weather was the perfect excuse to go out and walk at the park. Mama wanted to shed a few pounds too, so we agreed to walk at the park a few times a week. I read somewhere that walking was the fastest way to burn belly fat. I'm not sure how accurate that was, but I had to do something to make sure I didn't look like Miss Piggy at the wedding. I especially didn't want to embarrass myself again with Hakim's friend. I didn't even know his name, but I could spot him out in a crowd if I had to.

Mama was always so inquisitive about my life, but she had backed off in recent months to give me space, I had assumed. However, it had been almost four months since I lost Ronaldo and the baby. I guess she felt like it was an appropriate time to start prying again. On my way to drop her off, she rolled her window down and allowed the wind to blow through her short coily hair. I switched the radio station to a gospel after hearing a few curse words on the station that was playing. They had done a poor job of censoring the foul language. Mama and I started singing along to Kirk Franklin's "Smile" on Praise 365. It was a beautiful and positive song which we both loved. When the song was over, she looked at me and smiled.

"So, I see you are coming back to your old self as of late. Do you agree?"

I thought about the question for a few seconds before I answered. "I am coming around. It hasn't always been easy but I'm still standing. I finally made the top 25 at work so things are much better than last month."

"I'm glad to hear that." She placed her hand on my sweaty thigh. The radio station faded to static and I looked over and smiled at her. Her forehead and freckles were damp with sweat but she still looked so beautiful. Despite her flawless and effortless beauty, she was still alone.

"Hey, did you ever call that plumber guy?" I already knew the answer was no, but

I was compelled to at least ask.

She retracted her hand and replied, "No, I did not call him. I already told you that I wouldn't."

"Unless you needed his services..." I said.

"And I don't need his services. The plumbing at home works just fine."

It was so funny to see her get defensive. It made me wonder if she secretly liked him and was too embarrassed to tell me. She gave me a harsh look.

"What are you smiling for?" she asked me.

"Nothing." I turned my head back to the road. We were almost back to her house but I couldn't resist asking her more questions.

"So, you were never interested in him?"

If her eyes could kill, I would be a bloody masterpiece. "Why does it matter to you?"

"I mean, you are too pretty to be alone, so I want you to find somebody. What about at church? Are there any single men there that you may be interested in?"

"I go to church to hear the Word! I'm not focused on meeting a man at church! My God is the only Father and the only man I need in my life right now! If He sees fit to bring a man into my life, He will do as such when He is ready, and I will be obedient!"

As we pulled up to the house and parked, I could tell she was ready to go because she was sick of my questions.

Before exiting she said, "I have been without a man all my life. Starting from day one with no father, I still turned out okay. It is what it is. And what about you? Are you and Jamie still doing that online dating mess?"

I loved how she used the term mess for anything that she didn't like or agree with.

"Yeah we both are."

"Oh, and how is it going for you?" she asked sarcastically.

"I have been chatting with a few guys and don't worry, I already looked them up on casenet.com and they are not killers or criminals, okay."

She shook her head at me, closed her eyes and looked to the sky. "Lord please bless this child of mine!"

. . .

There was a thunderstorm and a tornado watch on the night of Kandi and Hakim's engagement party. The rain had no mercy on the trees and buildings. It had been constantly raining for hours even before the party began. I usually enjoyed staying home listening to the rain splatters on my window, but I could not miss Kandi's engagement party. She would never forgive me for it. I had three possible outfits that I wanted to wear. I hadn't weighed myself since I started walking because I didn't want to get discouraged so soon. I assumed I lost a few inches, but I wasn't expecting much in just two weeks' time.

The first dress was my favorite which was a baby blue bodycon dress with puffy sleeves. I was hesitant because of my bulging belly but I hoped that the waist trainer would work a miracle. I tried it on, but it didn't flatten my stomach as much as I wanted it to. The second option was a similar number in pink, and the final option, a light pink and navy-blue color block blazer dress. The third option won, paired with my clear pumps. This dress hid my belly perfectly. I felt beautiful as I checked myself in the mirror. I hadn't felt that way in such a long time.

I jammed to SWV as I got ready. My music was interrupted by an incoming call. I declined, but it rang again. It was Jamie.

"Hey sis, what's up?" I answered.

"Hey sis, why did my date for tonight just cancel on me?"

"Oh yeah? What happened?"

"This fool said he just washed his car, so he didn't want to drive in the rain."

"Wow...what if y'all took your car?"

"How about if I drive my car, I'm driving myself and not going to pick him up. He just messed up my whole vibe, I was trying to get my drank on tonight. I didn't want to drive."

"So, is this your way of saying you want me to pick you up?"

"Naw, you would be coming out your way to get me."

"Not really because I have to pick Mama up too."

"Oh yeah, that's right. Yeah, come swoop me up then. Call when you are on the way. Love you, bye!" My music started to play again, but minutes later it was interrupted by another call.

"Hey sis!"

"Hey sis," Kandi said sadly.

"What's the matter with you?"

"This rain won't go away. I've already had six people text me to say that won't be able to make it. I'm afraid others won't come either cause of the tornado warning."

"It's only a warning and the party doesn't start until two hours from now so that gives the rain a little time to slack up."

"I know but what if it doesn't? This night is special to me and I want everybody to come." She sounded like she would burst into tears at any moment.

"Girl, it's going to be alright. A little rain never hurt nobody. Granted some may not want to come out tonight, but those that truly love you all are still going to come. Get yourself together and start getting ready and don't worry about who won't make it."

She took a deep breath. "Okay I guess you're right. I'm probably overreacting."

"Yes, you are and you know I'm usually the queen of overacting so just chill out." We both laughed.

"Okay, I'm chilling out, but you know you never told me what you were wearing tonight?" she asked.

"Oh, I decided on this pink and blue blazer dress."

"That sounds cute, can't wait to see it."

"Thank you girl! Now go finish getting yourself ready and stop worrying."

"Okay see you soon."

"Hey wait, I know you said some people cancelled. What about Hakim's friend, is he still coming?"

"Oh yeah, Charles is still coming as far as I know.

"Okay cool," I said. I thought "Charles" was a nice name. It was good to finally be able to put a face with a name instead of just referring to him as "Hakim's friend with the hazel eyes."

"Make sure your wig is tight this time so it doesn't fall off," teased Kandi.

"For your information, I'm not wearing a wig tonight. I actually got my natural hair flat ironed this morning, so if any wigs go flying in the air tonight it won't be mine," I joked.

"Say what? I can't remember the last time I saw your natural hair straightened."

"I know, it has been forever. I just wanted to do something different. But hurry up and finish getting ready so I can too. See you tonight!"

I was intentional about getting my hair done so I wouldn't have to wear a wig. It was embarrassing enough that I had to be in the same room with Charles again, so it was imperative that I not have any mishaps with my hair again. Nikki, my stylist, did my hair for many years before I met Ronaldo. Luckily, she was able to fit me in at the last minute the morning before the party.

I hadn't worn many weaves before I met Ronaldo, but he thought I would look sexy with twenty inches of Brazilian Wavy or Yaki Straight, so I had Nikki install a sew-in. My scalp was sore from the tightness of the braids and it was a tedious process to remove the hair. I had noticed that many celebs and reality TV stars had begun to wear wigs that could easily be mistaken for their own hair. The hair appeared to grow right out of their scalps, which was a big upgrade in the wig community. I decided to try those instead of the sew-ins.

In the time I spent wearing those wigs, I failed to properly manage my natural hair. I neglected my hair to the point where my coils were stringy and damaged. As a result, I had to get it cut. I wanted to cry as all the hair fell to the floor. When Nikki was done, my hair appeared rather thick and healthy. The new length put my hair at shoulder length, and it was full of body. I loved my new look. All those wigs that were the object of Ronaldo's affection were graciously donated to cancer patients. I thought maybe I could keep one or two for bad hair days.

I had a plan to make a better impression of myself to Charles. I knew that first impressions meant everything, so I hoped for a notable second impression to replace the first. I knew that Kandi mentioned that he wasn't interested in dating yet since he just had a bad break up. I was fine with that considering my own situation and I felt that it was something that we both had in common. Commonalities were one of the best ice breakers I thought. My goal was to show up looking drop dead gorgeous and to start a conversation with him. I needed to show him that I was more than just a rowdy chick who had brawls at the bar, as Jamie called it. I couldn't put my finger on it, but I knew someway or somehow that night was going to be memorable.

. . .

"Hey Mama Carter! I haven't seen you in forever," Jamie said as she eased her way into the back seat.

"Hey Jamie," Mama replied. The scent of jasmine from Jamie's perfume was so strong I could smell it from the driver's seat.

"I'm so glad it stopped raining! Thanks for letting me ride with y'all."

"You are so welcome," I said as I maneuvered out of the parked space.

"Hey sis. I love your hair like that!" exclaimed Jamie.

"Thanks girl, just switching it up a little bit you know." I glanced at her through the rearview mirror.

"I see. I haven't seen your real hair in years."

"Do you like her hair Mama Carter?" Mama turned her head back toward Jamie before she answered.

"Yeah I love it too. I told her it makes her look younger."

"Aww you just saying that. I don't look younger, Mama," I said humbly.

"Well I think so, but you are beautiful regardless of your hair. As a matter of fact, you both are beautiful!"

"Thank you," Jamie and I said in unison. I knew that was an introduction for Mama to go into a speech.

"So, Jamie," Mama said as she turned her head toward the back seat. "Steph tells me that y'all been on some dating matchup love connection site or whatever it is."

"Yes ma'am. Loveconnect.com."

"Well whatever floats your boat but I tell Steph all the time that she should come to church and meet a nice man there and I think you should do the same."

"Mama, you can't just push that on her like that," I interjected.

Jamie replied, "Yeah, Mama Carter I understand what you trying to say but I recently realized that I'm not ready to settle down like Steph and Kandi. I'm just having fun right now."

Mama started playing with her newly painted nails. "Oh okay, I understand," she said quietly.

Jamie continued. "I thought I was over Jason and ready to move on but I'm still not over his death so every dude I meet is never good enough. I'm always comparing them to him. If I met someone that just swept me off my feet, then that's a different story but I don't think that will happen any time soon."

It had been five years since her children's father took his own life in his mother's basement. She hadn't discussed Jason or his death with me in years so I was shocked that she was so open and honest to talk about it with Mama. As a matter of fact at one point, she asked Kandi and me to never mention his name again because it bought back memories. We had obeyed her request with great caution.

"That's totally understandable. If you are still searching for healing, church is a great place to begin. Now how are those little girls of yours doing?"

"They are doing just fine. Ain't doing nothing but working my nerves, always begging for something."

Mama and I both laughed in unison.

"I know how that is, this one right here was so spoiled," teased mama.

"No, I was not spoiled," I protested.

Jamie chimed in, "Girl yes you were, your mama and Grandma spoiled you rotten."

I rolled my eyes at them. Within the blink of an eye, the rain started back up.

The small parking lot of the Community Center was rather packed when we pulled up. I was thrilled to see that they also had an attached parking garage so my hair wouldn't get wet. I drove around for several minutes before finding a spot on the third level.

"Can you grab my gift out of the back seat please?" I asked.

"Oh dang, girl I forgot my gift at home," said Jamie. "Oh

well I'll just take it to..." She stopped short and squealed, "Hey Steph, is this Granddaddy's car next to us?"

It felt like my heart paused as I quickly walked over to her side of the car to verify her suspicions. Low and behold, there sat Ronaldo's car. It was the same make, model and color with the same scratches on the rear. I took a deep breath in hopes to regain control of my heart, but I couldn't.

"Oh my God, yes this is his car. I know those scratches anywhere. But what is he doing here?"

"I mean this place has multiple event rooms so he's probably here for another event," Jamie added.

I shook my head. "I can't believe this. I don't even want to go in now."

"Sis, you can't let him ruin your night. Like I said, other events are going on tonight in separate rooms, so the chances of seeing him are pretty slim."

"I know but still, to be in the same building with this man is crazy to me. I won't be able to have fun tonight."

Mama interrupted us. "Baby, Jamie is right, you cannot let him ruin your night. This is Kandi's engagement party so just forget him. He is part of your past and trust and believe he will get his karma for what he did to you."

I accepted their advice although I didn't want to. The attendant at the front desk appeared unbothered and ready to go home for the night. "Engagement, retirement, or baby shower?" she asked, her voice flat and monotone.

"Engagement Party," I answered.

"Second floor, first room on the right," she said right before turning around to get on the computer.

"Thank you dear," mama added.

The party room was filled with much of Kandi's family with whom I was familiar. There were some strangers that I had never seen before who I assumed to be Hakim's family and friends. The venue was filled with purple and gold decorations, and balloons were afloat throughout the air. A picture of the happy couple was set up near the entryway. The portrait captured them on a bench at the park as Kandi sat on his lap. As I took in the details that surrounded me, I couldn't help but wonder if Ronaldo was attending a retirement party or baby shower that night. It was amazing how I had managed to never run into him after all the time that had passed.

Soft jazz music played in the background as the crowd mixed and mingled. We spotted Mama and Papa Collins first and headed over to speak to them. Mama and Mama Collin's hadn't seen each other in a while so they started to chat and catch up.

"I don't see Kandi yet, but I see Hakim right over there at the table. We should go speak to him and apologize to him about what happened last time we saw him." I whispered to Jamie.

"We already apologized to him," she said.

"Sending our apologies through Kandi is not the same as apologizing in person," I offered. I didn't wait for her to make another excuse. I grabbed her arm and she followed without much resistance.

He looked like he didn't know what to expect when he saw us coming toward him. Luckily, no one else was around him at that time to distract him. I decided to speak for both of us to make the task an easy and quick one.

"Hey Hakim," I said before I got too close.

He looked around as if he was looking for someone else, perhaps Kandi.

"Hey there, thanks for coming out to support us."

"You know we wouldn't miss this special night for our girl." I looked at Jamie, who hadn't uttered a word. I cleared my throat. "Well I don't want it to be awkward between us, so we wanted to sincerely apologize about what happened at The Daiquiri Factory. You know we didn't mean any harm plus we had a few drinks in our systems that night. Ain't that right, Jamie?"

She low key rolled her eyes at me. "Yeah we were a lil tipsy that night. We don't want no problems with you man," she said as she smacked heavily on a wad of gum. Hakim nodded and smiled.

"Man, I really appreciate y'all for saying that. I don't want no problems with y'all either. I can't wait to marry your friend, real talk, and I know how important y'all are to her. So, it's all good, apology accepted."

He opened his arms and leaned in to show us some love. I was glad he received our sincere apology. Kandi snuck up behind us flashing her pearly whites and dimples.

"I see y'all made up!" she exclaimed. She gave Jamie and I a two-way hug. The scent from her perfume was even stronger than Jamie's.

"Yeah we're all good now," replied Hakim.

"Good!" she exclaimed. "Y'all looking super cute tonight! Let's take a group picture. She already had her iPhone in hand. I wanted to tell her that Ronaldo was somewhere in the building but I didn't want to make that moment about me, so I kept quiet and posed for our selfie. She wasn't satisfied until she snapped about five or six pictures. Hakim blessed her with a peck on the lips before he slid off to talk to other guests. I had forgotten all about Charles before that point since I was consumed with the thought of Ronaldo being so close by.

The Three Amigas sat down at the nearest empty table. It was embellished with a gold tablecloth and a beautiful glass centerpiece. Jamie had no problem disclosing the information that I wanted to withhold.

"Girl you not gone believe who car we parked next to."

Kandi looked puzzled and moved her eyes from Jamie to me and then back to Jamie.

"Who?" Kandi asked.

"Grandaddy," Jamie volunteered.

I didn't say anything; I just waited to see Kandi's reaction.

"Grandaddy as in Ronaldo?"

"Yep," offered Jamie.

Kandi's jaw dropped. She looked as if she was struggling for the right words to say.

I began to speak on the matter. "Yeah, he is here somewhere in this building. I really feel some kind of way about it too. It's like part of me wants to run into him so I can ask for my money back and ask for an explanation on why he left me. Then the other part of me doesn't want to see his face at all."

Jamie chimed in. "Ooh I have an idea. Do you have a crowbar or something in your car? I can go bust his windows out real quick."

Kandi and I both laughed at her although we knew that deep down, she wasn't joking.

"No, girl I don't have nothing like that in my car. Plus, I'm not gonna let you get arrested for doing nothing like that. He's not even worth it."

"He's not worth it but he hurt you, so I want him to feel some hurt too."

"Aww that's so sweet of you." I mockingly kissed her on the cheek.

She pushed me playfully. "Girl get off me, you know I don't like all that mushy stuff."

"It's all good. Don't worry about him Steph. You have moved on to bigger and better things," said Kandi. She smiled at me as her eyes looked across the room. "Don't look back now but Charles just walked in."

My heart fluttered and I blushed at the thought of his presence.

Jamie looked back in that direction to get a glimpse of him. "Ohhh, y'all dressed alike too."

Kandi laughed, "You right, they are twinning!" exclaimed Kandi.

"Would y'all stop playing? We are not dressed alike," I said.

"Ain't nobody playing. Y'all both wearing pink and blue, said Jamie."

I wanted to look back so bad to see for myself, but I also welcomed the anticipation.

"Y'all kinda look alike so y'all would look super cute together," exclaimed Jamie.

Kandi nodded in agreement.

"Whatever, y'all just trying to get my mind off of Grandaddy."

"No seriously, y'all would make a cute couple but remember that he is fresh from a breakup. He specifically told Hakim that he wasn't looking for anything serious anytime soon, but I can still formally introduce you to him."

Jamie interrupted, "Well once he sees how dope my friend is, he will change his mind."

"Thanks girl," I said as I jokingly leaned in to kiss her cheek again.

"Well let me know when you're ready to be officially introduced. I'm gonna go mingle with some more guests so I'll catch y'all later," said Kandi.

The space started to fill up with more guests despite Kandi's fear that the rain would deter them. I finally spotted Charles from across the room. He wore a long sleeve light pink button-down shirt that I assumed was Polo, but he was too far away for me to confirm. His slacks were navy blue with a crisp crease. He even wore a navy-blue tie to match the pants which was a big turn on. I loved how he could look so hip one day and so classy the next.

Kandi and Jamie were not lying because the two of us looked rather adorable in our matching colors. We could look even better together as a couple and I secretly wondered how much time he needed to get over his breakup. It felt like it was a silly thing to wonder because I knew firsthand that there was no specific time.

Jamie didn't hold off from the liquor, but I only had two glasses of Amaretto Sour. I gulped them down quickly in case mama snuck up behind me. I engaged in conversation with one of Kandi's colleagues with whom I had previously become acquainted. I noticed as Jamie made her a way back to the bar. Moments later, I felt a tap on my left shoulder. I thought it was Jamie, but when I turned around, to my surprise, it was Karl. I was so happy to see him that I grabbed and hugged him tight. I was surprised that he showed up despite his reservations about his new soon to be brother-in-law.

"Hey Karl, I haven't seen you since the engagement night." I had to speak much louder than normal so he could hear me over the mellow jazz music that continued to play in the background.

"Hey Steph, how you been?"

"I've been okay, I guess. How about you?" I asked.

He looked rather tipsy already and it wasn't even nine o'clock yet.

"Man, I'm cool. I just hate that me and my sister not talking right now," said Karl.

"I know. I don't like it either. Y'all better work out whatever problems y'all have before the wedding."

He took a sip from the amber liquid that was in his glass. He was nodding his head, but it was more so to the melody of the music and not in response to what I had said.

"Man, you know I'm really protective and I just don't know dude that well."

I kept my eyes on Charles. He was laughing uncontrollably at something that Hakim had whispered to him.

"Well why don't you try to get to know him. I think he really loves Kandi, and you should give him a chance. I mean you were cool with all of her other exes and they turned out to be no good."

He took another sip from his drink. "You know what? Maybe that is my problem. I was cool with her exes and they turned out to be no good. So, in my mind I wasn't trying to get to know a new dude who I thought might hurt her again."

I snapped my fingers in a circle at his newly found revelation.

"Yes sir! I think that's your issue. I'm glad I could help you come to the conclusion. What would you do without me?" I joked.

He laughed at me. "I know, right? Well thanks sis. I guess I'll make an effort to be more supportive. I just don't want her to get hurt again."

I may have seen his eyes tear up with emotion. He wasn't usually the emotional type, but liquor does that to some people.

"I know. Nobody wants her to get hurt but she is grown, and she has made up her mind so just roll with it bro."

"Yeah, you right though," he said as he took a big gulp of his drink. "Oh!" he exclaimed after sitting his new empty glass on the table. "You not gone believe who I saw in the elevator."

My face tensed up with displeasure. "Please don't tell me you saw Ronaldo?"

"No. I didn't see him. The way you look though, I take it y'all not together no more?"

"No, we're not but who did you see then?"

"I saw Nappy Gappy and you were right. She looks so much better now that I didn't even recognize her at first. She was on the elevator with me and she looked over at me and asked if I remembered her. I knew she looked familiar, but I couldn't place the face."

"I told you she looked like a new person. Too bad she didn't get a new attitude to go with the new look."

"Right. She still had a lil stank attitude until I apologized."

"Did you really apologize?"

"Yeah I did. I was just a kid back then. Besides she preggers now so I really felt the need to apologize even though it wasn't my fault that the school started calling her Nappy Gappy." He chuckled at the ridiculousness of the nickname.

I had developed a jealousy for pregnant women, and I felt it rise. The liquor that I had numbed me a bit, but I didn't even acknowledge that part of his story.

"Well I still appreciate you for taking up for me back then and I'm glad you were able to apologize to her. I mean we were in high school and we are grown now so let bygones be bygones."

"True but sometimes people can't let go of things that happened in their childhood and they hold grudges. So, since I had the opportunity, I wanted to make amends."

"Good for you," I said to him. "I need another drink now. Where is Jamie?" I asked.

Karl quickly pointed out. "She at her favorite spot over by the bar," he said.

I guess she noticed Karl pointing at her, so she made her way toward me as I started walking towards her. As we got closer, she pointed to the left but I didn't know what she meant.

"Too many drinks. Come to the bathroom with me."

I scanned the room for Charles before I answered her. I spotted him near the snack table and Kandi was nearby as well. She could finally introduce us, so I figured it was a good time to go to the bathroom so I could reapply my lipstick and freshen up. Jamie didn't wait on me to answer; she just started to walk toward the door. I followed her outside to the hallway where the bathrooms were located. The coast was clear.

The bathroom was empty, but the sounds of the jazz and R&B music could be heard, creating an echo. Jamie's urine flowed loudly like a bathtub full of running water. I shook my head while I stood in the mirror, admiring my new look.

"Girl would you hurry up? This is the longest pee in history," I said jokingly.

"I'm almost done! Don't blame me, blame it on the alcohol!" Jamie said.

"I can't with you sometimes. Maybe you should have added getting sober on your vision board."

Jamie laughed, "Maybe next year I will; you know I'm still a work in progress."

She was right about that. She finally appeared from the stall and washed her hands. As she was drying them, she looked over at me in the mirror. "I can't believe one of the Three Amigas getting married."

"I know right."

"You know I always thought you would be the first to get married Steph?"

I was shocked to hear her say that.

"Why did you think I would get married first?" I asked over the buzzing sound of the hand dryer.

She shrugged her shoulders, "I don't know, I just did. C'mon let's go."

I wanted to tell her I felt the same way too, but it didn't really matter at that point. The coast in the hallway was clear again. We were almost back to the doors of our event when

Jamie stopped dead in her tracks. "Wait a minute. I left my cell phone in the bathroom, hold on," she noted.

She turned around and quickly paced back to the bathroom. As I waited outside the door for her to come back, the door to the event room opened and a tall figure emerged. My heart was pounding as my eyes connected with a familiar pair that were hazel in color. I needed support. I needed assistance with speaking. The plan involved Kandi being there as the middleman to facilitate the interaction between the two of us. But she nor Jamie was with me this time. My lips failed to come up with the right words, and I was drawing a blank mentally.

"Hey lil mama," Charles said. His voice was sultry and low. I wanted to run away but my knees quivered, and I felt like I was sinking in quicksand. My lips began to tremble.

"Hey," was all I came up with. I saw that Jamie was headed back over with her cell phone in hand, which was a relief.

"Ronaldo! Ronaldo!" Jamie screamed out into the narrow hallway. "Steph, there he is right down there! Ronaldo! Where my friend's money at you low down dirty dog?" Jamie sped past me and Charles like a lightning bolt. I turned my head and there stood a man with long dreads and a Burberry plaid shirt, just like the one Ronaldo had in my closet before he secretly removed his items. Is it actually him? I thought briefly before the man sprinted down the hall as Jamie chased after him. It was him.

"Don't run punk! Where is that money you stole from my friend?" Jamie shouted down the hallway.

The next thing I knew, I took off after them. "Jamie stop it! What are you doing?" I yelled, almost out of breath.

She had almost caught up with him, but the elevator saved him with the doors closing just as she was approaching. She leaned against the wall to catch her breath. I got up in her face to show my displeasure.

"Girl why did you do that?" I screamed at her.

"Girl when I saw him and remembered all that he put you through, I just lost it. Can you believe that he ran from me? What kind of man does that? He better be glad I didn't have my gun tonight."

"Your gun? You would have shot him?"

"Well I wouldn't kill him, but at least slow him down a little."

I didn't even respond to that. I wanted to be mad at her for embarrassing both of us, but it was hard to have any solid anger towards her. I couldn't believe I could run so fast in heels.

"C'mon let's get back to the party," said Jamie.

"I'm so embarrassed. I don't even want to go back inside."

"Don't be embarrassed. Nobody else saw us."

"Girl did you not see me talking to Charles?"

"Naw. I saw Grandaddy and didn't pay attention to nothing else," she said.

"Well I was in the middle of talking to him before I had to chase you through the hallway like some crazy person. I bet he thinks I'm a drama queen and he'll never be interested in me now."

"I hate to bust your bubble sis, but don't be living in no fantasy world about this man. You saw him one time before and that was it. Remember Kandi said he not even ready to date right now so don't get your hopes too high."

I saw nothing wrong with a girl living in a fantasy world. I had been through hell and high water. If a little fantasy kept me sane for a while, then let me have that moment and leave me alone, I thought.

Kandi came rushing out of the event room but seemed relieved to see us headed back in.

"What's going on y'all? Charles came and told me something was going on out here."

I responded, "Your friend saw Ronaldo and took it upon herself to chase him down the hallway. And me being a dummy, followed after them but he ran and made it to the elevator just in time."

Kandi put her hands on her hips, "Wow, I can't believe that happened. So y'all actually chased that grown man?"

She held in laughter that she didn't want to let out, but she couldn't help it when Jamie replied, "Yeah I chased him down and he ran like a lil girl." Kandi tried to stifle her laughter but failed. Their high pitched laughing continued as I stood silent, trying to sort through my feelings. The laughter ceased when they saw it wasn't funny to me. Kandi grabbed my arm. "I'm sorry for laughing. Let's go back inside. Mama Carter was asking where you were."

I followed her lead and when she went to open the door, it flung open.

"Oh! Perfect timing!" exclaimed Kandi. "Charles, I would like you to officially meet one of my best friends who is like my sister. This is Stephanie."

Chapter 15

I laid across my twin bed staring at the porcelain white ceiling fan as it twirled around in a circular motion. I wept silently in the privacy of my room. It was the spring semester of my tenth-grade year. I replayed our phone conversation over and over in my head. I wasn't sure if the excuse he fed me to justify the breakup was true. I almost begged him to give me another chance but the women in my life were too strong and they wouldn't approve of that. When he called, he didn't waste any time with me. He usually started off every conversation by asking what I was doing. That day he didn't bother to ask because he no longer cared.

"Hey Steph, we need to talk real quick," he told me over the receiver.

I had just finished a bag of Flaming Hot Cheetos and my fingertips were smothered with red cheese. I knew something was wrong by the tone of his voice.

"Um, okay hold on real quick." I closed the bag of Cheetos and slowly walked to the bathroom to stall the time. I knew whatever he wanted to talk about was not going to be good. I lathered the soap and water, rubbing my hands together vigorously as I contemplated the possibilities of what he might say. I took my precious time with a small hope that maybe he had changed his mind on giving me some bad news.

I held the receiver back to my ear and nervously said, "Okay I'm back. What's up?"

He cleared his throat and began to talk. His voice sounded more mature than it had ever sounded.

"This isn't working out. I think we need to just be friends," he said.

I paused for an undetermined amount of time.

"Hello?" he asked to make sure I was still there.

"Yeah, umm I never knew this was coming. You just told me that you were in love with me four months ago and now you don't want to be with me anymore?"

"I just think it's for the best. I never meant to hurt you but um, I'm a teenage boy and you know we haven't..."

I cut him off before he could finish. "Okay I get it. I'm not having sex with you so your breaking up with me. It's cool I understand."

"Please don't hate me. I don't want to cheat on you so it's best that we just end it. I know how strongly you feel about waiting until you get married. I respect that about you, I promise I do but I really think it's best for us to just be friends."

There was nothing more I could say to change his mind. I understood that as a teenage boy, he had raging hormones and built up tension that I couldn't help him release. Mama got pregnant with me while she was still in high school and she made it a point my whole life to keep me from making those same mistakes. Grandma Rose had scared me to death with the talk of STD's so the thought of sex as a sophomore in high school didn't appeal to me like it had for many of my peers. I had developed a negative perception of sex because I had been taught that it could result in an itchy vagina or a pregnant belly at a young age and I refused to have either. So that was the end of Rob and me.

I lost my appetite and my nerves that day. My body ached of numbness. Mama worked a late shift during that time, so she wasn't at home yet. Grandma Rose knocked on my door and told me to come out but the sadness in my voice and the declination of dinner raised concern for her. She didn't ask first, she just turned the doorknob and walked right in. She wore pink sponge rollers with a scarf tied around her head and a pink house coat with matching house shoes. She hovered over me and examined my weary face.

"What's the matter witcha chile?"

I closed my eyes and a tiny stream of tears began to fall. "Rob broke up with me," I cried, eyes still closed.

"Forget him then, it's his loss, not yours."

"But he told me he loved me. How can you do that to someone you love?"

Grandma Rose sat down at the edge of my bed. I opened my eyes.

"Chile, y'all young kids don't know what love is. You think you know but you really don't. Trust me you will look back on this moment and laugh at it. It will be such a small thing to you one day."

"I don't think I'll ever laugh about this."

"What did I just say?" She continued, "Look, men come a dime a dozen. I know you got your heart set on one right now but there will be many more after him. You have to understand that everyone you meet is not gonna always be around. People come in your life for a reason, a season or a lifetime. You gotta understand when the season is over for them. I promise you will be okay chile." She got up and grabbed my hand, clasping it between her own wrinkly hands before kissing it softly.

"Now c'mon and eat before this food gets too cold.

I wondered whether Charles had come into my life for a reason, a season or a lifetime or perhaps just by coincidence. My plans of making a better second impression than my first had failed miserably. He offered no small talk nor showed any interest in me the entire rest of the night at the engagement party. I pretended to deny interest in him as well. Jamie was actually right. I had to throw my fantasy out the window and catch up to reality.

. . .

Will2trill: Wyd?

LaRose: Laying down watching t.v...and what are you doing?

Will2trill::Just got off of work

LaRose: Oh ok cool... where do you work?

Will2trill: A factory that makes household cleaners

LaRose: ok cool..how long you been there?

Will2trill: 3 years..where u work?

LaRose: Ok cool and I work for Atlas been there 17 years

Will2trill: Dannnnggg thats a long time

LaRose: right lol

Will2trill: do you sleep with socks on or off?

LaRose: lol that was just a random question out the blue

Will2trill: lol i kinda got a foot fetish

LaRose: oh wow

Will2trill: you gone answer the question or naw

LaRose: lol socks have to be on

Will2trill: Noo you gotta let them toes be free

Will2trill: So i can play with them

LaRose: LOL

Will2trill: 4 real...i bet you got sexy feet

LaRose: nope I got claws lol

Will2trill: no you don't... let me see them sexy feet...send me a pic

LaRose: are you serious?

Will2trill: dead serious

LaRose: I'll send you a pic after you send you send yours

Will2trill: no it don't work like that i asked you first

LaRose: Maybe later down the line I'm just now getting to know you

Will2trill: Please please, I wanna lick every single toe before I suck them toes all night...so let me see them pretty feet baby

BLOCKED

DeeMee: Hey lady...how was your day?

LaRose: It was a long day. I worked 12 hours...feel like a hebrew slave but gotta do what I gotta do and how was your day?

DeeMee: 12 hours? dang that's too long I couldn't do that and my day was cool

LaRose: Yeah it is tiresome but I got sales quota to make plus the overtime money is good

DeeMee: ok queen I see you on your grind

LaRose I'm trying...what are you up to now?

DeeMee: Playing Modern Warfare on Xbox

LaRose: Oh really...oh ok

DeeMee: Yep...I keep looking at your pictures on the website...are these current pictures?

LaRose: I mean not current as in last week but they were taken within the last two years or so

DeeMee: Ok...this my number 314-555-1111 send me a pic of how you look at this very moment

LaRose: Sorry but my hair all over my head right now

DeeMee: So what...I wanna see a recent picture of you... need to make sure you not 50 pounds heavier now lol

LaRose: So if I was 50 pounds heavier you wouldn't want to talk to me no more?

DeeMee: It depends on how the 50 pounds look on you. I just want to see some more recent pictures of you

LaRose: You can view my profile and look at those pictures...I still look the same

DeeMee: Any guy on the site can look at those too... I want a special picture

LaRose: I don't really like sending pictures to someone that I barely know

DeeMee: are you serious?

LaRose: yes

DeeMee: I wasn't asking for no nude pics...just wanted a more up to date picture to look at

LaRose: I already told you the pics I posted are not that old. I promise I still look the same

DeeMee: Not sure why you are so difficult... only just a picture...I can see if I asked you to send a topless pic

LaRose: I'm not being difficult. I just don't know you like that and I don't want to send any pictures to you. Like I said if you want to see me you can just look at the ones I already have on my profile

DeeMee: It's all good... don't worry about it. You ain't that fine anyway

LaRose: BOY BYE AND YOU NOT THAT FINE EITHER!

BLOCKED

Nathan4Christ: Good morning beautiful may God bless you today.

Nathan4Chris: Good morning praying that you have a great day.

Nathan4Chris: Good morning, hope you have a blessed day.

Nathan4Chris: Good morning sending good vibes and prayers your way today.

Nathan4Chris: Good morning beautiful, hope you have a great day.

Nathan4Chris: Good morning Queen, I pray that all is well with you.

Nathan4Chris: Good morning dear, hope all is well with you. May God bless you....

. . .

The cool breeze was a blessing to us on a rather warm Saturday morning. Kandi and I were enchanted by the whisk of cool air that twirled around us when we reached the shaded areas of the walking trail. We both looked athletic yet cute in our Black spandex tights and tank tops. Perspiration flowed down my back, chest and stomach. Kandi only talked about her wedding planning from start to finish. I didn't comment much as she rambled on and on, sharing every detail. I wanted to ask her if Charles had inquired about me since the engagement party, but I assumed he had not as she would have mentioned it already.

"So, what do you think?" Kandi asked as we came to another stretch of shade on the trail.

"About which part?" I asked.

"About everything, do you like my ideas?"

"Yeah it seems like you have everything sorted out. I could have helped you more, but I know how you don't like to give up creative control. I'm sure it's gonna be the wedding of the year."

She looked at me and smiled. "Aww, thanks sis and yes I can be a bit of a control freak. I know you and Jamie would help out if I asked you but so far Hakim and I have it all under control with the help of my parents' money. We have been saving too to help out."

I had forgotten how privileged Kandi was. I wondered who came up with the idea for the bride's father to pay for a wedding. That was such a ridiculous concept to me. Perhaps I wouldn't feel that way if I had two parents that could pay for my wedding, if I ever had a wedding. Mama wasn't broke by any means, but she also wasn't a floating ATM machine either.

"Oh, one thing I forgot to tell you is that you'll be walking down the aisle with Hakim's frat brother, Malik. Kayla is walking down with his other frat brother Tyson. He is such a short and tiny man so he and Kayla will be same height. The frat brothers actually call him 'Too Short'." We both laughed. "And then Jamie and Charles are going to walk down together."

I wanted to ask why she didn't pair Charles up with me, but I knew she was going by height. Charles was tall and Jamie was taller than me.

"Oh, okay cool. I actually met Malik at the engagement party, and he seemed pretty cool."

"Oh yes he is really cool. You know I felt bad that I didn't ask Kimbella to be in the wedding but I thought it would be awkward to have his sister in the wedding and not have my own brother in the wedding," she said.

"Well, why don't you put both of them in the wedding since they are the siblings.

She wiped some sweat off her forehead. "Well he and I haven't been as close as we used to, so it seems kinda weird."

"Girl you gotta give him some credit since he did show up to the engagement party. Besides, I had a talk with him, and he claimed that he was going to give Hakim a chance."

"Tuh! Well I don't know what he told you, but he hasn't tried to give him a chance. Yeah, he showed up to the party, but he didn't try to make amends nor apologize to me or Hakim for his recent behavior."

"Well he seemed genuine about it, but I don't know. Hopefully, he will come around soon."

I attempted to change the subject because we were going nowhere fast with that conversation.

"Girl why did I have to block two men from the dating site?" I laughed at myself for the recollection.

"Why? What happened?" she asked curiously.

I chuckled a bit before I recalled the story. "The first guy started off a message with 'wyd'."

She replied, "Omg, enough said. That is so annoying."

"Tell me about it. To make matters worse, he confessed that he had a foot fetish and wanted me to send him a picture of my feet."

"Oh, he didn't want a selfie, he wanted a footsie?" she asked.

Both of us roared with laughter.

"A footsie. That's a good one. He got really weird saying he wanted to lick my toes and he wasn't taking no for an answer so I blocked him. The other guy wanted me to send him a recent picture to his phone. I told him that I didn't really know him that well, so I didn't feel comfortable. He had an attitude with me and eventually said I wasn't that cute anyway," I said.

"If you weren't that cute, why was he trying to get your picture then."

"Exactly! Ain't nobody got time for that, so he got blocked too."

"I know that's right sis. I'm sorry you're not having any luck but keep trying. We still got vision board goals to complete, remember?" she said with a smile.

"Yes, I remember. I'm doing my best not to give up on it but it's not easy. There are not many guys that are interested in marriage, so I have a smaller selection to work with. But I'm trying to get out of my own way and just trust the process. I saw this one guy who was super fine when I looked for new profiles but he hasn't sent me a message yet. I don't want to seem too desperate, so I haven't messaged him either."

"It won't hurt to message him."

"Maybe I will if he doesn't do it soon."

"Okay and what about the church nerd? Is he still sending you messages?"

"Girl, yes! He is very consistent. He seems really sweet but also kind of annoying. I know he's not my type, so I don't want to waste his time. I will probably respond to him to let him know to stop sending the messages."

"Well how about this: If you don't message the new cute guy, you should give it a try with church nerd."

"I don't know about that, but we will see."

The sun was beaming on our worn out bodies as the walking trail started to fill up with more people. Our one-hour session had come to an end. I could see my car straight ahead and couldn't wait to get inside and turn the air on blast.

Chapter 16

I was bored and had nothing else to do that night. Plus, I only had several small snacks throughout the day, so I was starving. It was a last-minute hookup so I wasn't able to do all the investigation that Jamie had taught me. However, he agreed to send a screenshot of his driver's license to me, and I sent it to mama in case he tried any funny business. My hair wasn't up to par either but luckily, I had saved my favorite wig for a bad hair day, so I threw that on.

I arrived at the restaurant early and sat at a table near the front door. I grabbed my phone to see the time and hoped he would stroll inside at any minute. I scrolled up to the camera icon on my phone; but not to take a picture. I just wanted to see how I looked and to make sure there was no purple lipstick on my white teeth. I decided on a natural face other than the lips. I also made sure my blouse, which donned a floral print, was adjusted so that I wasn't showing any cleavage. I didn't think he deserved a tease on the first date. I brushed back a few strands of hair that stuck to my face. I looked classy and beautiful, yet simple, which was the look I aimed for.

I didn't expect much from the date except a free meal. Then on the other hand, I hoped we would fall madly in love. If that happened, I could look back twenty years later and say that I almost didn't come on the date and almost risked not meeting the man with whom I would spend my life with. He and I would laugh at the irony of our first encounter. But who was I kidding? That was just wishful thinking. My thoughts were interrupted as my phone vibrated. It was a text message from my date. Thank goodness he had finally messaged me a few days after I had that conversation with Kandi. I was relieved because I didn't want to take Kandi's advice to reach out to the church nerd.

Three years had passed since the time I was preparing myself for my first date with Ronaldo. The raindrops tapped my rooftop as the thunder growled quietly. There were butterflies in my stomach prancing around as I sat on the bed and nervously wiggled my feet into my dark brown knee boots and zipped them up. I contemplated different topics of discussion that we could have on our date. I sometimes lost my train of thought on first dates. I would have all these questions to ask in my head, but my mind would go blank like a deer in headlights during the conversation. I didn't want him to think I was too boring. His past girlfriends were typical bad girls. I figured he was accustomed to the drama and unpredictability that a bad girl could provide.

"So, tell me about your past relationships. Why did you all break up?" I asked as I laid across my bed somewhere after midnight on our third phone conversation.

"Cause they were all crazy!" Ronaldo said.

I laughed at his answer. "What does that say about you? You have a thing for crazy girls?" He laughed at my question.

"Man, to be honest, I just ended up with girls that liked drama and things always went left. I told myself that I had

to try something different in order to get different results."
I loved to see a man who had learned from his mistakes and
wanted to do better.

"What kind of drama are we talking about though?"

"Too many to name but the top two was when one of my
exes slashed my tires and another time I was spit on."

"Spit on?" I asked curiously.

"Yep, she spit in my face."

"That's all bad. But hold on, women don't just do those
types of things for no reason. What did you do to them?"

"Oh here you go. I knew this was coming," he said casually.

"I'm just saying, it seems like you did something to hurt
them and that was their way to get you back."

"I didn't do anything, they were just flat out crazy and I
ignored the signs."

"Because men make women act crazy right?" I joked.

"Not me, they was already crazy. For example, my ex from
high school was the type to always listen to rumors instead
of asking me first. Someone told her that I was at the movies
with another female and she assumed that it was true. She
didn't ask or nothing, just came to my house late at night and
slashed my tires."

"Wow! So was it only a rumor or actually true?"

"Only a rumor. I think her friends were jealous of our
relationship or I had an identical twin out there that I don't
know about. Other than that, it was not me."

"Okay so after she slashed the tires, y'all probably broke up
and got back together the next week." I said.

"Nope. When I'm done, I'm done. There is no going back.
Same thing with the other ex, she accused me of cheating
but couldn't prove anything at all. She was so jealous, and I
couldn't take the accusations no more so I ended it with her

over the phone. She was mad so she pulled up at my homeboy house where I was at. All the fellas was in the basement watching a game and she came in going off and accusing me. I ignored her and still tried to watch the game while she yelled and screamed so that made her more upset. My homeboy tried to push her away and she finally was about to leave but she spit in my face before she walked up the steps."

I raised both my eyebrows at the story and had more questions. I changed my position and sat up to hear more of the juicy story.

"That is so crazy!"

"Tell me about it."

"I got questions though."

"I got answers," he offered as a response.

"Okay. First off, how could you break up with someone over the phone? That is so insensitive. Secondly why was she so adamant that you cheated without any proof? Thirdly how did she just walk into your homeboy house like that? Lastly what did you do when she spit on you?"

"Well I'm not a confrontational person so it was easier for me to break up over the phone instead of in person. In regards to the other question, my homeboy's wife let her in the house. His wife had no idea that we had been beefing so when she knocked on the door, she played it off like I had invited her there. Then she came down to the basement and started clowning with me. When she spit in my face, I was in shock and I didn't have time to react. I wasn't about to hit a woman, so I just let her go and washed my hands of her."

"That is too much drama for your mama." I shook my head at the unfortunate story.

"Who you telling?"

"You still didn't answer the question about the cheating."

"Oh yeah. She just said I started acting differently. She said she had a gut feeling because I came home late one night. But it was just all in her crazy little head."

I hoped he was being truthful to me. Even if he had cheated on his ex, I did believe that people could make mistakes and learn from them. I would never judge him on his past relationships anyway.

"Okay well for the record, I just want to let you know that I'm not crazy!" I could sense his smile through the phone.

"You don't seem like you are. You seem to be put together well which is why I want to get to know you better," said Ronaldo.

Mike: Outside

Stephanie: Ok sitting at a table right at the front when you come in to the right.

I suddenly felt a tingling sensation in my upper chest as I waited. I wondered what we would talk about or if he would even like me in person. I hoped he didn't talk too much but also hoped his conversation would be sufficient. I was extremely impressed by his looks on loveconnect.com and I wondered if he would look like the photo or if the lighting and filters had deceived me. For some reason I wasn't as nervous as I had been on other first dates so I took that as a good sign.

A light skinned man with a wavy low cut and a gigantic gold chain with a blinged out airplane medallion strolled into the building. It was him, but the lightning and angles of the photos I saw were a bit enhanced. I stood up so he would recognize me. He bounced his way to the table with a light smirk.

"Hey baby. Nice to meet cha."

"Nice to meet you too, Mike."

"You sholl is fine baby girl, let me get a hug," he said as he forcefully gave me an embrace to remember and regret.

"Thank you," I said as I gently escaped his captive embrace.

I was caught off guard not only by the hug but his country accent. He had told me that his family lived down south but they all moved to San Louise when he was sixteen. I was shocked that he still carried the southern twang in his voice after all that time. He sat down across from me and stared at me rather awkwardly. I tried not to stare back so I grabbed the menu to divert my attention. He did the same, and for a moment, we were both silently gazing at the menu. The silence peeved me, so I tried to break the ice.

"So have you ever been here before?"

"Naw shawty, I ain't neva even heard of this place befo ya dig?"

"Oh okay. Well this my third time and the food is really good."

"Yeah it better be good, looking at these prices. They steep as a mug." He began to giggle which displayed a railroad of gold teeth.

I giggled with sarcasm.

"I'm jus jokin baby. I'm a silly guy that's all, just jokes." He winked at me in a provocative manner.

"Well good cause I love a man with a good sense of humor."

The waiter came over and took our drink order. Mike asked for a Bud Light, but I only wanted water. That would make my portion of the bill a little more reasonable for him. I still hadn't made direct eye contact with him yet, but I couldn't miss all the metal in his mouth.

"You only wanted water baby?" he asked.

"Yeah just water for me," I said.

"Okay, so you one of dem goody two shoes that don't drink huh?"

I couldn't believe he was so bold to ask that. I also wondered why he kept calling me baby because we were nowhere near that level.

"Um, I wouldn't take it that far. I'm not a goody two shoes," I said while making air quotes. "I mean I do drink on occasion, but today is just not one of those occasions for me."

"Okay baby, my bad," he said as if he could sense the slight irritation in my tone.

The waiter came back to the table with our drinks and to see if we were ready to order. The waiter was a freakishly tall guy who was bald and wore thick glasses. I was ready to end the date already, so I wanted to order, eat and go as soon as possible.

"I'll take the Sampler Platter with blue cheese dressing."

"Okay ma'am, and for you sir?" the waiter asked.

"Well I'm still thinkin' but I wanna ask you do y'all got a dollar menu up in this joint?"

The waiter said snidely, "No we don't but McDonalds is just down the street."   I nearly spit out my water as I snickered at the waiter's witty comeback to Mike's foolish question.

Mike started to laugh too, which displayed all his golden mouth pieces. In his profile picture, he wore a red baseball hat that was turned backwards and a white tee shirt. I always had a soft spot for a man in a baseball cap, especially a red one. I had no idea about his gold fronts because his mouth was closed on the profile picture.

"I was jus playin my dude, just playin. But um, let me get a order of dem chicken wangs and mac n cheese."

"Okay I'll go put that order in for you now," replied the waiter in a monotone voice as he walked off.

"So, I see you really do have all the jokes tonight," I said.

"Yeah baby I like to have fun, I don't take life too serious, ya dig." Before I could respond, his phone started to vibrate. He stood up immediately and said, "Hey, I gotta take this call real quick, be right back!"

He rushed off. As he walked toward the door, I could see his boxer briefs since his skinny jeans were sagging. They were blue with red lobsters on them. Had I known he was such a big fan of lobsters I would have recommended we go to Red Lobster instead. The date was not going very well and Mike seemed like such a different person than I expected.

In the meantime, I witnessed a couple walking in with a small baby girl. They looked so content. The man held the baby's car seat while the woman carried the diaper bag. I admired how they worked together as a team. I wished it was me instead. An older white couple walked past them to exit the building. They looked like they were in their sixties and were adorable as they walked out holding hands. Would that ever be me at sixty years old? I wondered. The hostess escorted the couple with the baby to their table as Mike returned.

"My bad baby, that was my baby mama. I had to make sure the lil shawties was cool, ya dig?"

"Is everything alright?"

"Yeah everythang all good baby."

"So, you said you had three kids, right? Do they all have the same mom?"

"Well um, my three lil shawties got the same mama. But I might have a possible on the way but I ain't claiming that lil shawty til we take a DNA test."

I was glad to hear another term of endearment other than baby, but I could not believe he had just admitted that he may have another woman pregnant. That was the most ghetto revelation I had ever experienced on a first date. That darn red hat had bamboozled me. I acted as if I didn't even hear his last remark because I honestly did not care.

"Oh, okay cool. Well how old are the three kids that you know for sure are yours?"

"Umm they like five, ten, and fifteen."

"I see you spread them out five years apart."

"Fa sho but I sholl hope that lil baby ain't mine cause that dang on child support ain't no joke. You lucky you ain't got no lil shawties runnin round. I can't believe you in yo thirties and don't got no kids. Dem dudes you been messin wit was shootin blanks." He laughed at his own joke.

"Excuse you!" I said with an attitude.

"I'm saying the dudes you been wit musta had low sperm counts or either you the one with the problem."

"Well let me stop you right there. Just because I don't have any physical kids running around doesn't mean I've never been pregnant before. It's very insensitive to say that to a woman with no kids when you don't know the history. Plus, how do you know that I didn't want to be married first before I had kids?" I exclaimed as I rolled my neck and eyes at him simultaneously.

"Dang baby, I was jus joking again. My bad I ain't mean to make you all mad and go off on me. I'm sorry boo. Can you forgive me?" Mike asked as he gave me a fake smile. "You know you can't stay mad at this smile," and he displayed the mouth bling again.

I grabbed my glass of water and took a sip before I spoke again. "Oh, I forgot you've been joking all night so I should have known it was another joke," I said sarcastically.

"I'm sorry I made you mad. I wanna make it up to ya if I can."

The only thing he could do to make up for it was to walk out the door and never come back. My stomach growled loudly. I just wanted to skip conversation, eat and leave.

"Matta fact, I know what I can do for ya."

"No, it's fine. No need to do anything for me."

"But baby jus hear me out. I can make you famous."

He nodded his head repeatedly and rubbed his hands together as he collected his thoughts. "I can put you in my video shoot next weekend. You can be the main chick in the video."

"In your video?"

"Yeah shawty, memba I told you I did music. That mug gone be lit! My song called "The Golden Life" by yours truly Flight Mike."

He announced his stage name as if he were a big deal as he popped his collar on what now appeared to be a fake Burberry shirt.

"Flight Mike huh? Interesting name."

"I know it is baby, it's one of a kind jus like me. They don't make em like me no mo. I be flying all over these hatas."

Flight Mike had mentioned that he dabbled in music and I assumed it was just a hobby for him, but nothing too major. It was then that I understood the significance of the airplane medallion that he was wearing.

"Well you are definitely a unique person. Unlike any other I have met. Sorry, next Saturday I have to work so I won't be able to be your video girl. But thanks for the offer," I said before taking another sip of water.

I really didn't have to work on Saturday but that was an easy excuse to get out of being in the Golden Life video. There was nothing golden about him except the gold grills in his mouth.

"It's not on Saturday though. It's on Sunday at Fairmount Park and my homies coming out with they whips and motor bikes. We gone be doing stunts and bussin wheelies and all dat. And you can be in da car with me sitting looking pretty ya dig?"

His voice and his whole presentation annoyed me, and I needed to make an escape for the moment.

"I'm sorry, I still can't do it on Sunday either. I have to do something for my mama that day but I gotta use the restroom, I'll be back."

I grabbed my bag and stood up before I saw another couple walk into the restaurant. The gentleman had an awfully familiar face, but I couldn't place it. He held the hand of a pregnant woman who was dressed in a floral sundress with a wig that was like the one I had on.

I heard him speak to the hostess. "I have a reservation for two at seven thirty under Ronaldo Johnson."

Memories from the night I came home and found an empty closet and money withdrawn from my account crept back in my mind. My feet were planted to the hardwood floor. I wanted to move or yell out an obscenity, but I froze in disbelief. The pregnant woman noticed me staring before she whispered to him and he turned around. Our eyes met for the moment. My eyes were filled with anger, shock, disappointment and any other look that was equal to the 'if looks could kill' phrase. His bright eyes changed from happiness to regret, sorrow, and confusion.

"You can follow me now," said the hostess and they walked off into the direction of empty tables.

"Is somethin wrong baby?" asked Flight Mike.

"No, I thought I saw someone I knew. I'll be right back." I said.

I darted to the bathroom which was on the opposite side of where they were being seated. The couple who came in with the baby was seated nearby as well. The baby girl was crying hysterically as her mom rocked and held her to calm her down. The dad sat there, unbothered as he laughed and conversed on his cell phone. The couple didn't seem like the team they appeared to be when they walked in.

I finally reached the bathroom and wished there was a window so I could climb out and escape from the night from hell.

"Ugh! I can't believe this!" I exclaimed loudly. I didn't care if there was anyone in the stalls who could hear me. I immediately called Kandi and as soon as she answered I told her to hold on while I conferenced in Jamie. Once all of us were on the line, I revealed my situation.

"Please tell me why I just saw Grandaddy and Nappy Gappy together holding hands and she is pregnant! Do you hear me? She is pregnant!" I yelled.

"You lying!" replied Jamie.

"Are you serious?" exclaimed Kandi.

"I'm not lying! I'm dead serious. I'm at Edible Truths in the bathroom right now, on a date with this wanna be rapper dude who's wearing fake Burberry. I can't even believe this. I wanna go over there and beat both of them down right now. She lucky she is pregnant."

"Well I ain't scared to fight a pregnant chick. I'm on my way!" exclaimed Jamie.

Before I could reply, Kandi yelled on the phone. "No, you not gonna fight a pregnant chick! Neither one of you are. But what you will do is hold your head up high and you go back on your date and show him that you have moved on. That's the best kind of revenge honey."

"But Kandi, he took my money. He just left me without any explanation, changed his number and everything. He got another chick who is pregnant; someone that I know! I lost my baby cause of him!"

I slammed my fist into the bathroom stall, then followed up with a kick. The tears began to fall silently.

Jamie added, "Right and he had the chance to explain to her at the engagement party too, but he ran like a little---"

Kandi cut her off before she finished. "I understand that, but you are on a date right now. You are too classy to be fighting your ex and his alleged baby mama. Forget them and move on. Trust and believe they both will get the karma they deserve and it's gonna be worth more than the amount of money he took from you and much more than any physical altercation."

"I hear you Kandi, but Steph let me know what you want to do. My shoes are on already. You just say the word and I'll be there," added Jamie.

Although I didn't want to hear it, Kandi was right. Ronaldo did me a favor when he left. I stood with my back up against the stall and uttered slow subtle cries.

"Hello? Are you still there?" asked Kandi. I didn't say a word as I moved the phone away from my mouth. I could hear both of them yelling through the phone.

After about ten minutes in the bathroom, I regrouped, and decided to tell Flight Mike that an emergency came up and I had to leave right away. I rushed out of the bathroom and the lady was now bottle feeding the baby with an agitated look on her face. The dad was still on his phone, laughing and talking with someone else as if the mother and child didn't exist. It's funny how I had a whole different version in my mind of the couple's relationship.

As I approached the table, the waiter had just set my plate down. I couldn't help but look over in the direction of where my ex and his new baby mama were seated. They were no longer there. I scanned the restaurant to see if they had switched tables, but they were no longer there. I guess he was shook and didn't know whether I would confront them or not, so they left. I wasn't surprised; he was nothing but a coward anyway. Since they were gone and the food had arrived, I decided to stay and eat in hopes that it would help calm my nerves.

I was shocked that Flight Mike who I had dubbed as "Lobster Boxers" hadn't made a corny joke about me being in the bathroom so long. Luckily he didn't hassle me again about the video shoot once I reassured him I would be busy all weekend. There was a lack of conversation while we stuffed our faces, which I didn't mind. He seemed to be just as hungry as I was, if not more. The proactive waiter came over and laid the check on the table face down. Before he could walk away, Mike called after him, "Hey hey, we need two separate checks my dude."

The waiter's face turned pink from embarrassment. My face was red with anger as my mouth dropped. I had never been on a first date where the guy didn't pick up my portion of the tab. I mean, I had done him a favor by ordering water instead of a charged beverage.

"My fault sir. I'll be back then," the waiter said as he scurried away.

"Oh, I wasn't aware that we were going Dutch on this meal. It seems you invited me out," I said.

"Naw shawty this only our first date. I don't really know you and you don't really know me yet."

"But you asked me if I had plans tonight and I said no. You responded that you were hungry, and I said I was starving. Then you said let's link up and told me to pick a place."

He laughed at my re-enactment of our chat conversation. "Shawty that's right I said let's link up, let's get together. I neva said let me take you out on date tho."

I paused for a moment and took it all in. I didn't even have time to argue with a certified idiot with no class. "Wow!" That was all I could say at that moment. I knew my meal cost $16.99 so I reached in my wallet to get cash. I threw a wrinkled twenty-dollar bill on the table and headed toward the exit.

Chapter 17

"Mama I need to talk to you."

"What's the matter? Your eyes are red like you've been crying?"

We both took a seat on her couch. "Yes, I was crying because I saw Ronaldo and the waitress from The Breakfast Denn together and she was pregnant."

"Oh wow! Well you don't have any proof that he is the father."

"I'm pretty sure he is the father and it's not even so much about him. It's more so the fact that she is having his baby and my baby..."

"Steph, I know that still hurts you, but you know God don't make no mistakes."

I sighed, leaning back on the couch. I decided to ignore what she said.

"I can't believe this mama. He and I could have had a baby, but he is having a baby with her now."

She grabbed my hand and rubbed it gently. "I'm sorry baby but like I said, God makes no mistakes." I snatched my hand away from hers.

"Look, I don't wanna hear about no God and religious stuff right now!" I snapped.

Her eyes looked at me in shock and displeasure. She put her hand over her chest to further express her disbelief at my outburst.

"Baby I know you are hurting right now but the Lord won't put you through nothing that---"

I was exasperated. "Oh my God! I told you I can't do this religious talk tonight! That heffa is walking around with my ex carrying the baby that I should be carrying and you acting all nonchalant about it which is really pissing me off. How come your precious God didn't take her baby too? Why just mine and why am I the one who can't have kids anymore? Huh? What does God have to say about that mama?" I yelled out in frustration.

I couldn't believe I allowed myself to release those words into the atmosphere after burying them deep down in those bed covers the night I left from the hospital. Keeping the words contained and muted gave me a sense of hope that they were not true. Now the words "I can't have kids anymore" had been affirmed, and my secret had risen from the grave.

I reached for my purse and was headed to the door. My comments along with my newfound temper made mama upset and she tried to block me from leaving.

"You can still have kids Steph. One miscarriage doesn't stop you from having more."

"Well that's not what the doctor at the hospital told me, and my primary doctor confirmed it at my checkup too! You know,

I never told you cause I knew you would tell me something about it being in God's plan and I didn't want to hear none of that!"

She put her finger in my face and began to speak sternly, "Now you listen to me, and you listen good. For one, you will not denounce His name in my house! You are right. I don't believe nothing no doctor says. So if the doctors ruled it out for you, God still has the final say in that matter! You need to be thanking Him that you are still alive and breathing."

I had a lot to say to defend my feelings but I didn't know where to begin as my mind was being pulled in a million different directions. I looked up to my right to think of what to say next. I saw our family photo on the wall with Grandma Rose. It took me over the edge and I immediately missed and yearned for my grandmother's voice or presence again. The words finally came to me.

"Well maybe I don't want to be alive and breathing anymore! Maybe I wanna just die like June Bug and Grandma Rose! I lost a baby that I didn't even know existed. My boyfriend left me, took my money and now he is having a baby with someone else. I might be unemployed by the end of the year. I'm watching my best friend live out the life that I always wanted and what do I have?

I flung my arms around as I answered my own question.

"I have nothing! Nothing! Nothing! I have nothing and what happened to Grandma Rose was all your fault too! I don't want to hear about all this God stuff anyway cause you never even stepped foot into a Sunday service until after she died."

I felt my words cut sharp like a knife. Mama stared at me with eyes bucked and loaded. She didn't say a word as she drew her right arm up and swung it across my left cheek with massive impact. My reflexes wanted to return the favor, but regardless of my disposition, I knew I could never hit her back. She stood strong and erect as if she was ready to go a few rounds with me if I tried to retaliate.

Enough damage had been done at that house for one night, so I stormed toward the door to make my dramatic exit. The rain poured down outside, and the thunder roared as soon as I opened the front door. I stomped to my car in a bit of rage that doubled in sadness. I just wanted comfort at that time; the kind that only Grandma Rose could give me. I was determined to go visit her gravesite and I didn't care that it was a thunderstorm and after 9:00 PM. My car swerved in and out of the lanes as I sped through each street, barely stopping at stop signs. The tires slid a few times from the slippery roads, but that didn't scare me. I was invincible and didn't care about life or death at that moment.

When I finally arrived at the cemetery, it looked like an eerie scene from a scary movie. The bright lightning and heavy thunder were irrelevant to me. I needed answers, reassurance, or something to calm my sorrows. I had no umbrella, sweater or hood to protect me from the rain, so the droplets showered down on me. I walked across the wet grass, allowing mud and wet grass to cover my shoes. I trotted in between the tombstones using the light from my cell phone to help guide me since it had been so long since I last visited her.

When I finally reached her tombstone, I read the transcript out loud.

"Rose Vernice Carter, Beloved Mother and Grandmother"

The text was written in gold script with two gold roses on the left and right corner of the tombstone. A calming peace rendered through my wet body. I knew she wasn't there in the flesh, but her spirit soared through the storms.

"Hey Grandma Rose, it's your one and only granddaughter...I miss you like crazy. I miss your hugs and your words of wisdom." It hurt that I couldn't hear her speak back to me though.

The closest thing between us was the soggy ground and the marble tombstone. Before I knew it, my body was laid out on the slimy grass with my arms wrapped around it. It was so hard and wet from the rain, a contrast from her soft yet wrinkly skin. I don't know how long I laid there as my tears intertwined with the rain drops and melted on my face.

A New
Summer
Breeze

Chapter 18

The Miami heat grazed my forehead as I made my exit from the airport doors. The heat hit differently down south but was less humid than the Midwest. The sweltering summer heat was suffocating. It made it more difficult to speak or think about anything other than getting to a cool place with central air. Until then, your skin was at the mercy of massive perspiration and unwanted tanning. Thank goodness for the cool summer breeze that formed after the sunset. It was reminiscent of spring but slightly warmer. The air was fresh and crisp, and the calming waters nearby soothed by soul. A white man walked by dressed in full cowboy attire. His plaid shirt was rolled up at the sleeves and his blonde chest hair was displayed.

"Howdy cowboy!" exclaimed Jamie to the man. He didn't reply back. It was as if he knew she was trying to mock his attire. Kandi and I laughed as we found an empty bench to sit on while we waited for our Uber. Jamie put her luggage down and started waving her hands in the air to an imaginary song.

"Y'all ready to turn up this weekend? I know I am!" She playfully twerked in front of us and she didn't care who else watched.

"Girl get your butt out of my face," said Kandi, as she playfully kicked her in the rear. We all laughed.

"But yes! I'm ready to turn up too! This my last girl's trip as a single woman." She snapped her fingers up high in the air.

"What about you Steph, you good? You have been kinda quiet," asked Kandi as she turned her head toward me.

"Yeah you know I'm always down to turn up with y'all. But I can't stop thinking about mama and Ronaldo and---"

Kandi interrupted, "Don't even say it. This is my bachelorette trip and it's time to have fun. Take your mind off all the negative bull back at home. You know Mama Carter still loves you and when you get back home y'all will make up. And nobody even cares about Grandaddy anymore," replied Kandi.

"Yeah you right. I do need to clear my mind of all that while I'm here."

It had been two weeks since the outrageous night when I had the date from hell, a blast from the past and the biggest altercation with Mama that I ever had before. I wished I could rewind that night and delete it from my memory bank. I almost picked up the phone to apologize to Mama for yelling and being disrespectful toward her. I stopped short when I remembered the blow to the face and how she downplayed my revelation of not being able to conceive children. How could a mother be so insensitive to her child like that? I knew she loved God, Jesus and all the saints, but I needed her love and compassion at that moment. She was stubborn, so she had not called me either.

Jamie replied, "Yeah, loosen up girl. We only booked this trip last minute to help clear your mind."

I replied, "No, don't blame me. We all agreed we could have the bachelorette celebration down here too to kill two birds with one stone."

"I'm not blaming nobody. I'm just glad we're here."

"Man, this hotel is everything," said Jamie as she looked around the foyer while Kandi checked in at the reservation desk.

"Yeah it is super nice, but I expected nothing less with Kandi making the reservation." All of a sudden, I got a whiff of chlorine from the pool area. "Ooh, I wanna get in the pool. I haven't gone swimming in forever," I said.

"I know, me too. I bought this super cute bikini. Maybe we can meet some fine, rich men at the pool," said Jamie as she nudged me with her elbow.

Before I could reply, Kandi approached us with a concerned look on her face.

"Hey y'all, they said it's a problem with our reservation. I know I requested three rooms, but they only show two on my reservation."

"Can they add another room now?" asked Jamie.

"No, they claim to be booked for the weekend."

"Well if they only got those two left, we'll just have to make it work. See if they have any rollaway beds," added Jamie.

"They do. I already asked."

"Hey, I got an idea. How about you cancel the second room and get two rollaway beds, which will be cheaper anyway. Then we can pretend to be little girls again and have a sleepover together like old times!" I exclaimed.

I knew we were all grown women who were accustomed to our own space, but the nostalgic vibes came over me. I hoped for a least a 2-to-1 vote in my favor.

"Oh my God. I love that idea!" Kandi squealed. "Are you down Jamie?"

She scrunched up her nose. "I mean it would be cheaper so that's cool, and the sleepover idea is cool, but can we at least hire some strippers?"

Kandi playfully bopped Jamie on the head with the rolled up paper in her hand. "Girl I already told you I don't want no nasty strippers sweating and gyrating all in my face," said Kandi.

"But Steph and I do! I guess since you are the bride, we gotta respect that so a sleepover party it is. But we'll do that tomorrow night cause tonight we gotta turn up!" She raised her hand for a high five. My palm met hers in the air. I was ready to forget my troubles at home.

My morning was blurred with visions of dancing, loud music, flashing lights, drinking and roaring laughter from the night before. I wasn't sleepy anymore but the pains in my head were excruciating. An electronic charge surged my temples every thirty seconds or so. The Three Amigas had visited a few different clubs on the strip.

We danced all night like it was going out of style. Jamie joined us between her conversations with potential six-figure earners. The men in Miami were much more flashy and arrogant than the ones back home, which intrigued us. A cute and well-dressed white guy asked for my phone number, but I wasn't ready for jungle fever so I transposed the last two digits of my number in case he actually called. A few others shot their shots but nobody caught my attention the way Charles did at The Daiquiri Factory. Nonetheless, we all had fun as if we were in our twenties again. I felt free being in a different city and I had barely thought about Ronaldo, Nappy Gappy, my job, the miscarriage or Mama.

The chilling water that rippled my feet was a deep contrast to the warm sand tickling my toes. I laid face up on my oversized beach towel that was decorated with tie-dye. I was close enough to feel the new waves of water that came upon the shore, but not too close to be submerged in the water. The beach was such a serene and therapeutic place that I didn't want to leave. All three of us were still tired from the lack of sleep the night before but the club scene was well worth it to me. Jamie had fallen asleep face down on her beach towel. I threw a spare towel from the room over her to cover up her backside that was displayed in her new black Victoria Secret swimsuit.

Kandi on the other hand had made friends with a family consisting of a twenty-something year old woman and her son and daughter. She went out into the water to swim with them, so she left her phone with me. I noticed that Karl had called her. I started to answer so I could speak to Karl to thank him for officially taking my advice but decided against it. A week prior, he finally went to see Kandi and apologized for his behavior. He also extended an olive branch to Hakim. Kandi was so happy to have her brother back in her life.

After about thirty minutes, she returned from the water. It was perfect timing since the tide was rising. I was in the process of moving the towels further from the shore and waking Jamie.

"Welcome back, friendly Bob," I said to Kandi who was soaking wet in her one piece.

"And wake up sleeping beauty," I said to Jamie. Jamie hopped up quickly, refreshed from her nap in the sun.

Kandi grabbed a towel and dried herself off. I handed her the phone back when she was done.

"I wasn't trying to be nosey but you missed a call from Karl, FYI."

"Okay thanks," she said as she sat back down and looked through her phone.

I removed my sunglasses and slid them on top of my head. I looked over at Kandy. She was staring at her phone in disbelief.

"What happened?" I asked curiously.

She looked over at me for a moment but paused. "Nothing," she said quickly.

I had been friends with her long enough to know that "nothing" really meant something.

"Are you sure?" I asked.

She nodded and said, "Yeah, just a post I saw online, that's all."

The Three Amigas hung out at the beach for a while longer before having a nice dinner on the strip. I couldn't forget about what happened on the beach with Kandi, and I felt that she was withholding information from us. She always saw crazy posts and memes online and she was never really phased by any of it. Perhaps something had gone wrong with her wedding plans and she just didn't want to talk about it until she could get back home and fix whatever the issue was.

"Y'all, we gotta have our real slumber party tonight. We were out of commission last night," said Jamie as she opened the room with our magnetic key.

"Yes, yes, yes! Let's end our vacay with a bachelorette slumber party. I got a game I want us to play too," I said.

"What kind of game?" asked Kandi.

"It's called the Ex-Game."

"Oh yeah? How do you play that?" she asked.

"Well, this is in honor of you putting all of your exes behind and moving forward with your marriage. So, I want us to think of an ex-boyfriend and write his name on a piece of paper. Next you will tell us why the saying goes 'Exes are exes for a reason' and cut up the piece of paper with their name on it as a way to release the pain they caused us."

"Booooo! I don't like that game. We gotta play some nasty games at least since we ain't got no stripper," said Jamie.

Kandi burst into laughter at that, but I didn't.

"C'mon y'all. I think my game will be fun. We can play whatever game you want later Jamie but let's play my game first. Please, pretty please?" I pleaded.

They both looked at each other and decided with their eyes that they would do me the honor to play my game.

The first round of the Ex-Game was about to begin, and I wanted Kandi to start first since she was the bride to be. We all sat in a circle on the king-sized bed with the hotel notepad and pens in hand along with a pair of scissors that I had to borrow from the front desk.

"Okay since I'm starting. I am going to go back to my very first boyfriend ever. She laughed at the memory of it. "Remember when we were in the third grade and Bryan asked me to be his girlfriend, but he had actually asked other girls too and I was just the first one to say yes."

I most definitely remembered since I was one of the other girls.

I laughed it off with her. "Yeah I remember. But why are you going all the way back to third grade over a two-week relationship?"

"Excuse you. This is the Ex-Game, and he was my first ex so that's why I went back there," she said jokingly.

"Okay you're right, he is still your ex I guess," I said.

Jamie chimed in. "So, tell us the reason why he is an ex?"

Kandi grabbed the scissors and started to cut. "For one I saw him on Facebook recently and let's just say he didn't age too well."

"For real, what does he look like now?" I asked curiously.

"He looks like a hot ratchet mess. He got bad acne on his face and he's fat and sloppy now."

She continued to cut and cut some more. "Because of him I had issues in later relationships?"

"What do you mean?" Jamie asked curiously.

"Well, I had insecurity issues after that. I always thought that my boyfriends had other girlfriends or that I was just somebody that they settled for."

"Wow that's deep," I said.

"Yep. I never thought about that until I started doing premarital counseling and we uncovered things in our childhood that affected our adult relationships."

"That is crazy. I never knew that affected you," I offered. I guess there was a reason why I had never told her that I was one of the other girls who received a letter.

She cut the sheet of paper into itsy bitsy pieces that sprinkled over the ivory comforter.

"See, that's why I appreciate Hakim so much. He was upfront and honest with me in the beginning. He told me all about his ex. Remember the one that y'all beat down at the bar." We all snickered at the unpleasant memory. "He was very transparent about everything which made me trust him." she added.

"Aw that's good. Glad you found a real one. Now who is the next ex, is it Travis?" asked Jamie.

"Travis, Travis, Travis. The cocky arrogant son of you know what. He was too controlling. He tried to tell me what to eat, who to talk to, how to dress, how to wipe my behind. You name it, he tried to control it."

"Dang, Pretty Boy Floyd. I had forgotten all about him," I added.

"Exactly. He took more time in the mirror getting ready than me." She started cutting some more. "He made me insecure too. I always thought I was pretty, and he would tell me that I thought I was cute but that I wasn't that cute. Or he would tell me that if I ever left him, I would never find nobody better than him. The scissors went to action with every syllable as she spoke of him.

"Tuh! Well I'm glad you left him, and it seems you actually found someone better than him after all."

"Okay! I sure did!" We high fived each other.

"Alright, my turn, my turn!" yelled Jamie as she raised her hand like she was at school.

"Go ahead," I replied.

"So, my worst ex was Jamar aka Bob Marley. All he wanted to do was get high and smoke weed all day. He had no goals or nothing. He didn't even want to work, and he had the nerve to always ask me for money."

"Oh, you having flashbacks now? Is that why you want a rich man now because of him?" I asked playfully.

"Girl yes I am having flashbacks, he didn't have a car either, so I always had to be his chauffeur to drop off and pick up his weed." Jamie started cutting in a zig zag rhythm.

We all started to laugh at memories of Bob Marley. We called him that since he had dreads and smoked so much weed. "Boy, you know we put up with some crazy mess when we were younger," said Kandi.

"We sure did. But if it wasn't for us getting into an argument and me kicking him out on the side of the road, I would have never met Jason." She looked off into space as she revisited the memory.

"Oh yeah I had forgotten about that," said Kandi.

She continued looking up at the ceiling as she relived the scene again.

"He just pulled up beside my car and honked his horn at me to roll down my window. He said he saw me put some guy out of the car down the street. He wanted to make sure I was okay.

I thought that was so sweet of him and the rest was history for us." She paused for quite some time. "And now he is nothing but history." She reached for her drink of brown liquor on the table and gulped it down.

I felt so bad for Jamie. The game was supposed to be a fun male bashing game. I never planned for her to get all sentimental thinking of the death of her daughters' father. The entire atmosphere shifted, especially since Jamie was never the emotional one of the group.

I rubbed her on the shoulder. "I'm sorry sis. Jason was a great dude."

"Real talk, he was a great dad and great boyfriend to you," offered Kandi.

Jamie still looked off into space with her drink in hand. "Yeah he was. You know since we are getting all in touch with our feelings tonight. I think I know why I always say I want a rich husband."

"Why is that?" Kandi asked.

Jamie replied, "Because I don't think I will ever love again. My mind feels like if you don't marry for love you must at least marry for money."

"Girl, that makes so much sense. That is so crazy," I added.

Kandi nodded. "Yes, there is a lot of healing going on tonight. Amen!" she shouted.

"I just thought about something else. Maybe you use drinking as a way to numb your pain. Have you ever thought of that?" I asked.

Jamie looked over at me. "Yep."

"Wow," Kandi and I both said at the same exact time.

"Man, I wish there was something we could do or say to help you but---"

She cut me off. "No, it's all good. He is in a better place now so I just gotta move on with my life and take care of my girls."

Suddenly, Kandi's phone rang, startling us. Jamie went to the restroom while she got up to go check it. Although I was excited to play the Ex-Game, it was intended to be light fun and therapeutic, not too heavy and emotional. After all, it was something I made up.

I was prepared to rip up Dante who had many infractions. The biggest one occurred when he had another female over to my apartment while I was at work. I would have never known if the stupid female hadn't left her bra in between our sheets. He was too dumb to check the room and bed for any evidence of his wrongdoing. He was definitely an ex for a reason. Of course there would be the most recent ex, Ronaldo. His disappearing act was the worst thing ever. I wanted to rip his name to shreds, letter by letter for impregnating another woman and leaving me alone and childless. He reached an all-time low for any of our exes when he took my money from that account too. I was ready to reveal his sick fantasy of hair weaves and wigs. I couldn't wait to dispose of his secret which was sniffing my wigs and weaves. He said the smell of them aroused him. It became second nature for me to wake up in bed and feel him sniffing the strands in my head. It was rather weird when I caught him with his nose planted in one of my wigs in the bathroom in the middle of the night. They would have doubled over with laughter after those revelations but the mood had totally changed. I was ready to rip his name to pieces and leave him in my past for good.

When Kandi returned with a huge smile on her face. I assumed it was her fiancé. It was a big contrast from her face earlier at the beach.

"Hey so what really happened earlier today? Was it something about the wedding plans? Her smile faded and she just shook her head. "No, but just leave it alone Steph."

"Okay, fine I'll leave it alone."

Although she got quiet, it seemed as if she were contemplating whether to tell me or not. I wasn't sure what the big deal was.

Jamie had come back into the bedroom, a towel in one hand wiping her face, and her drink in the other hand.

"Jamie, do you know what was wrong with Kandi today?"

"No ma'am, I have no idea what was wrong with her. She's keeping secrets I guess."

Kandi couldn't resist and blurted out, "No I'm not trying to keep a secret but it's something that will hurt you and I don't want to do that."

"Something that will hurt me? I knew it was something but now you really have to tell me."

"Look I'm getting sleepy, let's just go to sleep," pleaded Kandi. "I'm just ready to go back home now."

I got in her face. "No, we are not going to sleep until you tell me whatever this is that may hurt me." Kandi backed away from me and Jamie butted in.

"So, if both of y'all got secrets that may hurt one another why don't y'all both just get them off your chest right now?"

"Wait, what are you talking about?" I asked.

She cleared her throat and came and whispered in my ear, "What happened in third grade?"

I could have punched her in the throat. Why was she bringing up something that occurred over twenty years ago? I smelled the liquor on her breath, so I knew it was the alcohol.

"What are you talking about?" asked Kandi.

"Tell her Steph, and then she can tell you whatever it is that will hurt you."

"Jamie shut up. You're drunk. There is nothing I can say that will hurt her but apparently something she knows will hurt me!" I exclaimed.

"I'm not drunk! I'm not sober! Leave me alone and go ahead and tell her. If you don't I will!" exclaimed Jamie.

"Tell me what? What the heck is going on?" asked Kandi.

"Fine, if I tell you will you tell me?" I asked.

She paused briefly. "Yes, I'll tell you if you tell me," she said.

I huffed and puffed before I began to reveal what I thought was a small secret that I now knew had created insecurities for her in her dating life.

"We're waiting," exclaimed Jamie after drinking more of her liquor.

"Shut your drunk self up!" I demanded. "Okay, so to make it short. I was one of the girls that Bryan asked to be his girlfriend back in third grade. It was nothing major like Jamie made it out to be. I never knew that you were so affected by that since it was so long ago."

"Well don't you feel good to have it off your chest now?" asked Jamie.

"I'm not talking to you right now." I said. "I'm sorry Kandi. I guess I should have told you back then but I didn't want to hurt you so that's why I never said anything. I hope you're not mad at me."

She had a calm look on her face. "No, I'm not mad." She scratched her neck and continued. "I already knew that anyway."

"What! How did you know?" I asked.

"Somebody saw him put the note inside your desk and they told me. That was the reason I broke up with him."

"Wow! Wow! Wow!" repeated Jamie. She started twirling around in a circle with the drink still in hand.

"Really? I never knew that you knew. We were kids then and we have moved on. Now what is this thing that is going to hurt me that you were refusing to tell me?"

"Well remember Karl called me today while I was in the water?

"Umm yeah."

"Okay so he also texted me too and um..."

"He um what?" asked Jamie.

"Well Nappy Gappy sent him a friend request on Facebook after they saw each other at my engagement party."

"Okay," I said as I waited for more details.

"And he told me that she posted a picture that her baby daddy, which happens to be Ronaldo, had proposed to her last night at Botanical Gardens. He wanted me to warn you before you found out from someone else. I was gonna tell you, but I didn't want to ruin this trip."

The words that were spoken put me in a state of shock, although the situation was not shocking. My body went limp and felt like a wilted rose in a dry vase. No amount of fresh water could bring me back to my life.

Chapter 19

Family and friends had planned to gather at the cemetery for the one-year anniversary of June Bug's tragic death. It was a beautiful sunny day, and the temperature was bearable; not too hot or too cold. Although Grandma Rose missed her nephew with everything in her; she was hesitant about going to the gravesite. As a matter of fact, she decided she would not attend, but Mama begged her to go as we finished our breakfast at the kitchen table.

"Why should I go to the anniversary of his death? Most people celebrate happy thangs for an anniversary, not sad thangs!" Grandma Rose exclaimed.

"You should still go because it's a way to keep his memory alive."

"His memory is always alive in my heart. I don't have to go to no tombstone and release no darn balloon for that. I don't know why Rhonda is doing all this anyway."

"Mama, she lost her fiancé a year ago on the day they were supposed to get married. It makes perfect sense for her to plan this. But if you don't want to go, we still going."

"Okay, fine. I'm not going," said Grandma Rose.

"Mama, I don't wanna to go either," I said. Mama let out a loud sigh.

"See what you did? Now Steph doesn't want to go."

"I ain't do nothing. If she doesn't wanna go she doesn't have to."

"No, she is going and that's that. I'm glad your sister in town so at least one of his aunties will be there. Now go take your bath so we can be ready on time," she said to me.

"Okay, I'll take a bath, but can I stay home?"

Grandma Rose yelled out "Yes" at the same time mama yelled out "No."

"You can't make her go if she doesn't want to," Grandma Rose declared.

"Actually, I can. She is my child and not yours." Mama turned to me and pointed her finger, "You are going with us. No ifs, ands, or buts about it. Now go and get ready now."

"Okay Mama," I said as I sadly walked out of the kitchen.

There was a straight line of cars parked along the curvy cemetery road. Everybody in our neighborhood loved June Bug and he made friends anywhere he went. It wasn't a surprise that so many people came to support. I noticed some of June Bug's friends in the crowd including Stanley who was scheduled to be the best man in the wedding. Mama and I rode with Auntie Mae, who drove down from Tennessee without her husband, We were last to arrive and join the crowd.

There was already a group of people surrounding his tombstone. Some people carried flowers. Mama found a violet artificial rose bush at Ventures that I proudly carried.

Chapter 19
======

I spotted a woman and a young boy around my age handing out blue balloons to everyone. The boy was brown skinned, four eyed and sported a box haircut with a part on the side. He was kind of cute from a distance. I wondered if he was Rhonda's son whom June Bug had wanted me to meet. I was happy to see blue balloons since that was June Bug's favorite color. Mama spoke and hugged the people that she knew. When the woman and young boy with the balloons reached us, the woman said, "Hey girl!" to Mama and reached and gave her a big hug.

 Mama replied "Hey Rhonda! I didn't even notice you at first."

Rhonda laughed and stated, "Yeah everybody keeps saying that. So glad y'all could make it. Give them a balloon honey," she said to the young boy.

He gave Mama a balloon first while Rhonda turned to Auntie and I giving us hugs. "I love those roses you got Stephanie; I know June Bug would have loved them."

"Thanks," I said.

"Who is this handsome fellow with you?" asked Auntie Mae.

"Oh, this is my son Nate. Honey, this is Shirleen, Stephanie and Auntie Mae. They were his family."

"Hello, nice to meet you," he said as he handed me and Auntie our balloons. He walked off continuing along with his balloon duty. I had a feeling that was him and he was even cuter up and close and personal.

"Where is Miss Rose? Is she coming?" asked Rhonda.

"No, she not coming. It's still extremely hard for her and she is handling it in her own way," offered Mama.

"Yes, my big sister is very strong, and she doesn't like to show her pain in front of others," added Auntie Mae. Rhonda's face looked so sad when she found out Grandma Rose wasn't coming.

"Oh okay. I do understand. Well, we will be starting in just a few." She walked off; her eyes cast to the ground.

"Oh my God, she looks so sick now! Do you think she is on drugs?" whispered Auntie Mae to Mama.

"Shhh! Auntie you know you can't whisper. We'll talk about that later. I hope she didn't hear you."

It was entertaining to see where Mama got her lack of ability to whisper.

"Oh, hush chile, she ain't heard nothing." Auntie rolled her eyes as she clutched her purse.

I had to admit, Rhonda had lost a significant amount of weight. She was unrecognizable to me at first glance. I hoped what Auntie Mae said about drugs wasn't true.

"Okay everybody, we are about to start now," yelled Rhonda over the construction that was happening on the other side of the cemetery. If anybody else wants to come up and say something, you can. But I just want to start off with a prayer. As a matter of fact, it was June Bug's favorite scripture, Psalms 23." she yelled out to the crowd.

Psalms 23 was also Grandma Rose's favorite scripture and she even bought us green mini bibles where she highlighted it for us to remember. Once she was able to get everyone's attention, Rhonda started her speech.

"The Lord is my Shepherd; I shall not want..."

I blocked it out. I wanted to stay home with Grandma Rose. I agreed that celebrating the anniversary of his death would be too hard. It was beyond hard and I didn't want to cry again. I had cried periodically throughout the year from missing June Bug. I was tired of crying, so I had to distract myself. I held onto the balloon string for dear life, focused on my grip to make sure I didn't let it go too soon. I did the same with the rose arrangement that I held in my other hand. I focused on a tree in my peripheral view. I blocked out the words and cries of others. I played a happy melody in my head to help block out the noise. I was relieved to finally see a sea of balloons rise to the sky, which meant the event was over. I finally loosened the grip of my balloon which floated up to the clear blue sky never to be seen or touched again.

. . .

I dozed off on the couch the Saturday after we returned from Miami. I laid across my couch ready to doze off at any moment. I was full of the macaroni and cheese, fried chicken, greens and cornbread that I whipped up just for fun. Well honestly, I cooked and indulged to alleviate my stress levels. I binged on recorded episodes of the show Shark Tank. I wished I would have gone to school for business or restaurant management instead of going for telecommunications. Someone should have told me to follow my passion instead of going for the degree that my nine-to-five had picked out for me. I would have pursued opening a restaurant, but I knew nothing whatsoever about business. I was, however, intrigued by the entrepreneurial spirit displayed on the show.

DING DONG... DING DONG...DING DONG...DING DONG.

I had just dozed off and was getting deep into my slumber when I was startled half to death by the doorbell. I immediately looked at the clock on the wall for the time. It was almost 8 o'clock and I had no idea who was ringing my doorbell unannounced at that time of the evening.

DING DONG...DING DONG...DING DONG...DING DONG.

I walked toward the door with the intent to look through the peephole before I spoke. Then there was a loud banging as if it were the police. I looked through the peephole and could see it was only Jamie and Kandi. I was relieved that it wasn't the police or some crazy man. However, I was annoyed at them for abusing my doorbell and coming over unannounced. I quickly opened the door ajar without unhooking the chain lock so they could stop causing a scene outside my condo.

"What are y'all doing here?"

"You haven't been answering my calls or nothing. Are you okay?" exclaimed Jamie.

"I'm fine," I said.

I really didn't feel like being bothered with them, especially Jamie. I still hadn't spoken to Mama since the night she slapped me. I still couldn't get over my ex having a baby with and marrying someone else so soon. Dealing with Jamie's antics was not my top priority at that time.

"Can we at least come in sis?" asked Jamie.

After careful deliberation, I removed the chain on the door and they walked right in. We didn't exchange our usual hugs. I closed and locked the door and headed back to the couch where they had already taken seats.

"I'm sorry that we just popped up on you, but you haven't returned any of our calls and Mama Carter called to see how you were doing too. You know I hated to be the one to break that news to you but, I wanted to see how you are doing now?

"It's cool Kandi, it is what it is. What did mama say to you?"

"Well she wanted to see how you have been doing. She wants to speak to you, but she wasn't sure if you were ready to talk yet. She is ready whenever you are."

I sighed and put my hand on my forehead.

"You really need to make up with her already," said Kandi.

Jamie jumped in, "Yeah you do, it's been too long already, and I also wanted to say that I'm sorry about what happened at the hotel. You know I was tipsy and when I get that way I can be off the chain. I should have never been an instigator by bringing up Bryan. But sis, don't be mad at me, blame it on the ah-ah-ah-ah-ah-alcohol." She sang the last part, mimicking the song by Jamie Foxx with rapper, T-Pain.

"You always blame your wrongdoings on the alcohol. You need to stop it or at least slow down on the brown," I told her.

Kandi intervened, "She knows that, and she is going to try to do better. Ain't that right Jamie?"

"Yeah all I can do is try," she said as she folded her arms.

"So, do you forgive her?" Kandi asked me.

"Yes, it's all good," I said hurriedly. "It was nice seeing y'all again but y'all did interrupt my sleep, sooo let's call it a night."

"Well wait, will you reach out to Mama Carter too?"

I sighed, "Sure Kandi. I'll reach out to Mama too. Now can I go back to sleep?"

Kandi flashed a smile that displayed her beautiful dimples. "Okay good, and yes you can go back to sleep after I tell you some good news."

I scratched my head in curiosity. "What good news?"

"Well, Charles finally asked about you."

She was correct about that being good news. My inner being was lifted into the clouds of happiness.

"What did he say? Did he ask for my number?" I asked casually while trying not to display too much emotion.

"No quite. It was very random. I stopped by the tuxedo shop earlier while they were there. We spoke to each other and started a little small talk. He specifically asked how you were doing. He remembered your name and everything."

I was beaming on the inside, but I played it cool. I wished he would have asked for my phone number, but at least the inquiry was a start. I guess I had made an impression on him after all. Or perhaps he felt I was a woman full of drama and only asked out of concern and nothing more.

"Just tell the man that she likes him," said Jamie.

"No ma'am. I don't chase men. If he is interested, he can chase me," I exclaimed.

Jamie added, "He won't have to chase you. You gonna be right there waiting for him to tag you."

. . .

Grandma Rose was dressed in all-white, donning a blazer and skirt. Her soft salt and pepper curls framed her slender face. Her nails were polished pink, and her makeup was flawless. She laid still and calm inside the all-white casket that was trimmed in gold. I stared at her in disbelief for an unknown amount of time. Reality hit me as somber music came from the organ.

That would be the last time I could see or touch her body. I was overwhelmed at the realization and tried to climb inside with her. Mama and Auntie Mae tried to stop me but I kicked and flailed around and ended up on the carpet sobbing. The music from the organ got louder, almost drowning out the sounds of my grief. I hoped that my cries of anguish would awaken her from the eternal slumber to comfort me in my time of my need. Instead, the organs stopped playing. She never woke up and the casket was closed forever.

Chapter 20

I was nervous to see her again after several weeks had passed us by. I was alright with moving on and pretending that the night never happened. I understood my delivery and tone was contemptuous and out of line, but my thoughts about religion at that time were valid.

Since she had reached out to my friends, I finally called her and she wanted me to come by so we could talk. When I arrived, Mama was nowhere to be found. I called her name and searched every inch of the house. I heard a door slam which I discovered was the back door.

"Hey Steph, I was outside if you were looking for me," she said.

What a difference a few weeks could make, I thought. She was already the lightest black person I had ever seen, yet she somehow looked lighter than before. She even appeared to be about fifteen pounds lighter and she smiled at me like we were strangers crossing paths in a grocery store.

"Outside?" I asked.

"Yep, it's such a nice day and I wanted to enjoy the breeze. I stopped and got us some Chinese food when I got off from work. We can eat outside since I brought up the old table and chair set up from the basement."

It was amazing how she pretended as if nothing bad had transpired between the two of us. I assumed she didn't want to relive the night either, but I was shocked that she hadn't grabbed me for a hug yet. I understood she probably wanted to take things slow, so I went with her flow as well.

"Really? You never go outside in the backyard!"

"I know. That's one of the things I wanted to talk to you about among other things that I need to get off my chest. So, let's eat our Chinese food and then we can talk."

I wasn't sure what she had to get off her chest, but I knew it was related to the harsh things I said to her that night. I always asked her to go sit outside in the back with me and she always declined so that was a pleasant surprise.

The cool breeze felt like ecstasy to my skin. Neither of us mentioned the dreadful night. We chatted over fried rice and egg rolls, but the conversation was light. It had been a long time since I sat outside on the concrete slab in the backyard to enjoy the weather. The table and chair set from Family Dollar had aged with the passing time, it came in handy for that lovely evening in nature.

When we were done eating, Mama looked over at me with a concerned look. I was nervous about how the conversation would go.

"Stephanie, I don't want to dwell on that night, but I must say there are some things that we must talk about and some things you need to know about me."

"Okay. What about you?" I asked curiously.

"I don't know where to start. I may jump around a bit, but I'll get it all out eventually."

She made it seem like it was something life altering. I yearned to know the details now more than ever, yet I was afraid that I may not like the outcome.

"Okay. I'm listening," I said.

"There were some things that you said to me that night that truly broke my heart."

"I am so sorry Mama. I didn't mean---"

"Nope just listen, don't be sorry. For one, you were so angry with God and so angry that your life wasn't going as planned. I had similar issues as you with having a miscarriage and being betrayed by a lover. As a matter of fact, I had a miscarriage while I sat outside in this very backyard. That's the reason why I stopped coming back here. The memory of that was just too hard to bear. Believe it or not, I was only sixteen and pregnant by the plumber that I ran into at The Breakfast Denn. You know, the same one you keep bringing up all the time."

I knew she never wanted to go out into the backyard, but I never knew the reason. I most definitely was not prepared for all the other details. When she had initially opened up to me about her miscarriage, I had assumed it happened later in her life after I was already born. I began to feel like I was seated across from a stranger that I had known my whole life. However, it made sense why she got defensive every time I mentioned the plumber and why she was so adamant that I maintained abstinence when I was a teenager.

"I have to admit that I was so in love with that boy. We dated my freshman and sophomore year until I found out he had cheated on me. I broke up with him after that even though I still loved him. I never suspected pregnancy because I hadn't missed my period. But one day I was out here just minding my business enjoying the cool breeze and then it happened." She got quiet for a moment and took a deep breath while I sat quietly taking it all in.

"So, in my eyes, everything happened for a reason and I lost that baby because I was too young and immature, and he and I were no longer together. I tried to explain that to you after you lost your baby. All I was trying to say is that God knew it wasn't right for you to share a baby with Ronaldo and it was the same for me too. As a matter of fact, some doctor told me that I may have trouble conceiving in the future but guess what happened two years later?"

I replied, "Um, you had me?" I guessed.

"Correct. So, when I said that God has the final say about that, I'm living proof.

"Wow, it's so crazy that we both---"

She cut me off, "Yes that is crazy, but there's more that I must tell you. When you blamed me for your grandma's death, that tore me up inside."

"Mama, I'm sorry, I didn't---"

"Steph, just let me finish please."

"Okay sorry."

"When I stormed out on Mother's Day; I had no idea that would be the last time I would see her alive. It hurt me to the core when she died two weeks later, and I blamed myself. I thought she died of a broken heart." She paused for a moment and I wanted to reply but I waited on her to give me approval to speak again.

"After she died, I was lost and broken. I really wanted to kill myself, but I thought about you. I couldn't leave my baby girl in this world alone. I ran out of options and the last option was the church."

Mama's eyes started to water, and she looked up into the sky.

"Christ and the Church saved my life. God told me that Grandma Rose forgave me for our last argument and for not speaking to her again before she died. That's how I managed to move past my guilt and go on with my life. People told me I should have sold the house, but I chose not to because I wanted to remain as close as I could to her presence since I felt so bad about our last encounter. It hurt me when you said you didn't want to hear about church and religion. I know the truth and I know that he is an awesome God, and He gave me a peace of mind."

I was glad that church gave her a sense of peace during that rough time. I hadn't intended to hurt her. I got beside myself that evening because I was dealing with a lot of emotions.

Mama looked down to me again and grabbed my hand. "Stephanie, I love you and I want you to have that kind of peace too. You deserve it! Please don't overwork yourself at your job. If it's meant to be, you will still have your job next year. If you don't, that is okay too. You will find something even better that you genuinely enjoy. I know Ronaldo left you and got another woman pregnant, but that is not the end of your story. Trust in the process and one day God is going to give you everything that you prayed for."

Well technically, I didn't get on my knees to pray for anything because it was useless to me, but I just nodded and listened to her. She still held tight to my hand, but she got quiet and stared at me as if she was waiting for a response.

"Can I speak now?" I asked.

"Not yet. There is still more to my story. I told you earlier that I may jump around a bit so let me go back to the last argument that Grandma Rose and I had. I know you remember that day when we went to stay at the hotel. You know I tried to surprise her with the new bedroom set for Mother's Day. This is what actually happened-" She paused again before she took a deep breath.

"Well, of course in order to get the new bed in we had to remove the old one. Under the mattress, there was a manilla folder that was full of papers. I paid it no mind at first, but I couldn't help but notice that my deceased father's name was written on the envelope. I was curious about the contents of the envelope since she was always so secretive about him."

I was really glued to the story; I needed some popcorn like I was at the movie theatre.

"I opened the letter, and I couldn't believe my eyes. She had lied to me. It turned out that he had not died when she was pregnant like I had been led to believe my whole life. In his letter he revealed that he actually tried to see me, but she denied him. Turned out she was upset with him because he lied about being married. I was so mad and hurt that I found a letter that was dated in 1968, which proved that he was still alive at least when I was four years old. I couldn't wait until she got home so I could confront her, and I didn't care that it was Mother's Day."

I had to be daydreaming because this could not be real. What in the heck was going on? Where did all the lies, deceit, and misinformation come from? How did we go from God to miscarriages to long lost letters? I felt like I was carrying a load of confusion and disbelief around my shoulders. I had to be day dreaming because this could not be real. I wished I never knew this truth. It would be less stressful if I continued to assume that the argument started only because Grandma Rose was upset that her room was tampered with without her knowledge. She was finicky about people being in her room so that was the theory I wanted to believe. It would be so simple to not know that my own grandmother had lied to her only daughter for years about something of great importance.

Mama continued, "I will admit, I threw the letter in her face and I said some really harsh things to her. I can't even remember everything I said but it was bad. It was so crazy because she stopped yelling at one point. She knew she had been caught in a lie and she could no longer defend her actions."

Grandma Rose always had a sharp tongue and had a quick witty response for anybody. The fact that she remained speechless during the confrontation spoke volumes.

"Did you try to find him to see if he was still alive once you found the letter?" I asked.

She continued to hold my hand, but she used the index finger from her other hand and shushed me. I couldn't believe my ears. This whole story sounded like a daytime soap opera and it made me want to change the channel. She continued holding my hand and even squeezed it tighter than before.

Mama continued on, "I felt so bad that our last argument was the worst and consisted of me yelling and calling her a liar and all the other harsh things that I said. It hurt even more that I wasn't able to tell her I loved her one last time."

The night when Mama slapped me was the worst argument she and I had ever had. I was more grateful than ever that I still had the opportunity to apologize and tell her I loved her.

"To answer your question, I wanted to look for my father, but I felt guilty. I figured she didn't want him in my life, so I wanted to stick to her wishes and I never tried to find him. My Abba, God, is the only father that I needed anyway. He helped me sort through all the trauma, all the lies, and all the bad things that occurred in my life. When I turned my life over to him, I became whole again because he healed me. If he can heal me then I know he can heal you too."

That day was just too much for me. I desperately wanted and needed a do-over. The grandfather that I never knew was resurrected from the dead. I couldn't believe how much of my family history was revealed to me in the backyard as I sat on an old white patio chair. It was ironic how I grew up with these people, yet I knew so little about them.

Mama let out a big sigh of relief. She took a big gulp from her Grape Vess soda and finally said, "I know that was a lot to take in, but you can speak now."

Chapter 21

I couldn't believe Kandi and Hakim's wedding date had finally arrived. The sun was glowing and the sky couldn't be any clearer. My hands were sweaty all morning and my mind ached with anxiety. I felt like I was the bride as I stressed over the hope that everything went according to plan with no mishaps. I paced back and forth around my room making sure I did not forget anything before I left. The jittery feelings that I experienced were annoying, but I managed to gather everything and head to the church.

I hadn't forgotten about Charles, but he was at the bottom of my list of things to wonder about. I was bummed that he wasn't able to attend the rehearsal dinner due to being out of town on business. I was excited to see him again at the wedding. The thought of his sexy eyes distracted me from the dysfunctional family secrets I had recently discovered along with my uncertainty of things. It was no secret that my faith was lost when I was just a ten-year-old girl but maybe Mama was on to something. I was still not officially over Ronaldo and the possibility of not conceiving again. I wondered if God could give me the same kind of peace that he gave Mama. I was confused, but it was neither here nor there. I had to focus on my best friend's wedding.

I forewarned Jamie that we would conduct ourselves as ladies the whole time. Fighting, throwing drinks, or chasing after people in heels was not allowed. She laughed at me, but she agreed. There were already a few cars in the parking lot when I pulled in. I got out of the car and went to the passenger side. I grabbed my duffle bag and dress which was still wrapped up in plastic. As I closed the door, a yellow Hummer with the windows down pulled up beside me. I felt the bass vibrating through my body as the upbeat tune of an old Ludacris joint from the year 2000 blared through the speakers. IT was right up my alley since that was my favorite era of hip hop. The music ceased as soon as the ignition stopped. To my surprise, the driver of the vehicle was Charles.

"I love that color on you," he said, noting our matching vehicles. It seemed that we had similar taste in our choice of colors..

I smiled like a schoolgirl. "Thanks. I love your color even more," I responded. He grinned.

"Did you need help carrying anything?" he asked.

"No, I got it. But thanks." Internally, I screamed at myself for not saying yes and allowing him to help me. That would have allowed more time for us to be together since he would have had to walk me to the women's waiting area. But it was too late. I always got nervous around him, especially seeing him unexpectedly. I did manage to call out, "See you later!" as I walked off carrying the dress with both hands and the duffle bag on my shoulder.

Kandi was still getting her makeup done when I got inside.

"Hey sis! This your last day as a single woman!" I yelled.

She screamed, "I know right! I can't believe it!" I wanted to hug her but didn't want to interfere with the makeup artist working their magic.

"Me either but I'm so happy for you though." Kandi gave me a big Kool Aid smile as she was getting her eyebrows done.

"Thank sis, appreciate it," she said.

The door opened again, and it was Kayla. "Hey auntie. Your hair is so pretty," she said.

"Hey niece! Your hair is too. I see your mama finally let you get some color in it."

"Just a little piece, but I wanted more," said Kayla.

Kandi interrupted, "You better be lucky you got that lil girl. Now show Steph the room where she can change into her dress and you can get your makeup done after me."

"Okay ma," said Kayla. I followed her to a room two doors down. My anxiety spiked as I entered the room. I did my best to ignore and regain my focus as the day went on.

Three hours later, the entire bridal squad was completely glammed up and ready to go. Kandi was almost done, and I assumed the men were ready and waiting on us. Mama had arrived early to see our dresses before the ceremony began. I was able to squeeze into my dress perfectly with the help of my walking schedule and a juicing detox that I incorporated into my diet a week before the wedding. Each of the bridesmaids wore a white mermaid-styled dress that had asweetheart neckline with a pink sash. I stood in the mirror shaking terribly as I held onto my bouquet of pink roses, which coordinated with the pink sash on my dress. I stared at myself with great intensity. How ironic it was for me to stand before a mirror wearing an all-white dress for someone else's wedding? Even though it was a bridesmaid dress, it could easily be worn as a less formal wedding dress as well. I only dreamed of wearing this type of white dress to attend my own nuptials.

I was infatuated with my hair, which had been styled in wand curls. My tresses had grown out so much since I got the ends clipped. Nikki only had to add a few hair tracks for thickness. I showed her a picture from Pinterest of a model with the same hairstyle and she was able to duplicate the look perfectly. The makeup artist gave me a natural look, but I insisted that whatever she did, I needed a pink shade of lipstick that was popping and she didn't disappoint.

I heard Jamie complaining about her makeup and Kayla talking to Mama Collins, but I focused on the sound of my heartbeat to drown them out. I realized my anxiety was the result of fear. I always feared that something bad would happen at a church wedding as a result of my one and only wedding experience. Internally, I had associated June Bug's sudden death with weddings. It was the sole reason I made up excuses not to attend every other wedding that I had been invited to. A mysterious illness or a prior obligation were common excuses, but no excuse would be good enough to miss my best friend's wedding.

The little girl who dreamed of a lavish wedding was now a grown woman who was terrified of the actual wedding itself. I would prefer a courthouse or even a quick beach wedding, but a wedding inside a church was no longer my desire. Mama walked into the room while I was in mid-thought. I could see her through the mirror, and she looked beautiful as always. I wished she had a man to share her life with, other than God. I finally turned around when she was done speaking to everyone.

"Hey nosey rosey," I said jokingly.

"Oh my God, look at you Steph! You're gonna make me cry!"

I gave a weird look and laughed at her, "No need to cry, it's not my wedding."

"I know, but you look so beautiful. I love the dress, makeup, hair and everything. You really look like your grandma today for some reason."

"I always look like her," I joked.

"Yes, but today you really favor her. I can't stop staring at you," she said.

She made me blush a bit. "Thanks Mama. You look cute too!"

"Thanks baby," she said. She stood directly in front of me and pressed down on my shoulders. She was firm but gentle. She whispered, "I know today is hard for you, but you will be okay. God does love you, so you have to love yourself too. Everything else will fall in place. I promise you."

I shook my head in agreement with her. "Thank you, Mama!"

For some reason I needed to hear that. I guess Mama did know me after all. I had never officially told her about my secret wedding escapes, but I guess she figured it out. She also knew how I yearned for my own life partner like I needed air.

"You're welcome baby." She kissed me softly on the cheek. "I'm gonna go take my seat now. See you later," she said.

When she left, I turned back around to the mirror. Her words had a calming grasp on me. *God does love you, so you have to love yourself.* Those words captured my attention and left a permanent mark on my brain. I continued to stare in the mirror, and I thought about the little girl who was so excited to attend a wedding for the first time. She was care-free and hopeful of the future. The whole world was at her fingertips and she was fearless. *Where had that little girl gone?* I knew my faith in the Lord had died but perhaps my faith in myself had died as well. *Did I not love myself anymore? Had I ever genuinely loved myself? I thought I did but maybe I didn't. I knew I liked myself, but did I love myself? Was that the reason I doubted so many things about myself? Even though I turned my back on Christ, did he still love me? Was that the reason I needed a man, to fill the void of a life without God? Was that the reason I still thought about Ronaldo from*

time to time when he should be out of my memory for good?
Was that the reason I was so jealous of others when they
accomplished things that I had not? Was that the reason I
was low key insecure about my being? Was that the reason
I was afraid that I would never find true love? Was that the
reason I couldn't turn my life over to the Lord? Did I not feel
worthy of His love if I couldn't love myself? To love thyself or
not to love thyself, was that the question?

My concentration was interrupted.

"Dang girl! How long are you gonna stare at yourself in the
mirror? You cute or whatever but it's time to go!" exclaimed
Jamie.

Charles and Jamie pranced down the aisle first to the song,
"Ribbon in the Sky". Jamie resembled a little chocolate barbie
doll. Her sixteen inches of Brazilian Straight with a middle
part, was a deep contrast to her usual short hairdos. I didn't
know what she was complaining about during the makeup
session because her makeup was flawless. She playfully stuck
her tongue out at me before she walked through the church
doors. It was her way of showing off that she was walking down
with Charles instead of me. I shook my head and laughed at
her silliness. "You ready?" asked Malik.

"As ready as I'll be." I said. We interlocked arms and
entered the church, flowing to the rhythm of the music like the
wedding planner had taught us the night prior. I was sure to
keep that fake smile on my face although I was terrified that I
might trip and fall. Luckily, the man who was the object of my
affection stood at the altar already and I pretended that I was
walking toward him. He looked like he had stepped fresh out of
a G.Q. magazine ad in his tailored white tux. His pink vest and
bow tie matched my sash, bouquet and lipstick. He exuded a
beautiful combination of swag mixed with sophistication. Our
eyes locked, just like they had the first night I saw him.

Hakim looked rather dapper in his tux as well. He carried
a laid-back attitude at the altar. He didn't look pressed or

stressed, but he had a serious look on his face. I couldn't tell if that was his nervous look or if he was just ready to kiss the bride already. Kayla and Too Short came down the aisle after us. They walked down rather awkwardly, and Kandi didn't exaggerate about his height. He was the same height as a twelve-year-old. Hakim's niece Shania and nephew Jordan were the flower girl and ring bearer. Shania, who was five years old, sped her way down the aisle throwing flowers as fast as she could. She was in a hurry to disperse those flowers and three-year-old Jordan was just the opposite. He took his time like a little old man carrying the ring. His mother had to eventually help guide him down the path.

When the doors of the church reopened, everyone rose to their feet. The sweet sounds of Tamia and Eric Benet's ballad, "Spend My Life with You" serenaded us. There stood my best friend and sister. Blood couldn't have made us any closer. She stood in the middle of both Mama and Papa Collins and they escorted her down the aisle. Kandi was absolutely stunning on this day. Hands down, she was the prettiest bride I had ever seen in person or on television. She smiled the whole time, flashing those dimples at every sight. The dress that she finally chose after trying on what seemed like a million dresses, was the perfect match for her style and personality. It was a ball gown with a beaded bodice at top and cascading ruffles at the bottom that formed a long train. She wore a half up, half down hairstyle with big bouncy curls. The tiara was the perfect accent, giving her the resemblance of a real life princess. I looked over at Hakim and the serious look on his face had transformed. He tried to hold it but the tears couldn't stop flowing. It was the cutest thing I had ever seen. Kandi's smile and dimples disappeared as she got emotional at the sight of Hakim's tears. It was truly black love at its finest. There was no doubt in my mind that the love was real. Even Karl couldn't deny the love. I saw him nod his head with approval for his little sister and I thought I saw him shed a tear too.

The ceremony was going fine. No babies cried, no cell phones rang out loud and nobody walked into the ceremony late. Even the wedding started on time which was probably a first in black wedding history. My nervousness had started to fade.

"If anyone can show just cause why this couple cannot lawfully be joined together in matrimony, let them speak now or forever hold their peace," cited the minister.

"I do!" yelled a voice from the back of the church. All the guests turned around to see who the person was. I knew things were going too well. My gut told me something bad was going to happen.

"Who is that?" Kandi exclaimed. Hakim covered his face.

"Hey, that's his ex-girlfriend that we beat up at the bar," "Are you serious?" I asked.

"Did she want another beatdown today or what?" Jamie whispered. She was right. That was Shay from the bar. At least my anxiety wasn't in vain. Jamie and I vowed not to fight at the wedding but I was down for whatever at that point since she had the nerve to ruin Kandi's big day. She started walking down the aisle toward the now distraught couple. A massive guy who could be mistaken for a bodyguard blocked her from going further. "I can't believe this," I heard Kandi utter to Hakim.

The big guy cautioned, "Ma'am get back, you can't come any closer." She tried to walk around him, but he continued to block her. Everyone got quiet and waited for the drama to ensue. I was ready to kick my heels off and get to business and I knew Jamie would be two steps ahead of me.

Hakim walked closer to his ex in a calm manner and said, "You can't do this today. I love that woman right there." He pointed his finger in Kandi's direction. His tone with her was incredibly careful and non-aggressive, which I took to be a calculated decision on his part. If he were too hostile with her, she probably would have returned the favor. "I love her with all my heart and her daughter too. I'm sorry but it ain't nothing you can say or do to change my mind."

She rolled her neck and smacked her lips. The bodyguard double continued standing between them. Personally, I would never try to crash my ex's wedding, but if I did, I would come looking like an Instagram model. I would make him do a double take and think twice about letting me go for good. However, Shay wore another cheaply made dress with a synthetic weave that was equally as cheap. I knew that looks were not everything, but she really had no oomph or class about herself. There was no doubt that Hakim had upgraded with Kandi.

"Okay, okay, okay. Hakim, you right! You got me looking like a fool in front of all these people."

"No, you made yourself look like a fool," yelled Jamie from the altar. Shay didn't respond continuing her conversation with Hakim with the bodyguard in between them.

"To be honest, I did come here to start some mess. I was jealous that you wanted to marry someone else so soon. But I can't lie, you never looked at me the way you just looked at her. I see for myself now that I can't compete with that, but I had to at least give it one last try. So, I'm bowing out gracefully." She held her hands up in the air in a surrendering manner. "You lucky sis, you got a good man right here," she said as she turned back around and did a stank walk toward the exit.

"Goodbye and good riddance!" yelled out Hakim's sister. The guests began to clap for the end of the villain's performance.

The whole scene felt like an act from a movie. The wedding party and the guests were the extras in the movie who waited quietly while the main characters hashed out their conflict on screen. It all happened so fast, yet it also replayed in slow motion. She held up the deuces sign with her two fingers as she made her exit without looking back again.

"I'm so sorry my queen," said Hakim after he rushed back over to Kandi. He got down in front of her on bended knee. "Give me your hand baby," he said. "I had no idea she would come here. It has been over between us for quite some time, but she couldn't accept me moving on. But she is gone for good now and I will never let her, or anyone disrespect you again."

Kandi had allowed him to take her hand and she looked down at him. "But how did she know our wedding date and location?"

"Baby I don't know. I didn't tell her. I'll find out how she got the information, but that doesn't even matter right now. I'm here for you and nobody is going to stop this. Please, will you still marry me?"

Kandi paused for a few seconds as she pondered if she could really trust him.

"Girl get your man!" Jamie shouted. The guests started to laugh and began chanting, "Get your man! Get your man! Get your man!"

Kandi couldn't help but laugh. I saw her look over to Karl, who gave her a thumbs up. "Okay. I'll still marry you baby," she said.

"That's what I'm talking about, baby." He got up from his knees and dusted himself off. "Carry on please. Where were we?" he asked the minister.

The rest of the wedding went off without a hitch and the reception was nothing but a good time. Everyone secretly talked about the wedding disruption but loved how Hakim diffused the situation. The reception venue was decorated so beautifully that it could have been posted in a luxury wedding magazine. The DJ was on point, the food was tasty, and no more exes attempted to break up the love connection. Kayla, Jade and Jamiya were having a ball with the other kids. They were doing the latest dance moves, which I thought were too complicated and ridiculous. What ever happened to the

MC Hammer Dance, The Running Man, The Butterfly or the Bankhead Bounce? Those were all dances from my era which were simple to learn and didn't require a YouTube tutorial.

The wedding party was seated at a long table in the center stage of the room. I'm not sure if I imagined things but it seemed like Charles peeped down at me a few times during dinner. I remembered what Mama had told me about loving myself and trusting God. If it were meant for us to hit it off, God would make it happen. That could be true, but I also had to put in some effort too. I took my chance and decided to start a conversation with him. I planned to wait until everyone was done eating. I mean he broke the ice earlier with the car comment. I took my chance and walked down to his seat while the rest of the wedding party mingled with others or danced on the dance floor. The most obvious conversation starter would be the unexpected wedding crasher. However, I didn't want to remind him of the bar fight. I decided to go with a lighter subject. He was in the middle of scrolling through his email messages on his phone when I snuck up on him.

"Hey there. Did you enjoy your food?" I asked.

He looked up at me like he was surprised that I came to speak to him. "Oh yeah, the food was fine. The mac and cheese wasn't the best but everything else was good. I'm a big mac and cheese fan so I'm really critical about it."

"Oh okay, I didn't even try the mac and cheese. I'm actually a big fan myself.

I have my own recipe that I use so I don't eat everybody's mac and cheese."

"Oh yeah? I may have to try your recipe one day."

OH MY GOD! I squealed on the inside. I was elated that the conversation was flowing so well, but I felt my face rising with heat as I blushed.

"Well actually it was my grandma's recipe and she passed it down to me."

"Okay cool. Hey, looks like they're about to do the bouquet toss. Are you gonna to try to catch it?"

My smile couldn't have gotten any bigger. "I would love to catch the bouquet!" I exclaimed.

He smiled too, "You better hurry up, looks like they're about to start."

Beyonce's famous hit, "Single Ladies", started to blare from the speakers and that was my calling.

A whole squad of single ladies gathered in the middle of the floor. I didn't see Jamie at first, but Mama strolled into the crowd too.

"Mama, I know you not trying to catch the bouquet," I said jokingly.

She shrugged her shoulders. "I'm just having some fun."

Kandi grabbed the microphone and did a roll call. "All the single ladies please, hurry up if you want to participate!"

Moments later Jamie ran into the crowd. "Throw it to me Kandi, my rich husband out there waiting on me!" she yelled. The crowd got a kick out of Jamie's amusing antics.

"Girl whatever," Kandi said jokingly. "Hey Steph, this is for you." She pointed to me.

"Bring it on, bring it on!" I yelled as I waved my hands in the air. The next thing I knew, Kandi turned around and threw the bouquet backwards. It came right toward my direction which I'm sure was her intent. All I could hear were screams and other noises in the crowd as I jumped up to catch. It was snatched up by the pair of pale hands right beside me.

"Oh my God! I caught it! I caught the bouquet!" yelled out Mama. She did a circular dance to commemorate her victory. I started to snatch it out of her hands just to be funny, but I let her have her moment. Everybody clapped and we continued having a good time.

"Yay Mama Carter! You go girl!" yelled Kandi.

"Sorry Jamie, I guess you'll have to wait on your rich husband," Mama said to Jamie. Jamie laughed so hard she couldn't even respond. I could tell she had been to the open bar a few times already.

I went back over to Charles to finish our conversation. As I approached him, he shook his head at me.

"Why are you shaking your head at me?" I asked.

"Because you almost had it and you let someone steal it from you," he said jokingly.

"I know right? I was so close. That was my mom who stole it from me."

"Oh yeah? Moms had the strong-arm game tonight I see."

"Yeah, she won it fair and square. Is your mom here tonight?" I asked. I assumed that his mother should be close with Hakim since they had been friends for a long time.

"Naw, she doesn't do weddings and receptions. Actually, I don't like them either. I'm only here for my boy Hakim."

It was so crazy that he and I had so many things in common. We both had bad breakups recently, both had yellow vehicles, both hated weddings and loved mac and cheese.

"Really? I feel the same way too. I don't usually do weddings either."

Before he could respond, Hakim came back to the table, "Hey man can you come outside with me for a second?"

"Don't mean to cut this short but let me see what's up with him."

"Okay no problem at all," I said. When he walked off, I missed him already. How could I be so infatuated with someone after a one-minute conversation? I had to be foolish, but it didn't matter. I was only glad that we finally broke the ice with one another. I was hopeful and confident that he would ask for my phone number by the end of the night.

Things started to wind down as the lights dimmed and red neon lights started to beam. They should have called it Red Light Special time. The D.J.'s smooth voice sounded over the music, "Hey y'all, it's time to slow this party down. I need all the lovers to the dance floor with the newlyweds right now."

Jamie and I had been on the floor jamming to some nineties hip hop music. She drunkenly stumbled off once the D.J announced he was switching the music up. We were almost off the dance floor when the bells from the song's intro rang and I heard Keith Sweat's whining voice shortly after. I stopped in my tracks, closed my eyes, raised my arms up, and sang along to the sweet sounds of the melodic tune. There was no way I would sit this one out, so I danced by myself, pretending I had a partner. I had no problem with doing so either because that song always took me on a natural high that I didn't want to come down from. Before I knew it, someone grabbed my hands, forcing me to open my eyes. Before I could say a word, his deep voice muttered, "This must be your song."

I gazed at him and smiled. "Yes, I love this song," I said.

Our hands were interlocked as he walked me a few steps over to the middle of the dance floor. We were surrounded by the others, everyone swaying to the rhythm. Once we had our place on the dance floor, he looked into my eyes seductively as he wrapped his arms around my waist. I raised my arms and rested my hands on his neck. We swayed together from left to right as I sang the verse in his ear. I heard him chuckle. When the chorus came on, I felt his body snuggle closer to mine. I continued singing, "There's a right and a wrong way to love somebody...." He was so close at that point, and his scent was intoxicating. I trailed my fingers across the top of his back as he moved his fingers up and down my waist.

I hadn't slow danced that intimately with anybody since my high school senior prom with Dante. That night was much different for me compared to senior prom with Dante. I felt extremely confident and sexy dancing with Charles. I thrusted my body with his and I felt an immense level of comfort in his strong broad arms. He must have felt the passion just as I did. He leaned in and serenaded me before he planted a soft and sensual kiss on the lobe of my right ear. I tingled with delight as I felt the sweet saliva from his juicy lips. I daydreamed that Keith Sweat performed a private show for us. I didn't notice anybody else on the floor, not even Kandi and Hakim. I wished for that moment to be frozen in time, but the song eventually concluded. Charles pulled back away from me, gazed deeply into my surprised eyes, and slowly released himself out of my embrace. The moment in time was over but it was forever embedded in my soul.

Chapter 22

I had begun self-reflection in the weeks after the wedding. So much had occurred in just a short time and it was all so much to take in. It was exhausting. I did some research of my own about self-love. Many blogs advised that loving yourself first was important before someone else could love you. I felt I needed to work on that more and accept myself for who I was, flaws and all. I could not allow Ronaldo to continue to have a negative hold on me. I had to forgive him for what he did to me so that I could move forward with my life.

Mama forgave Grandma Rose for withholding the truth about her father. Although, she was no longer alive to explain her version of the story, I was sure there was a reasonable explanation. If mama could forgive her then I could surely forgive Ronaldo.

Nobody was perfect and everyone had done or said something in the past that they were not proud of. Those two women were still my heroes because they raised me without the help of a man. Their strength was carried down to me, but I had denied it for years. However, I decided to make a conscious decision to own my strength as a single woman. I slowly started to understand that a man did not define my happiness.

I finally got rid of that leather coat that Ronaldo got for me and I sold the coffee table he had bought from someone on Craigslist. Those were the final concrete reminders of him that were in my condo. The plan was to finally start over fresh and view my life in a more positive way instead of dwelling on the negatives. I was in such a good head space that I didn't even care that Charles didn't ask for my number, not even after our steamy slow dance. I thought there was a connection during our dance but apparently it was one-sided. The old me would have freaked out and assumed there was something wrong with me but the new me wasn't fazed by it.

Self-love and self-care became my new lifestyle. I started cooking healthier meals for myself and continued walking a few days a week at the park. I added a Zumba class to the mix sometimes. I scheduled mani/pedis every two weeks instead of once a month. The negative thoughts that I would be single and childless forever were replaced with positive affirmations that I spoke over myself daily in the mirror.

"My name is Stephanie La'Rose Carter. I am smart. I am funny. I am a great daughter. I am a great friend. My future is bright. I am successful. I will find a husband and have a family one day. I am lovable. I love myself. I am capable of love."

It sounded silly to look in the mirror and talk to myself, but it was recommended from all the blogs I read. When I practiced it, I somehow felt empowered. I'm not sure if my mind was playing tricks on me, but those affirmations gave me a boost of confidence in myself and my future love life.

Ronaldo and the men from my past left me with bags of insecurities. It became my mission to unzip those bags and release all the debris. They were only meant travel with me through certain reasons and seasons of life. They were not worthy of a lifetime of my love. That's what Grandma Rose had tried to instill in me early on. They were meant to teach me lessons and those lessons were pre-tests meant to prepare me for the big exam when I finally met my life partner. Until he arrived, I vowed to focus on loving myself because nobody could love me as much as I should love myself.

Chapter 23

I was bored and uninspired at work, so I made it a point to go to the cafeteria every time I had a break or lunch, just to escape the monotony of my little office. I stopped putting in so much effort and it was like I didn't care to work that hard anymore for something that wasn't promised. I wasn't totally giving up on it, but the whole self-love thing that Mama hit with me had me thinking about my life on a much deeper level. I would much rather work hard at doing something that I was passionate about instead of doing something just for the bi-weekly paychecks. I hadn't even bothered to look at the top twenty-five sales for a couple of months. I just waited on Liz to come tell me where I stood on the list. She was much more consumed with it than I was.

On my morning break, someone left the TV on Channel 11 and I caught the end of "Paternity Court". It was a case of a thirty-five-year-old woman who wanted a DNA test to prove that the defendant was her father. The defendant admitted that he slept with the woman's mother in the past, but he believed another man was her biological father. The mother stood at the podium with embarrassment that she wasn't 100% sure who her daughter's father was. The case immediately drew a parallel to Mama and her biological father. The man whom she was led to believe had died while she was still in the womb had actually reached out and wanted to hold her and love her, but he was denied. Mama in return denied him when she didn't try to look for him once she found out the truth. I was compelled to call her and plead with her to try to find out whether he was still alive. I took a chance and called her work phone, unsure if she could answer. Luckily, she answered on the third ring.

"Thank you for contacting Hopewell Industries, this is Shirleen, how can I help you?"

"Mama it's me. Can you talk for a second?"

"Yeah, is everything okay?"

"Yes, all is fine."

"Oh okay, you scared me a little bit cause you don't usually call at work."

"I know but I really wanted to reach you now. I've been thinking about something, but I didn't want to upset you."

"Upset me how?"

"Well I just saw this paternity case and it made me think about you finding your father. I know you're gonna say God is the only father that you need but I want to know for myself as well. We got a whole family out there that we don't know about."

"Steph, I'm at work right now so I don't really want to talk about this."

"Well can we finish this conversation tonight?" Mama got quiet before she let out a big sigh.

"I'm sorry baby but I don't want to look for him or his

family. I've made it this far without them so I'm fine and I would appreciate it if you left this matter alone for good. Now I gotta go, talk to you later," she said before she hung up.

I shook my head at how stubborn she was, but Grandma Rose was stubborn too, so she got it honest. I wanted to see that letter for myself. I wondered if Mama threw the envelope away or if she still had it. I didn't want to upset her anymore so I decided I should just let it go. My break was almost over so I sluggishly got up to return to my office right as Judge Lauren Lake called out, "Mr. Johnson, you are the father!"

. . .

"So, tell me how married life's been treating you so far?" I asked

Kandi looked up in the sky with a grin. "It's everything that I could have asked for. My husband is so great. He helps me in the kitchen, he takes the trash out without me asking, he packs my lunch in the morning. I mean I couldn't have asked for a better husband."

"Well that's good to hear. Glad the honeymoon phase is not over yet." I added.

"No honey, not at all." She wiped the sweat from her forehead.

It was a scorching eighty-eight degrees. I was shocked to see so many people who walked, rode bikes and even skated around as the sunshine radiated around us. The waist trainer I wore around my belly was drenched with sweat and we had only been walking for a short period of time. I wished we would have walked later on that Saturday evening, but it was date night for Kandi and Hakim so she wouldn't be available.

"Well I'm super happy for you, but I do miss my friend. Seems like we don't talk as much since you got a husband," I teased.

"Whatever sis, we do talk. I mean I can't talk as much as I used to but---"

I interrupted her, "No worries, I'm just kidding with you."

"Okay, you better be kidding. Hello there!" she said to a friendly walker who waved to us. "But seriously, how have you been though?"

"You know, I have been really good. Honestly, I feel the best I've felt all year. I really think I'm back to my old self."

"Yay! I'm happy to hear that girl." She hit my shoulder to express her enthusiasm. "If you're back to your old self, your niece needs to come spend some weekends with you again. She said she misses you."

"Aww I miss her too. Yeah I'll have to plan a little slumber party for her, Jamiya and Jade."

"Yes, that would be good." Kandi cleared her throat. "Um, so I saw Charles the other day. He came over to grab something "You wanted to ask him what exactly?"

"I wanted to ask what his deal was? I mean I saw y'all on the dance floor and I mean the chemistry was undeniable." She clapped her hands for emphasis. "When I say that you and Granddaddy never had chemistry like that before! When I say you and Dante never had chemistry like that before! I mean it was such a connection that I couldn't explain."

I stopped her before she went on and on. "Yeah, I felt something too, but he didn't pursue anything after, so I guess he didn't feel the same. But it's cool Kandi. I'm not tripping off of him nor any man right now. I'm just focused on me right now."

"But what about our vision board?" Kandi asked as she pouted her lips out in an attempt to look sad.

"Girl my chances of getting married by the end of the year and Jamie finding a rich one by the end of year are pretty slim at this point. I'm gonna hang it up!" I laughed at the whole situation.

"No, no, don't hang it up yet. Look I'm going to tell Hakim

to give me Charles' phone number and I'm gonna have you call him."

I stopped in the middle of the trail. "Oh no you will not! I'm not gonna act like some desperate chick. You never know, he could still be in love with ex or it could be anything. I told you that I don't even like him anymore."

Kandi sighed and gave in. "Okay, I understand but what about the nerdy church boy. Has he still been sending you messages?"

I had totally forgotten about the dating site. Flight Mike left a bad taste in my mouth and I hadn't even considered anyone else after him.

"I actually don't know. It's been awhile since I went to the site. I need to just delete my account for real because I don't even have the energy right now for a man. I'm just learning to love myself again, you know?"

"Yes, I know and self-love is so important, but you know how I am about goals and stuff. Can you please go to your account and if he has sent you any messages recently go ahead and reply back and try to go out with him."

I didn't even respond to her. I looked at her like she was crazy and kept walking. She laughed at my lack of response.

"Sis, I know this sounds crazy, but I just have this gut feeling that he may be special. I can't put my finger on why I feel like that, but I do."

"Have you been smoking today?" I asked jokingly.

"No, you know I don't smoke but let's make a deal Steph."

"Do I look like Wayne Brady to you?"

Kandi started laughing and couldn't stop. At that point, I couldn't tell if the heat was more aggravating or her. The sweat drizzled down my back as I took each step. When she finally regained her composure, she offered me a proposition.

"I'm gonna leave it alone after this but please try to connect with him and see what's up. You can even delete your account after that, and I'll be done with asking you about it. But I do think it is worth giving him a shot. You never know, he could change your life. If not Charles, then it may be Church Nerd for the win."

Chapter 24

Nathan: Good morning LaRose. I was so excited when you sent me your phone number. I hope I'm not texting you too early. Please have a great day beautiful and I hope to speak to you later today.

Stephanie: Good morning Nathan. Sorry I sent you the message so late last night and no it's not too early to text me. Hope you have a good day too

Stephanie: Are you happy now. Church nerd was still sending me messages so I sent him my phone number.

Kandi: YAY!!!!!!!!!!!!! Thanks for taking my advice. Let me know how it goes and smile and be nice to him please and thanks.

I had neglected my honorary auntie duties all year, but since I was officially over my breakup with Ronaldo, I was able to get back into a regular routine. I planned to have Kayla, Jamiya and Jade all weekend long. There was a time when we had the fanciest of tea parties, baby doll hair appointments and

Easy Bake oven contests. Now they were older and stayed on Instagram, Tik Tok or YouTube. They were the cutest little girls who had turned into scrolling, dancing, boy crazy teenagers. The plan was to order pizza on Friday night and watch movies. Saturday we would go to the mall, go bowling and go eat at Red Lobster where I hoped not to run into Lobster Boxers, aka Flight Mike. On Sunday morning I planned to take them to the local carnival that was in town for the weekend.

They demolished the whole pizza and breadsticks. Jade fell asleep while we watched the first movie, *US*. I couldn't understand how anyone could fall asleep during a Jordan Peele movie. Kayla stayed up but every ten minutes, she asked me questions about things she didn't understand about the movie. Jamiya barely watched as her eyes were more focused on her text messages and Instagram. I had checked my messages from Nathan a few times, but he stopped once I told him I was watching movies with my nieces. I had to give him props for his consistency of reaching out to me all those months. He said there was something about me that grabbed his attention. He said other women were only looking for casual hookups or friendships, but he wanted more.

We ended the night with just one movie, and I decided to save *The Quiet Place* for another night. I texted Nate and told him about the disastrous movie night and he asked if he could call me. I had nothing else to do at that point as I let the girls have their freedom for the rest of the night.

"Hello," I said in my sexy voice when I answered the phone.

"Hey, you. It's good to finally put a voice to that beautiful face," he said.

"I know right. After all this time," I said.

I was glad that he was the type of guy who could carry on a conversation. He didn't just wait on me to initiate a topic, which was very refreshing. He never asked me to send him pictures of my face nor my feet which gave him major points.

As long as he didn't have a fetish for sniffing hair extensions or wearing black nail polish; he was alright with me. His voice was deep and raspy, which kind of turned me on. I had to say the voice didn't match his pictures. I expected him to have a high-pitched Steve Urkel voice. We stayed on the phone for five hours straight. That was a new record for me. The last time I stayed on a call that long was back in high school with Rob and Dante. I started yawning every few minutes toward the end of the call.

"Am I boring you now or you just tired?" he asked.

"Oh no, you not boring at all. I'm just sleepy. Did you know it was 3:00 AM?

"I did not. Where did the time go? I am so sorry, never meant to keep you up this late. I just really enjoyed our conversation."

We had talked about so much in five hours and the conversation flowed naturally without awkward silences.

"It's all good, time flies when you're having fun," I said.

"Yes, ma'am so true. I hope I'm not too forward in asking you this but I definitely wanna meet you very soon. I got the perfect place to meet for our first date too. It's a public space where you can feel safe."

"Where is this perfect place?" I asked skeptically.

"At the house of the Lord."

"At church?" I asked as I popped up in my bed.

I had briefly forgotten how much he referenced God and religion in his profile and messages, so I should have known a church date was right up his alley. He was more down to earth and secular on the phone than he came off on his profile.

In the past I had been invited to wineries, restaurants, movies, and even bowling, but nobody had ever invited me to church for a date. As a matter of fact, I had never visited church with any past boyfriends. Mama had invited Ronaldo and I many times, but we always made excuses not to go. We almost went one Easter because we were bored but decided the holiday crowd would annoy us.

"Yep, what better place could there be?" A tiny giggle escaped from my lips.

"What's funny about that?" he asked.

"Well it's just different. I wasn't expecting for that to be your answer. I must say my mama would love you from the bottom of her heart and she would tell me to look no further." I laughed some more. "She would probably say, 'Welcome to our family, Brother Nathan.'"

He laughed as well. "Yeah I'm sure your mama would love me. Most mamas do. I mean what's not to like?" he proclaimed in a cocky but joking manner.

"Well so far I haven't found anything that I haven't liked about you. We have had great conversations so far."

"Then it's settled. Service starts at 10:00 AM and I can text you the name and address. But wait a minute, when was the last time you went to church? I don't want the doors of the church to burn when you come in."

I absolutely loved his sense of humor and I couldn't contain my laughter at his last jab. "Really?" I laughed. "Don't play me like that!" I continued, "To be honest it has been a while."

"Why is that La'Rose?"

"Well," I sighed. "Let's just say God and I hadn't always seen eye to eye. It started after my cousin got killed when I was ten years old and then my grandma passed away some years later. I kinda pulled away from the church and my mama turned to the church after my grandma passed. There are also some things that have happened to me that had me questioning things. Not to mention the sermons are so long and so boring that I fall asleep. So, there you have it, those are my reasons. I guess you don't want to go out with me anymore now. You probably think I'm an atheist or something."

"No, that's not true. You just lost your faith in Him and that happens sometimes. You are human and you have feelings. I felt the same way when my stepfather passed away but I prayed about it."

I knew he had more to preach about, but I cut him short. "He won't put you through nothing that you can't handle," I said.

"Exactly! You took the words right out of my mouth!"

"Yeah, I knew what you were gonna say cause my mama says it a lot too. Man, she would really love you for real!"

He chuckled again. "I'm sure I would love her too. Now check your phone, I sent you the name and address of the church so see you at 10:00 AM on Sunday. And come as you are."

Saturday morning with the girls started a little later than I expected since I was up late on the phone like a schoolgirl. We finally arrived at the mall around noon and stayed there for a couple of hours. Each girl walked away with two outfits and a few accessories. We didn't feel like waiting in line at Red Lobster so we opted to eat at the food court instead.

I felt disrespected as all three of them sat with their cell phones in hand. They were so preoccupied as if the phone carried secret time sensitive information that they had to retrieve right away.

"Do y'all stay on the phone this much when your parents are with you?" They all burst out into laughter, but I missed the joke.

Kayla shook her head, "No, my mom doesn't let me stay on it all the time."

"Okay good, well act like I'm your mama today." I smoothly snatched it from her fingers. She didn't protest as she continued to laugh, revealing her missing side tooth.

I turned to the other two. "And what about y'all?"

Jamiya shook her head. "Our mama doesn't care. She is on her phone a lot too." "Hmm, Jade is that true or not?" I asked.

"Yeah it's true, she doesn't care for real."

"Well I'm not your mama, so give me those phones for now. We are gonna eat our food with no electronic distractions. Just food and conversation.

"Can we have it back after we eat?" asked Jade.

"Yes," I said. She handed her phone over to me but Jamiya hesitated a bit. "I know you are older than them, but this applies to you too boo-boo," I said.

"I'll just put it in my pocket," said Jamiya as she rushed to put the phone in the pocket of her denim cut off shorts.

"There used to be a time that y'all would talk me to death and ask me all kinds of questions. Let's eat our Panda Express and go back to the good old days."

"Okay, Auntie Steph, do you ever want kids of your own and a husband?" Jade asked in her sweet high-pitched voice.

That particular question cut me in thirty-five pieces across the small table. If there was ever a moment when I should have been careful what I asked for, that was it. I briefly wondered whether it was too late to give them their cell phones back so they wouldn't be forced to ask any more terrifying questions They all stared at me blankly, awaiting my answer. Since they couldn't go on social media, I became their entertainment. Instead of The Shade Room, they could call me The Steph Room.

I cleared my voice before I answered. "Of course, I do Jade. I just have to meet the right person to marry first and then we can talk about babies after that if it's meant to be."

"You don't have to be married to have a baby though." Jamiya tapped her little sister on the arm.

"Be quiet girl, you talk too much," said Jamiya.

"No, it's okay Jamiya. She is right. You don't have to be married but that's what I want though. Or shall I say that's what I would prefer," I said politely.

Sunday morning came and I had the decision of taking the girls to the carnival or going to meet Nathan at church. This decision would have been much easier for the old me because I would have declined the church date. However, Mama had kind of stirred curiosity in me about finding Christ and finding peace within. When he asked me out, I had totally forgotten about the carnival I had promised to take them to. I had about an hour and half to decide who I was going to let down. I could go to church then come back and get them for the carnival, but that would make my day longer. I wanted to go to the carnival earlier before it got too hot and crowded. In all fairness, they probably wouldn't appreciate the fun and games of the carnival like they did when they were younger. The games and apps on their phones along with social media were their new ideas of fun.

I called the other two amigas to let them know that I would be dropping their kids off early. Jamie decided that she would take the girls to the carnival since I had other plans, so it all worked out perfectly.

Nathan's criminal record came up as clean as the Board of Health when I checked on casenet.com but I still sent Mama the name and address of the church I was headed to. She was still stuck inside her boring Sunday service but at least she would see my message when she left. Just in case the church was a cult who tried to lock me up and make me sacrifice my life for a greater good, she would know where to come find me. I laughed at myself in the car. Who would have thought that I would choose a Sunday morning service over merry-go-rounds and funnel cake? What was really happening to me?

I was a little caught off guard when I put in the address for the church in my GPS and it led me to the big church by The

Breakfast Denn. That was the same church that Kandi told me was Charles' family church. I was nervous as I didn't want to run into him while I was with another guy. I thought I was over him, but it was still weird to attend his family's church and possibly run into him. At first, I wondered if he and Nathan knew each other and had bible study lessons together. That would have been so awkward but luckily Nathan confessed after the service that it was his first time at Mount Holiness. He told me the pastor of his church had passed away six months prior and he did not like the leadership that had taken over. He was in the process of finding a new church.

The congregation was rather large which was refreshing because it made it harder to run into Charles. Other than my paranoia, the service by far exceeded my expectations. Pastor Abraham was the best pastor I had seen in person in all of my thirty-five years of life. I stayed awake during his whole sermon. I was pleasantly surprised that I didn't nod off like I did at Mama's church or any other that I had been dragged to throughout the years. The pastor seemed so familiar and personable and his message was relatable. His words flowed and resonated like poetry to my ears.

I was just as amazed with Nathan as I was with the church. I had to give him credit because the pictures he posted on the dating site did not do him any justice. The nerdiness faded away in person and he was actually a very nice-looking man. He was respectful and just an all-around bonafide gentleman. He didn't even greet me with a hug. Instead he offered his hand for a handshake. Which was something I had never experienced before on a first date.

I couldn't wait to get inside the car and tell everyone about my experience. I guess Kandi was on to something about him. He walked me to my car, opened the door for me and he shook my hand again and leaned in for a smooch on my left cheek. It was the most innocent and sweetest thing ever.

"Thank you for coming. I hope you enjoyed yourself. Please drive safe and call me later when you get a chance."

"I sure will. Thanks again for the invite," I offered. I didn't specifically tell him how much I enjoyed the service, but I assumed he could tell since I didn't fall asleep.

As soon as I got in the car and reached for my phone, it was vibrating. I had turned the ringer off before church.

"Hey Mama, I was just about to call you."

"Steph are y'all okay?" she yelled frantically over the phone.

"What? Calm down, I'm fine what's the matter?"

"Thank God. I was so worried. Did y'all hear the gunshots?"

I was totally confused. I heard no gunshots and there was nothing abnormal going on in my current area.

"Mama, what gunshots? You are scaring me."

"There was breaking news of a shooting at the carnival and four people died."

"Oh my God, are you serious? I guess you didn't get my text because I didn't go to the carnival, but Jamie took them. Let me try calling her. I'll call you back."

I hung up immediately and tried to call Jamie. I hoped she and the girls were okay. To my displeasure, her voicemail picked up immediately. I tried calling her again and the same thing happened. Next, I tried Kandi, whose phone rang a series of times before connecting to voicemail. I even called the girls' phones and none of them picked up either which was scary because they always had their phones in hand. My heart pumped out of my chest and all sorts of negative thoughts crossed my mind. I was glad that I chose to attend Sunday service over the carnival. However, I was uneasy that Jamie had decided to go in my place. I would never forgive myself if something had happened to her or those girls. I tried calling each of them again and still nothing. For the first time in ages, I prayed to the heavens, "Please God, let them be okay!"

Chapter 25

I sat on the side of the pool in a brand-new bikini showing off the results of losing twenty pounds. I reclined in my lawn chair with my legs stretched out and crossed at the ankles. The water was a clear blue hue that was soothing to the soul. The strong scent of chlorine burned my nose a bit, but it was bearable.

"Stephanie! Stephanie!" I heard voices yelling out my name, but I couldn't see anyone. I looked around and eventually Jamie's head popped up out of the water like a scene in a scary movie, nearly causing me to jump out of the lawn chair. She laughed at me, pointing her fingers in my direction for my reaction. "Did I scare you? Why are you so scary?" she asked.

The same reason you're always drunk," I retorted

She chuckled at me, "I just like to have fun, that's all. We all can't be uptight like you. You know you used to be fun but lately you been so uptight. Loosen up!"

She made a big splash in the water that splattered all over me. The water was frigid, yet the sting was warm and inviting. So inviting that I got up and jumped in the pool with her to have a water splashing contest. We splished and splashed each other for several moments letting out joyous laughter and spontaneity at the same time. But she stopped and she looked at me in a serious manner, "Are you ready?" she asked

I waded in the water like a tadpole and asked, "Am I ready for what?" She glided over to me and said, "For this!" as she savagely pulled my head down into the water. I gasped for air but could not breathe.

. . .

After fifteen phone calls with no answer, I drove directly to Jamie's house. To my surprise her car was still there. That was a good sign, and I ran up to the door almost tripping up the steps to get to the porch. I barely had breath left in my lungs, but I still had movement in my hands to bang violently on the front door since I knew her doorbell no longer worked. I stood with my back up against the door and attempted to regain my breath. I grabbed my phone again and called her and still nothing. I knocked some more until I heard the locks unlocking from the other side. It was Jamiya dressed in a tank top and boy shorts. I was so relieved to see her in the flesh, alive and well. I was sure I looked like a mad woman with my hair all over my head, courtesy of the wind that blew through my windows as I sped to the house. She looked at me like I was crazy. I made my way inside the house looking around for Jamie.

"Is everything okay Auntie?" she asked.

"No! I have been calling your mom for the last 30 minutes and her phone is going to voicemail. I called you, Kayla and your sister and nobody answered. There was a shooting at the carnival, so I was making sure y'all were safe."

"Dang, for real? I'm glad we didn't go then, but yeah Mama passed out across her bed not long after you dropped us off and she wouldn't budge when I tried to wake her. We all ended up falling back asleep too since you woke us up early this morning so that's why we missed your calls."

"Whew, thank goodness. That explains it then, but I was so scared. I don't know what I would have done if I had lost any of y'all." I grabbed Jamiya and held on to her tight.

"Who was that banging on my door?" exclaimed Jamie as the entered the living room. Jamie's short hair was disheveled, and she looked like a wild woman too. She was dressed in a faded oversized t-shirt.

"What are you doing here?" she asked me. I let go of Jamiya and rushed over to Jamie and hugged her tight as well. She reeked of cheap men's cologne and alcohol and it was only noon.

"Girl you woke me up, what's going on?" she asked cluelessly.

"I'm just glad you're still alive." I held on tighter refusing to let her scent overpower my emotions.

He had answered my prayers just like that and I believed Mama was right about everything.

"Thank you, Lord," I whispered with my eyes closed.

Mama gushed and glowed at the details of me and Nathan's budding relationship. I felt like I had known him for longer than just one weekend. I couldn't explain it, but there was some kind of connection between us. Mama literally stood up and did a circular praise dance in my living room when I told her that I had thoroughly enjoyed church and considered going back.

"Amen to that! I tried to tell you a long time ago that you needed a man in church. I guess I couldn't get you back in the church, but He sent someone else to do it. Praise God! I love it and I tell you ain't nothing better than a God-fearing man."

She got up again and jumped in place." I couldn't do anything but laugh at her churchy antics.

"Yeah you right Mama, you told me, and I just couldn't see the vision. I always thought those types of men would be too boring for me and I would get tired of them too quickly. Or on the other hand, I put them all in the same category thinking they would be hypocrites so I was never interested."

"Yeah, I know what you thought, but I told you those thuggish boys with that swag sauce or whatever y'all young kids call it, ain't the right fit for the woman you are becoming."

I started massaging my feet, as they were tender from the wedges I had worn, which were a half size too small. I looked at her inquisitively. "Exactly what kind of woman I am becoming?"

Her eyes brightened and she flashed her pearly whites. "Well, I knew the day was coming soon, Steph. I think you are finally becoming a Woman of God! You got a long way to go but I think this is the beginning for you."

Mama's smile was so full of joy. I was happy that my going to church and enjoying it made her so proud.

Nathan and I had another late-night conversation that Sunday night. We both agreed that Mount Holiness was a church that we would like to visit again one day. We both also had work the following morning so we had a pact to end our conversation no later than 10:00 PM. Before we ended the call, he said there was a serious question he wanted to ask me.

"Ask away," I said.

"Okay, what would be your dream job or dream career?"

"Oh, that's an easy question. I always wanted to own a restaurant. What about you?"

"For me it would be to own my own art gallery."

"Oh wow, that's different. Are you a big fan of art?"

"Yep. I am. Are you?"

"Um, yes and no. I'm not an avid fan but my grandma had this painting in her room that I loved. It was a painting of sorbet flowers. Those are the pink, orange and lavender colored roses. I thought it was the most amazing visual and it just reminds me of her every time I see it."

"Oh okay. It sounds just as beautiful as you," he said.

"You sure know how to make a girl blush."

He laughed. "Well that's good to hear but I won't keep you any longer. It is ten o'clock on the dot now so have a good night."

"Goodnight," I said back.

My TV station was on Channel 4 and had become background noise while I was on my call with Nathan. The ten o'clock news appeared with the headline:

Fatal Shooting at Local Carnival today leaves 4 dead and 7 injured.

I turned the volume up to hear the latest development of the story. Apparently, some teenage kids had beef with some other teens from school. A fight ensued between the two parties and someone in the group started shooting. Only two of the teens involved in the fights were injured. The rest were innocent bystanders. It all happened toward the front of the carnival right between the merry-go-round and the funnel cake stand. My heart dropped like an elevator at the realization that the girls and I would have been there when the shooting happened had I not gone to church. Had we been there, it was possible that we would have made the ten o'clock news just like June Bug did in 1994. I could hear Grandma Rose's voice in my ear. "Chile, I done told you before, people come into your life for a reason, season, or a lifetime. That's the sho nuff truth."

Maybe Mama was right about God sending Nathan for me. Had Nathan come into my life to put my body in the church pews amongst the worshippers, Holy Ghosters, bible holders, and the anointed ones on that day? Did God place him in my life to protect me and my nieces from harm's way on that day? Was he the reason I laid peacefully in my bed and not in a body bag that night? Chills began to resonate all over my body, and I shivered at the thought that we could have ended up slain, bloody and in a life or death battle. The moment of reflection was humbling. I could no longer deny that God was real! He had saved me and now I had to save myself.

The urge to get down on my knees, clasp my hands together and thank God for the first time in twenty-five years was halted by a shrill sound. It was nothing more than a telephone ring, but it startled me because nobody ever called my home phone. Heck I didn't even know my own home phone number. I only had it for emergencies since it was free with being an employee of the phone company. I assumed it was the wrong number but as soon as the house phone stopped then my cell started ringing. It was an unfamiliar number, but I was curious to see who this mystery person was calling my home and then my cell after 10:00 PM.

"Hello," I said cautiously.

"Hey Steph, I hope it's not too late. It's me Ronaldo."

Chapter 26

The church benches were empty but there stood Mama at the pulpit with a gigantic black church hat. The brim almost covered her tiny face. She reached her hand out for me.

"Come closer, I have a surprise for you!" she shouted.

I slowly walked down the narrow church aisle with hesitation wearing an all-white choir robe.

"Hurry, hurry!" her voice grew urgent.

I sped up to match the intensity in her voice. When I reached the pulpit, she grabbed my hand and pulled me up. Then we walked to the back and stopped when we reached a small flight of steps.

"You go first," she said. I didn't question her and took the steps up only to reach two more steps that led to a white porcelain tub filled with water.

"Keep going," she said. I held on to the wobbly wood railing for dear life. I was about to step my bare feet into the water,

but I saw bodies floating. I immediately screamed out and tried to turn around but Mama blocked my escape.

"It's okay, they won't hurt you. Take a look."

I finally spoke, "I don't want to look."

"They won't hurt you; they love you." I covered my eyes.

Mama whispered, "It's okay," as she gently removed by hands from over my eyes. I closed my eyes even tighter.

"Don't you want to see Grandma Rose one last time? They closed that casket on you and you weren't done saying goodbye yet." I shook my head uncontrollably.

"What about June Bug? You miss him, right? He was like a dad to you, not a cousin. Wouldn't you kill to see him once more? Open your eyes, you can see them once more."

"No, no, no!" I shouted as I tried to get away from the pool. I struggled to get away.

Her voice turned high-pitched and wicked, similar to that of the wicked witch of the West.

"No need to be scared baby. If you knew God, you wouldn't be scared. Do you know Him?" she shouted in my ear as I still attempted to escape.

"Do you know God, Stephanie? If you don't, you need to know Him!"

. . .

"My garbage disposal is not working, can you come take a look at it when you get off?" asked Mama.

"After my walk in the park, I can come over, but I probably can't fix it. You might have to call your ex, Mr. Plumber," I said jokingly.

I had to use humor to disguise my ill feelings about Ronaldo calling me. I started to tell Mama about it, but I chose to keep quiet at that time.

"Whatever chile, I'm not trying to call him. Maybe you can look up under the sink and hit that reset button or use the little wrench tool and try to turn it on or something like that."

"Okay Mama, I'll see what I can do, but if I can't, you know there's a plumber on deck that can help you out. I'm pulling up to the job now so talk to you later. Love ya."

My office phone rang as soon as I clocked in and I assumed it was a potential sales lead, so I answered right away.

"Hello Steph, please don't hang up on me this time. I really need to speak to you."

His voice sounded pitiful and shamed to my confused ear. This was the same man who went radio silent on me for months and now he was blowing up all my phones. I didn't speak nor hang up, but I waited for him to say what he needed to say.

"Hello, are you still there?" he asked.

His voice annoyed my current existence. The fire that blazed under my skin, in my ear, and my throat created an invisible smoke that almost choked my lungs, causing me to lose the very wind I needed to respond to him. Was I having another bad dream? It couldn't be real. The man who abandoned me without a single word could not be calling me to utter any words to me after all this time. There was so much I wanted to say to him, but I froze up and just hung up on him again.

I went on about my day in the usual manner. I made two sales before lunch and I was mad at myself for not speaking up and telling him how I felt about him doing me wrong. But there was no need for that; he already knew that. I went to meet Liz downstairs for lunch and grabbed my phone that had been on silent in my purse.

314-555-5555: Steph I know I'm the last person you want to hear from but I need to talk to you... You do deserve answers and I want to give them to you... I'm leaving town for good tomorrow so I need to see you before I go please can we meet up to talk when you get off of work.

I started to text him back some vulgar and profane language, but I had been to church the past three weeks, and I didn't want to lose my newfound religion. I showed Liz the message and she encouraged me to meet up with him. I also forwarded the message to Kandi, Mama and Jamie for their opinion.

Kandi: Say what? He got his nerve..now he wants to talk after all this time but I think it may be good for you to get closure..Love you and I support whatever you decide.

Mama: God is a forgiving God so if he is sorry for his actions you can forgive him and move on. You don't have to meet up with him to forgive him but whatever you feel you need to do, please do. I'll pray that you make the right decision! Love you

Jamie: F*** HIM PERIOD!!!!!!!!!!!!!!!!

The rest of the day I contemplated what I should do. I did have a closure since I had moved on, but his explanation would be the ultimate closure. On the other hand, he got another woman pregnant and stole money from me so that was all the closure I needed. He sounded sincere when he picked up the phone though. I sensed pain and hurt in his voice so maybe he finally worked up the courage to explain his sudden disappearance. I replied.

Stephanie: I'll meet you at Howdershell Park at 6pm

314-555-5555: Ok cool see you soon

The nervousness took over my body for the rest of the day. I was already going to the park when I got off work to walk the trail. I changed into my workout clothes before I left. I had no idea I would see my ex when I packed my black spandex sports bra and black workout pants in my pink duffle bag. I had to admit, the athletic attire looked good on me and my new figure. The workout pants sculpted my legs, thigh, and buttocks like a high-end piece of artwork. My stomach was much smaller from the last time he saw it bare and it pleased me that he would get one last glimpse of what he gave up. My beauty was natural and not injected and manufactured like his new baby mama. I spotted a park bench not far from the parking spot that I pulled into. I sat my butt on the hot and hard green bench. I was there five minutes before six, so I waited on him impatiently. Luckily, my nerves started to dwindle down a bit since I was in position at the final scene only moments away from the conclusion and one step closer to getting back to my regular scheduled programming.

His car pulled up to a parking spot right next to mine. I wondered if he would even recognize me on the bench without my hair extensions. I was happy about that too as I didn't want to give him the pleasure of one last hair sniff. To my surprise the man who exited the car, had a low haircut. He no longer had the dreads that he had started over ten year prior. He wore a simple white t-shirt and black basketball shorts, and in his hands, he carried a bouquet of flowers. I shook my head. I wondered why he would bring flowers for me. I was all confused and I just wanted to get to the bottom of everything.

As he got closer to the bench, he smiled when he finally recognized me. My arms were crossed, and I had a serious look on my face. No smiles for me.

"Hey Steph," he said. "These are for you."

Did he expect me to be impressed by calla lilies? I assumed he did but he must have forgotten that my favorite type of flowers were roses of any color. How hard was it to remember that fun fact about me? I took the bouquet without saying thanks and laid them on the bench creating a space between the two of us when he sat down.

"So, what's up? Why do you need to meet with me now?" I asked with an attitude. He flopped down on the park bench and I noticed his black Nike slides and white socks. He took a deep breath before speaking and he looked into my face.

"I know you hate me right now," he said.

I did hate him but there was no need to verbalize it.

"Actually, I hate myself right now too," he said. His eyes started to water a little bit. I guess he wanted me to agree that I hated him, but I just pressed my back up against the bench and folded my arms again, waiting for him to get to the point.

"Okay, well let me just start by saying that you were a really good woman, and any man would be lucky to have you. The thing is I didn't think I was the right man for you."

I continued to listen without saying a word.

"I never felt that I was good enough for you. You had your big corporate job where you worked since high school. You had a college degree, money and good credit. I had rinky dink jobs here and there, and I never even finished high school."

I had to speak at that point. "I encouraged you to go back to get your G.E.D. though."

"Yes, you did, but I felt you were embarrassed by me. You never really took me around your friends that much or your family."

"I only have a few friends and I don't have much family in town, but you have been around the friends and family that I do have. So, what's your next excuse?" I asked angrily.

"See this what I'm talking about. You didn't value anything that I did or said. I can't help that you made me feel that way. Regardless whether you agree or not, I'm telling you that was my truth. I really felt like you were just tired of being single and you just got with me and you settled. It was like you were trying to make me out to be something else. You tried to change my whole wardrobe and everything."

Was he really complaining about wardrobe recommendations? I couldn't help that I liked matching outfits or colors with my man. Dante and I started that back in high school, so it was something that I was used to. However, that was not a deal breaker to leave me high and dry during the holiday season. I got so annoyed by him and we hadn't even been at it for five minutes.

I sighed. "Okay, whatever. What else is there?"

He began to complain some more. As he spoke, I realized that he looked better with the dreadlocks. I couldn't believe that the man who spoke was someone that I laid next to at night, talked to everyday, and planned to marry. My heart felt nothing for him now and he was a stranger to me.

"So that leads me to my next topic. Like I said, I felt that you settled for me and I didn't feel that you were in love with me and you didn't appreciate me either."

A couple walked by and nodded at us. We nodded back out of courtesy.

"So, one morning we went to The Breakfast Denn and I got up to use the restroom. This waitress had stopped me on my way back to the table. She literally told me that I didn't look happy with you and she slipped me her phone number."

"Gabrielle Abby?" I asked. He took a deep breath and paused before he finished. His eyes continued to well up with tears.

"Yes, I didn't even know that she knew you at that point. I just took it as she found me attractive and she tried to shoot her shot. So, at first, I didn't even call her. But remember that time I got us a new coffee table and had it delivered and assembled by the time you got off of work so you could walk in and be surprised?"

"Yeah."

"It took me almost three hours to put that thing together. You know I wasn't really that good at stuff like that. I thought you were gonna be so excited when you got home but you acted like it was no big deal. You didn't thank me, give me a kiss or a hug or anything. I told you I wanted to watch a movie that night in the living room, but you decided to go upstairs and go to sleep instead. So that same night I called her and we hit it off from there and the rest was history."

Did he expect some kind of gold medal for assembling a table? Wasn't he supposed to do those types of things as the man of the household? I did remember that night and I was really tired from working a ten hour shift so I couldn't help it if I was sleepy on that night that he was speaking of.

"She told me that she went to school with you, but she didn't know you like that. We messed around for a little minute and she kept telling me to leave you and come with her."

I assumed Gabrielle aka Nappy Gappy still held a grudge with me from our teenage days and made it her revenge to get back at me for the embarrassment she experienced in school. I wondered how long the affair lasted but didn't want to know. I continued to let him get things off his chest as it seemed therapeutic for him as he got rather emotional. Why was he so emotional when he was the one that left me dry, deserted and fiending for water?

"Okay, so I have heard enough. You left me to be with her and start a family with her and you took some of my money to---"

He interrupted, "Steph, I'm so sorry about that. I had lost my job and I knew that you would be disappointed in me, so I didn't even tell you. But she still accepted me, with flaws and all. That's how I fell in love with her and when she told me she was pregnant, I knew what I had to do. But I promise I'm gonna pay you all of that money back. When I leave tomorrow, I'm going back to Michigan and my cousin got a job lined up for me. I promise I'm gonna send your money back since that's the least I can do.

I threw my arms in the air. "Wait a minute! So, you lose your job, and your mistress gets pregnant, but you decide to take my money to pay for yall's expenses?" I asked sarcastically.

"I know it was wrong, but I also knew you would still be financially okay and I planned to pay it back."

"Well you do that! Please pay it back with interest too! Thanks again for the meeting. Have a nice life!" I hopped up to go start my workout, but he motioned his hand for me to sit back down.

"Hold on, hold on. There is more though," he said.

I was standing up at that point. "No, we're done! Just send my money and I hope y'all have a nice life together."

He blurted out, "She died Steph! She died delivering the baby. Her and the baby died."

I was so shocked at the new revelation. It became an even more uncomfortable setting than before. Usually I said 'Sorry for your loss' if someone died or offered condolences. But in this case, was I really sorry? I mean she was part of a problem that caused me a lot of pain, but I never wished death on anybody.

"Oh wow!" were the words that finally crept out of my mouth. I could tell he wanted to cry but he tried hard not to.

"That's why I wanted to meet up with you. What I did was wrong, and I felt that I got my karma for it. Her and I both did. I should have been honest with you instead of running like a coward. So today I am being that man that I should have been months ago. I never meant to hurt you. I pray that you forgive me one day."

I stood in front of the bench, my newly toned body hovering over him. At that point I wanted to tell him about our baby that also died. Would that make it worse for him? Did I want to get that off my chest like he had just done? Would it even matter at that point?

"Well, I never liked her even back from high school and she didn't like me either. But it is sad that she passed away like that."

"Thanks," he said as he wiped his left eye.

"I have something to tell you too." I rubbed my head as I wondered if I was making the right decision. "How can I say this? You didn't just lose one baby, you lost two."

He looked up at me in confusion. "Huh?"

"I didn't know at the time, but I was also pregnant when you left and I lost my...I mean I lost our baby on Christmas day."

He put his head down and covered his face for a few seconds. At that moment I wished I had kept quiet. Or maybe I needed to release that in order to officially move on from it.

"I am so, so, so sorry, Steph," he chanted.

"It's all good. My Mama and Grandma always told me everything happens for a reason." I grabbed the flowers on the bench. "Have a safe flight to Michigan and thanks for the closure. Goodbye Ronaldo."

I wasn't sure why, but I bent down and gave him a kiss on the cheek. It seemed like the right thing to do at that moment. I didn't give him a chance to say anything more. I jogged off and headed toward the trail. I stopped for a second and dumped the flowers off in the first green trash bin that I saw. The calla lilies sank down in the trash mixed in with all the debris of papers, food wrappings and other junk. I exhaled deeply. Instead of walking, I sprinted around the trail for the first time and didn't look back.

Chapter 27

It wasn't quite fall yet, but the weather was already cooling off a bit and it was getting darker earlier. I wasn't complaining at all because I couldn't wait for the autumn leaves to transition in color and drop onto my lawn. Fall made me think of my school days when a new school year started, and the anticipation of what the rest of the year would look like. There was always a calm but nervous feeling that numbed my body. The chilling winds swirled around my mind and body and created an ecstasy between us.

What should I wear to karaoke? Should I wear jeans, a cute top and heels or a jumpsuit with a denim jacket and wedges? I opted for the jumpsuit; a glittering gold one with matching wedges, which would be great for my stage performance, I thought. I was so enthused when Nathan suggested karaoke. The last time I had done karaoke was the same night Ronaldo went missing in action.

Nathan and I had begun to spend a lot of time together. He

told me I could call him Nate instead of Nathan. I told him he could call me Stephanie instead of La'Rose.

"I love that name, La'Rose, it's so unique and it has a ring to it. Does anybody else call you that?" he asked one day as we sipped milkshakes from the new Culver's that had opened up around my way.

"Nope. I love my middle name too, but nobody calls me that. I'm either Stephanie or Steph to everyone else. I was only LaRose on the dating website."

"Well now somebody does call you that and that will be me. I don't want to do the same things that others do because I'm different," he said.

I really enjoyed hanging out with him which was rather surprising. He was not the snooze fest that I had anticipated him to be. He actually had a good sense of humor and we were able to talk about politics, pop culture, movies and TV shows. We just had a good time in general. He did reference some scriptures in the bible from time to time, but it wasn't overkill. As a matter of fact, I was interested in what he said in relation to the bible. I guess I was slowly becoming the Woman of God that Mama had prayed about. We met at eight different churches for eight consecutive weeks. The last two were decent enough that I didn't fall asleep, but the pastors didn't compare to Pastor Abraham at Mount Holiness Church. I secretly wanted to visit that church again, but I was afraid I might run into Charles since that was his family's church.

I wished I had given Nate a chance much sooner than I had. He always paid for both of our meals when we dined out and never dared to ask for separate checks like Flight Mike did. He opened doors, pulled out chairs and constantly gave out compliments. He even surprised me with a dozen red roses which meant everything to me. I placed them in the center of my new coffee table. I wanted to personally thank his mother and stepfather who groomed him at an early age of how to be a gentleman. He needed to teach other men that chivalry still existed.

On karaoke night, he called when he was outside, rang my doorbell and waited outside the car for me to come out. As I approached the car, he greeted me, took my hand and provided a solid but sweet kiss on my cheek. He drove a white Chevy Traverse that was clean on the inside and even cleaner on the outside. He never played any of the secular Rap or hip hop like Jay-Z, Drake, or Lil Wayne. Instead he played gospel rap music from Lecrae and some others whose name I didn't know. The beats sounded like trap music beats, but they were rapping about their love for Jesus instead of women, drugs, and fancy cars. He looked so handsome bobbing his head to the beats and I couldn't help but do the same.

The parking lot of the venue was almost empty. There were only about eight to ten people inside. It was an old, country looking establishment with old portraits, cowboy hats and bandanas on the wall. I even saw a stack of hay over in the corner. The waitresses wore cut off denim shorts, plaid button-down shirts tied at the waist and cowboy boots.

"What kind of place have you brought me to?" I asked sarcastically. He couldn't help but laugh at my question. He looked around as well.

"Were you looking for flashing lights, a big TV monitor and a stage?"

"Um, yeah, pretty much," I said.

"Howdy partners, is a booth okay?" said that hostess that walked up to us with menus in hand. Her stringy hair was pulled up in a ponytail and I noticed she had severe acne.

"Yes, a booth is fine," said Nate.

"Okay, right this way," the hostess said. We followed her to a booth with carved writing on the table. "Here you go and just so you know; tonight is 90's karaoke night. And also, you can carve a message or your names or whatever you want on the table." She carefully dropped a utensil in the middle of the table for us to use.

We both chanted, "Okay thanks."

"Your waiter will be with you shortly. Enjoy."

"Woo hoo!" Nate said jokingly. "Nineties night, what do you think about that? What requests do you have?"

"I don't know yet. There's so much to choose from! I love, I mean love 90's music with everything in me! It just takes me back to my childhood you know. It brings back memories and just makes me feel some kind of way."

He nodded and gave me a look that I didn't quite understand.

"My name is La'Rose and I'm a simple girl looking for a husband to start a family with. My ideal date can just play me a 90's R&B jam, send me some roses, and take me out to eat sometimes," cited Nate in a playful girly voice.

I was in absolute shock that he memorized and recited the first few lines from my online dating profile. I was flattered but it was also kind of creepy. I found a way to look past the creepiness to focus on the flattery.

"Very impressive! Bravo!" I said. I gave him a sitting applause. "How in the heck did you memorize that?"

He chuckled a bit.

"I don't wanna to tell you just yet. You will think I'm crazy."

"What?" I exclaimed.

"Just chill out, I'll explain in detail later if you give me a chance. For now, let's focus on the food you want to order and the songs you want to sing. The night is yours La'Rose."

There was a small monitor for the words and a makeshift space for the stage, but we made it work. Two drunk white girls and a guy were my only competition that night. The girls were both thin with long flowing blonde hair, wearing tight mini dresses and dirty flip flops. They channeled former pop idols of the time period. They teamed up for classic Britney Spears jams such as "Oops!...I did It Again" and "Genie in a Bottle" from Christina Aguilera. I went through a pop phase in the late 90's so I thoroughly enjoyed their drunken renditions. The guy, who was very over the top, did a great impersonation of Right Said Fred's, "I'm Too Sexy". He was so into it that he literally unbuttoned and removed his Hawaiian-themed shirt and threw it out into the bare crowd. He closed out his performance with N' Sync's popular tune, "Bye Bye Bye".

I was afraid that the country, hicktown like establishment wouldn't have access to many African American songs but I was wrong. My first selection was Brandy's first single, "I Wanna Be Down" which got the small crowd hype. I mimicked the hand dance that she did in the video. "No Scrubs" from TLC wooed the crowd and the two drunk girls got up and sang along in the audience. I motioned for Nate to come up and sing with me, but he laughed and shook his head.

"I can't sing," he shouted.

"So, what, it's just fun, there's nobody here anyway," I shouted back to him.

"No thanks, I'll let you have the spotlight. I'm enjoying watching you."

He sat back in his seat and folded his arms. My singing voice was nothing to brag about at all, but I was just having fun. I wanted him to have as much fun as I did. I got down from the makeshift stage and tried to grab him to follow me. He laughed so nervously and blushed at the thought of going on stage. I finally persuaded him once the cowgirl inspired waitresses chanted for him to join me.

"Okay I guess I'll do it," he said reluctantly. I was so happy, and I wanted us to sing a duet together. I recalled seeing Babyface and Toni Braxton's hit "Give you My Heart" in their book of songs, which was on The Boomerang soundtrack.

Nate mentioned that Eddie Murphy was one of his favorite comedians in one of our phone conversations, so I'm sure that he loved that movie. I hadn't heard that song in forever, but the words came back to me once the beat dropped. I had forgotten that the chorus referenced making love and that was nothing that he and I had discussed yet. He seemed to enjoy himself despite his uneasiness at first. We danced and flowed together perfectly to the beat and the song became the background to our melody.

"How did you hear about the place?" I asked on the car ride back home.

"I googled karaoke spots and that one came up. It was the advertisement for a 90's night on Thursdays. I know it wasn't the fanciest place, but I thought you would like the 90's theme night."

"Wow, you did research. I really like that. It's okay that it wasn't the fanciest place. It's not always about that, it's the fact that you put in the effort so that speaks volumes."

I was barely impressed when we first walked in, but everything turned out fine. I enjoyed us carving our names into the table and the drunken white friends that we made. Even the pizza that I was unsure of ordering proved to be tasty. It was unfortunate that it gave me bubble guts and I secretly longed for my own bathroom toilet.

He turned to me with a smile. "Yeah, I put a little effort in so I'm glad you appreciated it."

That made me think of when Ronaldo told me that I didn't appreciate him during our relationship.

"But I wanted to address something really quick," he stated in a matter of fact way. He turned the gospel rap music down so he could be heard clearly. Had I done or said something wrong during that night? Was he mad that I fronted him out and brought him up to sing with me? The night breeze was the only sound that reverberated in the car.

"What's up?" I asked curiously.

He cleared his throat as he approached a red light at a busy intersection.

"Well, there's something that you need to know about me." I bucked my eyes in preparation of his secret. I knew he was too good to be true I thought.

"I've been celibate for the last nine years and I'm saving myself for marriage," he proclaimed.

My mouth flung open so wide that a baseball could have fit inside. I hadn't had relations in forever either, but I couldn't imagine being without sex for nine lonely years. Well, at least he has been intimate before and isn't an almost forty-year-old virgin, I thought.

"Wow!" I said. "That is commendable. Most men can barely wait for nine days, let alone nine years," I exclaimed.

He laughed, "Right. I used to be that guy until I turned my life over to Him." He pointed his finger up at the sky. "It is a process. It's not easy; I'll tell you that," he said with a slight chuckle.

"Wow," I said again as I didn't know what else to say. This man had the most will power I had ever seen in my life.

He did the usual routine of opening the car door for me, then escorting me to my front door. He gave me a friendly hug and kissed me on the cheek again.

"I hope what I told you doesn't change things between us," he whispered in my ear. His voice came across even raspier and sexier than it had been before. Our bodies were the closest they had been during our short dating situation.

"No, it doesn't change anything," I whispered back.

I scrolled down my Instagram feed as I sat on the toilet. I wished I had declined those last two slices of pizza because my body was paying for it. I received a call from Kandi while I was in the middle of reading the comments from the latest post on The Shade Room.

"Hey sis, what's up?" I said.

Kandi smacked her lips. "I was just seeing how your date went tonight?"

I put her on speaker phone and continued with The Shade Room comments.

I smiled at the memory of a great night. "Girl it was so sweet. So, he remembered that my dating profile had said that I loved 90's music so he found a spot that had a 90's karaoke night. He really put thought into it, and we sang a duet together too."

"Aww, too cute. He seems like a sweet guy."

"Yes, he is really sweet. He still opens the doors and all that too."

"Well I told you I got good vibes from him."

"That's so crazy, I don't know how you felt vibes like that from someone you never met."

"I think it was the fact that he was so persistent, so I was like he must really be interested."

I sprayed some more air freshener. I was done handling my business but I was so comfortable that I wasn't ready to get up just yet, plus my left leg had fallen asleep. When I had read enough comments I went back to the home page and saw that I had a new direct message.

"Very true. He is interested in little old me."

I shook my head and then clicked on the red symbol in the top right-hand corner of Instagram. There was a picture of a nice looking African American man in the circle and his screen name was charlesjustcuz. Was this who I thought it was? Kandi said something else, but I blocked her out for a moment. I clicked on the message that read:

Hey lil mama..how are you? I've been thinking about you and that secret mac and cheese recipe since the wedding. I found your profile from a wedding post that Kandi tagged you in.

I screamed so loud that my neighbors probably heard me even though the walls were super thick.

"Oh my God! I knew it! I knew there was a connection that night. I knew I wasn't crazy!" I screamed.

"Huh?" Kandi asked. "What are you yelling about?"

"Girl, your boy sent me a message on IG just now and it reads as follows: Hey lil mama...how are you? I've been thinking about you and that secret mac and cheese recipe since the wedding. I found your profile from a wedding post that Kandi tagged you in!"

"Is that from Charles?"

"Yes! Yes! Yes!"

"Wow, so he hit you up on IG huh?" He could have just asked me for your number though. So, are you gonna respond?"

"Of course, I'm gonna respond. I've waited for him to reach out to me for the longest."

"Wait, don't respond back just yet."

"I'm not. I don't wanna to seem too thirsty, so I'll wait until the morning to respond back."

"Okay good but I thought you were over him since he didn't pursue you after the wedding?"

"I did say that, but I only said it because I didn't think he was interested in me. I wasn't gonna chase after a man, but this message shows that he is trying to pursue me now. He said he thought about me and our conversation. I bet he also remembered that passion between us on the dance floor."

"I understand where you're coming from, but months have gone by and he just now decided to reach out to you. I mean Charles is a good guy, but I don't want you to forget about church nerd because..."

I zoned her out again and I couldn't wait until the morning.

Hey Charles, it's funny that you feel that way because I thought about you after the wedding too. I'm glad you found me and reached out <insert smiley face emoji>

"Girl, I replied already!"

"I thought you were going to wait."

"I know but I have already waited long enough."

I had meant to tell Kandi that Nate had been celibate for nine years. But that didn't matter anymore. Thoughts of Nate and Charles twirled around in my mind but those of Nate got flushed down the toilet and suddenly disappeared.

Chapter 28

Charles couldn't talk on the phone much because he traveled a lot for his marketing job. Our main line of communication was Instagram. He was in Atlanta, but said he wanted to see me when he got back to town and asked if I could make him that famous mac and cheese that I had bragged about. I was pleased to tell him yes. Nate on the other hand continued to call me as he always preferred phone calls over texting.

"Are you sure that everything is okay? You have seemed a little distant lately."

"No, everything is fine. I'm just a little tired. I have to go to my mom's this morning to help her out with something."

"Oh, I thought you went to bed early last night."

"I did but I tossed and turned all night," I said. In reality, I had tossed and turned as I was messaging Charles.

"Sorry to hear that you didn't sleep well. I'm also sorry if I'm questioning you too much. I just wanted to make sure I didn't scare you off when I told you I was celibate."

"It's all good Nate. You didn't scare me off," I said.

I remembered reading an article on how preacher Devon Franklin, husband of actress Meagan Good, was celibate for ten years. Nate was not the only man who practiced celibacy. Heck I hadn't had a warm body in my bed since early December so technically I was celibate too. I didn't judge him. I respected his morals more than he would ever know.

"Well I hope you have a good day today. Do you have any plans?" I asked.

"Yeah I'm getting ready to take my son to his youth bowling league game and after that we will stop by to see my moms."

"Oh yeah, I forgot that you do that on Saturdays. Which bowling alley is it again?" I asked.

"Kingpins Lane."

"Oh okay, I know exactly where that is. He is ten, right?"

"Yep, ten going on twenty," he said. We both laughed. He rotated weekends with the son's mother and had him every Tuesday and Wednesday.

"Sorry to cut you off, I just pulled up to my mom's house. She has someone coming by to do some work and she wanted me to be here with her."

"Oh, okay cool. Talk to you later. Hope you get some rest if you can later."

"Thanks," I said before I hung up.

Mama paced around the house and dusted off tables that had no dust on them. I knew it was just a coping mechanism for her nervousness. She also didn't want anyone to come into her house and think that she didn't keep a clean home.

I was glad she went ahead and took my advice and called Mr. Plumber. It took her long enough to finally do it, but she was left with no choice when her dishwasher flooded. That morning she wore a faded purple robe, but I knew she would change into everyday clothes before he arrived. She also wore a satin pink and purple floral scarf tied up in a big knot at the top of her forehead.

"Good morning Mama. Are you ready to get those pipes back working? I mean are you ready to get the dishwasher and garbage disposal back working?" I knew that would get under her skin. She didn't respond as she gave me a nasty look with squinted eyes and pouty lips. I cracked up as I walked over to her and planted a kiss on her right cheek. "I'm just playing Mama."

"I know you better be playing," she said as she kissed me back on my left cheek.

I began flipping the channels to find something interesting to watch until the plumber got there.

"What time is he supposed to come again?" I asked.

"He said he is making me his first appointment at 9:00 AM."

"Oooh the first appointment. That means you are special!" I teased. I finally found an episode of Martin to watch. Mama walked over to me on the couch and pretended to hit me with the duster that had turned from white to more of a grayish color as it had been used. We both laughed.

"It's ten minutes to nine now, so when are you gonna put some clothes on?"

"I don't need to put clothes on. I'm going to my room when he comes so I want you to let him inside. The money to pay him is already on the kitchen table."

"Wait a minute. I thought you wanted me to be with you while he was here. I didn't know I was doing all the dirty work for you. You're not gonna show your face at all?"

"Nope," she said and plopped down, right next to me on the couch.

I understood there were personal issues between them from back in the day but that was old news, and the garbage disposal and dishwasher was new business. I believed there was more to the story.

"Are you really still mad at him for cheating on you or are still in love with him?" I asked. She didn't respond.

"Are you going to answer the question?" I repeated. She refused to answer and laughed at Jerome in The House on Martin. "Or is it just too hard to face the first man that you almost had a baby with?"

"Was it hard for you to face Ronaldo?"

I almost answered but I was saved by the bell. He had arrived a few minutes early. Mama jumped up and hurried off to her room.

The plumber, whose name I found out was Barry, was a fine older gentleman. The salt and pepper gray in his beard was very becoming and his eyes seemed warm and inviting. He smiled at me when I opened the door.

"Good morning," I said as I signaled for him to come inside.

"Good morning young lady, you must be Shirleen's daughter."

"Yes, I am, nice to meet you. You can follow me to the kitchen."

I could see how Mama had fallen for him. He seemed charming enough and was easy on the eyes. He was in good shape for his age too. His ring finger was empty.

"Is your mom here?"

I wanted to tell him she was afraid to see him again, but I opted for a simpler answer.

"Yes."

He looked around as if he was waiting for her to come around the corner into the kitchen but he didn't say anything more. He just started to assess the problem. I walked back into the living room to give him privacy to work his magic.

About thirty minutes or so had passed. I had briefly dozed off on the plush couch until I heard a shuffling sound. He scurried out the door to get some more tools I assumed.

A voice from behind me whispered, "Baby do I look okay?" It was Mama and she had changed out of her faded robe into the outfit that I got her that she had never worn before. It was a gray 2-piece set from Ivy Park. The t-shirt was tied up on the side and the black and gray stretch pants accentuated her figure. She completed the look with a pair of big silver hoop earrings. The scarf with the knot on top was now gone and she had displayed her beautiful natural curls.

"Yeah you look just fine," I said.

The screen door closed, and he was back inside with a new garbage disposal in hand. He lost his breath and almost dropped the garbage disposal when he saw her standing next to the couch looking like a young hot girl.

"Shirleen, it's so good to see you! I'm so glad you reached out."

"Hey Barry," she said. How's it coming along under that sink?

"I'm working on it right now. C'mon back I'll show you."

Mama glided off behind him and I felt the chemistry as soon as their eyes locked.

Mama didn't have to answer my earlier question; I could tell she was still in love.

Chapter 29

The mac n cheese was in the oven and I could see from the oven window as the four cheeses melted and bubbled to perfection. I had about thirty minutes to get dressed before Charles arrived. He had been back in town for a few days and was so excited to taste my mac n cheese recipe. Luckily, that was the weekend that Nate had his son so that eliminated him asking me out on a date. I no longer chatted with Charles on Instagram as I finally asked for his phone number so I could give him my address. I was paranoid about typing my home address on social media because I didn't trust potential hackers.

I got all dolled up just to sit in the house with Charles, but I didn't go too crazy. I put on a blue form fitting maxi dress and blue furry slides. I pulled my hair up into a bun and tied a blue turban headband around it. He texted me and told me he was outside right after I was fully dressed. Butterflies swarmed in my body and I couldn't contain them. In addition to the mac n cheese, I also made fried chicken, greens and homemade mashed potatoes to go with the meal. I grabbed the expensive plates that I had never used and waited on him to ring the doorbell. A few minutes went past so I assumed he was doing something in the car. I went to look out the window and his Hummer was parked outside. He leaned against the passenger door as if he was waiting on me to come out. I opened the front door and yelled out, "Hey Charles, what are you waiting on?"

He threw one hand up to wave at me. "Oh, I thought you were gonna bring it outside to me. But okay I'll come in real quick," he yelled from outside.

I was flabbergasted by his response. What did he mean he will come in real quick? I had cooked a home cooked meal to be eaten on expensive china in my dining room. It was not meant to be bought outside in Tupperware bowls to be eaten at a different location. When he got to the door, the funk entered before he did. He glistened with sweat all over his biceps and his tank top was wet in some spots as well.

"Sorry," he said. "I just came back from the gym. I really didn't want to come inside sweating like this."

"Oh okay, I understand," I said although I didn't really understand. I wanted to hug him, but I had just gotten out of the shower and he needed one badly. I wondered why he didn't go home to shower before coming over.

"Dang girl, it smells good in here. I've been craving this mac n cheese all day."

I blushed at the compliment.

"Thanks, I also made chicken, greens and mashed potatoes too." We had reached the kitchen and I motioned for him to take a seat at the table.

"Okay cool. Who did you cook all that for?"

I wanted to say, "I cooked it for you idiot!" He didn't even let me answer.

"I hope not for me. I just worked out, so I don't want to eat that much. I was gonna eat the mac n cheese in small portions for the next few days." I tried to keep my composure and not look too pissed off.

"No biggie, I can take my mom a plate and I can eat leftovers tomorrow," I said with a straight face.

"Okay cool, do you have plastic containers? If not, I got some in the car."

"No, no need. I have plenty," I said. My back was turned to him as I put my fancy dishes unused, back in their normal spot and reached for the to-go containers. All my hard work in the kitchen was for nothing.

"That chicken does smell fire though. You can go ahead and throw me two pieces in there. I can't resist."

I literally threw the pieces in the container as I couldn't contain my disappointment. I almost reached for a recycled grocery bag to put his to-go container in. I decided he wouldn't get the luxury. I put my face back on before I turned around.

"Okay here you go. I hope you enjoy."

He got up and took the container as he thanked me again. On his way out he browsed my family photos.

"Is that your Mom?" he asked.

"Yes," I answered.

"She is pretty. She kinda favors my auntie." I wanted to tell him that I didn't care about his auntie. He continued, "Thank you so much Stephanie. I know this mac is about to be on point. I'll text you later and tell you how good it was." He chuckled a bit as he and the funk walked out the door. I found nothing to laugh about.

Charles: Girl this chicken and mac n cheese is the BEST that I ever had in my LIFE! Real talk! I'm not even playing.

Stephanie: <heart emoji> Thank you so much! Glad you enjoyed it!

Charles: Hey I want to talk to you some more about something. Do you have any plans tomorrow morning at 10:30 am?

Stephanie: I'll still be at church then but I can do 11:30

Charles: Ok cool, what church?

Stephanie: I don't have an official church home yet but I planned to visit Mount Holiness church again tomorrow

Charles: Are you serious? My grandfather is the pastor there.

Stephanie: Yeah I know. Kandi told me already. Btw your grandfather is so amazing. I've only been to his service once and I really enjoyed it. I didn't see you the time I went.

Charles: Well my ex and I used to go sometimes but I stopped going when we broke up but anyway let's do 11:30 then. We can meet at the Breakfast Denn since it's near the church. Have you ever been?

Stephanie: Yes I Love their food but I had a bad experience the last time I ate there but I don't think I will have that problem anymore so see you at 11:30 then

I had just pulled up in front of Nate's house when Charles texted me about our Sunday morning date. I was pleased to hear that he loved my cooking after all, even though my evening didn't go as planned. I was even more pleased that I never had to worry about running into Charles at Mount Holiness while I was with Nate. I was even more excited when he finally asked me out on our first date. I had to call Jamie and Kandi to let them know because Jamie clowned me when I told her I got all dolled up and took out the new china for a five minute encounter and a take away container.

Since I had so much food left, I made plates for Nate and Mama and decided to drop them off since my Saturday evening didn't go as planned. I really did like Nate too, but I just wanted to see where things could possibly go between

Charles and I before I fully committed myself to falling for Nate.

"Come on in," he said when I called to tell him that I was outside.

"Um, isn't your son home though?" I asked nervously.

"Yeah, but he doesn't pay the bills here, so come on in."

I was shocked that he wanted me around his son so quickly. If I was a single mother, I would wait at least a year to introduce my child to anyone. I would be afraid to bring someone in if I wasn't totally sure they would be around for the long haul.

I expected for Nate to have a small bachelor pad, but I was amazed when I walked in to freshly shined hardwood floors and an open foyer. It was a brick ranch style home with beautiful furnishings and exquisite paintings throughout.

"I love your house and all your paintings," I said.

"Thanks, my mom helped me decorate it."

"I was about to say. It sure looks like a woman had something to do with this." We both laughed and he gave me a tour of the three bedrooms, living room, family room, dining room, kitchen and the man cave in the basement. The door to his son's room was closed, but he barged in and found him lying across the bed with a PlayStation controller in his hand and a wearing a headset.

"Manny, I want you to meet someone. This is La'Rose. La'Rose this is my knuckle head son Immanuel, but we call him Manny." He nodded, then he took his right hand off the controller and waved at me.

"Hi Immanuel, it's nice to meet you!" I exclaimed.

Immanuel was a replica of his dad. He wore glasses too but had a mohawk haircut. His complexion was like peanut butter and his room was junky in contrast to the rest of the house.

"What kind of name is La'Rose?" I overheard him say after the door closed.

Nate warmed up his food and ate on the sofa next to me in his man cave while some unfamiliar movie played on Netflix. He was hooked to my cooking too within a couple of bites. He scraped his plate and licked it when he was done.

I laughed at him, "Now you're going too far with licking the plate. It wasn't that good," I joked.

"Yes, it was! I wish I had seconds," he joked, but I could tell he was also serious. I hadn't planned on staying that long, as I still had Mama's food in the car that needed to be dropped off as well.

"I'm glad I was able to see you tonight," he said as he scooted closer to me. "You smell so good, just like Victoria's Secret mixed with hot chicken grease. I love it." We both broke out in laughter. After about thirty minutes, I let him know that I still had to take Mama's food to her. "Dang you leaving me already?" he said.

"Sorry, but we will see each other at church in the morning remember? I have to go meet my friends for brunch right after that, so I'll just drive my own car and meet you there," I said.

"Oh, y'all having a little girl's brunch time, huh? Well that's fine because I have to drop Manny back off to his mom in the morning. Then I'm going to pick my mom up to visit church with us."

"Wow, I'm meeting the whole squad I see," I said rather uncomfortably. He must have noticed my unease.

"Do you have a problem with that?"

"I don't know. It's just kind of early to be meeting parents and kids in my opinion. Or maybe it's not. I have been out of the dating scene or a while."

He scratched the back of his head as if he thought of how to respond. Then he took his glasses off and laid them on the table. I was waiting for his response when he grabbed my hand.

"I hope I'm not coming off too strong. I just know that you are the one for me. I also know that it may take you some time to realize that. So I will be patient."

"How do you know for sure?" I asked curiously.

"Well, remember the night of karaoke when I recited your dating profile info? I told you that you may think I was crazy but let me tell you why." I waited impatiently to know the reason.

He took a deep breath before spilling his guts. "I have been lonely for a long time and I wanted a wife. Not just any wife. I wanted my soul mate, but I had some things I had to work out in my own life. God was still working on me before He sent love into my life. When He was ready for me, He came to me and told me that I would find my wife on that particular dating site. I was a little skeptical at first, but I trust Him so I gave in. I saw your picture and your profile, and I knew it was you. I also knew that it wasn't going to be easy to get you, so I went in with great patience. My God also revealed that you needed me to bring you back to center. I don't really know how but I had to be and will be obedient to him."

I felt like I was a character in a love novella. His words were so sweet and captivating. It moved my soul, and I believed every word that came out of his mouth. He continued on, "The day you finally responded back to me was on 7-11 at 7:11 pm. The seventh month of the year on the eleventh day and the seventh hour and eleven minutes. My lucky numbers were 7 and 11 and I knew that was my sign. So, that's the reason why I don't have a problem with you meeting my family. In my heart I already know you will be a part of my family someday."

I was at a loss for words. He was so sure of himself and this 711 sign thing. It all sounded like a fairy tale love story and I wanted to believe it, but I wasn't totally convinced yet. I wanted to be a part of a caring and loving family and there was a possibility that I could have that with Nate someday. But why had Charles come over, dripping with sweat and flexing his muscles and those sexy brown eyes? Even though he had upset me, that passion we had on the dance floor that night was something I couldn't let go of. I had to give Charles one more chance at our brunch date. Then I could see which man would truly be the right one for me. I wished God could talk to me or give me some kind of sign to help me with life altering decisions.

Chapter 30

I felt bad that I lied to Nate about going to brunch with my friends after church so I intentionally came in a little late so that I could slide out of church before he would see me. I found the back of his head in the crowd and sat about seven or eight rows behind him. The woman who sat so close to him had to be his mother. That was also another reason I sat in the back. Although he thought I was going to be his wife, I had to make sure for myself. My plan was to sneak out about five minutes before service ended so I wouldn't have to run into them. About thirty minutes into service, his mother emerged from her seat and headed to the exit. I assumed she was headed to the restroom. I made it a point to check her out as she walked by. She wore a pair of Mary Jane pumps and a black and white polka dot dress. Her black hair was pulled back into a sleek bun but her gray edges were very distinct. I looked into her eyes and her face and it felt like I had seen those eyes and that face before. As she walked by, I scrambled my memory bank to try and figure out who she was. Pastor Abraham was just about to stand at the pulpit when Nate stood up. He had a black purse in his hand, which had to belong to his mother. He walked back toward the church doors and of course he spotted me since I was on the aisle seat. My plan had not worked. He attempted to sit down in my pew, so naturally I scooted down.

"I was looking for you," he whispered as soon as the Pastor began his sermon. "Sorry, I was running late today," I whispered back.

As soon as his mother pranced back in the church, he held his arm out to get her attention. He scooted over to make room for her to sit with us. I still wondered how I knew that woman. She wasn't just a cashier at a grocery store I shopped at or a former co-worker. She was someone that I knew but for the life of me, my mind drew blanks. Charles texted me during the service and had to cancel our brunch date. I was mad again, but I got over it quickly because I was thoroughly enjoying his grandfather's sermon. He really had the gift of gab and his familiar presence was something that I appreciated. I felt something come up in my soul, but it wasn't the Holy Ghost. Maybe it was the guilt for lying to Nate. He officially introduced me to his mother once the service was officially over.

"Mama, I want you to meet someone special. This is La'Rose. La'Rose this is my mother, Rhonda." We shook each other's hands and stared at each other in a familiar way.

"Hello dear, you look so pretty," she said.

"Thank you and you too," I said. I realized who she was when he told me her government name. The last time she saw me was at the one-year anniversary of June Bug's death when we released the blue balloons up to the sky.

"Are you related to someone named Rose Carter?" she asked. "You look just like her."

"Yes, she was my grandmother!" I exclaimed. "I'm Shirleen's daughter. You knew me as Stephanie.""Oh, my Goodness! Little Stephanie! You're all grown up now. C'mon give me a hug baby."

We crossed over Nate, who was in disbelief that I knew his mother already. We hugged each other with great force.

I wanted to cry because I remembered her on the ground screaming out in tears when June Bug was killed right before their wedding. I wanted to cry because I remembered the pain that I saw in her eyes the day we released the balloons. Her and I both felt the same kind of pain once in life.

"Man, this is crazy. Look how the Lord works!" Nate exclaimed. I was ready to let her go but she held on to me super tight like she didn't want to loosen the grip.

She was crying the tears I felt internally. Nate exclaimed, "Ma, what's the matter with you?"

She tried to speak but the words couldn't come out. "June... It's June...Family"

"Huh?" he asked again, concerned about his mother. She finally released her grip around my body but reached down to grab my hand. We turned around to face Nate with our hands interlocked.

"Baby, she is June Bug's family. This was his favorite little cousin who was more like a daughter or a niece to him. I'm just so happy to see someone who was a part of him."

It gave me great pleasure to hear those words, even after all the time that had passed.

"Wait a minute. Are you serious? He always talked about you. He wanted me to meet you."

"Oh my God! Yes I remember. He talked about you all the time too. He considered you his son and we were supposed to meet at the wedding to play together."

He grabbed my other hand.

"This is so crazy." He stared into my eyes and I gazed into his through his glasses.

"We didn't meet then, but we were certainly destined to meet each other in this lifetime."

Chapter 31

"It was really good talking to Rhonda after all that time. I'm glad you gave her my number to call me," Mama said.

I stalled time on the phone with Mama as I waited at the table for Charles. I kept track of the time and he was about twenty minutes late at that point.

"I told her we should go see a movie, go to lunch or go shopping sometimes," Mama said.

"Yeah that would be cool for you to get out of the house more. Maybe you can hang out with Barry the Plumber sometimes too," I exclaimed. Usually she got uptight and defensive when I mentioned him, but she let out a cute schoolgirl giggle.

"Or have you already been hanging out with him behind my back?" I asked.

"Chile, I am a grown woman. I don't have to do nothing behind your back or anyone else's, you got that?"

"Yes Mama, I got that," I said back playfully. "I see him

coming now, I gotta go." I hung up the phone and placed it inside of my purse in case Nate called. I had lied to him again and told him that I was going to the mall with Kandi in hopes he wouldn't call during my date. I felt bad about lying to him again, but he wasn't my boyfriend though. We were not exclusive yet, so it wasn't his business.

"Hey, hey," Charles said as he approached the table. I wondered whether I should stand up for a hug or if he would hug me while I was still seated. He did neither. I took it that he wasn't an affectionate guy.

"Hey Charles, how are you?"

"I am good now. I hope you are too."

He said as he squeezed his athletic body into the small booth. The waitress had already left water on our table and he took a sip directly from the glass as soon as he sat down.

"I want to thank you so much for your patience. I'm sorry that I had to keep cancelling on you. My job can get really hectic sometimes with deadlines and launch days so thanks for taking time out of your Wednesday evening to come meet with me. I appreciate it."

He was lucky that he was undeniably cute because three cancelled dates would have got any other guy blocked already. Besides, at least he let me know beforehand that he had to cancel.

"Oh, it's no problem. I understand things happen."

"Yes, they do, as a matter of fact I was late tonight because I had to meet my dad and grandfather at the church to pick up some paperwork. Thanks again for being so patient with my tardiness too."

"It's all good," I replied with a bright smile.

"So, speaking of church, you said you like my grandfather's church, right?

"I do. So far, he has no competition in my eyes."

He took another sip of water. "Oh yeah? That's nice to hear. It's funny how he went from fixing cars to fixing souls." He laughed at his comparison.

"Was he a mechanic before?"

He browsed his menu, but I already knew what I wanted since I had an extra twenty minutes to decide. Without looking up from the menu, he answered. "Yep, he had his own auto repair shop called Harry A's Automotive down on the North Side. My daddy runs the shop now so if you ever have car trouble let me know."

I was honored that he wanted to know if I ever had car troubles and how his family's auto shop could help me. I was even more honored to be on our first date. From the moment I first saw him, I thought he was perfect. I never thought in a million years that we would be seated across from each other on a date. I never thought we would have practically made love on the dance floor at Kandi and Hakim's wedding. I hope he remembered the passion. He ordered his grilled chicken salad and suggested I order the same thing. I didn't protest but I really had my eyes on the salmon. I allowed him to be the man and followed his lead. Once the waitress took our order, Charles got right down to business with me.

"So, do you know I'm still thinking about the chicken and mac n cheese you cooked?" he joked. I smiled politely.

"Girl, I'm serious. You got something on your hand. Now you know I work in marketing and I have a great opportunity for you. That's why I've been trying to meet up with you. I don't do business over the phone or via message."

"What kind of opportunity?" I asked inquisitively.

"Well you told me that your grandmother passed down a lot of her recipes to you right?"

"Um, yeah."

"Okay, I can make you a household name." He pointed his

finger toward me and then he moved both of his hands in a circular motion to indicate a cloud. "Here is the big picture: I can get you in touch with the right people to create a cookbook out of your recipes. You can sell on amazon.com and on your own website. We can set you up with major cooking shows on big networks to show off some of the recipes"

"Whoa, a cookbook is something that I have never thought of doing."

"That's the beauty of it. That's why I am here to guide you. I will market all over on Facebook, Instagram, and Twitter. We will even do photoshoots to help advertise and so much more."

Charles switched his charm over into salesman mode. He fast talked and advertised like he was in the office pitching me the deal with a Power Point presentation. I couldn't deny that it was a good idea, but my recipes were private. Grandma Rose was a private person so I didn't think she would want her recipes shared with millions around the world. I preferred to cook the recipes and leave people in awe of the taste and coming back for more instead of duplicating the recipes. Maybe it was selfish but that's how I felt. I also felt a little let down that our first date in my mind was more like a business proposition in his mind. I assumed he felt nothing during our dance at the wedding and that I was just another female that he could use to capitalize on instead of date.

"Um, sounds nice and all but I can't totally say yes today. I need more time to consider."

"The time is now! Deals don't wait around. I promise this is a deal of a lifetime."

"Well, I'm not saying no. I just need more information."

For the remainder of the night he tried to convince me that a cookbook was my calling. After dinner, he held me with a tight grip and kissed me on the cheek outside the restaurant. We were as close as we were on the dance floor that one magical night. I wasn't sure if his closeness was genuine or just a way to get me to accept his cookbook scheme.

Charles: I hope you enjoyed your food tonight and let me know when you are ready to do business

Nate: Hey are you home yet?

Stephanie: Yes I enjoyed dinner sir, thanks again for a great evening

Stephanie: Yes I'm home now, I spent too much money though lol

Nate called my phone immediately and I answered. I was in the middle of removing my off the shoulder blouse and floral bell bottoms, so I put him on speaker.

"Hey you," I answered.

"Hey," he replied, but not in his usual cheerful manner.

"What's the matter?" I asked.

"Check your phone," he demanded.

"Okay, did you send me a picture?"

"Just check your phone," he said. I slipped on my Pink leopard nightgown by Victoria's Secret and went back to my text messages. Under his name there was no picture of anything so I was confused as to why he insisted that I check my phone. About ten seconds later I realized that I had violated Texting 101. I accidentally sent the message intended for Charles to Nate so I was busted. How could I be so careless? I guess that was the reason why I never played the field in my younger days. Multi-tasking with different guys wasn't my best sport. I froze up as I didn't know how to explain the mix-up.

"Hello?" he asked sarcastically. My existence was frozen and I wanted to melt from the embarrassment.

"Yes, I'm still here."

"Did you check your phone? I mean your text messages to be exact."

I held the phone and quietly answered, "Yes, I did. I'm so sorry. I---"

"It's cool. I never officially asked you to be my girl yet, but I thought you knew how serious I was."

"But---" He continued and talked over me.

"I'm not mad at you for going out with someone else. But I am mad that you lied about it. You could have been honest with me." I thought I heard thunderstorms come out of nowhere and I feared that God was going to strike me down for lying to a true man of God.

"You have every right to be upset. I am terribly sorry. I just didn't want to hurt your feelings and tell you that I was interested in someone else too. I never gave them a chance yet, so I wanted to compare the two of you. I'm so sorry."

"Tuh. I don't know who this other brother is, but there is no comparison."

I was shocked that the church nerd turned his swagger up to a hundred. It was definitely a turn on.

"But if you still want to explore him and other options, please do so. Just let me know when you're ready and no need to contact me until you are one hundred percent ready and not a minute sooner."

"So, what are you saying? Are you done with me now?" I asked concerningly.

"I never said that.""Well you just told me not to contact you anymore!" I exclaimed.

"La'Rose, I said don't contact me until you are one hundred percent ready. That means when you get done comparing me to other folks that will never compare. I already told you what God told me. Maybe you need to reach deep down and try to have a conversation with Him so you can be sure yourself."

I was furious at the conversation but even more furious at myself.

"Well I'm in the bed now so I'm getting off the phone. Do what you have to do, goodnight."

The phone call ended, and I sat alone in the middle of my bed, legs crossed with my head in between my lap.

Chapter 32

"A cookbook huh? That's dope, I love that idea," exclaimed Jamie on the three-way call with Kandi and me.

"Yeah it's a great idea but I don't really want to expose my grandma's recipes."

"Well you don't have to list all of them. You can just list half and keep the other half private," added Kandi.

"Yeah I guess I could. I really wish I could open up a restaurant. That's always been my real dream."

"That's a great idea too. He can probably help you with that too. But other than business, how are you two getting along?" Kandi asked. I wanted to exaggerate and say we had fallen madly in love through our random text messages, but mostly the messages revolved around him and all he had going on.

"We get along just fine," I said. I secretly wanted to feel the same sparks I felt at the wedding and the very first time I saw him at the bar. I hoped those sparks would reignite once we spent a little more time together.

Jamie chimed in, "What about Church Nerd? What's going on with him?"

"What about you going to AA, what's going with that?" I joked although I was also serious. We all laughed but it was more at my timing of the joke than the joke itself.

"Whatever, I'm taking it one day at a time. I'm weaning off slowly. I can't just give up alcohol cold turkey. But anyways, are you and Church Nerd still good or what?"

"Yes Jamie, we're still good." The lie bounced right off my tongue like it was nothing. How was it that I was such a liar after going back to church and taking steps of regaining faith? I could hear Grandma Rose's voice yell out, "The devil is a lie!" I had already lied to Nate about my whereabouts which backfired on me so I came clean to them about my texting mishap.

I naturally learned to replace Nate with Charles. Unlike Nate, Charles never offered to pick me up. I wasn't so against it at first because I could ride in my own car and listen to my own music and avoid awkward car rides home. We met each other at designated restaurants of his choice on four different occasions. We sampled different types of salad or vegetable dishes. After Caesar, Strawberry Mango, Chipotle Chicken, and Avocado Ranch, I wanted to go on a salad hiatus. I was relieved that he still asked me out even after I declined his cookbook deal. He still tried to bring it up from time to time, but I stood firm on my decision.

I was shocked when Charles invited me to his father's retirement party and even offered to pick me up instead of meeting him at the venue. The invite spoke volumes to me in a way that I hadn't expected. A man didn't bring a woman around his entire family if he wasn't really interested. I had a tiny glimpse of hope that he and I could possibly have something special. I already respected his grandfather so much and loved his sermons so it would be a pleasure to be acquainted with their family. Kandi had warned me beforehand about his bad breakup, so I assumed he was just taking things extra slow with me on purpose.

When I got inside his Hummer, I noticed we were color coordinated again in black and white.

"Great minds think alike," he said. He looked sophisticated with a crisp white button-down shirt with a black and white color block tie, black slacks, black loafers and no socks. I hated when guys wore loafers with no socks, but Charles pulled the look off. I opted for a black and white blouse, black pencil skirt and black pumps. My hair hung down my back and was parted in the middle. It was nice to sit up so high in his truck, but it was also awkward since it was my first time.

"Nice ride," I told him. He smirked at me.

"Thanks," he replied. The windows were halfway down and the cool wind blew strands of my hair around in multiple directions. The wind blasting through the window and music coming the speakers were the only sounds inside the vehicle for much of the ride. I tapped my fingers on the door handle as I thought of something to talk about. I turned my body toward him to speak.

"So, you know I was surprised that you invited me to your dad's retirement party."

He looked over at me in the passenger seat. "Why were you surprised?"

"Well, inviting someone to meet your family is kind of a big deal to me." He stopped at a red light.

"Hmm. It's not really that big of a deal. This is not the kind of event that you go to alone. It's like a protocol to come with a date."

I was offended by his answer. It seemed like he only used me so he wouldn't have to come alone. "Protocol huh?" I asked sarcastically.

"Yeah, that's just how my family is. They are always asking me and other single family members when we are getting married, so they are just really big on relationships and stuff."

"I understand, but we are not in a relationship. Maybe you can call it a situationship but not a relationship."

My last words were not meant to be comical, but he somehow found it to be funny. I gave him a nasty look.

"Sorry, I didn't try to laugh. The word situationship was pretty funny to me though. But what I was trying to say is that marriage in my family is very important. They don't believe in divorces and they think everyone should be married or at least dating someone in hopes of marriage."

So, was he saying that he may want to marry me one day or not?

"I mean they don't care if the person cheated; divorce is not an option. So many women and some men have been cheated on, but they will never leave. Even my grandfather cheated on my grandma back in the day. She found out years later, but she wasn't gonna leave him anyway."

"Pastor Abraham?" I asked.

"Yep."

"Wow, I never would have guessed. But everyone makes mistakes sometimes. Nobody is perfect," I added. I was shocked to hear that the man I recently started to worship had been an adulterer at one point in his life. Still, the conversation had diverted into another direction. I wanted a more direct answer to why he invited me, and it seemed that he only did it because everyone else would be attached to a partner and he didn't want to be left out. That still had nothing to do with bringing up Pastor Abraham's infidelity. I figured he tried to take the heat off himself, but I was bored and ready to play with fire.

"Okay so back to my original statement, I was surprised that you invited me to a family event. So, correct me if I'm wrong: You knew that everyone else would be coupled up, so you didn't want to be the odd man out?"

He cleared his throat as he made a right turn at the light. "Well kinda. I mean I do like you too. Trust I wouldn't bring just anybody around my family."

I sat up straight and folded my arms, "Okay," I said. I rolled my eyes as I recalled thinking that this night might be special. I thought I was special to him to be in a big room full of his closest relatives and family friends in such a short period of time. How stupid and naive I was to think he would be a better fit for me compared to Nate.

He tried to be a gentleman as he extended his arm for us to walk inside, arm in arm. What a great impression he and I made entering the venue that way, with matching black and white outfits. To the naked eye, we looked like a solid couple, but we were strangers who were still getting to know each other. The more I learned about him, the more turned off I was.

The event space was decorated with white, black and silver decorations. Frankie Beverly and Maze blasted on the sound system and I was introduced to his father who was retiring from the family's auto shop. He was a very nice-looking older gentleman who was a fast talker. He was turning the business over to Charles' older brother. They were practically twins, but the older brother was about thirty pounds heavier. I met a slew of family members and friends. They were all cordial and sweet to me and I had seen a few of them at church.

We ran into his aunt in the buffet line. I was excited to hear that they had chicken wings, pasta, beef brisket, and shrimp and no salads at all. I figured that dinner would be the highlight of my night other than officially meeting Pastor Abraham. Charles' Aunt Rosalyn was stunningly beautiful. I recalled the first time he saw mama's picture and said that she resembled his aunt. Mama was still prettier, but his comparison was on point though.

"Is this your new girlfriend, Charles?" Rosalyn asked as we waited in the buffet line. I felt embarrassed for him as his face turned apple red.

"No this is my friend. We're taking it slow, Auntie," he responded.

"Okay now, she is a pretty girl. Don't take it too slow now or you may lose her." She walked off, hands full with two plates and a drink. We both looked at each other and smiled. I hated how much I loved his smile.

"I do appreciate you coming with me tonight, real talk."

"No problem," I said as I filled my plate with bow tie pasta in alfredo sauce.

"Don't get too much. I know you're still trying to watch your figure," he added. I was so excited for a good meal and his comment ruined my moment. I chose to ignore him and continued filling my plate with whatever I pleased.

After dinner, I sat at the round table all by myself. Charles had gotten up to throw our plates away but had apparently got lost. It had been over thirty minutes that I sat there looking stupid, waiting on him to return. I could have at least made small talk if there were other guests at our table. I didn't personally know anyone else there. I still hadn't seen the First Lady nor Pastor Abraham either. Thank goodness I had a cell phone. I swiped and scrolled through social media to keep busy. Another ten minutes had passed, and I was annoyed and ready to go. I contemplated calling Jamie to come pick me up. I happened to see Charles across the room making small talk with two of his cousins. Maybe he forgot I was there, so I decided to get up to go to the restroom which required me to walk past him. I pretended like I didn't even know him as I was almost out of the party room. He yanked my arm as I tried to slide by.

"Hey, are you good?" he asked.

"No, not really but I'm going to the bathroom."

"What do you mean, not really?"

"You just left me over there by myself forever. But let me go, I have to pee." He didn't offer an apology or an explanation, but I knew he could sense my frustration. He said nothing to appease me, he only released my arm.

As I walked to the bathroom, I finally spotted the famous Mount Holiness couple. The First Lady wore one of her big church hats and a bad plaid blazer with the matching skirt and heels. Pastor Abraham was stylish with his own plaid suit as well, with a pair of shiny Stacy Adams and a black fedora. My eyes were pleased at their union until I got closer. I noticed tiny freckles on his face that were too small to be seen from my view of him in church pews. Pastor Abraham looked me up and down and stared at me like I was a bum on the street who didn't belong at the venue. I had not done anything nor did I look a certain way to get that type of reaction. I had planned to speak, introduce myself, and praise them for their awesome church but I no longer felt compelled to do so. Something didn't feel right so I kept going toward the bathroom. When I was done, I called Jamie to come get me and I left without saying goodbye to Charles.

Chapter 33

All I could do was think about how good Nate had been to me during the early months of our courtship. He opened doors, allowed me to order whatever I wanted, he sent me roses and he wanted me to be his wife someday. How ironic it was that I had been wanting a man to marry all my life, and when I finally got a good one, I had to be so stupid to run him off. I was glad Mama wanted me to come by. She said she wanted to show me something at the house so I knew whatever it was would be something to take my mind off Nate for the time being.

When I walked into the front door; there was a mysterious glow to her appearance. She had dyed her hair honey blonde which was a perfect match compared to her usual sandy brown colored hair.

"Hey Mama. Your hair is cute," I said as I made my way to the couch next to her.

"Thanks baby," she said.

"So, what you want to show me?"

"I'll tell you about it in a moment but first tell me exactly what happened with you and that Charles boy?"

I stretched my arms up above my head before I answered.

"Well he only invited me as arm candy, but he only showed me off when we first got there and after we ate, he left me at the table by myself. I thought it was rude and tacky, so I had Jamie come get me."

"Oh my. Did he call to see what happened to you?'

"Tuh, it took him thirty minutes to call me after I left the party. How did it take him that long to notice I was gone? I didn't even answer his call; I just texted him back and told him I left because I was being ignored anyway. I don't know what's wrong with him or his family. I saw his grandparents in the hallway and the Pastor stared me down so hard; it was so crazy.

"Well the Pastor probably stared at you because you're so beautiful. You know old men love to look at pretty young girls." She laughed. "But now that you're done with that Charles boy you should reach back out to Nate. Now he is a true Man of God."

"Well I think I messed things up with Nate. He is such a Man of God and I'm only a Baby Christian. He probably needs a more mature Christian woman anyway."

"Well you can't look at it that way. Yes, he has had a strong relationship with God for many years and you are just now finding your way back. Did you ever think that he can help you get even closer to God? Don't try to compare his timeline to your timeline. I think you ought to call him. I've been talking to Rhonda and she said he was still very fond of you."

I smiled on the inside when I heard that he was still fond of me after he caught me in a tiny white lie and basically told me not to call him back until I was done playing games.

"Really? I thought he hated me now." I sighed. "I mean I do want to call him, but I'm scared."

"Scared of what?"

"Well, he told me that God spoke to him and revealed that I was his future wife. Nobody has ever told me that before so if that is true then I want God to speak to me and reveal that he is my future husband too."

"I understand. He will reveal the truth to you in due time. He may be imperfect to your eyes, but he is perfect for you. I honestly believe in my heart of hearts that Nate is the one. I need you to pray and ask God to speak to you or give you some kind of sign so that you can know this too."

"Okay, I will pray about it." I looked up to the ceiling and asked, "Mama have you ever been so close to getting everything that you asked for and you got scared? Because that's how I feel; I feel like Nate is too good to be true. I felt like if things kept going so well that eventually something bad was going to happen."

"Baby, that ain't nothing but God. You are getting everything that you asked for because you are finally being obedient. You are praying. You are believing again. You are getting your faith back. I prayed for this to happen and it's all just coming together now. You must trust the process and not sabotage your blessings. You deserve true happiness, you hear me?" She grabbed my chin and raised it up as a means for me to look directly in her eyes. Her words had yet again touched me. She was right. Why did I think I didn't deserve happiness? Why did I drop the ball when my desired love goal was almost attained?

"Yes mama, I hear you! I really needed to hear that. Thank you so much!" We leaned in for a hug before we peacefully returned to our original positions on the couch. "Well enough about me. What's going on with you? Does this have something to do with Barry the Plumber?"

She chuckled a bit. "Well Barry and I have been spending some time together here lately. He has been going to Bible Study and to Sunday service with me. We've had some date nights and we're enjoying each other's company." She sounded like an airy teenage girl describing her first love. The reality is that he was her first love, but they were going through a new phase almost forty years later.

"Aww, that is so sweet! I'm so happy for you Mama."

"Thanks baby. You know it was so crazy that I hadn't had a man in so long that I became numb to it. For some reason when he turned that garbage disposal back on that day; he also turned something on inside of me. I want to actually thank you for pushing me to reach out to him. You know I was so angry with him over the past, but he apologized so much that I had to forgive him. I mean God forgives us for our sins so how could I not forgive him for something he did when we were teenagers?"

"You got a point there. Well I'm so happy for you both. "Are y'all a couple now?"

She got quiet and stared at me for about three seconds before she reached in her shirt pocket and flashed a princess cut diamond ring in my face.

"Hold up, hold up! Is this an engagement ring?" I shouted. "Oh my goodness!" I screamed as I snatched the ring and examined it.

"Well Beyonce said "Put a ring on it" and he did!"

Chapter 34

The chirping birds and sunshine interrupted my morning sleep. I laid in bed for a few minutes before my bladder forced me to skip to the bathroom. I grabbed my cell phone first to check the time. I assumed it was some time after 9:00 AM but my phone displayed a much earlier time of 7:11 AM. The same thing happened the night prior when I fell asleep watching a recording of Shark Tank and woke up at exactly 7:11 pm. It dawned on me that it was the same time that I finally reached out to Nate on the dating site but for it to happen again seemed pretty ironic.

"Haaaaahh!" I screamed before I jolted to the bathroom. "Is this a sign? Is this a sign?" I asked myself and God. After I washed my hands, I did the old 90's cabbage patch dance in the bathroom mirror. "I think those were the signs I've been looking for!" I screamed again.

I looked through my call history one more time to make sure I hadn't missed a callback from Nate. I was compelled to finally accept my calling for true love after the talk with Mama. I had called Nate twice and I left him a message seven days prior but he never returned my calls. I even prayed all week for God to speak to me or to at least give me a sign or confirmation. I started to call Nate again, but I decided against it. Maybe it was only a coincidence that I woke up at 7:11 that night and again that morning. I was probably tripping.

The happiness and screams halted as I thought about how ridiculous I sounded. I laid back in bed and attempted to go back to sleep, but I tossed and turned in and out of the satin sheets. My stomach started to growl, and I craved for biscuits and gravy, so I showered and headed out to get breakfast. My original thought was to call in an order at The Breakfast Denn. I changed my mind because The Breakfast Denn had become a bittersweet place for me. Their food was the absolute best, but I now associated it with being the place the led to the demise of my relationship with Ronaldo due to Nappy Gappy. Then on the other hand, The Breakfast Denn was the same spot that reunited Mama and Barry the Plumber which was a great thing. All of a sudden, a flashback came to mind when that old man freaked me out, staring at me through the window there.

My mind wandered briefly until the hunger pains kicked back in and I remembered I was trying to get breakfast somewhere other than The Breakfast Denn. I was so hungry and had no groceries so McDonald's would have to do it.

I was annoyed to see not one, but two winding lanes of cars waiting in the drive through. I never usually ordered inside but something told me to go in and place the order instead of waiting in the drive through lanes. Jamie called me as I opened the door to enter the restaurant. I wondered why she was calling so early in the morning.

"Good morning sis, what's up?" I answered.

"Hey Steph, I didn't want nothing. I just saw you turn into McDonald's."

"What are you doing up this early in the morning in my neck of the woods?"

"Girl I was out at the casino all night. I was so tipsy and didn't want to drive home. I should have taken Uber but I didn't want to leave my car up there, so I waited a few hours to sober up."

Thank goodness there were only two people in the line in front of me which was a big difference compared to the herd of cars outside.

"Girl, I thought you were going to slow down on the drinking? It's getting out of hand."

"Oh, here you go. I forgot you are a Christian now who wants to judge me. I told y'all I would stop, and I am but give me time; it's a process," she said in the tone of a defensive alcoholic.

"Jamie, hold on. Yes, I want to order the biscuits and gravy meal with an extra biscuit and an orange juice," I said to the young boy who barely looked to be of working age.

Jamie didn't hear me say hold on and she continued to speak. I heard her ask, "Has Church Nerd called you back yet? If not, you need to pull up on him."

The young boy handed me the receipt and I moved toward the rear to allow the customers behind me to step up to place their orders. I took note of my ticket number so I could be prepared when they called my number. It was Order # 711. I laughed out loud. I would be a fool to deny a third sign in less than 24 hours. I wanted to moonwalk across the newly mopped floor. God answered my prayers and gave me another sign that I prayed for just as Jamie asked me about Nate.

"Girl, you gonna think I'm crazy but I asked God to give me a sign to officially tell me if Nate was my future husband and I just got confirmation."

"Sis, don't I always tell you that you overthink too much? Why can't you just go with the flow?"

"I know I do overthink too much. I can't help it but I'm trying to do better," I said jokingly.

"I'm shaking my head at you. You didn't need to ask for a sign. You should have known he was the one. You said you missed him, and you even thought about him when you were out with Charles. Please call that man again and if he still doesn't answer, go to his house then. Don't miss an opportunity at happiness because of your pride. Forget your pride. Jason is long gone, and I will never get him back. You still have a chance at true love so go get that man girl!" I hated her drunkenness but drunk people always told the truth. She was absolutely right, and I was going to get my man.

"Ticket Number 711!" called out the young boy.

"Okay Jamie, thanks so much, I gotta go."

I grabbed my food bag and practically skipped out of the restaurant.

"I got my sign! I got my sign!" I sang in my head. I called Nate's phone and it rang and rang and rang before going to voicemail.

"Nate, can you please call me back. I'm sure about us now. I'm sorry that I had a few doubts, but I got the signs from God that I prayed for. Please call me back!" I pleaded in the voicemail. I threw the bag of food in the passenger seat and headed straight to his house like Jamie suggested. If he was going to let the phone ring without answering; I was going to ring his doorbell and bang on the door until he answered. I prayed that he would call me back before I made it to his house, but he didn't. It didn't matter though because he was going to see me that day whether he wanted to or not. I had all the courage and faith that one could possibly have, and I was so sure of myself.

When I finally arrived at his house, there was a Caribbean blue Chevy Spark parked outside. It was clearly a female's car. That was probably the reason why he had not returned my calls. My heart sank down deep into my gut and I wanted to cry. I was still starving so I pulled into his driveway and ate my breakfast while I debated whether I should go to the door and ring the doorbell and confess my feelings or let him and his new lady who drives the Chevy Spark live in peace while I bowed out gracefully? I wanted to call Jamie back and ask but I already knew her answer. I called Mama instead and asked for her advice.

"Slow down baby, slow down," she said. I assumed that I jumbled my words together as I briefly tried to explain my scenario.

"You say you got the sign from God that you prayed for? And you drove to Nate's house but there is a woman's car there?"

"Yes! My question is should I go to the door or should I just leave?"

Mama still sounded half asleep, but she said, "Steph, I don't think another woman is there."

"Mama, this car is a little bitty car. This car is clearly a woman's car, I promise you."

"No what I'm saying is that I don't think he would have a woman staying there with his mother being there. I talked to Rhonda last night and she was spending the night with him because today would have been June Bug's birthday. Today and the day he actually died are always hard for her so she was spending the weekend with Nate and his son." My heart was suddenly restored. It was so touching that she still held June Bug near and dear to her heart after all the years that had gone by.

"Are you sure?" I asked.

"Yes, that's what she just told me last night."

"Okay Mama! Thank you so much for that info. Back to the plan. Wish me luck and talk to you later."

I nervously stepped out of the car with my Adidas stretch

pants and t-shirt. My hair was pulled up in a bun and looked like I was headed for a workout instead of stake out. I rang the doorbell three times before I finally heard footsteps creeping to the door. A sweet voice called out, "Who is it?"

I answered, "La'Rose. I mean Stephanie." The door crept open and there stood Rhonda in a silk white and pink robe and a pink scarf tied around her head. She looked surprised to see me.

"Hello Miss Rhonda. I'm so sorry to come here unannounced but I need to speak to your son. It's really important."

"Hey baby, nice to see you again but he is not here. Manny's bowling league is headed to Columbia for a tournament," she added.

"Oh okay, I didn't know. Are they already gone?" I asked.

"Not yet. They are meeting at the bowling alley and scheduled to leave at 9:30 if I'm not mistaken."

"Okay. Thank you so much Miss Rhonda. I need to catch him before he leaves." I jetted off to the car.

"Is everything okay?" she yelled after me.

"Yes, all is good, thank you!" I called to her as I waved and slipped back into the driver's seat.

Usually I could get anywhere in town in fifteen minutes. I hoped that would be the case as I only had about fifteen minutes to spare before he would be leaving to go to Columbia. I came to a rolling stop at a few stop signs and sped through two yellow lights which helped me arrive a few minutes before 9:30. As soon as I turned into the parking lot, I saw a small shuttle bus turning out of the parking lot. I raced right behind the bus as fast as I could, but two other cars had beat me. I tried to call Nate again and I still got no answer. I followed the bus, and was willing to drive to Columbia if I had to. I called him back and still no answer. It slightly reminded me of all the calls that Ronaldo failed to answer. I continued to blow my horn to get the attention of the bus. However, the only thing that now needed my attention was the gas tank as the low fuel light illuminated on my display.

Chapter 35

I started honking my horn to get the bus driver's attention to pull over once the other two cars had turned off on different roads. I blew my horn and yelled, only for nobody to hear me. "Please stop the bus, please!" I pleaded. The low fuel light kept distracting me. I banged my fists on the steering out of frustration as I still managed to keep up with the bus.

Suddenly, my phone rang. I lit up like Christmas when I saw Nate's name flash across the screen.

I answered, "Can you please tell the bus to pull over real quick? I'm right behind you. I need to talk to you now."

"Huh?" he asked.

"I need to talk to you before you go, did you get my messages? Please tell the bus driver to pull over for a second," I said frantically.

"La'Rose, I'm not on a bus. I'm in the parking lot at the bowling alley right now. Our bus is a little late"

"Are you serious? I'm following the wrong bus? Okay, I'm turning back around. Don't leave yet, I need to talk to you." I hung up as I felt our conversation would be better in person instead of over the phone. I bet that bus driver thought I was a crazy woman blowing my horn like it was nobody's business. I started to feel at ease, but I hoped he still wanted me after the time that had passed. Regardless, I was prepared to shoot my shot with him.

It seemed that the bus had arrived shortly before I returned to the parking lot. Parents and children had already started to load the bus with their bowling bags and shoes. I spotted his vehicle right away. He leaned against the back of his trunk looking so handsome. Nothing was imperfect about it. I pulled up right next to him and jumped out of the vehicle. He looked flabbergasted by my intense emotions, but I hugged him with all my might.

"I missed you," I said with passion. I was pleased that he whispered back with the same sentiment.

"I missed you more," he added.

I released his body, stood firmly in front of him and stared into his four eyes.

"Listen, I know you don't have much time. But I just need to tell you that I am sorry, and you were right. There is no comparison to you. You told me not to contact you until I knew for sure. Last night and this morning I got three signs that I believe were from God. Even before the signs, I think I knew but I just wanted that same confirmation from God like you did."

"Girl come here and kiss me." His lips opened the key to my heart. His key fit perfectly into my lock and he was so gentle and loving once he opened it. There was no denying that I had fallen in love with a man that I never expected to. Isn't it funny how love works out? Isn't it funny that the person who I dismissed for months was actually the person that I needed in my life? I didn't want our moment to end but I knew he had to get going.

He pulled back and stared at me, "I'm so glad you feel the same. I knew you would one day."

"Somebody is really cocky I see," I joked. We both laughed.

"Naw, I'm not cocky but my faith is cocky though." I nodded my head to that.

"That's a good one," I said. "Did your mom tell you I came looking for you this morning."

"She texted me. I'm sorry that I missed your calls. I left my phone in the duffle bag that was still in the trunk, so I wasn't able to check my phone until we pulled into the bowling alley lot."

"Oh okay, that makes sense but what's your excuse for not calling me back this week? I called you twice."

He grabbed my hand, "Babe, I'm sorry. I didn't know. My phone went dead. They call it the white screen of death so I couldn't get my calls or texts or anything, so I just literally got this new phone two days ago." He flashed his upgraded phone to further back up his story.

I gave him a look. "Okay, you better be glad. I thought you didn't want to talk to me anymore." He grabbed me again, held me and kissed my neck.

"Don't play with me. You know I would never do that to you. I was just waiting on you to realize it. I didn't want to pressure you, but I honestly didn't get your calls.

"Hey dad, we gotta go!" yelled out Manny as he stood behind the bus.

"Hey Manny! Good luck in the tournament today!" I yelled out to him. He waved at me and yelled back, "Thank you!"

"Well I'll be back this afternoon. We're going to June Bug's grave this evening if you want to come." Of course I wanted to go with them to celebrate June Bug's life. I could stop by Grandma Rose's grave too.

"Yes, I wanna go too honey." It was interesting how his new pet name rolled off my tongue so naturally.

"Okay, well see you later cutie. Let me get out of here before the bus leaves me," he joked. He kissed me again and ran off to the bus as Manny waited on him.

It was such a beautiful sight to see my future husband and future stepson run off together. I would be the first of the Three Amigas to have a stepson. I would finally have a first in our little group. I already loved his son too, just like he was my own. I waited for the bus to drive off before I got back into my car. I heard my Grandma Rose's voice in my ear, "When you miss one bus, there's another one coming in fifteen minutes."

I had a good hearty laugh as I re-entered my car. I missed the first bus, which was not slowing down or stopping for me despite my excessive honking. But Grandma Rose was right. The bus I needed was just around the corner waiting on me. I exited the parking lot listening to Monica's "Why I Love You So Much" and headed straight to the gas station to refuel my tank.

. . .

It had been almost two months since Nate and I had officially become a couple. It had also been about two months since I learned the truth of my identity. I was afraid to tell Mama. Her and Barry the Plumber were cute and so in love. She was in a happy place in her life, so I didn't want to stir up raw emotions for her. On the other hand, I needed to release the burden so that I could be free of the secret.

"What's the matter?" Nate asked as I plopped down in the passenger side of his car wearing my Sunday's best.

I leaned in to give him a kiss before I sighed and answered his question.

"Well, I really want to go back to Mount Holiness. I don't get the same kind of feeling at Mama's church or any of the others we have been to."

"I understand but I want you to be comfortable. We can still try other church homes too until we find another match. Or do you want to tell her and just get it over with?" I paused for a moment thinking of my answer.

"I don't know yet. I'm still praying about it, along with my job too."

Chapter 36

Judgment Day at Atlas had finally arrived after a long, hard year of job uncertainty. My stomach was in knots all morning and I couldn't stop my bowel movements. I supposed it came from being so nervous about whether I would have a job in 2020. After my last bathroom stop, I saw I had a couple of messages of well wishes.

Kandi: Good luck sis, I hope all goes well for you today, Love Ya!

Mama: Good morning..I tried to call you. I guess you were in the shower. Just letting you know I prayed for you this morning. Leave it in God's hands.

When I got inside the elevator, I wondered how many more times I would be privileged enough to ride up to my office. It was bittersweet to see the Christmas decorations that were hung up every year and I wondered if that would be my last year seeing them. I saw people scattered about the office and the usual quietness was replaced with loud talk and chatter.

Chapter 36

There was a long line of employees who waited to see the final sales report sheet that would determine their fate. I decided to go to my office first and wait until the line went down. There were two big boxes in front of my door which was an indication that I didn't make the list. I grabbed the two boxes and went inside the office where I found a glass vase filled with sorbet roses on my desk. They were a replica of the same ones from my favorite painting in Grandma Rose's room. That made my heart smile amongst the sorrow of losing my job. I already knew they were from Nate and I wondered how he pulled that off so early in the morning. There was a card attached, which read:

My Dear La'Rose, No Matter what happens today. God has a bigger plan for you!

Love, Nate

I just loved him so much. He was so caring, thoughtful and considerate. I felt so blessed to have him in my life. The year before that around the same time, my life seemed to have fallen apart but most of it had been pieced back together. As I was in mid-thought, Liz came into my office carrying a box. She was one of the top sellers so I knew she was in the top ten without a doubt.

"Did you see the list yet?" she asked so excitedly that she didn't even say good morning.

"Hey Liz, I didn't even look but someone did me a favor and left my boxes to pack up so I got the hint."

"Steph, go look at the list please."

I didn't see a reason to look except to confirm my walking papers in person. I guess she wanted me to see how close I was to the top 25 but almost didn't count.

"It was such a long line; I'll wait until the line dies down."

"C'mon girl, you need to see this." She put her box down and grabbed me by the hand to follow her. She made her way through the crowd and walked past all the people until we got to the front.

"Excuse me for one second," she said to Larry Rogers who was the one looking at that time. She told me, "Look at the two yellow highlighted lines."

I moved in a little closer, "I'm sorry Larry, excuse me." I followed her directions and focused my attention on the two yellow highlighted lines. The name at the top read "Elizabeth David" which was Liz's government name. She was #7 in sales. To the right of the line the words RETIRED were written in black ink.

"Retired? You didn't tell me you were retiring." I said to her.

She smiled, "Would you hurry up and read the other yellow line please before these people get mad that we butted them."

"Okay, okay!" I exclaimed. The other line that was highlighted was further down the list and read, "Stephanie Carter". I was #26, but to the right of the line were the words "Job Save by #7 to #25" was printed in the same black ink. My eyes had to be deceiving me. If I read it correctly, I was about to be out the door because I was one spot off from the 25 ranking, but I moved to #25 since Liz was retiring. Liz could not stop smiling. It was then that I knew that my eyes had not deceived me. We both started screaming and jumped up and down for joy.

Nate took me out to some expensive restaurant that I had never heard of to celebrate on the night that my job was secured.

"Honey I can't believe Liz saved my job. I'll forever be grateful for her."

"I know right. I'm so happy that you're happy, but I told you that you were gonna be good regardless. I got plans for us."

"What kind of plans?" I asked curiously.

"I can't tell you now. Everything is still in the making right now."

I gave him an inquisitive look before looking through the expensive menu.

"Well alrighty then. I trust your lead so I'm sure your plans are going to be epic, whatever they may be."

"Yep, you know everything's falling into place except that one thing. I can tell that you're still struggling with telling your mom."

I leaned back in the chair a bit.

"Yeah it is weighing heavy on me, but I prayed about it and I decided that I have to tell her."

I was so afraid to tell her. I thought she would be mad at me for prying and sneaking into Grandma Rose's old pristine room. It happened the same night that I confessed my love for Nate before Manny's bowling tournament. After we all went to the cemetery to visit June Bug and Grandma Rose's gravesites, I wanted something tangible to feel closer to her so I opted for the tarnished rose brooch that I knew stood on her dresser in her room. While I was in the room, I snooped under the mattress and recovered two letters from my grandfather that Mama told me about.

After that night, I lost count of how many sleepless nights I stayed up, enchanted by the love my grandfather had for both Mama and Grandma Rose. I kept the letters safe in a new manilla envelope along with the rose brooch.

Harry A.

60 Firewood Drive

San Louise, MO 63000

Rose Carter

213 Gates Street

San Louise, MO 63000

Dear Rose,

I am truly sorry from the bottom of my heart. I never meant to hurt you and I pray that you forgive me one day. I wanted to tell you that I had gotten married but I didn't want to hurt you either. You know it's not all my fault. You did leave me, so what was I supposed to do? I eventually moved on with my life. I never thought we would run into each other again. I was just so happy that I had one last night with you so I didn't want to mess that up by telling you I was married. I'm sorry for everything but keeping me away from my child is not the way to handle things. Please reconsider and reply back to me. I hope you will let me spend time with our precious baby girl. All in all, I will always love you Rose.

With Love,

Harry A.

Dear Rose,

I have not heard back from you so I assume you are still mad and punishing me. If that's how it's going to be then I will sneak and see her. As a matter of fact, I saw her playing outside in the yard with June Bug the other week. Yes, I try to get a peek in since you wont allow it. Our daughter is so precious; she favors me and not you. I wanted to run and grab her and take her with me but I couldn't hurt you like that. Just let me see her please. I am begging you. You can't keep my child hostage. Let me explain something to you Rose. Yes, I am a married man now but not a day goes by that I don't think of you. Your beauty was timeless and I was often in awe and at a loss of words when I saw you. I still envision that beauty in my mind too. Our love was different and unexplainable. Even though I'm married, you don't understand how much your love flows through my body, my veins and most of all my heart. My wife is not as strong as you are. She couldn't take it if I ever left her. I'm kind of stuck in the situation and I will be a man about it. Don't get me wrong, I do love her too. However, the love that you and I share is rare. I know you still love me too because I feel it and the longer we are apart; the stronger it gets. Please let our love child get a chance to know me.

With Love
Harry A,

The passion and love that exuded through those letters was almost bone chilling. My long-lost grandfather carried a genuine love for my grandma and mama. I couldn't help but to be impressed. I understood how she hated him for consenting to sex with her while he was married, but she couldn't deny his words of expression for her or their child.

The name Harry A. rang a bell to me and I racked my brain trying to figure out where I heard it, but I kept falling short of an answer. Something told me to google the address on the envelope and maybe I could drive to the address or surrounding neighborhood to get more clues. The directions to that address came up as a business which was Harry A's Automotive Shop, which was the same shop that Charles said belonged to his grandfather before he became a Pastor. The riddle had been solved. Harry A. was Pastor Harold Abraham. Pastor Abraham was Harry A who was my grandfather.

"If Pastor Abraham is my long-lost grandfather, that would make Charles my cousin. How gross!" I yelled out to myself before I almost fainted.

Chapter 37

The Sunday before Christmas was the first Sunday that we planned to attend Mount Holiness again. Nate and I both agreed that none of the other churches that we visited compared to Mount Holiness and we came to a consensus to make it our church home. I also thought it was a way to be closer to my newfound flesh and blood.

A part of me was afraid to see Pastor Abraham again because I was ashamed to step foot in his church as the offspring of his love child. However, Nate reminded me that what Pastor Abraham did in his younger days was not a reflection of the man he had become. I agreed and came to the understanding that we all make mistakes in life and nobody is perfect. One thing I could say from those letters was that the man loved Grandma Rose with all his heart.

The sanctuary appeared to be more packed than usual but it was probably because it was the holiday season. I felt something on my heart all week and I invited all of my squad to come to service. I was more than excited to be back to the church that helped bring me back to my religion. The ten-year-old girl who lost her religion was now a baby Christian Woman. I was thankful for Mama who stuck by me through the years and prayed for me to come back across the threshold.

Our church pew consisted of myself, Nate, Manny, Rhonda, Jamie, Jade, Jamiya, Kandi, Kayla and Hakim. I invited Mama and Barry the Plumber too but they were nowhere to be found, which I wasn't really surprised about. I really hoped she would change her mind, but I understood how hard it would be for her to step foot into a church that belonged to the father that she never knew personally.

On our brunch date, she shook her head casually at the table once I finally found the courage to tell her of my findings. I expected more of a scene from her though.

"I guess it makes sense how you felt a familiar presence from him. And then you said Charles had an aunt with the same features as me. She continued to shake her head. It makes sense why he stared at you like that at the retirement party too. It was like he saw a ghost I guess."

Mama gave me another revelation without even trying.

"Oh, my goodness! Mama do you remember I saw an old man staring at me through the window at The Breakfast Denn?

"Um, I vaguely remember," she said as she took a gulp of orange juice.

I clapped my hands for emphasis. "Mama that was him! I just thought about it. That was him! He seemed so familiar because we were related but I had actually seen him before. It makes so much sense now. Remember Nappy Gappy told me that some old man paid our bill that morning. That had to be him," I exclaimed.

"Oh yeah, I do remember that now. Well, I guess it was meant for me to tell you about those letters so you could go play detective." We both laughed and I was relieved that she took the news far better than I had expected.

"Can you pass me the salt," she asked, attempting to change the subject. I realized that she was more affected by the news than she wanted to portray.

"Mama don't dismiss this. This is major news. Your dad is actually still alive, and I found him. You know he begged to see you and he really loved both of you. You really should come to the church and try to meet him?" I pleaded.

"Baby just let it go. That man had over fifty years to try to find me. He wrote two rinky dink letters and then gave up, so I gave up on him too."

"But Mama did you look at the address where he sent those letters? It was not the current address which means when Grandma Rose moved, he didn't know how to find you anymore. And you thought he was dead for half of your life. My dad really is dead, and I can never talk to or see him. You at least have the opportunity to."

"Chile, like I told you before, my Heavenly Father is the only father I need. Now don't let me stop you from going to his church. That has nothing to do with me. I do thank him and Nate as well for bringing you back to the Christian side. Now are you gonna pass me the salt or what?"

I passed the salt, and I was done with it.

The choir and the sermon were as great as usual. I was deeply fed by my grandfather's words, his tone, and his delivery. Nate sat close to me and his Burberry cologne was very inviting. He had his arm around my neck, and I felt so protected. We all sang, praised, clapped our hands and enjoyed the sermon. I still didn't catch the Holy Ghost, but I was happy to be inside my desired church location.

I would have been happier if Mama was there to see me as I stood to my feet for the altar call. It was as if my body moved on its own without even thinking. Nate and I both got up and walked toward the altar, hand in hand. Rhonda gave us the thumbs up for approval. The church aisle leading to the front of the church seemed never ending. I hoped I didn't have tissue stuck to my heels since everyone in the congregation stared at us.

When were almost to the altar, I felt someone tap me on the shoulder. I was caught off guard to see that it was Jamie. She had tears in her eyes. I immediately grabbed her hand.

She whispered to me through the tears.

"I'm tired of fighting these demons sis. I need to be saved."

I gave her hand a squeeze as I led her down the path with us. When we finally reached the pulpit, I was shocked to see my estranged cousin, Charles, sitting in the front row with the slacks, no socks and loafers that I hated. He was seated and holding hands with a young white woman with long blonde hair and a black dress that was cut too low for church. I wanted to vomit knowing that I had the biggest crush on him before I knew we were related. It was funny how things ended up, considering I lusted for Charles in the flesh not knowing that he was my flesh in blood. God made no mistake when he never allowed anything intimate to happen between us. I wished him and his Caucasian boo the best. Everything worked out the way it was supposed to in the end because the love I shared with Nate was ordained agape love that was on a different level.

Jamie, Nate and I stood in a single file line with the other sinners and backsliders as the church leaders grabbed each of us by the hands and prayed with us. I didn't even make eye contact with my grandfather. My moment was bigger than him, Mama or Grandma Rose. This was my moment to publicly come forward to make a new spiritual commitment to Jesus Christ. I knew the next steps would involve becoming an active member of the church and getting baptized by him.

If Mama knew what I was doing on that day, she would probably say to me, "If your Grandma Rose knew you had found him, and was getting saved at his church, she would probably rise up from her grave!" I would then tell Mama, "Well, in Jesus name, LET HER RISE!"

Epilogue

There were three minutes left before the year 2019 would be a part of history forever. The new year ahead was going to be a great year for myself and those around me. I could feel it resonating in my bones. I could taste the sweetness of it like it was stuck in between my teeth.

I was in a solid relationship with someone and I knew marriage would be somewhere around the corner. In addition to that I gained a highly intelligent and funny soon-to-be stepson. Nate was open to more kids if God blessed me with the ability to conceive again. He was also open to adoption, so however God saw fit for us to grow as a family was all that mattered to us.

It was so amazing that I reunited with Rhonda after all those years and that she and Nate continued to keep June Bug's legacy alive. I still had my nine to five job, so I wasn't going to be unemployed in the upcoming year. I even received a $6,000 check in the mail from Ronaldo that was signed with the memo, "Merry Christmas." He didn't add the interest he owed me, but I was thankful that he did the right thing at the very least and returned the money. I no longer hated him and prayed that he was doing fine in Michigan with his family.

I was more than thankful that my faith had been restored. I had lived the majority of my life without any spirituality and I had to see that my life was much more fulfilled now. I would never ever denounce Christ again as long as I lived, and I got on my knees every night and thanked Him for His grace and mercy. I was a Believer again and I was beyond grateful for all my blessings.

I couldn't believe that I had discovered my long-lost grandfather, whom I thought had died over fifty years ago. There were so many things I wanted to say and ask him. I knew it would be hard to speak to him in a church setting and around his family so I wrote a letter and dropped it in the mailbox on our way to the hotel. All I wanted him to do was serve as my pastor in public and my grandfather in private.

Everyone in my hotel suite was having the time of their lives at my 90's themed New Year's Eve Party. There were big gold hoop earrings, baggy clothes, and bandanas just to name a few of the iconic trends. I finally got the man who was down with matching outfits from time to time, so Nate and I both wore black and white oversized baseball jerseys, baseball hats flipped to the back, stone washed jeans and Jodeci boots.

Everybody was full from the fried chicken, potato skins, spinach artichoke dip and buffalo chicken dip that I whipped up. Not to worry, I packed workout clothes for the hotel fitness room to burn those calories the next day.

All the kids were in the bedroom probably on their cell phones. Manny wasn't able to come since he was with mom, but Nate and I planned to facetime him after the ball dropped. Jamie hadn't had a drink since the altar call so she kept busy by eating every chance she could. Although she didn't get her rich husband or red vehicle, she was going to be rich in more meaningful ways. She was scheduled to attend AA meetings after the new year, so I was more than proud of her. Kandi and Bro Man cozied up on the couch as he rubbed her new baby bump. Jamie realized that we hadn't coined a nickname for Hakim like we did with our other lovers, so he graciously became Bro Man on Christmas. Karl was passed out on the couch already, but I was sure all the noise and commotion at midnight would awaken him. Mama and Barry the Plummer played Spades against Mama and Papa Collins at the table. Rhonda stood over them laughing at the two men as they talked trash to one another. She was happy to be in the presence of June Bug's family, and even happier that her only son had found true love, just like she had with June Bug. Mama kept making unnecessary hand movements with her left hand to show off that engagement ring and she was the happiest version of herself that I had ever seen.

Jamie made the announcement after stuffing more chicken in her mouth that we had sixty seconds before the New Year. The girls came out of the room so we could all watch the countdown of the ball dropping on TV and Karl popped up too, just like I suspected. Those people on the screen were all bundled up in their coats, scarves, and hats in the freezing cold. Liz was out amongst those people. Since she retired early, she wanted to travel all around the world and Times Square in New York was the first stop.

I was seated on Nate's lap as I observed and took everything in. My new reality and outlook on life meant everything to me and for my loved ones. What a difference a year could make, I thought. My vision board goals were not completed for 2019, but I knew my 2020 visions were going to be right on the bull's eye.

"Five, four, three, two, one...Happy New Year!" we all screamed to the top of our lungs.

. . .

February 14th was always known to the world as a day for lovers. For me it was also the day that I got cut out of my Mama's womb.

"Thirty-six where?" I said as I looked at myself in the full-length mirror in my red fitted jumpsuit. Although I was closer to forty, I looked closer to thirty. I was told I still had a babyface and had good genes. I had to give credit to my consistent workouts and smaller food portions as part of my success too.

It had been a good day thus far and I was happy with myself. I was not only happy because I was in a relationship. I was happy with myself in general. I thanked Mama for reiterating that self-love speech to me and all her speeches about faith. When I began to walk in faith, the whole game changed for me and I was thankful for all her years of prayer. I was even more grateful for all the blessings that had been bestowed upon me even after one of my darkest hours.

My cell phone rang as I continued to admire myself in the mirror. It was Nate and he called to tell me he was outside. I rushed out the door as I was buttoning my red peacoat. I noticed there was a trail of pink rose petals going from my front door to a long white limousine.

"Aww, this is so sweet!" I said to myself. Nate stood against the limo door with a black peacoat, black slacks and a pair of shiny Stacy Adams. He had a fresh line-up and was sporting a trendy new pair of frames.

"Happy Birthday, My Valentine," he said in a smooth and seductive voice.

I had no idea where we were going. I asked him several times, but he was tight lipped. After twenty-five minutes of driving, our limo driver finally arrived at our destination. It was an empty parking lot inside of a small strip mall in a prestigious part of town. I was really confused as I assumed we were going out to a fancy restaurant. The limo driver opened the door for us and once again there was a row of pink rose petals leading from the limo door to the door of an empty business space.

"Where are we?" I asked curiously. I walked on the soft petals which I was sure felt like silk to the bottom of my heels. He didn't say a word, but he pulled out a key from his pocket and unlocked the door. He turned the light on and continued to guide me until we came across a back room. There were two white chairs with a small white round table that was beautifully decorated for a romantic dinner. There were more rose petals that circled around the table and I began to hear the sweet sounds of "Her" by Isaac Carree play out of nowhere. The lights were dim. He still had my hand in his, but he got down on one knee and pulled a box from his back pocket. This was the moment I had waited for and this was nothing like what I had envisioned in my mind.

"Stephanie La'Rose Carter, I have waited all my life for this type of love. You have made me the happiest man on earth. This agape love that I share with you is love from God. I'm your Adam and you're my Eve. I love you with all my heart, no in between. We were created for each other and I promise to take care of you like no other. I want to spend every day with you for the rest of my life. So, on this day I want to ask you, will you be my wife?"

By then the waterworks were already flowing.

"Yes. I'll be your wife!" I exclaimed.

"Yeah! Yeah! That's what I'm talking about!" He got up, slipped the beautiful diamond ring on my finger and planted a big one on me. I felt like the world was mine.

He hired a personal chef to cook our dinner for the night. The chef created a surf and turf meal that was remarkable. We drank sparkling water out of wine glasses and toasted to a great future.

"This is so, so sweet. You have really outdone yourself honey," I said. "Oh, excuse me, I mean you have outdone yourself fiancé." We both laughed.

"But I gotta ask, why did you pick this place?"

"I'm glad you asked that. So, remember one of our first phone conversations when I asked you what your dream career was and you said it was to have a restaurant?"

"Um, yeah."

"And you asked me the same question and I said I wanted to have an art gallery?

"Yes, I remember."

"Well this is our new building. The front will be a spot to have different artists come display their work. There will be tables for our guests to eat. Back there will be your spot, the kitchen."

"So, wait, this is really our own building? You got to be kidding me?"

"Nope this is ours. We can live out our dreams. I know we both still have jobs, but I figure we start off small and open on the weekends to start out until we get big enough and then you can quit your job."

This couldn't be real. It had to be a fantasy. All I could say was, "Thank you Jesus for sending this man to me!" This couldn't be real. This had to be a fantasy. I couldn't wait to tell Mama, the other two amigas, and Liz if he hadn't already told them. Maybe Mama and I could have a double wedding, I thought. Once we were finished eating, he said he had another surprise for me. I wasn't sure if I could take any more surprises. He grabbed my hand and led me to the front of the building to what looked like an easel that was covered up with a cloth. He told me to do the honors of removing the cloth. I was shocked to see a replica of the painting that I loved to look at above Grandma Rose's bed. It was absolutely beautiful, and it immediately made me feel warm inside. I felt her presence inside the building.

"This will be the first painting we will put up in the building in memory of your Grandma," Nate said.

I pinched myself to make sure I wasn't dreaming because I couldn't believe that my 36th birthday was the best day of my life. I was speechless about everything that he planned out.

My new fiancé swept me off my feet and my legs dangled as we made our way back to the limo. I looked up into the misty blue skies ahead of me and God finally spoke to me! It was no longer a feeling in my body or an obvious sign of His presence. I heard a voice from within and it was pure music to my ears. His message was calm, sweet, and reassuring. I replayed the words in my head like the chorus of a song over and over and over again.

THE
END

Made in the USA
Monee, IL
28 December 2020